The Severan Prophecies

A Novel of the Roman Empire

Also by David Chacko

Price
Gage
Brick Alley
The Black Chamber
White Gamma
Red Bishop One
The Shadow Master
A Long Way from Eden
Like a Man
Less Than a Shadow
The Peacock Angel
Graveyard Eyes
Martyr's Creek

The Severan Prophecies

A Novel of the Roman Empire

David Chacko

Foremost Press
Cedarburg, Wisconsin

David can be reached at his website at
http://www.davidchacko.com
or by email at david@davidchacko.com

Published by Foremost Press

ISBN-10: 0-9789704-6-2
ISBN-13: 978-0-9789704-6-8

For Nancy Klein

EPITOME

Should I say I mean to set accounts straight?

Ask not how many men have spoken those words in the history of Rome. The answer is: all of them. They would like the story of their lives amended, and above all, justified. I will not do that. My purpose is to set down a record of the life of the most remarkable man ever to be known as the Emperor of Rome. He ascended the throne when he was fourteen years old and died when he was eighteen. Yet he was an emperor. And a man.

Some say he was more—a demon come from the worst place in Hades to visit disgrace on Rome. These men have stated their case. After his death, the Senate proclaimed the *damnatio memoriae* upon the emperor. The name of Marcus Aurelius Antoninus was stricken from every place in the empire. His statues were thrown down and his coinage withdrawn from circulation. All memory of him as emperor, or even a man, was erased.

The vilification continues to this day. Two men who call themselves historians—Cassius Dio and his pupil Herodian—have issued their verdict on Marcus Aurelius Antoninus, but it must be said their viewpoints are skewed. Dio was a creature of the emperor who was overthrown by Marcus Aurelius Antoninus and the men around him—by us.

This record of course is written in blood, the same medium in which much of the history of Rome is written. Marcus Aurelius Antoninus changed history by restoring a dynasty that had been usurped. When he accomplished that against all odds, he reformed the institutions of Rome as they had not been reformed since Great Augustus reshaped the republic into an empire. He meant to change everything, including our traditions and gods.

Men of vision can bring forth vital change. That thing has been done before and will be done again. At some point, Rome will redefine herself. The need is there, citizens. We crave a new day with an eagerness that our ancestors, looking forward into the blank space of the future, would not recognize.

I'll start my story at that point, where exhaustion presents itself like a ghost to be filled with more permanent forms. Beginning a life is an arbitrary choice, but when dealing with Marcus Aurelius Antoninus no uncertainty exists. I was present when his destiny was announced. No one recognized it because the words were spoken by an outlaw. That day in the legion camp of the most savage outpost in the Roman Empire, we witnessed what we thought was a disturbing incident in the life of an old man—the Emperor Septimus Severus—who was his uncle.

The day was dark, and we were upon darker business. For months, we had tried to subdue the barbaric Celts who inhabited the island of Britannia like their personal pigsty. Our campaign was marked by great success when we met our enemy on the field of battle, and greater casualties when we did not.

It was that kind of war.

BRITANNIA BARBARA

The Year 210

THE BLUE MAN

The Blue Man was someone who never should have appeared when he did. An anomaly, a manifestation of the gods, he arrived like a thing out of time.

He had been hunted down by scouts led by a Phrygian tracker who had gained fame by fetching a white leopard to the Secular Games. The Phrygian claimed to be guided by the Great Mother, but I trusted more in the senses of his dogs. Mild creatures with wide jaws and nostrils of nearly the same span, they nonetheless did the bidding of Caesar.

It was the fate of our expedition that the emperor accompanied us. Few Caesars fought with their armies, but Septimus Severus was an uncommon man. The first Roman emperor from Africa, he embodied the energy of that continent. He brought the empire from the chaos of civil war to order in the seventeen years of his reign, and he did it at the frontier many of those years, sharing the hardships of his legions and the reversals of fortune that are the soldier's lot. Perhaps it was the life so much like a lottery that caused him to believe in luck.

I shared Caesar's belief, but had no idea why this big stinking man had been brought to me. He was blue where he was not brown, painted the peculiar color milked from the glands of eels. He had no boots or sandals. The torque that circled his neck was steel. Most barbarians liked torques of gold. It said something of these northern Celts that what they valued was a harder substance.

"He should be cleansed before entering the emperor's presence," I said. "He's sure to carry every kind of vermin."

"I have orders, Tribune. This one appears as he was made."

"Orders from whom?"

"Above," said Oclatinus, raising his eyes to the sky.

I did not press the matter. Oclatinus was a *frumentarii*, who in ancient times were the collectors of the corn. Their universal presence in the empire eventually caused the emperors of Rome to decide upon their use as spies. From that point their numbers had grown, as had their power. The frumentarii could be ignored, overruled, or defeated, but not for very long.

"I can't believe he appeared naked to your eyes."

"There was a rag tunic on his body," said Oclatinus, "but being filthy, it was discarded."

And if the torque had been made of gold, it would have disappeared, too. The frumentarii were nothing if not collectors. Their corruption was the most certain thing in life.

"Has he a name?"

"He has nothing but what you see, Tribune."

"A rank?"

Oclatinus scoffed. "You know how it is with these people. The one with the biggest stick is king for a day. Unless that silly paint on his body means something."

I thought so. No Celtic tribe was well organized, but their customs were rigid. Everything about them meant something.

"Does he speak Latin?"

"He doesn't speak at all, Tribune. This is the rankest piece of meat in Caledonia. Our trackers had been all over those swamps three times. It was so cold their piss froze before it hit the ground. They slept with the dogs to keep breath in their bodies and had to fight bear for their breakfast. Imagine what they thought when they found this animal inside the base of a tree."

"An oak tree?"

Oclatinus looked to see if my question was serious. When he decided it was, the frumentarii spoke quietly. "I didn't think to ask, Tribune. But if you wish, I'll order the tracker brought here. At the moment, he's being treated by the surgeon for the bites he received."

I did not ask who had put his teeth into the tracker. The Blue Man had obviously partaken of his first meat in weeks. His long body was taut and his ribs enumerated like the rungs of a ladder. Though he seemed strong at the core, his flesh plaited with muscle, he had reached the point where he fed on himself to survive.

Most naked men show fear when faced with their captors, but the Blue Man had shown nothing until his brown eyes flashed when he heard the word "oak." "Knowledge of the oak" was the Latin translation of his creed. That is, if he was who he seemed to be.

"What's your name, priest?"

The Blue Man did not reply, but his eyes said he understood.

"I'm going to tell you something you may not know. All men can be made to talk, even if they have no story to tell. I think you do. You and your kind are supposed to be extinct."

Again, the Blue Man said nothing.

"When you get inside, make up your mind to perform. It's the only way you'll survive."

The Blue Man no longer chose to feign the idiot. He brought both hands forward from behind his back, slowly, holding them out to show they were empty.

My sword, always at the ready before the door to the emperor's chamber, came to his throat. Oclatinus drew his sword, and at the sound of quickened blades the guards from the entrance came running with their weapons drawn. In an instant, the Blue Man was ringed by metal the way his barbarian charm ringed his neck.

"Oclatinus, you fool!"

"He was bound! Tribune, I swear this man was bound!"

"Your oath would do us no good if he were allowed to pass. You know the penalty for endangering Caesar's life."

Being flogged to death was the prospect Oclatinus faced. "Ask the guard," he said in a bad voice. "They'll tell you he was secure!"

I looked to Lepidus, centurion of the guard, who nodded. "Yet now he's unfettered."

"I can't explain it," said Oclatinus. "But you called him a priest. Is he a sorcerer?"

I raised my sword to the Blue Man's neck above the torque. The image of a snake had been graven into the twists of steel. Yes, he was a sorcerer.

"Tell Oclatinus what it means to have knowledge of the oak."

The Blue Man's smile spoke of what it meant to go against Rome—the long months in hiding, living on roots, bark and nuts, drinking foul water, and on a good day, blood. The teeth were stained brown where they were whole, and blackened where they were broken.

"This fellow may not look like much, Oclatinus, but he's an important man of the Caledonian tribes. If I'm not mistaken, he's a Druid."

Oclatinus blinked. "A *what?*"

"They're no longer enemies of the state. Druids were priests of the Old Religion. They made sacrifice by burning their captives alive in wicker cages. They read the movements of the burning men to decide the future. Often, the interpretations went against the interests of Rome."

"A political agitator," said Oclatinus. "Does he know the Latin for that is dead man?"

Oclatinus dropped his sword from the Druid's third rib to the cloth that hung at his loins. He dallied, moving his blade in circles, then with a snap of his wrist cut the cloth. It dropped to the ground, leaving the man's blue belly and his softest parts exposed.

"A cock like a bull," said Oclatinus. He took the man's member on the flat of his blade, then moved the blade forward until the sharp tip touched his scrotum. "You nearly cost me my life. Now we'll see what your joke costs you."

The Druid did not look at the weapon between his legs. He spoke with an accent that rolled our precise tongue. "Go on. Take my manhood. Fools prize most what they have not."

The Druid might have known that a servant of Caesar would never destroy his master's booty; but Oclatinus was not the most forgiving man in the empire. Even as I put myself between them, I wondered what kind of man, naked before his enemy's sword, would throw out a challenge he could only lose?

One answer presented itself: a man who had no fear of death.

I had never seen one before.

* * *

And I should not have seen one in the antechamber of the most powerful man on earth. The priests called Druids had once been dominant in the Celtic tribes that stretched from the forests of Germany to the Western Sea. Believing that their souls traveled after death, entering the spirits of men still alive, they reckoned they were immortal. Armed by that belief, they were the most fanatic leaders the legions of Rome ever faced.

They were not supposed to be found on the northern frontier of the empire now. More than a hundred years before, in the time of Claudius Caesar, an expedition had been sent to exterminate the Druids, who were a constant problem. The priests of the forest had been hunted down man by man over the length of Britannia until they were driven into a cul-de-sac on the island of Anglesey off the western coast.

That place on the rim of the world was the center of their religion. The legions under Seutonius landed on Anglesey from boats and deployed for battle, but were not met by the enemy, who hid in the forest. Eager to engage them, Seutonius ordered his men forward. They had advanced a mile into dense wilderness, their scouts confused, when the enemy struck.

Let it be known that the legions wavered when faced by an attack from men who did not believe their essence would be extinguished. Were it not for the discipline that told our troops that everything that bleeds must die, the priests might have carried the day and bridged their legend from Britain to their cousins in Gaul until the empire tottered. Fighting naked as was their custom, arising from pits dug in the ground, dropping from trees, causing chaos among our cavalry, attacking from all directions, the Druids bore on our formations and with their broadswords inflicted heavy casualties.

In battle, where success depends on shock, the priests could not be thrown back. When their comrades died on our shields, they employed those bodies for which there was no longer a use to vault overhead into our ranks. When their swords became useless because their limbs had been hacked away, they bit off pieces of our flesh with their teeth. And when their attack was finally broken and they were driven back to the edge of a cliff overlooking the sea, many of these men jumped to the rocks below rather than allow their enemy the pleasure of the kill.

The Druids were destroyed to the last man and their bodies decapitated. Every dwelling on the island was put to the torch. Hounds were put to the earth to discover their hideouts in underground culverts and caverns. Divers searched the shore for grottoes and caves until they ended at the beginning of the circle. Last, since the Druids worshiped trees, all the trees were slain.

I know these things because my great-grandfather, Marcellus, told them to me. The Destruction of the Druids was the greatest tale my *pater familias* related to the child on his knee.

They were colored men, he said. Blue is the sacred color of the Druids, and all those men who did not believe they could die were painted blue.

* * *

I would have secured this Druid in double irons, and ringed him permanently with steel, but shortly afterward, the emperor's first son, Antoninus, who was known as Caracalla, informed me that his father wished to see his prize now. "Serve him up," is what the young man said, as if speaking of the next course at a banquet.

I did not contravene the word of Caesar's successor. Caracalla was insane even then, but who could tell? The emperors who rose to power by force, like his father, knew what it took to stand astride the world. Caracalla and the palace brats like him were born to live a fantasy of unlimited power. Nothing that can be said about him is untrue. Yes, he was undersized, snouted like a boar, and wished to punish all the world that was well made. Yes, he once threw a soothsayer to a den of lions, and when by a miracle that man emerged whole, Caracalla had him killed for surviving.

There was no lesson in that save the obvious, which should never be ignored. I had the Druid led into the royal chamber by Thrax, who was eight and a half feet tall and half as broad. Flanking the Blue Man were Praetorian Guards with swords crossed under his throat. The priest ignored Thrax, and the others, as he disdained everything. His only concession was the way he held his hands before his crotch. That proved he was not a complete barbarian.

"Caesar, the prisoner."

The emperor looked up from the map on his camp table. Geography was the most natural thing in war, but what the legions fought was the miasma of the swamps, the bitter weather of the highlands, and an enemy who did not give battle. After the villages were burnt, the cattle slaughtered, and the women and children sold into slavery, nothing was left to fight. Our sentries were sometimes found with their throats cut and our scouts hanging by their entrails from trees, but no armies of barbarians came against us. The standing battles for which Septimus Severus was famous were denied him. All he had gained were casualties in excess of thirty thousand men.

The frustration showed on his face, which in official portraits was benign and mystical. The image was cultivated. Caesar was a short but powerful man with brilliant eyes that exerted the force of his person. His full head of hair showed the gray of his sixty-two years, but it was a nest of curly ringlets, and his beard, too. Only his unbreakable will did not show. As he looked upon his prisoner, the months of blood and sweat to no point seemed to descend on the Blue Man, as if the evils of this campaign had taken form.

"Bring him wine," said Caesar. "The man looks chilled. Or is blue his natural color?"

The court, led by Argentocoxus, a Caledonian, laughed. They were joined by the demented sounds of Caracalla and a fair-haired boy of seven years who sat at the emperor's left. He was Caesar's nephew, the most beautiful boy in Britain, whose name was Varius.

"I should like to be painted like that," he said with a smile. "All in azure blue."

Caesar looked fondly on his favorite, whom he loved more than his two sons. "We shall ask him about his methods and art, Varius. Perhaps he will reveal his secrets this day."

One of Caesar's body servants brought a chalice of wine to the prisoner, who turned his head away. I did not blame him. The wine given to the legions on this campaign was infused with horehound to ward off the chest complaints caused by the weather. It tasted like gall.

"He will drink," said Caesar. "His tongue must be loosened."

So the prisoner drank. Another servant appeared to hold back the Blue Man's head while the first poured; but those barbarian shoulders were so high that the services of Thrax became necessary. The giant grappled the Blue Man down to his knees by the hair, and held back the head until his eyes stared at the ceiling and the mouth opened in spite of itself.

Drink the gall, I thought. Resistance will only make your death more painful.

But he would not swallow. The wine welled up in his mouth and ran over his matted beard to his chest, adding a red stain to the blue dye and mud. When the chalice was empty, the servants stepped back. That was the moment when the Blue Man spewed a blood-red gusher of wine halfway to the table at which Caesar sat.

No one spoke. In the air lay a mist created by the Blue Man's expulsion, hovering like a curse.

"It seems he isn't thirsty," said his countryman, Argentocoxus. A short stout Celt who had come over to us, he walked in his chesty way to stand before the Blue Man.

"Yes," he said. "I know you."

The Blue Man spat. The attempt was manful, and the gob of spittle landed at Argentocoxus' feet. On his sandals, in fact.

"He's one of Barradnach's people," Argentocoxus said. "Barradnach was a minor chieftain with tribal quarters near Kopay. I remember this one. Before he chose to pursue the ways of the dark past, he was educated in a Latin school. In other words, he understands us."

"A lie," said the Blue Man as he rose to his feet, boosting his voice in the same strong way. "I learned nothing there. No man of power could learn anything in that place."

"Hear him, Caesar!" said Argentocoxus. "What stands before you, daubed like a clown, is a powerful man."

The emperor stirred as if he might come to meet the two Caledonians. But Caesar rarely taxed his gouty legs. He rarely left the praetoria, and when he did, traveled in a litter.

"I'll tell you something true," he said to the praetoria. "Long ago in Gaul, I spoke to men of the Celtic tribes about their customs and ancient practices. They said that the old ways were lost, because all their priests had been lost. Now, I find that's untrue. Tell me, Druid, where did you learn the things that mean so much to you?"

"In the forest," he answered. "There a man can be free. Yesterday, it might have been on this ground, until the legions destroyed the hearts of the trees. That is the way of Rome. Nothing sacred can stand. Nothing remains unpolluted. The earth itself must be paved with stone to carry the orders of Caesar. The fruit of the vine is poisoned with filth. You wash your bodies in great baths but can never be clean. The oak that speaks lays silent as boards under your asses."

Caesar heard the words, ignoring the insults. "If the oak speaks, what does it say?"

"That you will never leave this island alive."

Everyone now knew what the Druid meant by power. Measuring his death in his words, he spoke them directly, flagging a challenge in to the man who ruled all the world worth having. You will die soon. You will die here.

The praetoria was silent. Even Caesar seemed daunted. Everyone knew he followed the sun god Mithras, believing in the zodiac and its interpreters. Set in the ceiling of the praetoria was a mosaic displaying the houses of the planets and the symbols that spoke the future through the heavenly bodies. Everything could be found there but the part that "observed the hour" when Severus was born. That day—that hour and minute—was his secret.

"As a seer you take the well-trodden path," said Caesar. "Telling an old man he will die one day on campaign is like saying the sun will rise in the east. That's not power. It's like the man who stumbles from his bed in the dark but unerringly finds his pisspot."

"You would hear more, Caesar?"

Severus smiled at the Blue Man. "I would be entertained."

The Druid's eyes roamed west of Caesar until they focused on Caracalla, who stood by his father's side, bored, as ever, by the import of words.

"Since we speak of piss, know that your son and heir will die in it." The Druid's eyes leered as if he saw far into space where distance warped as time; as if he were reading the future. "This Caesar will meet his end reeking of animal waste in the most terrible place in his empire."

Caracalla, whose future had been spoken, laughed. "*My* empire? So I'm to be Caesar. Now there's a happy thought."

The rest of the company followed Caracalla's laughter. Even Caesar seemed amused. He had two sons. Geta, the second, was sane, and only one year younger than Caracalla. He was at Eboracum to the south with his mother.

But the Druid was not done with his prophecies. He waited until the laughter passed before he spoke again to Caracalla. "You will be more than an emperor," he said. "Your destiny is to fill your mother's lap with blood."

"Enough of that!" said Caesar harshly. "We do not speak of women here, least of all the empress. Nor do we speak of blood just yet."

The Druid heard his fate spoken, but turned to Caesar as if he had forgotten him, like a coin bet on a board. He spoke with scorn. "Since we speak of women, know they will come to rule your empire, Septimus, whose name means the seventh. All the manly virtues of Rome will expire within the time of your house.

Your men will become women. And the treasures of your gods will be looted."

"You prophecy doom with every breath," said Caesar. "I wonder, could it have to do with being a prisoner? And the feelings in your breast? Tell me truthfully, Druid."

The Blue Man closed his eyes as if to show his presence was as great as Caesar's. No one moved. No one blinked. Even Caracalla gave his attention, or rather, went over to the brooding that was the other side of his madness.

"I have more clarity in my thoughts than I had thought possible." The Druid opened his eyes and brought them to the boy Varius. Caesar's nephew seemed entranced by the figure in blue. More, he seemed transfixed as the Druid raised his hand and pointed at him.

"This is a Child of God." The Druid lost his balance and staggered. "In him is the beginning and the end. He will prepare the way for all that follows."

"That's better," said Caesar, patting his nephew's knee. "We would have our prophets recognize fate in every form, especially when the form is so perfect."

"Can we have more?" said the boy. "I wish to know more."

"What awaits you, Varius, is all you can wrest from life," said Caesar. "The gods point the way, but fate must be taken by the hand. When I was the legate in Gaul, I had a dream one night where a stranger appeared and took me up to a high place. There, I could see Rome and all the world. As I gazed down on the land and sea, I laid my hands upon these things as one might an instrument that could play every mode. And they all sang together."

"In perfect harmony," said the boy.

"In the dream, yes," said Caesar. "Five years later, Emperor Commodus was assassinated in his hunting theater. Two pretenders bargained with the Praetorian Guard for the throne so they might be be Caesar. When I saw that shameful scene, I marched down from the north with my legions. I disbanded the Guard, dismissed the pretenders, and named myself emperor."

"And slaughtered half the Senate," said Caracalla, very pleased. "That was the best thing you did, Father."

Caesar turned from his perfect nephew to his imperfect son. He seemed to want to right the family imbalance when the Druid began to rant again.

"What begins in blood will end in sacrifice!" he said. "Hear me!"

We listened. His voice was inhuman, beyond the ken of all we know. A strange substance pulsed from the Druid's lips, fetid and blue, filling the praetoria with a deep stench.

"One God!" he shrieked. "One God above all others!"

He fell to his knees as if driven down, though no one touched him. The guards with drawn swords were staring. The servants were awed. They listened to the words that seemed jerked from the Druid's mouth.

"This god will not be the sun that you worship, Caesar. He will be both dimmer and brighter. He comes from the east, but is understood by none. The future of your empire belongs to the man who will seize and hold his worship!"

Varius bolted from his chair. He ran three steps toward the Druid, but stopped short. He looked at those eyes that struggled with starvation and the blast of alcohol.

The Druid looked at the boy as a destination. "You will rise up to be the greatest man in the world," he said. "And your name will be *scorned* to the ends of the earth."

"Enough!" Caesar slammed his hand on the table. "Remove him!"

The Druid was given to Caracalla, who had him taken from the praetoria to the gate of the encampment. There, the prisoner was crucified by his genitals. He hung upside down, long and bitterly, as was the custom with criminals.

THE DYNASTY

Shortly afterward, Caesar's health turned worse. He withdrew to Eboracum south of the Hadrian's Wall, where his wife and younger son, Geta, kept court. The Great Campaigner traveled in a litter all the way. Caracalla assumed command of the expedition against the northern tribes, which he conducted with furor but no success. His only concern was to gain the confidence of the army. Caracalla had taken that much counsel from his father. The man who controls the legions is de facto Caesar.

At Eboracum, the emperor fell into a decline. I heard rumors by Oclatinus, who had been promoted to proconsul, that Caracalla bribed his father's doctors to hasten the emperor's end; but I cannot speak to the truth of that. The frumentarii advanced information on all subjects without knowing the truth, or caring for anything but their power. That spidery thing should always increase, the organization grow ever larger, until it was indispensable.

In Britannia, the frumentarii were very busy. They learned that Caesar, who doubted Caracalla's stability, would name both sons to joint command of the empire after his death. That meant the corn spies must jockey in two directions, casting seed that could be worked no matter who won.

The end came, as it seldom does, expectedly. The tremendous energy that was the hallmark of Septimus Severus expired one afternoon as if on schedule. Caesar turned from the report that he had been reading and told his attendants to send immediate messages to his sons. He put aside the medallion he always wore, which was the missing portion of the zodiac where the hour of his birth was recorded, and lay on his bed. At the same moment, two eagles swept down on the palace gate, paused in midair as if taking on some unseen burden, and climbed swiftly out of sight.

Caracalla barely had time to reach his father at Eboracum. We rode in the from the north on a moonless night in the third month of winter over ice-covered roads, killing three horses and two slaves who could not maintain the pace, so he might take the hand of the brother he loathed, walk to the side of the father whose end he wished with all his might, and hear the words Caesar spoke on his deathbed.

"Be good to each other, be generous to the army, and pay no heed to anyone else."

The last words of Severus went unheeded. The army recognized both sons as Caesars, but the brothers refused to recognize each other. Even as they bore their father's ashes back to Rome, the young emperors kept separate quarters. Their relations were so strained that when we reached Londinium, the chief port of Britannia, each traveled with his contingent of Praetorian Guards, refusing to have any contact with the other.

As a Tribune of I Gallica, I accompanied Caracalla with the party of the Mother Augusta through Gaul. Always, we mirrored the movements of the legions under Geta's command, following the same roads and never losing sight of the brothers bound so close in hatred. We would have gone on all the way to Rome in that tandem but for the illness that Severus' nephew Varius contracted when we crossed the dangerous passes of the Alps.

Caracalla was furious at the delay and determined to arrive in Rome not a step behind his brother. Nothing would stop that from happening. I understood the urgency when he called me to his praetoria on the verge of a cliff with a drop of six hundred feet to jagged rocks below. Each man who came to Caracalla walked a narrow path along the cliff. He tested his courage. Twice.

"We're going ahead," he said as he sat in his bath with a whore. "You'll have charge of the Mother Augusta's party and bring it safely home. Must I impress you with the gravity of this mission?"

"My lord, I understand."

He looked up at me with that nose stolen from the lowest animals. "I doubt you do. It grieves me to leave the imperial nephew in poor health, but I cannot tarry in this place. Varius will recover from his illness."

"Yes, my lord."

"You will see to it."

"I will do everything possible, my lord."

"Do more," said the emperor. "Make up your mind to his recovery. If anything happens to my cousin, I'll have you in the hunting theater against twenty leopards."

I had not known Caracalla loved any man so well that he noticed their absence. What he loved was torture. I wondered if the whore knew he had bitten the nipples off the last one.

"My lord, you may rely on me."

Caracalla stepped from his bath. Two servants rushed with cloths to hide his nakedness, but he did not notice them. He stood before me dripping dirty water with one hand on his whore, who was beautiful, and the other holding a finger to my face.

"You will have a sword for the leopards," he said. "A wooden sword."

* * *

I wondered if Caracalla wanted his cousin to recover. I had no idea of his true feelings for Varius, but his lust for the entertainment of blood could not be satisfied. Nor did I fault his memory. Madness often has facilities that exceed normal bounds.

It was my luck that the imperial nephew in two weeks regained his health from spotted fever and retained no blemishes on his body. We resumed our journey and had a late arrival in Rome a fortnight later. Thus I earned the gratitude of Julia Domna, Severus' wife, who was still the Mother Augusta of Rome.

She was thankful for my efforts to secure Varius' health, which included sending to Verona for a physician who had treated my family for a generation. She was even happier to reach Rome, where she could assert herself. Julia Domna was the only link to the leadership Severus had provided. The sons respected their mother not only as the author of their beings, but as a source of good sense. Skilled in the management of bureaucracy and the language of governance, the Mother Augusta had practiced those talents as Severus' partner.

She would have done the same for her sons, but even the vestige of sanity fled as the division of power between the brothers carried to lunatic heights. After Geta and Caracalla led the public ceremony to deify their father, they divided the royal palace into halves. Each half had its own entrance, while the connecting doors and passages throughout the vast complex were barricaded. Two competing sets of Praetorian Guards kept watch at every point of access.

The factionalism found its reflection in the city. Instead of a court, two shadow governments arose. In the Senate, a man was either Caracalla's or Geta's. Though he was more often the latter, enough politicians accepted Caracalla's money to make every issue a contest. When cases came up for trial, both sides strained every lever of power to have the verdict rendered for their clients, destroying every notion of fairness at law. Even the priests who read auguries from the bowels of animals were bribed to discover signs of favor. The circus games grew so riotous that the streets were in turmoil and dangerous. A man wore blue or he wore green, and woe to the citizen who found himself in the wrong color.

Never was Rome so divided. The sun came up each morning like the last day before doom. I was glad when orders came from the Mother Augusta, telling me to repair to the capital of Gaul as Prefect of the City. I arrived at Lugdunum the second week of March. The distance from Rome caused me to acquire news of the next weeks at secondhand.

The differences between the emperors grew. Geta and Caracalla tried to settle the issue with poison, each subverting the other's guards, servants and tasters, but the plots were foiled each time. It was Julia Domna who exposed the assassination attempts and kept the brothers alive to be at odds. She was the only person in the empire who could speak to her sons, and the only one capable of effecting a compromise.

For weeks, the Mother Augusta toiled between the fratricides, carrying proposal and counter-proposal in an attempt to return sane rule to the empire. Finally, she had success when she put the matter in terms of territory. The brothers made a board game of the empire, trading provinces and peoples like coins and shuffling borders like cards. In the end, they settled on a plan of division. Geta would have the east as far as Syria, while Caracalla took the west.

It was while negotiations were underway that Geta decided to meet Caracalla in their mother's apartment so they should come to a final agreement. The reason Geta agreed to such a dangerous course is unknown. He might have thought he was safe because his mother always favored him, as did most people. He was not the first man to be seduced by numbers.

Geta lost half an empire, and his life, when Caracalla's men broke into the apartment with daggers drawn. The murder came furiously. Those who saw the Mother Augusta afterward said that her lap was steeped in the blood of her second son, and that on her hand was a gash given as she tried to intercept an assassin's blade. Geta had died in her arms.

In the days that followed, so was Rome swept by a tide of blood. Caracalla's Praetorians raged throughout the city. Carrying the death lists of the frumentarii, they murdered Geta's supporters in their homes, in the baths, on the streets, at their suburban villas, and even in the temples. How many died no one knew, but they were thousands upon thousands. Half the aristocracy of Rome, including my uncle and his first-born son, disappeared under the onslaught.

And the army held for the winner.

SYRIA

Six Years Later

ANTIOCH

I spent four years as Urban Prefect of Lugdunum, the capital of Gaul, before I came east in the winter of 217 to serve the emperor in his campaign against the Parthian Empire.

I would like to report that we defeated our enemy, but Caracalla spent most of his time outfitting his army. He raised a cavalry of elephants to emulate Hannibal, the African leader he took as his forefather. He armed several legions with the weapons and uniforms Alexander the Great had used when he set out against the empires of the East.

It was a play of war with armies that never knew battle. The Parthians had no idea of our intentions. When they learned that they had come under attack, they were slow in raising their armies. By the time they came against us, Caracalla had raided several towns, looting and burning and setting his lions loose on the inhabitants. Satisfied that he had inflicted damage upon his enemy, he withdrew his legions and retreated to winter quarters at Edessa.

We spent a miserable season in barracks that led to a rainy spring. I was as bored as any soldier in my command until a day in early April I was summoned to the quarters of a man who would have an impact on the empire far out of proportion to his stature.

Marcus Opellius Macrinus was a Prefect of the Praetorian Guard. Like many men who rose to prominence under Severus, he was African. His black hair and beard were tousled in curls, and his nose had been made so big that it looked like a replacement fitted with no special skill to his face. A lawyer in his youth, Macrinus had exchanged public slander for private misrepresentation without reference to morality. He had no need of that serving Caracalla.

"Marcellus Decimus, I called you here to say I'm assigning you to serve as questor at the garrison of Raphanae."

I said nothing. At best, it was a lateral move. A wiser man might have called it a demotion for things done too well.

"You're disappointed," said Macrinus. "You'd rather stay here to fight the Parthians."

"If that's to be done."

"It will not be done," he said. "At this moment, peace is being made."

"So this campaign undertaken at such expense produces nothing for Rome."

"That's not for you to say. Nor is it my business to explain the realities of power to a battle commander. The emperor needs the services of a loyal man to maintain peace in Syria. You may refuse the assignment of course."

If I wanted to die under the breath of lions. Caracalla ate with them, slept with them, and fed them better than his body servants. More than once, he fed them his body servants, so those great rank cats might partake a haunch or arm while it was still warm.

"I accept, Marcus Opellius. Am I to take full control of Upper Syria?"

"You will have those duties, though you understand the Mother Augusta has taken up residence in Antioch. You must defer to her in all matters. Most men might find that difficult, but I understand you are a friend."

"I respect her judgment more than any. Except, of course, the emperor's."

"Then the choice is good."

Macrinus smiled, a thing he never did to his superiors. "I would like you to leave immediately. Talks with the Parthians are proceeding well, but the emperor wisely does not trust their words. You will be tasked with bringing the garrison to readiness. Be prepared to move at once in case negotiations do not come to a successful conclusion."

"So you expect trouble."

He clasped his right ear where a hole had been bored for the placement of jewelry. "The emperor tries to anticipate the future.

At this moment, he is preparing to make offerings at the shrine of Sin to ensure the successful end of this war."

"Sin? Is that not a temple of expiation?"

"The emperor has nothing to be forgiven for. But he submits to the will of the gods."

Greater lies had been spoken, but I did not take this as Macrinus'. A man who hated himself like Caracalla will seek a better self through magic. Wherever his army tarried, the emperor sought out sanctuaries where healing was done. To what purpose? The part of Caesar that wanted healing was not his body. But expiation for his crimes—that made sense.

"I'll leave at once, Marcus Opellius. Shall I give my farewell to the emperor?"

"That won't be necessary."

* * *

I counted myself lucky not to chance an appearance before Caracalla. He spent his life searching for what he lacked, never imagining it was a conscience. Surprisingly, he retained power throughout his reign. Although hated by the patricians, the people were his.

The rest he left to his mother. Julia Domna ran the business of the empire, following her son to war, as she had done with her husband. When he spent money on the legions that could not be paid, she found the means. When he slaughtered half the male population of Alexandria in Egypt on a whim, she consoled the grieving mothers, of whom she was one.

We were all like the Mother Augusta, who had seen her son murdered, yet served his murderer. I should have gone from Edessa to my post at Raphanae in the south, but I chose as a matter of policy and politeness to bend my journey and pay my respects to her.

Antioch, lying on the Orontes River, was the capital of the East. Blessed with a fine climate, surrounded by hills and one great mountain, the city attracted the best dancers, actors and athletes to its theaters and amphitheaters. Here, pleasure was the only principle, and the sun the focus of every act.

I entered the city on the sixth day of the Great Mother's Festival that would end on the seventh with the Games. The city was overwhelmed. The Avenue of the Caesars, as wide as ten chariots, could not be crossed by a starving dog. All the population between the aged of five and fifty turned out to revel. Every second man was drunk and every third a pickpocket.

Every woman was a chance at love, and they roistered in the taverns and hung from their balconies, shouting to the throng below and stripping flower petals on their heads. Music came from everywhere as harps filled the air, but other sounds came, too, heavy and pulsating. Drums and tambourines. Flutes and clarinets, and a strange haunting sound, like a hunting horn.

I took the passage through the perfumer's quarter. Though the mixing rooms were shut, the air reeked with the aromatic gums of hartshorn and fleur de lys. A group of men came along with casks of wine and perfume. They drank the first and shook out the second, flinging it to the passersby, men and women alike. "For the Mother!" they cried. "For the Great Mother!"

At the end of the passage, I found the street where the palace lay on high ground above the river. This bastion of state three stories high with a forty-column front would see no petitions presented today. The bureaucracy had been shelved until after the games.

That made the reception I received at the entrance to the palace surprising, especially since I had sent a letter ahead. The guards, two mutes with axes, crossed their weapons when I gave my name, refusing to allow me through.

"Stand down! Marcellus Decimus commands you!"

Confusion showed in their eyes; but they could not speak and would not step aside.

"Must I ride you down?"

I had my hand on my sword, but stopped at a movement from the terrace above. The figure that passed with a tunic belted around an obese body must be Humilis, the Mother Augusta's chamberlain. When I shouted to him, he stopped.

"Marcellus?" he said, peering forward, as if unsure of his identification. "Is that you?"

"Yes. I would see the Mother Augusta, but the guards have their axes and apparently their orders."

Humilis nodded, but again, as if unsure. "Whence do you come?"

"From Edessa."

"Edessa," he said. "Who sent you from that place?"

Something was wrong, and at Edessa. Surely it was bad. "Chamberlain, I'm on my way to Legion III Gallica at Raphanae to be questor. I wish to pay my respects to the Mother Augusta. I will gladly surrender my sword if you tell me what has happened."

The Syrian looked at me long. His double chin and overshot jaw seemed to make his face even fatter. I could not see his lips move within the layers of flesh.

"What do you know about the emperor, who were so lately by his side?"

Regardless of the things I knew, and more I had forgotten about Caracalla, my heart faltered and my words came poorly. "I know the emperor goes on pilgrimage to the Temple of Sin. Nothing more."

"But there is more, Marcellus. Much more."

"What has happened?"

"The emperor is dead," said Humilis, bowing his head. "Assassinated by his troops."

* * *

I now understood why my welcome was difficult. Though I was known by the Mother Augusta's entourage, I came from the army. I might be part of the plot, which was not necessarily concluded. The logical course after murdering an emperor was to exterminate his family.

"When did it happen?"

Humilis was slow with his answer as we stood in the doorway before the atrium. The universe that had been as orderly as it was rich had become a lethal maze. At any moment, assassins might burst through the door, killing indiscriminately.

"We just had word of his death. It happened yesterday. The emperor was on his way to the Temple of the Moon when he stopped by the side of the road. He had been having trouble with looseness in his bowels. And while he was thus engaged—"

"Who did it?"

"The word we have is of a lone assassin. The man was part of the emperor's bodyguard. Julius Martialis."

"Martialis?"

"You know him?"

"He's an Evocati."

Humilis paused heavily. "And if I might know who they are—"

The ignorance of most civilians about the military—the most important thing in their lives—was appalling. That never changed, even at the highest rank; even when it killed them.

"The Evocati are the most trusted of the Praetorian Guard. They are the Recalled. Every man puts in twenty years before he retires from service. He's brought back because his conduct has been exemplary. I knew Martialis in England. He was as good as any."

Humilis smelled a plot now, another plot. "We were told that Martialis was angry because the emperor executed his brother."

"Perhaps. I did not think he had a brother, but that may be unimportant. It would be better if we put these questions to him."

I'm afraid that won't be possible," said Humilis. "We are given to understand that after this man slew the emperor, he attempted to escape on horseback. A mounted Guard brought him down with a javelin."

"And killed him."

"Completely."

So a single throw from a charging horse at a target moving away rapidly killed Martialis. Not impossible. Convenient. The only man who knew the motive for Caracalla's death was dead. The only man who could tell exactly how it happened could tell nothing.

"I must speak to the Mother Augusta at once."

"She's in deep sorrow," said Humilis, sharing that emotion with sudden intensity. "You understand. First one son. Then another."

And last, an empire. "At once," I said.

* * *

I never looked upon Julia Domna without recalling the paintings and statues I had seen all my life in the fora of Rome, in basilicas and at country crossroads, in temples and inscribed on coins. Every representation was the image of a goddess.

She was not the portrait of Roman beauty, for she encompassed more than Italy. The black curls that fell over her brow, her bold but forgiving brown eyes, and the slow turn of her mouth, spoke of the softer lineaments of the east. Age had made its inroads, etching its passage, but that beauty haunted her face like the space in a triumphal arch.

The Mother Augusta crossed the room and took me to her breast. Here, Geta had bled to death, Severus had dallied, and her brilliant court of philosophers found a patron.

"Marcellus, you came quickly."

"I came without knowing, Mother. Accept my sorrow."

She did so gravely. "He was mine, but never his own."

"I understand he was on his way to the Temple of Sin when he was slain."

"He went at my suggestion," she said. "The Temple of the Midnight Sun is the holiest place in the east. There, the past may be forgiven if the penitent enters in the proper spirit. I've heard it said that the man who sees the moon as a god will be his own ruler. But the man who sees a goddess will never know peace."

"Your son always saw a goddess. What we know from the cradle is seldom unlearned."

She turned to face her terrace above the street. "How can any man unlearn the fact that the world has been vouchsafed to him like an egg? My son was obsessed with death. Even his dreams were corrupt. He told me of them. His father and of course his brother pursued him in sleep relentlessly. They carried swords, menacing him. I told him the only place he could find relief was at Carrhae."

"*Carrhae?*"

"Yes," she said. "He was on the high road to Carrhae, wherein lies the temple, when he was murdered. What a terrible place. Can there be a more terrible place to a Roman?"

No. At Carrhae, a Roman army had been destroyed to the last man by the Parthians. The legions' eagles—its standards—were lost. Carrhae was the exact location of hell.

"Do you have further word on the circumstances of his death, Mother?"

"You think that's important?"

"No, Mother. Except as it tell us of his killers."

She turned from the street and stepped to the image of the sun embedded in tiles at her feet. This land was hers, its people, language and deities. Her homecoming charmed her as the violence chilled her soul.

"You do not believe in the wrath of the Evocati?"

"Martialis may have guided the sword, Mother. It would be of more use to know who guided Martialis."

"But not why?"

"We know why, Mother. What remains unclear is who will be emperor."

The lines that rimmed her eyes mimicked the rays of a sun. "The name being put forward is Oclatinus Adventus."

Julia Domna may have been deranged by grief. *Oclatinus?* The frumentarii. He had gone from proconsul in Britain to be one of the two prefects of the Praetorian Guard. He had risen as swiftly as butchery could lift a man, but not to this height. Never.

"Mother, what you say is impossible."

"Of course. This wretch has been put forward as emperor, but not confirmed. They are already saying he's not the man to lead the troops in the East once more against the Parthians."

"Which means the real killers are hiding."

"They're testing the waters," she said in the voice that guided the political maneuvers of the court. "I expect within a week—perhaps three days hence on my husband's birthday—the pretender will show himself. It will be said Oclatinus has not the stature. That he is tainted by his life as a torturer. Many reasons will be given, except the real one, which is that the killer of my son does not wish to be known for his deed."

"Who is it?"

"There are two prefects of the Guard," she said. "Two men of equal power, except that one is senior."

Oclatinus was first, the second Macrinus. A tenacious man, his problem was his low birth. The son of an African fisherman would not easily be accepted by the Senate, though he could count on the army.

"So it's Macrinus. I must tell you, Mother, I'm surprised he organized the plot."

She agreed. "I too am surprised, though perhaps I should not be. You know I managed my son's correspondence."

"He was lucky in that, Mother."

"Usually. But two weeks ago I received a letter from Titus Mysticus in Rome. He's the astrologer in whom my husband placed so much faith—and my son, too. This man warned of a conjunction involving danger from a prefect of his Guard. I forwarded the letter to my son, but do not know if he read it."

"You think the letter was intercepted?"

She shrugged. "My son often detailed administrative matters to his aides."

So assassination had become a defensive act for Macrinus. My reassignment was a way of disposing of one loyal man. That could not be believed in any era pretending to sanity.

"What will happen to us, Mother?"

"I will die in Antioch."

She was saying that the Mother Augusta was irrelevant to the new order. They could not strip her title, but they could put her aside. She would do what Macrinus should have done when faced with an impossible choice. She would destroy herself rather than be dishonored.

"What of the rest of the family?"

"Marcellus, that depends on you."

"I don't understand."

"The dynasty must not die with me," she said with the strongest emotion she had shown. "There are two male heirs to the throne of Septimus Severus. They're the children of my nieces, Julia Soaemias and Julia Mammea. The eldest child, whom you know, is nearly of the age when he will receive the *toga virilis*."

That was the boy I had known in Britannia, who almost died of fever in Gaul. He was thirteen now. His name was Varius, and he was the final element in the prophecy.

"What is it you want me to do, Mother?"

"You know I am Syrian."

"Of course."

"I was born in the city of Emesa, the daughter of the high priest of the Temple of El-Gabal. Have you been to that place?"

"No, Mother."

"Like Antioch, Emesa stands on the Orontes River, but not far off is the desert. If my nephew could find his way to Emesa, he would be welcome at the temple. They would look after him with vigilance. Should something untoward happen, like the appearance of troops in the night, my people would know. A hunted man could vanish."

"I understand, Mother."

"Please do not understand too quickly. What I ask is as dangerous as it is vital."

"I will follow your orders."

"Are you prepared to leave immediately?"

"We should leave the palace as soon as possible. But darkness is best for the journey."

She came closer as the declining sun behind her put soft light around her. Her voice seemed clear but in shadow, like the voice of a priestess. "They will come for him. You must be ready."

"That will be my work, Mother. Varius will not be taken alive."

She took my hand again. "I say Rome knows no men but stand in this room."

* * *

While the Mother Augusta went to fetch Varius—no servants, no witnesses—I moved to the balcony overlooking the street. The panorama and the nature of the day were awesome. The crush of humanity in the streets had grown and seemed to have a destination—the forum. Centers of enthusiasm coalesced before moving on—men in black, along with others in rose-colored garments. Where they gathered, the drums, flutes and horns were loudest. I saw one group who were wielding weapons and dancing.

As I watched, I knew what might take us from the city. The *galli* were out. The eunuch priests of the Great Mother, so revolting they were forbidden the streets of Rome, had taken over Antioch for the festival and left to riot. Even with long swords and axes, the eunuchs were more effeminate than any woman, their skin as smooth as cheese, their bleached hair reaching down past their shoulders, their faces painted with white lead and rouge. Their garments were garish tunics of silk that clung to their limbs as they danced, belted at the waist to accentuate their womanly curves.

It was hard to imagine how they came to be what they so pitifully were, but I knew the cult of the Great Mother began in this palace with Julia Domna. Every man who spent a coin saw her image on one side and on the other, the goddess of the earth, Cybele. For most purposes, they were the same. And for mine.

"Varius!"

The boy led the Mother Augusta into the room, and his mother, too. He tried not to smile—his natural mode—but when he saw me he pushed aside the gravity of the day. I hardly had time to vacate the balcony when he clapped me on the back.

"Marcellus, it's been too long."

Half his lifetime. But Varius had gone to adolescence with none of the burdens others knew. Nothing was goaty, nothing blemished his blond, aquiline profile. His form had elongated as he grew to adult height. Except for that, it was, as Septimus Severus had said, perfect.

"You've not suffered by the years, Varius."

"They feed me hummingbird tongues," he said. "And red mullet now and then."

"I'm glad you're well, but we'll leave the delicacies behind. Has your mother explained we must travel fast?"

"And far," he said.

"You will want to temper your enthusiasm," said his mother, whose name was Soaemias. "Your life will depend on it."

"I understand."

She did not think so, and in that she was like all mothers. In every other way, Soaemias was so beautiful that motherhood seemed foreign to her. She was the opposite of Julia Domna—blonde, tall, with skin like a white rose and of strange translucence—like fine glass, but not with its tints or brittleness. Her lips were a darker color of rose and her hair spilled from her tiara. Her eyes were bold, trapped between blue and violet, and her voice was sensual, though she tried to sheathe it in iron.

"I like none of your promises, young man. Understand for the first time in your life that you do not make them to me so they can be broken. The words you speak are to yourself. You must do everything Marcellus tells you—without question. Your disobedience will mean your death."

"Yes, Mother."

Varius had rendered himself meek and mild, although it ran against his preference. His mother recognized the actor in him, but could say nothing more to earn his compliance.

"I will guard his life, Soaemias."

"Then you have my eternal gratitude."

"Princess." I bowed to her, taking her eyes close before turning to her son. "Are you ready, Varius?"

"I am, Marcellus."

Soaemias intervened again. "Would you not have provisions for the journey?"

"We can't be burdened with supplies. Nor should the servants be aware we're leaving. If possible, they should be gathered in one place for the next hour."

"They could be killed," said Soaemias.

"That shouldn't be necessary. Can we pass from the palace unseen?"

The Mother Augusta answered. "There are two passages underground," she said. "The first exits at the mint. The second leads directly to the Temple of Cybele."

"We'll take the latter," I said. "We can move fast once we reach the temple."

"I'll go with you," said Soaemias. "I've been a sponsor to the galli."

I had not known that the goddess approved of women at her temple, but if an exception was made, it would be Soaemias. Perhaps only men who were not quite men would be immune to her beauty.

"See that my horse is taken to the stable on the far side of the perfumer's quarters. Have another readied, too. At the temple, we'll require two full sets of the priest's clothing."

"A disguise."

"Yes."

The Mother Augusta demurred. "It's possible Varius, an unbearded boy, could be taken for a priest of the Great Mother, but I have grave doubts about you, Marcellus."

"Paint my face."

* * *

The passage underground was not what I hoped. Timbered for the most part with cedar, it had been constructed long ago but not generously. Even the thirteen-year-old Varius could not decide to stoop or crawl. Two adults moved slowly and clumsily, gathering insects and bruises. The cloak I carried, and the wigs with long plaits we had from the palace, stifled the flow of air and turned sweat to mud before we were far along. The lantern, though perforated, guttered more than it lit the way.

We labored in the passage just short of an hour. That was slow, but good. We would arrive at the temple near dusk. The deeper we penetrated, the more pursuit—when it came—would falter over the same ground.

From the rear, Varius and I heard only Soaemias, whose labors were forceful. Did she go on like that in bed? Her husband had been sent as the legate to Numidia, a place she chose to shun. I could not imagine a woman of her beauty and temperament abiding the absence of love. Casual gossip said the princess took it where she found it.

But they always said that when a woman looked like that. This time it might be more truth than rumor. Some women used men like objects, and divorce like a change of sheets. The market in slaves with a share of beauty and lusty private parts was great for the last two hundred years. If the Roman Empire fell one day, the reason would be a parcel of Caucasian slaves whose blond locks and long cocks drove the price of a promising fuck beyond the reach of the richest patrician lady.

Was I wrong? Bitter? Did I mention that the body of Soaemias was more perfect in its way than her son's? Have I described the scent of her perfume, which I had never encountered before nor could identify? Have I not expounded on the virtues of a life in billet in the legions? What does a condemned man desire more than a last supper?

I left those questions at the tunnel door, where we came suddenly. It was not quite a door but a smooth place recessed in limestone at the end of the passage. It had no lock, only an iron-ring pull that would not yield to my hand.

"It wants the key," said Soaemias.

She sidled close by me in the passage, relieving her girdle of a thick shaft of iron with a haft that ended in two lead balls. Yes, the device was suggestive. It was exactly what the galli lacked.

In the wall by the door Soaemias tipped back a wedge of stone and inserted the key in a slot hidden beneath. When she struggled, I closed my hand over hers and we pulled together. In the airless passage, her perfume rose powerfully.

"We're in," said Varius.

Correct. The door tipped ajar as the wedge of stone had done. I felt the pop in my hand through her hand, and leaning forward, my body pressed against hers, I drew the door aside.

"I'll go first," she said.

I watched her hips and slippers disappear through the opening that gave no light. Next went Varius with the lantern. As I put myself through the doorway, Soaemias took the hood from the lantern and transferred it to a sconce on the wall.

We entered the repository of the cult. Stone heads of the great cats sacred to Cybele hung on the walls—panthers, tigers, leopards, and lions. The eyes of the idols glowed with gemstones, as if pleased by what they saw—a burial ground.

On the floor, staggered in stone pods, were corpses of the high priests. These were the remains of men who had no issue but must have monument. Their faces were carved in the tops of the sarcophagi in hard lines of marble, and the eyes wandered in the flickering light.

"Step around the coffins," said Soaemias. "The foot that touches any part of the archigalli will be the one that rots away."

"A superstition?"

She did not return my sarcasm. "Perhaps it will be as you believe."

She was serious, and I did not know how to treat her devotion. I would never know that to the end. "Lead on."

Passing the lantern to me, she took the sconce from the wall and moved toward a dark space in the far wall like a second passage. Varius and I followed across the room. The boy's smile, always at the verge of his lips, seemed pressed in stone, like the faces of the archgalli. It was good if he borrowed his mother's seriousness.

We left the mummies in their crypt and moved through the gap in stone, where Soaemias disappeared. Two steps along, we saw she had gone up a steep flight of stairs. This place was old by the way the stone steps had been worn concave. At the top, where Soaemias waited, lay another door as old.

The Genius of Eternity within the zodiacal circle was graven in the stone. It was the constant in every religion of the empire. The study of the heavens that began in the East had been raised to science by Severus and his son. It was now reinforced by the solar calendar. Seven days, seven planets. Twelve months, twelve houses. Logic.

"We may encounter priests or corybants within," said Soaemias. "I will speak to them."

"You expect trouble?"

"I can't say. Today the Great Mother's servants are in a state of grace and permitted things usually forbidden. They're encouraged to explore the limits of their devotion."

Was she saying that in the temple we would find behavior to exceed the dancing and banging in the streets, the sword play, all the ecstatic states that came to the attendants of the goddess? The corybants—those men in rose-colored garments—were as intoxicated as the galli. They were always armed.

"If we keep out of sight of the priests, I see no danger. If we encounter them, beware."

"We're ready."

Soaemias put her hand against the door and pushed it open. She looked both ways, then entered a hallway with Varius and me behind.

We were near the central part of the temple where the smell of incense was overpowering. Outside, the drums beat like a muffled call to arms. The flutes and horns were more urgent. The marble floors, strewn with rose petals, wavered beneath our feet. The ceilings frescoed with the figures of the zodiac seemed to wobble. I hardly noticed the statues in their niches, nor did I see a stand of weapons or an escape route. I stopped when Soaemias stopped in front of a bronze door, opened it, and beckoned us inside.

The room we entered was an ablution and dressing area. Against the far wall was a pump that fed running water to a spout. The floor, tiled with the figure of Attis, the castrated son of Cybele, sloped to a drain in the middle. Along the sides were stalls that held the paraphernalia of the priests—silk tunics and belts and slippers, amulets in bronze and gold—as well as ceremonial vessels consecrated to the Great Mother.

My concern was how to hide my weapons beneath the priestly garments. The dagger was not a problem, but my legion sword, though short, could never be concealed under a belted tunic. There seemed only one solution: dress as a corybant, and carry weapons openly.

"The store is plentiful," said Soaemias, indicating a large chest near the door. "Here."

Exactly there, and locked. I tried to force the lion-headed clasp with my dagger but had no luck. Finally, I inserted the edge of the sword blade between the lid and hasp, and with some exertion freed the hasp from the hinges. The noise as the hasp broke was surprising—a crack and pop that could have carried far.

But I found two ceremonial swords inside. They were finely made and trimmed with legends of the Goddess in Syriac script, but not of strength or weight to withstand the stress of battle. We should not have to worry about that. I wanted a weapon to slash, and if necessary, kill quickly. When durability came to be the issue, we were dead.

I had been entrusted with the life of a boy who a few hours ago was on line to the throne of an empire, but now was a target—unless I believed the mad words of a man who painted himself blue. I was less sure of his prophecies than of the history of Rome, where men of no name, like Septimus Severus, had risen to command the world, while others born to it, like Caracalla, came to a bad end, their underwear heaped on their boots by the side of the road.

If the life of an emperor was in my hands, the young man had best be quick thinking and well-spoken, which Varius was; tall enough to pass for a man, if that's what the galli were.

"How do I look?" he asked.

Bizarre, but convincing. Varius' blond hair, continued to his waist by the plaits of the wig, shifted the lines of his face toward the feminine more easily than I imagined. When he put his hand on his hip and flounced his hair, I would not like to meet him in a brothel.

"You make a fine recruit," I said. "Next, we'll see how you dance."

Varius did that with a light step. He might have gone into a spin, like a corybant, but suddenly the door to the ablution chamber blew open.

Three men entered the room on the hunt. The first two were corybants in the same rose-colored tunics as myself, armed, like myself, with swords. The last, a broad-shouldered man in the black tunic of the galli, wore a string of pearls from the coils of his hair down his chest. His eyes were bloodshot and bulging. His face in white lead was like a bleached mask. The mouth beneath his hooked nose roared.

"Sacrilege! Defilers of the Mother!"

Soaemias immediately stepped forward. She shielded her son and allowed my free hand the full range of my sword. No accident. She knew what she was doing.

"These men, two acolytes, are under my protection, Archigallus."

The Archigallus, chief official of the temple, looked at Soaemias as if he did not hear her words or heed any. His face swelled beneath the lead paint as if yearning to be free of restraint. I was reminded of the other painted man I had known, and the changes that occurred in him.

"You come from the palace," he said, as if that were an execration. "The Palace of Not. The Palace of Nevermore."

Soaemias' face reflected fear. Word of Caracalla's death had spread. What the Archigallus said was that the authority of her family had been diminished forever by an assassin.

"We will leave the temple now," she said. "We have no wish to interfere with the rites of the goddess."

"You *have* interfered!" he said in a voice that rose to a shout. "You brought the taint of *lust* inside this temple! This is *pollution*!"

The Archigallus took one step forward. The odor that arose from his body was not incense but the putrefaction I first encountered in the praetoria of Septimus Severus in Caledonia.

"Who are you?" he asked.

"A friend of the Mother Augusta."

Soaemias had mirrored the steps of the Archigallus in reverse. She now stood at my side as she whispered. "Be careful. He's drugged."

"You do well to hide your words," said the Archigallus as if speaking to an animal. "Those who slink into the precincts of the holy temple to violate the sanctity of the Mother, to falsely assume the garments of her priests and blaspheme the things that are held sacred, cannot be allowed to prosper."

"Our apologies to the goddess, whose servants you are," I said. "But we must pass."

The Archigallus put his arm out and opened his hand. Without prompting, the corybant on his right filled the large palm with his sword. "You will not pass," he said, clasping the sword and drawing the blade onto me. "You will surrender your weapons."

"I think not."

His eyes did recognize refusal. "Do you know the penalty for polluting the Temple of Cybele? It's death. You will know it now— or in the arena with the wild beasts—but it will come."

When I saw the veins on his arm stand out as he clasped the sword tighter—as he readied himself—I took out his throat so he spoke no more. The sharp blade cut to a depth of a thumbnail, but it was enough to sever the artery. The last thing the madman knew was the spout of hot blood that gaped onto his chest and spread down his body.

The Archigallus dropped his sword to the floor as his hands went to his throat to close the wound. He sunk down as I turned to the corybant on the right—the one who retained his weapon. He was an adept who could halve a fly in midair, but he understood that he faced a man who knew battle.

He should have waited for his rose-colored mate to reclaim his sword, so they could close together. Instead, he feinted to my left. I threw up my arm as if reacting to the move. When my hand came back down, it brought my slave-hair wig hard into his face. He batted the wig aside, but his concentration had been disturbed for an instant. And that, too, was enough.

I took him down low, across the belly, and when he closed his hand around the guts that began to escape his body, I hit him again from the back.

In the same motion, I turned to meet the man who had stooped to pick up the Archigallus' sword from the floor. It never occurred to me that my response would be late. I had kept the second corybant at the corner of my vision and I knew where he was, how far he must travel, and the angle of attack. I judged everything correctly but the speed.

He was already there. He was where he was supposed to be and the thrust came from the angle I thought it would, but I could not get outside it. I was dead, I knew it, and I had already begun to experience the journey that begins at the moment when the mind does not want to die but the body knows it must.

The sword blade came in low, piercing my thigh but not with a great deal of force. The corybant's blow had been altered. It stopped. He stopped. When I stepped back, staggering, his sword fell from his hand before it dropped from my body. I watched it fall but did not hear the sound it made.

He said, "Too late," as if apologizing, then dropped to his knees so hard on the tile that the bones seemed to shatter. He dropped onto his belly. Only then did I see the double-bladed ax fixed at the base of his neck.

Soaemias placed her slippered foot on the man's shoulder. She pulled the ax free. "Your dagger," she said. "I'll make sure they're dead."

* * *

We did not pass directly from the temple. In the clothing of the Great Mother's servants, we walked down the hallway and across the open courtyard of the inner precinct, heads bowed, ceremonial bowls in our hands, moving behind the massive altar before climbing the long stairs to the propylaea.

The stairs continued to a great height until halfway up we reached a ramp that sloped down to the forum, where a massive crowd had gathered. Once we dropped down the canted wall and entered that enormous swell of humanity, we could pass out of sight among them.

We could not afford to be seen by anyone, and we could not let our pursuers know that a man had been wounded. They would find it hard to follow the trail of blood, since it was little. My wound had been tightly bound by Soaemias from the linen at her breast.

She had proven herself a Roman mother with a Syrian heart, but I was worried about her son. Varius had not taken the blood well. He had vomited in the drain, and he could not bear to assist his mother in binding my wound. At last, he cried.

When we came out onto the edge of the ramp above the forum, he stopped and stared as if what before him was not a sea of people but a blow to his innocence. The thousands in the crowd knew only one center of attention—the altar of the Great Mother and her priests.

The noise that had steadily risen as we came down the ramp shrieked like the keening of every mother since the beginning of time. The tambourines and flutes and clarinets and drums made a roaring pulsating din, and the trumpets were like the mooning breath of a mountain. The sounds were so loud that they became as one sound, its beat the heartbeat of the crowd. Anyone caught in this gathering was in thrall to the galli, and the numbers this day were vast.

"I leave you here," said Soaemias, speaking intimately but casting her voice above the clamor. Taking my hand, she kissed it.

"You will have a message of our safe arrival, Soaemias. A morning dove."

She smiled. "Is that your genius?"

"A gentle one, Princess."

She released my hand slowly. In her lingering touch was thanks, and a promise I did not think was imagined. "May we not always be bygones," she said.

She turned from me and kissed her son on the mouth. Varius spoke to her, but I heard nothing save the last word, which I read from his lips—"curse."

Soaemias smiled at her son, holding him. "A man rarely speaks of such things," she said. "A member of the imperial family, never."

And touching his breast, she was gone.

It was the act of a magician. I watched Varius' face, trying to find courage in it, when I looked back for her among the crowd. No trace. Had she dropped down and vanished among the throng? Was there another passage back to the palace on the slope of the ramp?

No, it was the fading light. Darkness had fallen not slowly but suddenly through the dusk. After we made our way through the crowd, we would travel the rest of the way cloaked. Antioch was the only city in the empire that lit the streets at night, but those lamps were nothing like the sun. We might be safe until we tried to pass through the city gate.

"Help me down, Varius. This should be our last passage afoot."

* * *

The boy did as he was asked, which was more than it seemed, for my wound had begun to bleed. We made our way across the length of the forum, and Varius kept his body in front of mine, protecting my leg from the crowd, which increased by the moment.

The people in the square were more than devout now. They were crazed. Their movements mirrored those of the galli who whirled around the altar like painted wheels, their long hair whipping to and fro, their amulets glinting in the red light of the braziers, their loose garments like burning gauze. As they danced, they leaped high in the air as if they had saddled the wind. Wielding their swords and axes in furious pantomime, they transmitted the thrill of danger to everyone, lofting it like drink or drug to the throng.

It was a lunatic mob we traversed, a single body with no mind but what could be taken from the altar. When the madness could go no further, it did. The largest of the galli, more than seven feet tall, jumped to the center of the altar, looming over the stone of the Great Mother like a lover. He made motions like a lover. His hips moved fast and faster. His hands clutched the sky as if it were naked and within his grasp. Screaming words that could not be heard above the music and the noise of the crowd, he took a sword over his head, swinging it in wider and wider arcs until the other priests gave way.

The giant commanded the stage. To the beat of the drums, he began to bring the sword lower in smaller and smaller arcs until the blade flashed before his face and over his outstretched arm. There, it lingered. Slowly, as if leading the beat of the drums, he began to chop.

The first strokes did not break his skin of his arm but came close. This gallus was a performer, a professional. He was playing with his flesh as he played with the crowd.

Then he did it once, twice, thrice, and everything was real. The sword blade bit into him. Blood burst from his arm below the shoulder, and lower, on his biceps and forearm. Again. And again.

Blood ran over the stone of the Great Mother as if from the darkest part of the heavens. The eunuch's eyes spun and his head swayed to the rhythms. He was saying that he was sated. The goddess was sated. This part was done.

"We'll not make headway," said Varius, shouting into my ear. "We'll have to wait for the climax. Look. The acolyte. He's the one to watch."

The altar was high, and I was taller than most in the crowd. We were part of the crowd for being among it. The only thing that kept me from slipping into the same frenzy was the pain in my leg.

Then the delirium rose a count. On the altar, a second man commanded the stage dressed in the same garments, but differently made. His hair was the length of a man's and his skin unlike a woman's. He was young. Taking a place before the sacred stone, waving his arms furiously—as if he was demanding attention or moving to his own demons—he unbelted his tunic and dropped his clothing to the ground.

Everyone looked on as if they were looking in a window. The naked acolyte was made like a man in every way, even to his member. And that was erect. It seemed unnatural, but in no way remarkable. Every other man in the crowd might have owned to being erect, and every other woman to being dilated in her parts. That was the message the drums conveyed to their blood.

The man on the altar held a piece of glass in his hand. Not a dagger. Not a sword. He took the jagged glass and put it between his legs as the drums increased their beat and grew louder. The cymbals crashed in a crescendo. At the same time, the galli began to beat their shields with their swords.

The man screamed until the veins in his neck stood up like ribs of fire. He could not be heard—nothing of his rage came to the crowd—but the sound was more powerful for being silent. Everyone entered his mind and body through that dark well. Everyone shared the force when with a violent movement of his arm he severed his testicles from his body.

He held fast. He held onto them and held them aloft. As the blood ran down his arm, he displayed those two poor orbs in a sac that had linked him to immortality. He shook them gently once, then fiercely, sprinkling the altar with drops of his blood. He was telling everyone this was the climax, the consecration, his first moment of his life as a half-man and priest.

As the beat of the drums and tambourines, the wail of the clarinets and horns, and the clashing of cymbals and shields rose to a crescendo, the newest gallus flung his old and useless parts into the crowd.

Quickly, the frantic mass closed on itself as women clamored for the bloody remains.

* * *

We saw two more men castrated that night as we passed through the crowds in the forum and the streets to the stable where I had left my mount.

It was the most degenerate spectacle I had ever witnessed, but it had one useful effect. The attention of the people was always on the man who held the glass in his hand. It seemed that shard of the most renowned export of the province of Syria was part of the ritual. It seemed the bloody parts were always held up like trophies and thrown to waiting women, who prized them.

What would those beggars think in the morning when they looked down and saw what was missing? Were Syrians different than other men? Did they like the idea that what they were would end with them?

Who knew? The streets were bright with torches set in orderly rows before each building and massed at every crossing. Even the smoke seemed perfumed and obscene. I did not think we were noticed at the temple, but we had been seen in priest's clothing. When word came to the streets of the killings, we might have to fight. I was glad we had taken the time to wash the blood of the eunuchs away and stack the bodies in the weapons chest. It was too bad the chest could not be locked down to buy more time.

And Varius had to hold firm. He seemed affected less by the slaughter of genitalia than the loss of whole men. He had never looked away as those testicles were cut off, nor did he vomit. As we continued as well as my leg could go, skirting the passage through the perfumer's quarters that would cause more pain, I tried to probe his thoughts.

"Do you understand these rituals, Varius?"

"Not altogether," he said. "I've heard it said that becoming a eunuch combines in one body the qualities of a man and a woman. It seems that neither sex offers a perfect communion with the goddess. A third is necessary."

"You speak like a philosopher. Have you been in Antioch long?"

"A month. I came with Mother when she decided not to go with Father to his post." Varius smiled late. "It was said that the emperor requested her presence. And he might have. After Antoninus exiled his wife, he trusted no women but the ones born to his family."

"And we thought he was crazy."

"He did not sleep," said Varius. "When he did, his dreams were haunted by demons. Perhaps that is madness."

He spoke factually, telling of a relative he had not liked, but a relative nonetheless. Until yesterday, his cousin had ruled the world and made it a rich place for his family. They were all on his mother's side Syrian, but Varius had been raised at court. He had never known his ancestral homeland. That meant not many people knew him here.

"You understand the situation, don't you?"

"I believe so," he said.

"You must be sure of one thing. The new emperor cannot tolerate your presence in Antioch or Rome. The easiest thing is to remove you from the scene. He will try to kill you, and he will not announce his intention. If we reach Emesa, he may allow you to live. The city is loyal to Rome but has no direct Roman rule. The priests of the temple govern. They are your family."

"That I know."

"Then know that every Roman soldier is an assassin working for the frumentarii. Every Syrian we meet may be in the pay of the frumentarii. We are in a race to Emesa. Anyone who stands in our way must be removed."

"Killed?"

"If necessary."

Varius did not like the choice. He had not liked it at the temple and did not like its place in his future. "I could cut off my balls," he said. "That would mean the end of it."

"Is that what comes first to mind?"

He smiled in his usual way, which had left him at the temple. "I'd rather keep them," he said. "I might find a future use."

"Perhaps you will tonight."

The reason: we had stopped at the head of the square first from the Eastern Gate. The street to the left led to the tanneries, the street to the right to the stable, and directly ahead was the only exit from the city in the area. At times, a guard was mounted there, but not on a holy day when most of the population took to the streets. No guard had been at the post when I came through earlier. Now, three Roman soldiers were on duty. Every person who passed was being stopped, and looked over, but only if they were leaving the city. That was bad.

We moved down the street toward the stable, where we were lucky. As we turned the corner, the mood of the crowd turned. They no longer harmed themselves in celebration, but others in anger. The cry of "Sacrilege!" arose like the beat of the drums. Swords and daggers came out. They were telling anyone who would listen, which was everyone in the city, that the Great Mother had been defiled and her priests murdered in her temple. Armed men roamed the streets until they become armed bands, screaming for the blood of the "fish-eaters."

"They're not looking for us," said Varius. "They're after Christians."

And welcome to them. The followers of Christ were the most fanatic sect in the empire, and Antioch was their home. They ate fish, sacred to the Syrians, and tolerated no god but their own. When trouble broke out, their death warrants were the first signed by the mobs.

My hope was that mayhem in the streets was as good as time, but I doubted if it would be enough to draw the guards away from their post. They were soldiers.

"We have a diversion," I said. "Now we need luck to get us through the gate."

"You don't think our disguise is good enough?"

"Those guards will speak Syriac. We'll be safe until we open our mouths."

Varius nodded. "I know some of the language, but not enough to convince a native."

"We can't chance it then. We'll ride through the gate. At twenty paces spur your horse."

He looked at me as if disappointed. "Won't that be dangerous? The guards will stop us."

"I'll engage them. Your job is to make sure you get away."

He shook his head. "You'll not make it through," he said. "Not with your leg."

"That's my concern. It's irrelevant to the heir to the throne of Caesar."

Varius looked at me as if trying to read the warp of my life, or any life that might come to a sudden end. "I think I understand. You're going by the prophecy, aren't you? The words that a criminal gave to us."

I wondered if he remembered the Blue Man. He was a child when those words were spoken, and so I wondered.

"I go by the word I gave the Mother Augusta."

* * *

I had more affection for my stallion, Bacchus, than I did for all the animals and things of Syria. He was lampblack, Parthian, trained in battle. I often thought he sensed its coming, and sensed it through me. A rider and his mount are one when what is ahead is unknown but for the danger. They share things that are not shared even by a man and woman.

Bacchus responded to ten commands with fidelity. Nine were common. The last was seldom heard by any man alive. When I cried "Victory," he charged the man at whom he was directed. He struck with his speed and mass, trampling the smaller things that stood in his path. I believe this is what he lived for, though he knew, as I did, that it was a last measure.

"Channel as close as possible behind me. A lane to the right should be clear."

Varius looked at me with an uneasiness that had nothing to do with his mount. A decent horseman, he seemed to have established a rapport with the animal that had been brought to the stable. Perhaps it was one of his own.

"And if you go down, Marcellus—"

"Keep riding. Stop for nothing. The road to Raphanae veers south about fifteen miles outside the city. A horseman like you should be able to make a hundred miles a day. Be sure to skirt the barracks at Raphanae and continue on to Emesa."

Varius gave the Latin salute with the first three fingers of the right hand. "To the gods!"

"And keep your mind on your horse."

I put Bacchus at a walk as we came into the square that led to the Eastern Gate, which was nothing like it had been minutes before. A group of ten men were flogging with knotted whips another man lashed to the base of an obelisk. He might have been a Christian, or one of their priests, who were not much different than corybants. He screamed, they screamed, and one sound was indistinguishable from the other. On the far side of the square, coming from the street that led to the tanneries, another mob herded a family, including children, toward the gate. The ditches outside the walls would be filled with Christian dead by morning.

I felt lucky but not remorseful. The passions fanned by the orgies of Cybele were bound to find an outlet, and any excuse would do. Letting blood first hand was better than the arena. We found ourselves knowing that when one of the Mother's revengers turned from his group and headed our way, dragging a Christian girl by the hair.

"Galli!" he said. "You who have suffered for the Mother!"

He screamed at Varius—at both of us in our costumes—and he was as drunk as passion could make a man. As he came closer, I saw a long curved dagger in his right hand.

"Will the Mother accept this Christian filth for her own?" he asked, jerking the girl's head to the side, exposing her neck to the knife pressed to her flesh. "I give her to you!"

She was a pretty girl about fourteen who probably enjoyed life until he cut her throat, and like garbage, dumped her, bleeding, to the ground. In the same motion, he turned and walked back to the friends who hurried toward the gate to deal with the rest of the family in the same way, the same deliberate repetition, the completion of the cycle we had created.

I noticed almost too late that Varius was about to vacate his mount and go to the girl whose blood ran across the stones in a flickering pool. I took him by the shoulder hard just as he swung his leg over.

"Let me go!" he said. "Get your hands off me!"

I looked into a face glowing with pity. "Have you never had a life dedicated to you?"

"What?" he said. "What are you saying?"

"You must expect this—you must demand it—of every man and woman in your empire."

"Then I don't want it!" he said. "Never!"

"Therefore, you won't have it."

He wanted to tell me what I could do with his empire that never was, and where I could put all the things that would never be, when something took control of his emotions. He snapped the reins in his hand and set his face ahead.

"They're right, you know," he said without looking back. "There's only one god."

I took his word. The family and the rioters had reached the gate, and it was the only advantage we had. My leg could not stand another shock; and Varius would never make his way through the gate unless I made it for him.

Would he obey? How much had he left behind with that girl? There was one way to find out. "Victory!"

Bacchus' charge put me back in the saddle and his heavy hooves pounded the stones. I knew the guards would hear the sound of an oncoming horse, but they did not have warning. I was within twenty yards, then ten, when the three turned to meet their fate.

The man on the right was Bacchus' destination. He was a bull from his belly to his neck, a rooster in his legs, and eyes as big as a statue. He did not move when he could have, and when he made his decision, late, he turned and tried to dodge as Bacchus came onto him.

I remember the shock of collision through the great body of Bacchus, the impact as it traveled through three bodies to my own. Then all I knew was I had hit the ground. I hit hard; my vision was blurred. I saw Bacchus rearing on my right. Someone was down on the left and two men were coming ahead. My leg was numb.

I could not get up. I tried once, twice. I felt a strange sensation, an absence of pain and thought as the world whirled around me.

Suddenly, the two men who were almost upon me blew away. A horse and rider blew through the gap. It was the roan gelding with Varius on his back.

I believe he would have run me down, too, but my third try at rising was the one that worked. I made it to my feet in a blur of darkened colors, I had Bacchus by the withers, he was pulling away and I was pulling myself up by his mane.

We were gone.

EMESA

We were all night on the road to Emesa, traveling Trajan's New Highway, centuries old but as good as the day it was built. Roads like these, ten layers thick and faced with cobblestone, were the means by which Rome kept the rule of the world. The legions put the stones down, maintained them, and held the vast web of empire together. If there was a better foundation of government, no man had yet thought of it.

Our problem was the traffic. It was not less at night than by day, as carts filled with produce and hard goods left the hinterland, hoping to arrive in the city before first light. Coming on them in the darkness, veering to pass, veering back to avoid collisions with vehicles that were nearly invisible on the other side of the road, put pressure on my wound that I would have given much not to deal with. It had begun to bleed again.

The pain kept me awake and in the saddle. We were never headed by riders on the road to Raphanae. Twice we passed detachments of soldiers, but they were clearly not looking for us. Five miles before we reached the garrison where I had been posted by Macrinus, we turned east along a secondary road until we rejoined the thirty-foot highway on the other side.

By then it was nearly morning. We had paralleled the Orontes most of the night, but south of the city of Apamea the river vanished. Only the broad mountains to the west remained as a guide. They were a strong barrier to the coast, shutting off the interior from the port cities except by scattered toll roads through the mountain passes. To the south lay the ancient heartland of Syria, called Phoenicia, and to the east the deserts of the interior.

We took the latter way. Soon after we entered on the final leg of our journey, we stopped at a way station to water our mounts. Among the several small buildings stood an inn. It was little more than a roof to keep out sun and rain, but it seemed so inviting I lost all sense of where I was. The pain that had kept me awake through the night eased, and as I sat beside the cistern, I slid into sleep. The next thing I remember was the sound of Varius' voice as it seemed to come softly, but not out of place, from the painted mouth of the archigallus.

"Are you feeling better?"

No galli were in sight. Varius bent over my body close. "Yes. I had a dream."

"You lost a lot of blood," he said, rolling up my trousers to the thigh. "I bought a piece of seric silk inside. Who knows, it may even be clean."

I looked away when he unwrapped the bandage on my leg that had been made from his mother's garments. I could not tend myself, nor did I want to know how the wound looked.

Surprisingly, Varius, who disliked the sight of blood so much in Antioch, did not shrink from it here. That was good. Away from the shadow of the palace and the shade of his mother, he seemed to grow into himself rapidly. Another day on the run might call a man from a boy. That would be one of the strangest phenomenon in life were it not so common.

"All the colors of the rainbow," he said. "I think you may lose this limb if it does not receive attention."

I looked now. The wound was suppurating. No colors of the rainbow were so sickly. "It will receive attention when we reach Emesa."

"The city is still some distance," said Varius. "The innkeeper promised we have four hours ahead of us. Perhaps more."

"You told him where we were going?"

Varius closed his eyes and puckered his lips. "I'm afraid I'm new to this life. Of course, I erred."

"I can tell you the man who owns this inn is not new to it. If he doesn't make timely reports to the frumentarii, he's a fool who's missing a ready source of income. And I doubt that he is."

Varius smiled. "He seemed like a fool."

"I'm sure that serves him well. You might ask yourself what disguise will serve you best in the future."

"I haven't really thought about it. Must I?"

"If you want to live. If not, continue as you are."

He grew serious, more so than at any time since we left the palace. "It's true that everything has changed," he said. "Everything I knew is gone. I suppose it does no good hoping for a return."

"It will do great harm if all you do is hope. Now help me up. Are the horses ready?"

"For the last hour," he said.

"I slept an *hour?*"

"I didn't want to awaken you. You were never more peaceful, Marcellus, than when you were the questor of your dreams."

I had no answer for his words, which were as natural as his new and filthier beauty. I would pray to the gods to visit him with common sense. I hoped this prayer would be answered, but knew not when.

* * *

The countryside we traversed after leaving the inn was like none I had seen. We still traveled the high ground well above sea level, but it was as if we had entered a long valley of dark drifting sameness. I do not know if my perceptions were keen, but the ground appeared as strewn with gravel, or rocks and boulders thrown down by volcanoes, or gathered in masses of sheet-like stone that had been poured like batter on the earth. The tones were grave and heavy, black and gray and every shade of the night. They were the same bitter colors that the earth, our mother, spewed in her fury.

The miles of broken basalt were good for nothing that grew. It seemed like a corner of the earth into which all the debris had slid. I would have felt that at any time, but chills and weakness touched my limbs. The sun pulsated in my body. It grew in the sky, burgeoning like a storm, until it rained down without relief. The biggest rocks began to give off strange aureoles. The aureoles began to spark. The pain in my leg seemed to lessen, which was very bad.

We were three hours out when I lost consciousness.

* * *

I remember being placed in a litter with two mules and a shade hung over my head to keep back the sun, and I remember the sun declining. No voices came to me that were familiar. I searched for Varius but did not find him. Then darkness fell as if it were permanent.

The place where I awoke was a large vault of basalt completely enclosed. The ceiling was low, less than five feet above my head, sparkling with bright but dark minerals embedded in the mass, which meant a light was near. I turned my head to see two candles burning, putting out a smell of beeswax and myrrh on a ledge niched into the wall. That's when I saw the eunuch.

Bent to his work with mortar and pestle upon a table, he seemed to take no notice of my awakening. He had the boyish skin they all had, but its smoothness was enhanced by having no hair on his head. A man like an egg. His nose was small and his chin seemed to exist to vanish. Only his eyes were salient—as pale as bone buttons set close together in his face.

"Where am I?"

The eunuch did not start at the sound of my voice. Continuing to knock the pestle about in the stone bowl, he spoke in Latin in a high voice without accent. "You are in the Temple of El-Gabal in Emesa."

"Is this a prison or hiding place?"

The eunuch smiled like a hungry bird. "We thought it best, since it was your wish not to be seen, that you be placed out of sight."

"And the boy who was with me?"

"Varius is safe."

"Where is he?"

The eunuch poured the contents of the mortar into a glass of wine, which he brought to the stone bed where I lay. He sat on a stool at the side of the bed. "It would be best if you don't know. Only two men have that information, and one, by now, is in no position to act upon it."

I suppose he meant that Varius had been conducted to a secret place by a man who would not return from it. That may have been wise; it was certainly Syrian.

"The boy is my responsibility."

"No longer, Questor. He is among his people."

What he said was correct. The way he said it was impeccable. If he told the truth, my mission as set out by the Mother Augusta had been accomplished. But that did not account for my feelings, which were the instincts of a soldier.

"Your name?"

"I am Gannys," he said.

I waited for him to finish, but he did not. Eunuchs often gave up the rest of the their names along with the other things they had lost. At least Gannys, unlike the ones in Antioch, did not appear to be armed.

"How is my leg?"

He did not answer. With a fine touch he unwrapped the bandage that covered the wound. When he whisked the bandage away, I was amazed. The badly colored gash on my thigh was nearly gone. What remained looked like a surgical incision that seemed to be healed. No discoloration, pus or swelling showed. It was as if nature's curative powers had accelerated to unheard of speed while I slept.

"How long have I been here?"

"Two days," he said.

I was surprised, but would have thought longer by the way the wound healed. Two days was much too long, of course. "You're a fine doctor."

"Since my birth, I've been a servant in the house of Julius Bassianus, the high priest of the temple," he said with a sitting bow. "One skill I acquired in his service is some knowledge of the art of medicine. I learned what I know from the great Galen, who also served this family. In addition to his unmatched knowledge of the human body, he was a believer in the healing power of sleep, and the secrets that could be obtained from dreams."

"Did I talk in my sleep?"

"Yes," he said. "But truthfully I could glean little from your words. You spoke mostly of glowing rocks."

As I should have. I recalled them among the rubble, which may not have been where I was. I was there, I was here, I was where my mind took me.

"The mixture in that cup. I am to drink it and return to sleep?"

"It will help," he said. "I think when you awaken, you will be able to function without reference to your wound."

I had the feeling he was right, but trusted nothing about the man. Was that due to my prejudice against his kind?

"Hold your potion, Gannys. First, I want proof that Varius is alive and well. Second, I require a morning dove."

"Your pardon?"

"A morning dove must be sent to the Princess Soaemias in Antioch."

"I will see that the bird is delivered," he said. "But I would be less than honest if I did not tell you that the princess is no longer in Antioch."

I felt a sudden pull of emotion, much stronger than I could have imagined. I did not ask myself why. "Where has she gone?"

"She came here to be with her son. To make her life his life." Gannys put forth the glass so I might drink. "She arrived last night and has been twice to see you. She will return, I'm sure."

That Soaemias had visited me in this place was flattering, but under the circumstances it fed my impatience. She should never have come to Emesa. Even if she traveled unobserved, which was unlikely, her presence would become known to almost everyone. And that would include, quickly, the frumentarii. On their heels would be the legions.

I swung my feet to the stone floor. Knocking the cup aside, I raised Gannys from the stool by his robes, which were priestly. "Take me to her."

* * *

Two guards stood at the end of the short passage that led from the underground chamber to the surface, but Gannys did not call them out. That proved, more or less, that we were on the same side. The guards were Emesene archers, the best at their trade afoot or ahorse. I served with marksmen like them on every frontier in the empire. Their presence as auxiliaries with the legions was the one of the reasons Emesa retained its independence from Rome.

"I hope you did not station men where Varius is being kept. There could be no better pointer to spies."

Though Gannys was taken aback, he answered quickly. "Where he is, there is no one."

"Is he in proximity to his mother?"

"No."

We emerged from the tunnel at a lower level on the acropolis that loomed over the city. Under the walls of the temple stood a long building like a tenement. I had seen other hovels like it close by temples in Syria. Small rooms all in a row, with smaller periods of occupation. They were cells really, and the means by which the temples prospered. In the cells, women prostituted themselves for the glory of a faceless god.

The temple above the sacred whorehouse was grand. Fronted by a propylaea sixty feet high with columns of red marble meant to awe the faithful, it was the first in a series. Behind lay an octagonal courtyard nearly as high, joined to a second courtyard of huge proportions. I could not see the god who was honored, but his temple rose at the end of the courtyard in six columns of green marble. There was no doubt who ruled this city, or to whom the wealth flowed.

Below in the distance the Orontes River appeared like a benign serpent, holding the city in its coils, making the dry lands bloom. The river was in full spate, pale green with melt-water that turned the valleys deeper green. Emesa could have been a smaller, leaner Antioch but for the dark tones that the prevailing stone lent to most of the buildings.

And the acropolis would have made a fine defensive position in any other age. The hill was not tremendously high, but it dominated the city. The lower part of town, to which we began to descend by way of a steep path, held the apartment buildings, the homes of the rich, the amphitheater, the circus, and several large markets. In almost every house would be running water, public and private baths in every district, and to carry the flow passages cut through the rock. I was certain that the tunnel we had traveled once was a conduit for water.

"Do many strangers pass through the city?"

"Enough," said Gannys. "We're on the main trade route from the East. Caravans come often from Palmyra with Oriental goods."

"Those should not be our chief concern. What of visitors from the west?"

"Caravans do proceed to the east," he said. "We have steady traffic to the temple. Some are Roman soldiers."

I was glad Gannys knew that. Perhaps he ran the whorehouse, too. "Any concentration of more than two or three men should be tracked. The authorities should be notified."

Gannys nodded. "I've already seen to that."

"Are you the chief administrator of Emesa, too?"

"Yes," he said.

I was surprised, but would have to adjust to the idea. A man could perform that work, a woman if she were aggressive, but a thing that was neither? It was not so much a question of mind, but instincts.

"Where is Princess Soaemias staying?"

"At her home." Gannys pointed to the center of the lower city and a dwelling so large I had thought it was a complex of apartments. "It's there, just beyond the baths."

"I'll go to her, Gannys. Station the two keenest-eyed men you have at the summit of the acropolis with orders to report any movements of men in a body."

"If you think that's necessary."

"It's vital. Like all precautions."

* * *

In front of the palace of Princess Soaemias, hung with cypress boughs to honor the recent dead, stood two men occupied with little but themselves. They were dressed like Syrians, whom the gods had blessed with fine weather and ample leisure.

The palace suited the family of the high priest of Emesa, which was also the family of the Severii. Sprawling for two acres in the center of the city, it was surrounded by a twelve-foot wall with placements for defense at each gate and right angle. The fortifications had obviously been thrown up to guard against incursions from the desert tribes. There was no defense against the disfavor of Rome.

I walked past the entrance, turning into a side street lined with date palms, and near the head of the block, lemon and lime trees. Because Emesa was an old city, its plan did not conform to the Roman model, but like Rome itself took eccentric turns. In back of the palace stood two sets of stables pierced by an alley and flanked by a wider street leading to the spice market.

I found no guard on the back gate. Slipping the thong on the lock, I entered without notice. The only resistance came from two brown dogs with dark muzzles, who barked until one of the servants came to calm them. That fellow demanded my name but not how I had come so close to his lady. He led me through the kitchen—a model of Roman technology—to the major domo, who accepted me for delivery to the next station.

We went by turns to a garden completely hidden from the street. It was heavily planted with colonnades that led to a portico. Statues of the gods and the Severii, some of whom were the same, gathered like an audience around a pool of cascading water. A gazelle grazed on the grass. A morning dove, yes, cooed from the branches of a tamarind tree. And sequestered under a red roof, Soaemias sat on a bench surrounded by massive blooms of the season as she dictated a letter to one of her freedmen.

I felt as if I were interrupting an idyll until her violet eyes saw me. With a small movement of her hand, the servant and freedman vanished into the recesses of the house. Instantly, we were alone.

"You are well, Marcellus."

I sat on the bench beside her, inhaling the smell of flowers and what I imagined were more subtle scents. "Yes. Completely."

As if she had no wish to quit her role as my nurse, she touched my thigh at the wound. The pain that my journey from the vault created fell away completely.

"I'm happy to hear that," she said. "Varius told me of your trials. I think no man could have done the things you did."

"They were not so much. And gladly done."

She smiled, and it was not lightly done. "Then I think you'll be happy to know I've just received word from the Mother Augusta. Macrinus, our new emperor, has guaranteed her safety in Antioch."

"So it's Macrinus."

"No other," she said. "The murderer comes forth to admit his deed. He apparently has no fear of the gods."

"But that is good news—if the usurper plans to honor his word. The Mother Augusta will be safe."

"He likes the Mother Augusta alive for the moment, and he knows Varius escaped," she said. "But I don't think he'll march against this city. He needs our good will—and our archers—to guard against the Parthians."

"Then all is well."

"As good as it seems," she said. "Your service to this family will never be forgotten. Whatever we have is yours to demand."

"I will take only what is freely given."

She withdrew her hand from my thigh and put it to her breast. "Then take me," she said.

* * *

Roman women are like others in bed, but more exacting and mindful of their pleasure, which becomes the pleasure of their mate. For that reason, they are more exciting, and when they are also Syrian, they are more skilled. Mouth, tongue, vagina, work as one. The communion never ceases. The end, when it is found, is found together, and the sensations are like music that was composed elsewhere, written nowhere, and taken to the last note as if the figures were the prelude to a complex orchestration. Finale. Then, if they are truly Roman and completely Syrian, like a coda comes the intrigue.

"Two guards are at the back gate now," she said as she stood at the window. "Archers."

"I'm glad to see that Gannys awoke from his administrative sleep."

She turned her focus back to me. Her eyes consumed my body again as if she had been satisfied, but only for a time. "You told him it was vital," she said. "I had word of that."

"Yes."

"But only to have this."

She turned around, parting her silk robe to her hips, revealing her breasts and the nipples that were the color of her lips, the thighs that were as perfectly formed as her breasts, and the tuft of fleece that was darker now and matted with come. Romans hated silk, of course. It was soft, degenerate. The way it clung to the limbs, the way it displayed the form of a woman like an invitation, the way that it could be partially invaded by the eyes. Romans loved wool. Pain. Some Romans.

"Yes," I said. "No."

"So you believe that Macrinus will violate his oath to the Mother Augusta."

"He's moving slowly, but with the legions behind him. He cannot be resisted. He can be delayed and at some point he may slip badly. Macrinus is not a brilliant man, as we know."

"Is that a qualification for the office of emperor, do you think?"

"Of course not. But for intrigue, yes."

She smiled at the thing she liked, which was so well combined with the other thing. As she sat beside me, the smell of her sex and what she had drawn from me were a provender of earthy scents. The breeze from the window could not drive it away.

"Do you know," she said with her finger at my lips, "that Macrinus has promised to deify my cousin?"

She watched my face for the ghost of dismay, but did not find it. The god Caracalla. That seemed right. He was never much of a man.

"Macrinus wants to link his name to the dynasty as close as he can," I said. "He was born with nothing to nothing in a village on the coast of Mauritania. He needs all the sanction he can find to appease the Senate and the people."

"He's trying to hide his complicity in the death of my cousin," she said. "We have it on good word that Macrinus was with the party that journeyed to the Temple of the Moon."

"So he went to guarantee the result."

"It seems," she said. "My cousin was apparently so distressed he could not control his bodily functions. He apparently stopped at the side of the road to relieve himself. The entire guard apparently looked away to vouchsafe the emperor's privacy at such a moment. That, apparently, gave the assassin a chance to strike."

"I always doubted Martialis in that role. Now doubt seems to surround everything."

"What we know is that my cousin was slain on the way to the temple," she said. "All else, according to an eyewitness—a loyal member of my cousin's bodyguard—is a fabrication."

And if she was right, the Druid's prophecy had met its first failure. Its verification was of rumor. I felt a mixture of disappointment and happiness, but the disappointment fled.

"I'm pleased that Varius is out of the usurper's reach."

"You have great affection for him, don't you?"

"It's hard not to. After the way he performed on our journey, it would be impossible. He did very well."

"More for you than for his mother, I think."

"Of a different kind."

"I sense something between you two," she said. "Something private. Why were you so willing to risk your life to secure the most dangerous man in the empire?"

"For this," I said, taking her in my arms.

She let herself be kissed. She returned the kiss, but with a reserve that was telling. When it ended, she put her finger to my throat. "Perhaps I'm missing something that should be plain. I'm Varius' mother, who must love him. I look at him as the fruit of my body. But the way you look at him is much different. And yet your lust is not for boys."

"How do you know?"

She laughed. "Credit me with some insight. Some things can be learned from a life in the palace of the emperor. I've seen slaves bled to death for the pleasure it lends to a man's orgasm. I've seen the look of lust in a man's eyes change lives. Millions of lives."

"So you love power."

"What I love is not the issue. You're evading my question. What do you share?" she asked again. "The two men I love."

I did not miss the intonations of her words, or fail to note that they were easy to give. "Varius and I shared one special day in Britain."

"What happened on that day?"

"A man died. He was crucified."

"A criminal?"

"Of a sort. This one pretended to know the future."

She looked at me closely. "What did he say?"

"You should ask Varius."

"I don't have Varius," she said. "Perhaps I never will again. I said farewell to my son."

"Is he completely safe?"

"Yes," she said. "Except for what will happen to him on the mountain."

She had already said more than she should have, but probably not all she knew. I saw no point in holding back superstition. "The man who died that day was a subversive—a priest. All the things he told have come true until this day, when suddenly they did not."

I saw the highlights in her eyes change color. The Roman blue gave way like a latch to Syrian violet. I wondered if that dichotomy was stable, and if I would ever be able to tell.

"What were the things, Marcellus?"

"He said your cousin, Caracalla, would die in the worst place in his empire."

"*Carrhae*," she said, like the curse that it was.

"Yes. But he also said your cousin would die reeking of waste."

She sat up on the couch, her face marked by fear. I reminded myself that she linked to the cult of the Great Mother and Astarte. Her beauty and intelligence had been placed in the service of bizarre gods at an early age.

"What did you say?" Her voice was higher and touched by urgency. "Tell me *exactly* what was said."

"Very well. The priest opined that Caracalla would die stinking of piss, which we know to be untrue."

She said nothing for longer than the Blue Man must have hung on the cross. I had not watched his agonies, and I was not pleased to watch her struggle to control her voice.

"Do you know the rituals of the Temple of Sin?"

"Not at all."

"Before the emperor set out for Carrhae, he would have observed the following: to be dressed in black; to be consecrated to the deity with prayer, fasting, and a mood of humble sorrow; and last, to be drenched in a perfume made from incense, poppies, and the urine of a goat."

I watched her eyes from which logic had fled, as it had from the world. "Now I wish to know what was said of Varius."

"That he would be Caesar."

* * *

I had barely related the sum of the Blue Man's wisdom when Gannys appeared at the door to the bedchamber unannounced. He was obviously in a hurry to impart news, but he came to the inner sanctum of Soaemias as if he knew the way. What gave him pause was the sight of me on her bed. Before he spoke what had come to him, he gave me a look that I did not like.

"A cohort of soldiers is on the way," he said. "They're three miles from the city."

"Do they come by way of Raphanae?" I asked. "Or Apamea?"

"The latter, I believe," he said. "Some are in uniforms of the Praetorian Guard."

"Then they come from Macrinus."

"It would seem."

I didn't know what was wrong with Gannys that would cause him to equivocate about such a thing. The Praetorian Guard was the emperor's personal weapon. They were sometimes used in battle, but because they made such big targets, were usually kept by for work on a smaller scale, like selective killing of enemies of the regime.

"They've come for Varius."

"And you."

"They're not looking for me, but what happens next will be carried out by me. Now where was the last place Varius could have been seen?"

"The spice market," said Soaemias. "He left—"

"That's enough. I don't wish to know more."

She looked at me with fear now, and I suppose it was for the men she loved. "I won't have this," she said. "Not on my land."

"There's nothing you can do. The Guard might be beaten back, but the legions would follow, as many as necessary."

"Something can always be done," she said, turning to Gannys. "Fetch Drusus."

I wondered what would answer her summons—a giant like Thrax, a master of siege warfare and elephants—but the young boy who appeared minutes later was more remarkable than any cipher of my imagination.

He was an apparition. Drusus, of twelve or thirteen years, had blond hair with a curl, blue eyes, and lips full and well formed. His skin did not partake of the blight of adolescence, nor did his limbs outgrow his body by much. Except for his hair, which was long, he was as near a copy of Varius as any human being could be. He looked like, and perhaps was, his twin.

"Drusus, you will accompany the questor. Do nothing but what he wills. And on no account will you speak."

"Mistress." He bowed.

"Gannys, see that his hair is trimmed. At once."

Gannys also bowed. He quickly took the boy from the room.

Soaemias looked at me, which she had been careful not to do since Drusus entered the room. "I should have his tongue cut out, but that would arouse suspicion."

"I don't think that's necessary. But it would be wiser for you to disappear like Varius."

"I'll take your advice, which has been an oracle to me."

"As Drusus was to me."

She took my hand to remind me that simple gestures are best, and the most final. "You feel I owe you an explanation."

"No," I said. "The fact that he exists speaks for itself."

"But what you don't know is that Drusus is the product of the body of a slave girl who once served our household. He's six months younger than Varius. That's because my husband took himself to her while I was pregnant."

What she described was common among Roman men who had the means to afford a comely slave. Most wives accepted the practice— and some gladly—except those who could afford not to.

"I'm surprised you kept the boy."

In her smile, which was quick, I saw her pain. "I could have sold Drusus. He's quite beautiful. But it's a myth that the imperial family may do whatever it pleases. In some ways, we're more closely bound than our slaves. I realized Drusus might one day perform an important role. He was kept for that purpose. Believe me, there was no other."

"And are there others . . . like him."

"None," she said. "The woman who bore him was destroyed."

I did not ask by whom. That seemed clear, as were the reasons why she seemed to hold no affection, or other emotions, for her husband.

"Does anyone know of the boy's existence?"

"Very few outside this household."

"Then what you're proposing might work—unless Drusus speaks."

"He would not do so unless under torture," she said. "And I doubt that he will live long enough for that. Custom holds otherwise."

"But if he should speak?"

"Then he does. And Varius will be more distant."

* * *

She supplied me with a uniform, one of her husband's, though she did not say so. It lacked the insignia of questor, but was in other ways acceptable. I should not say what more she gave, or promised. It was what the condemned man longs for but never receives.

Drusus and I mounted the horses that had been readied at her stable, and in that he was unequal to Varius. The black mare did not like her rider. She fought Drusus every stride of the slow gait that we kept up along the street toward the spice market. She may have sensed something strained in his demeanor. An aura seemed to hang like a pale omen at the nape of Drusus' neck where his skin was so new to the sun.

Although he could not have anticipated this day, Drusus must have known from an early age that he was the image of Varius, a counterfeit that could be taken from circulation at any time. If he were intelligent, he would have put his heels into the mare's flanks. But he was a boy, and though a slave, did not believe that he could really die.

The market square we entered from the south was large and fragrant. The hundreds of stalls lining the quadrangle and an acre of bins in the center was the reason Emesa had grown to its size and wealth. The city stood on the fringe of Roman control. Caravans came across the desert with the precious spices of the East—ginger and cloves from China, sesame, cardamom, and coriander from India, cinnamon, allspice and aniseed from the islands to the south.

If I reached down from the back of my mount to carry off the large parcel of saffron that lay under a belled glass, I could with its proceeds buy a villa on Capri, a parcel of slaves, or perhaps a seat in the Senate. But when we halted near the first row of stalls, those dreams returned to the ether.

Almost immediately, a cohort of Praetorian Guards appeared from the north on the far side of the market. Their uniforms were the same as regular soldiers of the legions, but their size marked them out. Each man stood more than six feet tall, and many cleared six and a half. Everything was outsize, even to their swords, daggers, and spears. On their shields, visible as they grew closer, was their symbol of power—the scorpion.

The first rank fanned out east and west to make a slow closure around the square. Clearly, the frumentarii had done their work in Emesa. I was glad to see Gannys had done his, too. He had increased the guard at the market, which would be three or four men monitoring the flow of money and precious spice. They now numbered a dozen or more, including four archers who stood atop the buildings at each corner of the square.

The troops closed the three sides of the square, then I felt them at my back. They would not attack me or the boy, because they had no orders for it. The man who gave the orders arrived as the last of the soldiers peeled back to give him the entrance through their ranks. He rode a speckled black stallion. I knew him.

Oclatinus Adventus rode toward me like a conqueror, his ceremonial breastplate gleaming in the late sun. He had been emperor for a day, perhaps two, while Macrinus took the pulse of the legions. When Macrinus decided the soldiers did not seem to mind a murderer as their leader, Oclatinus was invited to resign before taking office. That was good for everyone.

Accompanied by a dozen outriders of the Horse Guard, he cantered across the square as if nothing lay in his way. Several tables set up with spice crumpled under the advance, several men in black robes turned and ran, and another, who did not believe in the inevitable, screamed as he was hit, spun around, and trampled.

"Curb your mount," I said to Drusus, whose mare had started at the noise.

Drusus struggled with the reins. The mare coughed and stomped the ground, and I thought I saw a flash of teeth as I turned my attention to the riders. They halted ten yards away.

"Greetings, Oclatinus!"

He glanced toward the boy, but returned my words formally. "Questor, I see you do not travel alone. Would it be too much to ask who is your companion?"

"His name is Drusus."

Oclatinus looked closely at the boy, sampling his clean lines like a connoisseur. "He's of the clan Bassianus, I'd guess."

"Absolutely."

"And you came with him from Antioch?"

"We travel under the protection that Marcus Opellius Macrinus extended to the family of the Mother Augusta."

"Yes, of course." He turned to the tribune and moved his arm lazily. "Seize them!"

The tribune and two of his men put their mounts forward at once, breaking into as much of a canter as the aisles of the spice market allowed. It must have been the mass of horseflesh bearing down on us that produced the reaction from Drusus' mare. Suddenly, she bolted.

Her charge was swift and powerful as she rammed through the gap between the tribune's mount and the Guardsman on his left. Drusus had the reins in one hand but no control of the animal. He hung on desperately, flailing from side to side, as the mare careened into Oclatinus' stallion. Before the Guard could engage horse or rider, the mare made a leaping thrust, clearing a table with open packets of spice before crashing headlong into the next table in line.

The belled glass smashed and precious saffron blew like powder on the wind. The mare blew ahead wildly, turning completely around, thrashing and rearing high. The tribune, who followed close, took the brunt of her charge, her hooves clanging his armor, but he got hold of her mane. Leaning forward, he grappled with the mare. He had already put his hands on her rider when the first arrow struck his throat and clawed a piece of it away.

Two more arrows came quickly, striking his Guardsmen in the back and putting one of them down. At nearly the same time, Drusus took three arrows, two in the chest that bracketed his heart, and another that obliterated his eye.

He was dead when he hit the ground, but the reins were still wrapped around his wrist. The mare dragged him alongside and under her belly through the blood and spice until she was bludgeoned to a halt by three Guardsmen with axes.

THE PLEASURE DOME

In the next nine months, during which I never saw the sun, I wondered what had happened on that market day in Emesa. Immediately after the barrage of arrows struck, I looked back over my shoulder on trajectory. I saw no archers atop the buildings where the arrows must have been discharged.

It seemed clear I had been deceived by Gannys or his mistress. From the moment the decision had been taken to substitute Drusus, no thought was given to sparing his life.

They left to the gods, and our new Caesar, the question of why they should want to destroy the cousin of the deified Caracalla, the last hope of their line. I never knew the answer, but when asked, I gave my response. The boy who died in the market was not Varius Avitus Bassianus. His name was Drusus. His death was a mystery to me, as his life had been.

"Then why did you transport him from Antioch to Emesa?"

"Because I was asked to."

"By whom?"

"The Mother Augusta of Rome."

"Did you not think it strange that a slave boy should receive that sort of attention from such an august personage?"

"Yes."

"And you asked no questions."

"None."

"Where is the pretender?"

"I don't know."

That answer, repeated often over a period of weeks, cost me considerable pain. The *speculatore* who asked the questions would turn to the *questionarii* whose job it was to extract an answer. Both were specialists in their conjoined departments of the frumentarii.

When I badly wanted to tell them what they wanted to know, I was rescued by the fact that I could not tell what I knew not. They never believed me, but I was all they had. It seemed clear by their questions that they did not have access to anyone who could supply better information. The Mother Augusta, Soaemias, and the eunuch Gannys, were clearly beyond their reach.

Communication with the world outside my cell in Apamea, a city that lay on the Orontes between Antioch and Emesa, did not exist. The only thing of consequence I learned was of the death of the Mother Augusta in June of the year 217, the exact date of which I cannot offer. The commotion in the streets outside the prison was as great as at the height of the celebration for Cybele. When I asked the guard the reason, he told me that the finest woman in the empire had starved herself to death rather than submit to the new order.

"And you should try it, too."

I thought of that. I had lost most of my fingernails, which would return, and the sight of one eye, which probably would not. My nose could be rebroken to allow the free passage of air again. It seemed important to think that everything that was damaged in my body would mend, or find some means of compensation. That made up for being forsaken by those to whom I had dedicated my life, and after a while, even by those who wanted to take it.

One day the frumentarii did not come to my cell. That happened soon after the death of Julia Domna. I did not think the two events were related, or that a change had been signaled. What relation did the death of my friend and patron have to this filthy cell in Apamea? How could that tragedy work for my betterment?

My existence was an anomaly. The Roman state did not believe in lengthy imprisonment. This prison, though substantial, served a region that included four separate provinces, and served them with room to spare. Exile to a distant island in the Middle Sea was often the punishment for a man of my rank. Death was cheaper, and in almost every case the preferred option.

Still, that did not happen. Nothing happened. Days passed and became weeks but the frumentarii did not return. The worst thing about their absence was that I missed their presence, though not their attention. My torturers had been all I could call my own. They were the people with whom I shared my days. I had no contact with anyone else but the guards.

I did not think it was a a ploy. It seemed no one cared to disturb my solitude. The question was why they should continue to stand the expense of my incarceration. And why I should permit it.

Perhaps the Blue Man kept me alive. The words of that grievous lunatic seemed my only hope. He had been correct in every particle of his prophecies to this point.

Piss, I thought, over and over. Every time I went to the bucket and every time I felt a need to go to the bucket, I thought it. In the end, it was the precision of the Blue Man's clairvoyance that mattered. It was impossible to believe that a Roman emperor had been drenched in the urine of an animal while he journeyed to be absolved of the blood-guilt he had created. To think that anyone could know was absurd. And to think, as I did, that the last part of his prophecy was the very thing, and the only thing, that could save me.

A bad bet. The man who controlled the legions controlled the empire, and Macrinus would not let his hand slip easily. He might be assassinated, but only by his troops. With the example of Caracalla fresh in his mind, Macrinus would take precautions with his safety. Certainly, he had purged the Praetorian Guard to reflect loyalty to himself and no other.

I was left to hope for a miracle in which I did not believe. Varius might become emperor by some mischance, his reign might usher in a period of universal peace, but that day need not include my presence. My life was forfeit. My death did not matter to anyone.

That's what I thought until the day I opened the bucket of gruel that was brought to the cell just before sundown. When they were generous, they put in a potato, which they had done on this afternoon near the end of October. I picked up the potato and moved it to my mouth with the sensational greed that comes from starvation when suddenly I spit it out. I looked at it again in my hand where the single word had been carved into the soft gray flesh.

SOON, it said.

* * *

Then another month passed. I received no more messages by any medium, and I began to doubt the one I had eaten. I might have thought it a joke by a cook or a guard, but at the same time my life in the cell changed for the better. The food improved. I began to receive fresh vegetables, and once a week, the meat of a recently dead animal. The guards were more friendly and talkative. No question they were being bribed.

I soon began to have an inkling of what had transpired in the world, and what events led to the improvement in my life. The youngest guard, therefore the most corrupt, told me one day of the progress of the legions in the land of Rome's ancient and most stubborn enemy, Parthia.

"Artabanus, king of the Parthians, came after us. He invited Caesar to give battle, and Caesar accepted. There was a big engagement at Nsibis. Three days it carried. Cohort after cohort went to bloody ruin. My brother was there, so I know, but in the end it came to naught."

"No winner was declared?"

"The grave diggers," he said.

They had been the beneficiaries more than once in the open country of Parthia, where the legions were at a disadvantage against the cavalry and archers of the enemy. Carrhae was not the first or last disaster, only the greatest. Revenge had been taken on the Parthians many times, but in the end the landscape won. Only Alexander the Great had conquered the Parthians. He had simply run past them in his fury.

"Did the army get off intact?"

"Most of it," he said. "But it might be better if they hadn't. Those boys are mad, I tell you. Caesar backed off after all that blood was spilled. Retreated. Now, I hear, he's talking peace and a ransom to the enemy."

That was all the news the jailer had to impart, and though it was woeful for the empire, it was good for those who looked for change. Macrinus was vulnerable. Neither the army nor the people liked defeat in any disguise.

So I was encouraged, but found no evidence the news meant something. All I had heard from the world beyond my cell was a lone word that could have announced my death better than the end of captivity. When the Saturnalia began in mid-December, I lost hope again.

It was terrible to hear the revelry in the streets below at every hour of the day and night. The festival that began with the winter solstice was the happiest and most peculiar of all Roman celebrations. Seven days it lasted. During that time, business was suspended except what was necessary to the state. Presents were exchanged and parties held at every house, even the lowest. The lowest, indeed, could become the highest, since one of the customs held that masters must reverse positions and serve their slaves. The pater familias who valued his dignity removed himself from the premises, hiding out with friends until the holiday passed.

Conditions in the prison deteriorated during this period. The guards changed shifts so often it was impossible to know who would appear on any day. They doubled shifts for the festivities at home and debauchery abroad. They were inattentive to their duties, as men are wont to be whose minds, and often their bodies, are elsewhere. Excrement mounted in the buckets. Food diminished and sometimes failed to appear in the buckets. One day, they arrived in the same bucket. The straw grew black and lousy. Tempers, which were never good, flared into anger and beatings. The noise of men screaming grew to match the somewhat different sounds that arose from the streets.

The end of festivities came slowly. Time was confused, though I notched the days on the stone wall. I was not sure that the seventh day had arrived until I awakened that night to a clamor. Every man on my corridor seemed to shout.

"Again!" said one voice. "Take him down!" Two other voices, at least two, cried with all the strength left in them. "Take me! Please, please, take me!"

I heard the keys pressed into the lock and stepped back in shadow with the piece of iron I used to scratch away the days lodged between my thumb and forefinger. It was a poor weapon that I should not need. I knew what was happening, but my mind could not accept it.

The man who stepped through the door as it swung open wore the uniform of the prison guard but was certainly not one of them. He stood tall and clean, a model Roman except that he was slim and light on his feet. In his right hand he held a short sword, and in his left the kind of cloak that was always worn by the guards against the fetid damp of the place.

"Put this on," he said, throwing the cloak to me. "We'll be out of here on the next ferry."

I caught the cloak and slipped it over my shoulders. It was wet.

"My name's Florianus," he said with a Greek accent.

He stepped aside at the door and waved his hand, so I should vacate the space between four walls that was all I had known for nine months; but for what seemed like an even longer time, I did not move. When he finally shouted, "Out, dammit!" I bolted into the corridor.

The prisoners were at the slits in the doors of their cells if they had them, and the ones that did not were screaming within blank walls. "Take me! Take me!" Hurried by the noise, trying to adjust one good eye to quick motion, I stumbled on an object in the badly lit corridor. I caught myself on one hand as I went down, then slipped to the floor though I was barefoot.

Slipped on blood. It was warm, it pooled on the stones, and it had come from the body of one of the guards. He was the youngest one, who had imagined that tomorrow he would be rich. I wore his cloak. His bloody cloak.

I took his dagger and rod, which I knew to be hard vine stock. When Florianus shouted again, I got to my feet and began to make my way along the corridor, following his angular form.

We could expect trouble, but might be lucky. Most nights, the caterwauling could be heard all over the prison, but this was the last of Saturnalia. The guards who had been routinely drunk throughout the festival would be no less now. They would not come to our corridor unless it was to quell the disturbance with their rods.

Florianus slowed at the junction of two corridors where a small desk stood unattended. "We take this left," he said. "When we reach the end of the corridor, there's a double door. It leads to the rampart, where we'll put down the rope." He opened his cloak and patted the coils of hemp wound around his belly. "The horses are at the base of the aqueduct."

The thought of a waiting horse lit my mind. Nothing else had done that. I took the lead up the passage, made the turn, and when I saw three guards moving down the corridor toward me, I did not slow my pace. I put out my hand as if hailing them on the street.

"Have you something warm and wet?"

"There's a Greek freedman in Number Five," said the guard on the right, the first and closest, who stopped. "But you'll have to grease his asshole first."

His mates laughed, and he laughed, too. Just as they did, I laughed and hit him with my rod, looping the blow as hard as I could across the side of his head. As he staggered and fell, I pushed him against the second guard, who had his sword out.

We hit the wall together. I heard hard metal clashing behind me as Florianus engaged the third guard, but I wanted to avoid that. I did not trust my vision for sword play. I had to keep the weapon of the second guard, a burly man whom I suddenly recognized, so close that it could not be brought to bear. He would have to go for his dagger, like me.

But he refused. He got his hand on my arm just below the elbow, and I got mine on his wrist. Still, he swung his sword. He was strong enough to bring it onto the back of my neck and shoulder. I felt it pierce the cloak, but not deeply. I felt it again. And I felt his grip slackening on my arm.

The months of bad food and no exercise blunted the thrust of my dagger toward his throat as he pushed my arm high and higher. When it was nearly past his cheek, I lunged with the last of my strength and still did not have enough. He brought the sword onto my shoulder again. I felt it bite deeper, felt the blood it made, felt the hollow in my belly where my strength had gone.

He felt it, too. "Number Thirty-Seven," he said, bringing his sword down again.

When I felt the blade at my shoulder, I dropped. He started to follow me down, but his hold on the dagger lightened. I kicked out, the ball of my foot burrowing into his groin. When he lost wind, I ripped my dagger from his hand, rolled, and coming back up, put it in his eye.

I held it until the tip of the blade found the back of his skull, for he did not want to die. He seemed to grow stronger for an instant, and to begin a bellow before he went limp. When he let go of his sword and dropped away, I turned to Florianus.

He and his man stalked each other. Both were bloody. The guard held his side where a sword found flesh. Florianus had a gash on his face. Blood from his neck rolled down his chest.

I picked up the sword of the first guard. "Over here," I said.

The last guard knew something had happened on his left. The sounds of struggle had ended, and when he glanced my way, he knew that his would end soon. He made his decision. Feinting hard at Florianus, he put his feet to work, lunging down the corridor and away.

I might have caught him and killed him. He held his side while he ran, lurching like a hunchback. But that would have taken time, and I did not know what was waiting around the next corner. I looked to Florianus.

"Are you able?"

He nodded, but did not answer. I was afraid he was hurt worse than he looked, which was bad enough. Putting my shoulder under his, I walked him to the end of the corridor to a bolted oaken door.

"The key," he said, nodding to his girdle.

I found it quickly, noting his weak voice and the fact that he could not manage such a small thing. The key was old, but it worked. The door opened to the cooler air outside.

That first breath of air was the best of my life. With one labored step, we moved to the ramparts looking out over the city. Night lights gapped in the darkness all over Apamea, the citizens were in the streets for their last bout of celebration, along with the Legion II Parthica, who garrisoned this place. If I had to guess, Florianus was one of those on leave for the night.

"The rope," he said.

I began to appreciate trouble ahead with a man who could not undo the means of salvation gathered at his belly. Florianus bled worse than I thought. Blood had begun to sheet down his neck. He slumped against the wall while I unwrapped the coils, which were wet. When finally I got them unraveled, I held in my hand fifty feet of rope. The drop over the side looked like all of that.

"I'll go first. If you have a bad time, ride the rope down. I'll be there for you."

He shook his head. "Leave me," he said. "Go to the villa of the Sextus. One street north of the aqueduct to the junction of the road. Then east to the river."

"We'll go together, Florianus. You on my back."

We managed that somehow. The rope went down well enough, double knotted to a truncheon on the rampart. I backed him up to the wall and doubled us up, but felt his grip around my neck was weakening. I hoped that did not matter. And it would not as long as he held.

I was lucky his make was slim, but even so it was tricky hoisting a double load over the rampart into dark space. I lost the hair on my chest before I got the rope in my hand at the proper length and braced my legs against the outer wall. The stones were huge, and the mortar that gave the best purchase was far apart.

Too far. The wet rope slipped in my hands. I felt my feet beginning to slip and my legs trembling. It took all my strength to reach the next small indentation where my toes could grip better, and it was not by much that I stopped the slide.

The extra weight made the descent hard to control. Alone, I could have walked it down step by step. I could have been half-way to the ground, with no worry about a guard putting his nose over the side, or how my arms had begun to ache, or the feeling that Florianus was losing his grip around my neck.

"Keep hold," I said. "It won't be long."

"I can't," he said, whispering.

"Lock your fingers. You won't slip if you—"

I heard him sigh. I felt his hands around my neck easing away like a glide into sleep.

I let out my hold on the rope and walked the stones faster. I missed the next band of mortar, the next, and the next. We were sliding, gaining speed, we were nearly out of control, when my hands met a knot in the rope. My left hand went through the knot fast, burning, nearly breaking, but the right, the stronger, bumped and held. For a moment, we stopped completely.

And my burden fell away. It was a strange feeling. My back had been hot and heavy. Now, it was now light and cool.

I heard Florianus strike the ground at a great, almost infinite distance. It was a deadened sound with no aftermath.

I let myself down the rest of the way with bad hands and no heart. It was no more than twenty-five feet to the bottom, but it took a long time to reach. The bloody rope did not quite reach that far. I dropped the last six feet onto hard ground.

It was bedrock upon which the stone walls had been laid, and it was jagged rock upon which Florianus lay. He was still. Nothing I said roused him. I could not see well within the shadow of the walls, but no air seemed to leave his nostrils. The blood flowing from his wound had lessened. It seemed to have stopped.

I felt his pulse, very faint, just before it stopped.

* * *

Two horses waited at the base of the aqueduct, as promised. I rode hard along the outcrop that followed the forty-foot masses carrying the water of life. I had heard voices from the ramparts of the prison that were distant but much too close. When I cleared the junction of the road, I put the flat of my sword to the horse that bore Florianus' body on its back. With luck, the animal would carry him to a place where he could be buried with honor. There was no honor in saving the life of a prisoner of Caesar and being known as the man who did it.

The city glowed stubbornly in the last hours of Saturnalia, but the road that led east took me into the countryside darkness. The land was hilly, with orchards that had left a faint smell of fruit. All the land around Apamea was given over to dry farming.

I had some doubt as to how I would find the villa of Sextus from others along the way, but the horse, a piebald stallion, had none. When we neared the river and a familiar scent came to his nostrils, he shook his head and began to canter for the barn. That spoke of a good master, whose name I did not know, but could guess. It might be Sextus Varius, who had begun his life as a provincial Roman from Apamea. When he married into the family of Septimus Severus, his fortunes changed for the absolute best. In time, the husband of Soaemias and the father of Varius became a rich man and a member of the Senate.

The preparations at the Villa Sextus were more than casual. I expected to be challenged at the gate, and my attention was directed that way. But as soon as I turned off the road toward the entrance, three men scattered in my path ahead, one taking his life in his hands to wave down the stallion and lay hands on his neck. Four more mounted men appeared from the tall brush and trees that screened the villa from the road.

Emesene archers. Their bows, curving back to form the three sides of a triangle, were unmistakable even in the darkness. Probably, at least two more men lay in position to take down intruders who bulled through the sentries. The horsemen were disciplined, led by a short ramrod whose face was as tightly wound as a bowstring. He did not like it that one rider had appeared where two were expected, and he wanted nothing from me but silence.

I gave it all the way to the villa, which capped the rise above the river like a dark eagle. Its long wings spread to enclose the court of a working farm, and the smaller divisions of a pleasure villa. Though the shutters were drawn, the interior gave off bright light—and more guards—when we entered. The furnishings within were rich, and the paintings showed good taste if not the hand of a master. Likewise, the marble bust that dominated the atrium. It was of a Roman senator who bore a resemblance to Varius, if that boy had been corpulent.

I stopped to study the bust when a voice with a burr like unfledged iron seemed to converge from several directions at once.

"Leave us, Aziz."

"Yes, Princess."

A woman stood in the doorway to the inner rooms. Tall, stout and blonde, she had spoken with the authority that comes from a life at the highest levels. If she had told Aziz to open his veins, her tone would not have altered in the slightest, nor would her expectations.

"I am Julia Maesa," she said. "Welcome to our home."

Did she mean this villa, Syria, or the world? Julia Maesa was the richest woman in the empire. She was the sister of the Mother Augusta, the mother of Soaemias, and grandmother of Varius; yet she bore little resemblance to her family. In spite of the hair piled in ringlets, the heavy makeup, the gown of red silk, and the jewels that populated her body, age had plucked her beauty. Her eyes were small where her sister's were generous, her skin sallow where her daughter's was clear; her body as heavy as Varius' was graceful. Only her flaring nose seemed remarkable and Roman, commanding her face like fasces.

"I'm honored, Princess."

She came across the room as if on a cart. Her body seemed not to move beneath her floor-length gown. It was as if one of the figures painted on the wall had broken loose, endowed with the power of speech.

"You're bleeding," she said as she stopped at close range. "Is the wound serious?"

"The blood is mostly of others."

She smiled warmly. "The blood of others. That's always better, isn't it? Especially when the blood is so base. You *are* the man I've waited for."

Her daughter was the woman I waited for, but I bowed to her. "At your service."

She clapped her hands. Two servants entered the room before the sound traveled four walls. "Fetch Incitatus with his medicines," she said. "And have Generedis prepare the barge."

While the servants scurried off with their orders, Maesa took the cloak from my shoulders and examined my wounds. She had done this before. Blood gave her no pause.

"May I ask about Florianus?"

"He's dead."

The hand that probed the wounds on my shoulder and neck left off a bit, but her next question was direct. "Will his body be discovered?"

"In time."

Her hand relaxed on my shoulder. "Florianus will be missed. He was a devoted client of my son-in-law, Sextus, whose house this was."

I did not mistake the tense that described Soaemias' husband. I thought Maesa had deliberately stressed it. "The house no longer belongs to your son-in-law?"

"Rest easy," she said, teasing. "My daughter has been widowed less than three months."

* * *

Still within darkness, we put into the river on Maesa's barge. The Orontes was known as unnavigable, but with a shallow draft and a good pilot that could change. There was no moon in the sky, no lights upon the shore, but the pilot knew this run of black water well.

His family had served the priest-kings of Emesa for seven generations, he said. When the temple of the Jews fell in Jerusalem and her people scattered, the most fortunate had come upon the Orontes. This river was as good as the Jordan. Moses should have led his people out of Egypt right to this place.

I could not follow his genealogy, or his maneuvers at the helm. Moses was apparently his god, though it might be his name for the river. His allegiance definitely lay with the clan of Bassianus. Jews who had left their homeland were often loyal and a credit to the empire, while those who remained were ungovernable. They had rebelled so often, and been slaughtered so often, that it was remarkable any were left. Stubborn, warlike, with no head for trade, Jews were the opposite of the cunning, mercantile Syrians. Unless they were both.

"Where did you say you were a soldier?"

"Did I say I was?"

"I can't remember," said Eli. "But something about you smells of the barracks. Do you stand at attention when you fuck?"

"In part."

"What part is that with a Roman?"

"The same as you. The difference is how it's brought to bear. And upon what."

He laughed, but never took his eyes from the river. It seemed he could discover things in the darkness that were invisible. "Are you trying out the old witch? Is that why you're talking so foolhardy?"

"She's a catch from all I've heard. As rich as Croesus and twice as smart."

"You hear it right," he said, spinning the wheel and taking us closer to the shore than seemed safe or reasonable. "When Macrinus ordered her out of Rome, she brought half the treasury of Italy with her. Six ships filled with gold is what I hear and some of what I've seen. But it's what you don't hear that will get your cock tucked inside a Syrian amulet."

"You speak from experience."

"Seven generations. The women of this family are the bane of mankind. They're all as beautiful as your Venus, even the old bitch when she was young. But there ain't a man been born who could master them. They do what they want, and they do it as many times as there are stars in the dark sky."

"A challenge then."

"Keep thinking like that," he said. "But get the money first. It's a dangerous thing that Maesa's doing. Ain't a Caesar been born will stand for a rival."

"Especially if he wasn't born Caesar."

"How many been born that way?" he asked. "And how many made by the army? This Caesar, I hear, is pissing around Antioch, dressed in silk like a Syrian, taking himself to every whore in the city. It's like he needs a woman—a new one each day—to tell him he's got the biggest stick. What is it with soldiers and whores that they need each other so bad?"

"It's exactly what you think."

"No. It's exactly what Maesa thinks. If she's right, Rome will have its first empress."

I doubted everything the Jew said, but mostly I doubted the Jew.

Never doubt a Jew.

* * *

Still within darkness, we rode the current past Apamea, holding to the middle of the river before going inshore to slower water after we passed the town of Pella. The sun rose at Larissa on the right bank, where we let out a small sail. It was as if we had joined the progress of the clouds as the Orontes rolled between loose green hills. Waterwheels flashed at every space that was open to villages and orchards. A succession of small towns appeared like knights keen to prosper in a land of eternal spring.

As we came to Epiphania, Julia Maesa summoned me to her bower. Her quarters, which exhausted half the space on the barge, were curtained in muslin and pressed gold. I entered her presence as she reclined on a couch draped with green silk. I saw she had been refreshed by a nap. Her face was creased like a nut and the absence of body servants. I searched it for the legendary beauty Eli had guaranteed, but except for the nose, which was imperial, and the bones, which were good, my conclusion was that Julia Maesa was three hours older.

"We should reach Emesa by early afternoon."

"If the river continues to run." She indicated a gilded stool with her right hand. "Please sit by my side."

She looked better at the lower angle, as she was aware. The flesh that sagged seemed merely ripe. The body merely overripe.

"I should allow you the opportunity to enjoy your freedom, and indeed you will have that when we reach Emesa, but I'd like to discuss the future with the knowledge that our time is constrained."

"As you wish."

"My family owes you much," she said. "But I must tell you I will ask more. I request your commitment to our cause. And I want you to know I do not engage the service of good men without compensation. You will have four hundred thousand sesterces if you follow this venture to its end."

She sat back on her couch as on a supine throne, unaware that she had insulted me. I had no doubt that her knowledge of men was always calculated in coin. Most of her recruits would have taken the money and fallen at her feet. I might have, too, if the sight of my right eye had not been lost, along with other things, in the service of her family. Proper payment could hardly be determined.

"I'll have eight hundred thousand sesterces."

Her reappraisal took the best part of a mile's passage down the river. A village wended by the window of silver net. The sky darkened. The lines that extended from her eyes to the break of her hair seemed to contract and darken. She was deciding how much I was worth. Or if she could escalate her demands.

"My sister, the Mother Augusta, held a high opinion of your character," she said at last. "She trusted you with the thing we hold most precious."

I said nothing.

"Silence is often a good thing," she said. "I understand you were assigned as questor of the garrison at Raphanae."

"In a just world, I would be still."

"It's crucial that the garrison be delivered to us. I cannot imagine that our plan will succeed otherwise."

It was my turn. She wanted Raphanae and Legion III Gallica. That was logical, but far-fetched. Raphanae, like all Roman camps of any size, was impregnable unless an enemy went against it with siege weapons and an army. Add to that Caesar, such as he was, who took his repose at Antioch, where he could call upon at least five legions, and given time, more.

"Perhaps you should tender me a delivery date. When will Macrinus be assassinated?"

To prove she was humorless, Maesa spoke without irony. "That event, though much anticipated, seems impossible in the near future. The usurper has been careful to pay his Praetorians well, and to ensure the loyalty of his prefects, who are his picked men. You will recognize their names. Julianus Nestor and Ulpius Julianus."

It was as if there were a shortage of names in the empire, and a shortage of professions. Both men had been high in the ranks of the frumentarii everyone hated so much. "You're serious."

"I would not be," she said. "Macrinus is."

"These appointments will go down in the Senate of Rome like fish in the belly of a Syrian fanatic."

"The Syrian would have a better time," she said. "He'd vomit. The Senate, for their part, approved the appointments. That happened some months ago, while you were imprisoned."

I should not have been surprised. The Senate had almost no power except during those periods of transition when emperors were being made or deposed. Then they bid for the throne and all they could carry away.

"Macrinus made a blunder. It will not bring him down, but if he makes more—"

"I'm confident he will, but not that the Senate will seriously affect the course of events," she said. "In the meantime, his prefects guarantee his safety. That is the price he paid."

"Then we must wait."

"But not long," she said with excitement. "Macrinus may have bribed his Guard, but he reneged on a promise of better pay to the legions. They are, shall we say, restive."

"Why would he do something so foolish?"

"Because he was defeated in battle and called it victory," she said. "The reason he stays in the East is to make his peace with the Parthians. The numbers being bruited about are fantastic. He will pay King Artabanus of Parthia three hundred million sesterces in reparations. And more in bribes."

"Three hundred *million*?"

She smiled as if money were the source of her amusement. "Now you see why he cannot pay his legions as promised."

I understood now why Macrinus' beard was long. He could not afford to shave. An emperor without funds was a man on the brink. If a rebellion were fomented, he would be forced to confront it himself. He could not stand another loss, however small, but he did have an unassailable position to which he might fall back.

"What will stop him from calling up legions from the west?"

"He cannot," she said. "When the news of the death of my nephew reached the frontiers, the Dacian tribes sensed weakness. They attacked, but were bought off for the time being. The Armenians also attacked and are being bought off. It's possible that not one denarius remains in the treasury to buy off enemies. If Macrinus withdraws troops from the western frontier, the result will be chaos throughout the empire."

"He may risk that."

"But the legions on low pay will not take the risk with him," she said. "Not for another misadventure."

"Then all that remains to be done is split his legions here. That is my work."

"You will have all the assistance you need," she said. "And you will have the eight hundred thousand sesterces."

Just like that. I should have asked for a million. Or her daughter's hand. Clearly, Maesa would gamble everything to gain back the empire for her family. It was a formidable gamble.

"This will not end the expense. The overthrow of an emperor does not come cheap."

She smiled. "But the experience can be rewarding. I assure you there is enough money to see this through to the end."

"Who will be Caesar?"

She patted my arm. "Why, Varius, of course."

I expected no other answer, yet the possibility seemed to take on the shallow rhythm of the inevitable, like the spirit of the river that rolled under our feet. What had the Jew called it? Moses?

"I should like very much to see Varius again."

"You will," she said with a quick turn in her speech, which was no more than a change of rhythm. "But you must understand he is not the same boy you knew. He is . . . changed."

"How so?"

"Varius is nearly a man."

* * *

I slept after we talked. I dreamt of moneychangers gathered, as they often were, near the entrance to a temple.

I was disappointed that I did not dream of orchestrating pieces of the empire, as Septimus Severus had done, but that position was taken in the present and future. If the words of the Blue Man were to be fulfilled, and Varius ascended the throne, it was clear who would work the levers of power. It would not be a thirteen-year-old boy, no matter how much he had grown.

Women will come to rule your empire, Septimus . . .

That blue bastard should have been crucified *before* he spoke. He had planted the seed of the future as surely as there was a future. We lived out his prophecy as he had designed it.

I had stopped asking myself *how* it was possible for that priest to see into the future. By omens, prophecies and dreams the gods communicated their will. If I did not believe it, that was my problem.

When we put in at Arethusa, I bathed in the river and donned a clean tunic like any man might wear. It was important to look like that man, though I would regret living his life. Nor did it seem that was necessary soon. After my bath, I joined Maesa for a repast of pheasant, ostrich eggs, melons, pears, and the most wonderful sesame cakes ever made.

The garrison of Raphanae sat west of Arethusa twenty miles distant. We were on the points of a triangle between the post I had never reached and the city of Emesa down river. If the garrison was subverted, all lower Syria might come under the control of Maesa's family. Every major road south passed through Raphanae and Emesa. The passage to the Hauran and Judea could be blocked. Only the sea would remain open to Macrinus.

Seen like that, Maesa had found a bargain at eight hundred thousand sesterces. If the garrison were brought over, it might prove the price of the empire. Delivering it was the question.

"It will be difficult," I said as we reclined on her couches for a meal like all Roman patricians in every part of the world. "I'm a fugitive. My movements will be hampered. If I go near the garrison, I'll be arrested."

"You need not be concerned," she said, passing the silver slaver that held the cakes. "The garrison will come to us."

"With their swords drawn."

She laughed. "Exactly. When we arrive at Emesa, you'll see what I mean."

* * *

She was too coy about a matter that could mean my life and her hopes, but I put aside my impatience until we reached the city. At the forward part of town, we abandoned the barge and entered a litter that awaited the pleasure of Julia Maesa.

It was nothing less than a portable house borne on the shoulders of a dozen burly slaves. The chairs on which we sat were silver with cushions depicting scenes of battle. The tented roof was silk, embroidered with images of the sun and moon in gold and silver thread. The walls were sheets of transparent stone through which the world was glimpsed as a moving frieze.

Could there be any doubt that was how people of her wealth viewed the world? The universe could be observed, sampled, or put away for a better time. It never need be truly inhabited, or compromised with.

Twenty archers flanked our passage through the streets, but I saw no sign of new fortifications that would repel an attack by legions who could be at the gates in a day. No additional guards were on duty in public places.

The only evidence of augmented security were the structures that had been erected on the acropolis. There were several, but one was large, a bastion at the base of the temple, sprawling along the hill for a significant distance in every direction, surmounted by a shimmering dome.

We were headed that way, where Maesa's surprise awaited me. What was it? Clearly, the acropolis was a proper place to fortify. It presented the steepest ascent in the city and the most enclosed structures. Even the Temple of El-Gabal had been enclosed by walls, as was never done with temples of Roman gods.

As we climbed the hill, turning along narrow streets in the oldest part of town, I caught glimpses of the domed building. It changed but stayed the same. The walls were a deep blue that seemed too bright and metallic for paint. The entrance was a double-door of immense proportions. Embedded in the blue walls were brilliant objects in silver and gold. I did not see what they were until we drew closer, and then I was distracted by a greater curiosity.

The litter slowed and stopped as we approached the great dome. In our path, clustered and chattering, stood a train of women, all young, along with several men who were not much older. They were dressed in silks of the most costly sort, but they did not look like costly beings. Instead, they looked like the most exquisite things of their kind that had been gathered from the bountiful poor of every nation.

At first glance, I saw three Chinese so petite that an artist in porcelain could not have rendered better. Two Caucasians from the north country, blonde and tall, four sleek blacks from beyond the Sahara, Greeks, Carians, Egyptians, and others who could not be classified by the eye, or nationality. The only thing they had in common was their uncommon beauty.

"What do you think?" asked Maesa. "Is there one who meets your eye?"

"They would meet the eye of a blind man. But the Egyptian, she's special."

"I'll send her to you."

I could protest later if I felt cheated. Now, I wanted to know more. When the litter began to move again fitfully through the crowd, I put my questions.

"Do they all belong to you?"

"To the temple," she said.

"Prostitutes?"

"They will serve the god with their bodies," she said as if correcting my error. "It is the service for which they were engaged. And were born."

"How many are there?"

"We do not have a final accounting yet," she said as if she kept the list herself. "Another caravan is due from Palmyra any day. A second ship should land at Balanae tomorrow with a consignment from the West."

And if they were like these? What would happen to the business and pleasure of the empire if all the comely women gathered in one place? This place.

"Are they all slaves?"

"Not all," she said. "The terms of their contracts vary. I would not have the god served by those unhappy in their position. They are, after all, our warriors."

She reached to the golden pull at her side and rang the bell that alerted the bearers. They halted near the entrance to the great blue and gold structure. We alighted as quickly as an old woman and fragile man could onto the broad marble steps.

I saw it all in that moment. The size of the structure was immense. Each wing of the building carried two hundred yards along the crown of the hill under the temple. The dome that spanned the center was as large as the Pantheon. The golden doors shone in the sun so brilliantly they blotted the sight of my good eye. A multitude of gold and silver ornaments shrieked from the walls like infernal advertisements. The gold were phalli, the silver more modest, like receptacles that might be the hollowed moon, or a chalice, or the recesses of the female body.

I remembered this had been the location of the barrack-like rooms where the temple prostitutes performed their devotions of the flesh. As it was now, in more spectacular form.

Maesa swept her arms to include all the immense pleasure dome. "Will this suffice, do you think, for the drawn swords of the legions?"

THE APOTHEOSIS

I never answered the lady.

Princess Maesa seemed to have devised a logical solution to advance her cause. When word got out about the pleasure dome, the legions would storm the city, but not in battle gear. Were it not for Roman discipline, the garrisons of Syria would be depopulated in a day. The troops knew the women who worked in these temples did not charge a fee. Sacred prostitutes accepted what was given—and it might be a token—as a gift to the god.

If the soldiers were discontented with their pay, feeling they had been cheated by an emperor who promised more, their good will toward the Temple of Emesa would be a resource to draw upon. The man who was the symbol of the temple—the high priest of El-Gabal—would be the recipient of their good will. In Emesa, that position was hereditary. It fell by right of birth to the male heir of the clan of Bassianus.

Varius. Several times I asked Maesa where he had been sent, but her answers were evasive. "A high priest is not made overnight," she said coyly. "Nor should he be unmade before he has the chance to rule. Come along, see the rest of our temple."

She meant the whorehouse, of which she was proud. Never had I seen such a collection of erotic wonder. The huge coffered dome was like a pebbled vault set within the bounds of the heavens. The floors were set with intricate mosaics; the niches adorned with sculpture; and the walls painted with scenes of pastoral beauty and the ideal human form; but everywhere the emphasis was on the sexual and the fantastic. Things were done on those walls that my imagination had not touched upon even during those lonely days of imprisonment.

Machines induced greater means of stimulation. Harnesses were suspended from the ceiling, so that a woman, or boy, might be lowered from above onto the phallus of a man who did not have to move an inch while he lay his back. Couches and chairs operated by hidden gears allowed bodies to be positioned in ways that a contortionist could not exceed.

One room held kegs of silphium—a stable contraceptive. Another kept jars of scents and oils mixed so well with civet and ambergris that they could arouse the senses of the dead. Yet another held wines and drugs to call forth performance from the barely living.

There were more aphrodisiacs than could be named, and enough to insult the virility of the troops; but they were necessary to guarantee the performance of every man in every situation. Large amphorae held not only spices like nutmeg, vanilla and cubebs, but foods like pine nuts and asses' milk; along with more exotic items such as deer penis, and the dried crushed bodies of the green blister beetle that some called Spanish fly. Finally, to whip the legions from ecstasy to ecstasy, an orchestra had been gathered in a gallery under the dome, including a giant organ that resounded through every room like the pipes of Pan.

"What do you say, Marcellus? Adequate?"

"Just like home."

"You must have been born to an interesting place."

"I was born to the garrison. The only thing a Roman soldier values more than his shield is his collection of pornography."

"I like to think this experience is more tactile," she said.

"Absolutely. But I wonder how Varius will fit in as whore-master."

"A teenage boy?" she said with a smile. "We'll have to post guards to keep him away."

"That won't work. Unless he's changed more than I imagine."

"He may be," she said. "He's had rigorous training to assume the duties of high priest."

"Exactly what kind of training is that?"

"I really don't know exactly. Religion was never the focus of my life. You'll have to ask my daughter."

I planned to do that.

* * *

On a hill south of the acropolis, I was given a villa with fourteen rooms, a bath with hypocausts, a dining room that hung over the valley like a hawk's nest, a guard of ten archers, a staff of fourteen servants, and the Egyptian prostitute, whose name was Philomene. I wanted none of those things, but thought it imprudent to refuse.

I repaired to my villa late in the evening, still having not seen Soaemias or her son. They were together, I was told. Varius prepared to assume the duties of the high priest. Any time after the opening of the whorehouse should be suitable for his unveiling.

I was worried that Varius would be exposed to danger by appearing in public, but Maesa dismissed those concerns. "He will not be permitted to leave the sanctuary, and Macrinus does not dare violate it. The Syrian legions will not stand for blasphemy, and they are all he has."

It seemed he had less than he imagined. Maesa gave a list of key officers at every post in the East who had committed to her cause. I recognized the names and knew some of the men who bore them. They were all her "clients," which meant that she had tendered bribes for their allegiance. Additionally, she named senators from the cities of Emesa, Apamea, and Antioch.

The rest of the empire was in dispute, even Africa. Though most of the officials of those provinces owed their positions to the Severan dynasty, Macrinus, an African, had made his share of appointments. Likewise, Maesa was not well-connected in Britain or Iberia, but in Gaul, Pannonia and Greece selected officials had given their word to commit at the proper time.

"And there are some things," she said, "that even you must not know."

I went to bed thinking of those things, and nothing else. Of course. I had sent the Egyptian to the physician to examine her health.

And I was sorry for a time.

* * *

I awakened in the night knowing someone was in my room, but nothing more. That bothered me, because I usually had a prescient sense of an enemy nearby. It was my only connection with the invisible.

The guard was posted for the night, although I had not personally seen to their placement. That was a mistake. The shutters in the room were closed on this winter evening. There was no moon.

I held my breath until I heard breathing. And a movement— cloth, smooth cloth, like silk. It came from left side of the room. Not the doorway but from that direction. I made a movement of stirring in bed, but only to have a view of that thing.

Something touched my shoulder. Lightly. It was leather, but hard. A riding crop. No, a whip. I opened my eyes wide.

"I thought I'd find you with your Egyptian."

"A man gets used to celibacy. In time, he's said to prefer it."

Soaemias laughed, but the pressure of the whip increased slightly. "Don't lie to me. She is the image of Isis. A goddess of the Nile born in a garbage pit. I saw her when she came in. In fact, I chose her. But not for you."

I drew her to me, pulling the whip until my hand reached the stock and her body touched mine. "What do you have in mind? A whip across my shoulders? Or an arrow in my back?"

When she tried to withdraw, I pulled the whip hard and pulled her down to the bed. She gasped when I rolled and pinned her beneath me. Her eyes looked into my eyes because they had nowhere to go.

"Do you plan to rape me?"

"I plan to have an answer."

Her blue-violet eyes did not waver in the darkness. Her response seemed to come from them. "It was Gannys who did it," she said. "I'll admit I gave him the authority to act as he saw fit. But the decision to fire was taken by him when he felt the moment demanded it."

"Do you say that to all your lovers?"

She hesitated as if she were deciding to be a princess or a woman. "I had no idea that he would have Drusus killed. I was as surprised to learn that it happened as you were to experience the reality."

"Then you do not control your servants."

"Or my lovers."

Yes, she was a princess. She knew she had the advantage. She could feel me harden between her legs.

She cherished that hardness so slowly that it seemed like prison time once more. An absence of time. She took my cock inside her like the rising of the moon, searching for pleasure by the smallest measures until we were belly to belly.

She was wet, releasing fluids like a man. She kept coming unlike a man who needed surcease when once was done. She held my buttocks, telling me how to discover the movements and pauses that she liked. That I liked. That I would like to last forever. And it seemed to last nearly forever until in a sudden burst of time we came to a gulping, bellowing end.

I would never know if she had lied to me. The best I could hope for were these nights stolen from the gods.

* * *

"Your friend is a terrible man," she said. "He came with his troops to my house, where he tortured three of my servants until they died. If they had known anything of value, I'm afraid your life would have been lost, too."

I felt her lips moving against my chest. It was as if I could read her words best through my body. The one thing I did not doubt was her tenderness. She seemed to keep it in boxes within her that opened to the ones she loved. She closed them quickly, but left a memory of the contents to cherish. I had never been with a woman so abandoned, and then so peaceful.

"You were wise to leave the city. Oclatinus did not come to his position by force of mind. His business is buying and selling the minds of others. He rose from the torture chamber to the highest circles of power without any qualifications at all."

"Do you know he was sent back to Rome after he left Emesa? Macrinus appointed him co-consul and prefect of the city."

In other words, the most powerful man in Italy. That seemed like another large blunder. "His blackmail must be better than I thought. Oclatinus is no more capable of being prefect than being emperor. He can barely read and can't write without consulting the skills of his slaves."

"It seems Macrinus realized that. Oclatinus was relieved of his duties quickly."

"Macrinus' judgment is consistently poor. We're lucky to have an adversary like him."

"The fall of Macrinus is foreordained," she said. "The gods have spoken on that matter."

"How so?"

"Many signs have been seen," she said in an altered voice. "They appeared in Italy and the East, gathering over the empire. All relate to the anger of Vulcan. He is a powerful god."

"Volcanoes are powerful things."

"He is their spirit," she said. "An earthquake destroyed five villages in Bithynia on the day Macrinus ascended the throne."

"That's terrible news for those people."

"The god of fire is a terrible god," she said. "In the East, he's also the god of the sun, and so brings warmth. But the Vulcan of Rome has no mildness. His wrath is fire."

"If Macrinus believes that, too, the battle is half won."

"How can he disbelieve it? On the day of celebration for the god, tremendous thunderstorms visited Rome. Never was so much lightning seen. It struck the hunting theater with fury. The building was hit many times by gigantic bolts. Fire raged, destroying everything around it. Even though rain poured from the heavens, and the fire brigades emptied the aqueducts, nothing could stop the flames. The finest sporting venue in the Roman world was consumed."

I tried to imagine as a gutted shell that huge stadium where so many pageants had been staged, where so many skillful men fought and died, and where so many wild beasts were killed. I could not. The Coliseum was a symbol of Rome as much as the palace of Caesar.

"That's a serious problem. Bread without circuses is a dangerous thing for an emperor."

She held my eyes. "Always so practical. You don't believe in the gods, do you?" She grasped my arm hard. "You who are their instrument."

I could not see her eyes well enough to tell if they had changed color. I did not like the feeling in her body when she struck these moods. The other things could be dealt with, but this intensity about the supernatural I did not understand.

"I believe in power. If the gods have it, I believe in them."

"You demand a demonstration. More villages must be destroyed to confirm your faith."

"I'll settle for Varius."

"He'll soon by done with his passage," she said. "That's when his safety will become your charge again."

She did not want to talk about the subject. At no time had she mentioned her son's name. It was the one thing that she excluded from her bed, but now was the time to bring it in.

"How is Varius?"

"Very well now," she said.

Now? Her words left something unsaid. "Was there a time when he was not well?"

"He was affected by the death of his father," she said without emphasis. "That's not surprising in a boy of his age, although he and father were hardly close. A void opens, and must be drawn shut. The priests are good at things like that. They know the channels of the mind. They can slake any fear, or promote the same in the minds of unbelievers."

"I don't agree with that, Soaemias. They can affect people who believe."

"One day you will see the truth."

"In any case, losing a father can be terrible to a boy of his age. The direction it takes is uncertain. He may become paralyzed. Or heedless."

She moved away by small measures in the dark, as if the subject demanded retreat. "I was worried. He seemed to lose his bearings for a time. They called me to the mountain to be with him, because the priests feared for his life."

"Why?"

"He had an accident," she said. "As part of his training, Varius was required to sit upon a high rock for three days without food or drink. On the night of the second day, he fell from his perch. One of the bones in his arm had to be set, and he struck his head hard enough that it gave everyone great worry. For some time, he could not speak."

"He might have fallen asleep up there. That would be natural."

"The priests did not think so," she said. "As one of his tasks, Varius had been made to practice descents from high places. He had been taught to break his fall at the last moment, and tumble free as he struck the ground. But those things should never be done at night."

"It would have been better if he fell on the priests. These practices don't make sense, even as they form a passage."

"It's a passage the high priests of this family must make," she said. "That has been so since the beginning of the Ba'al."

Ba'al meant lord or master. All the gods of Syria were called Ba'al. All the gods of Syria were deranged, including El-Gabal, whose name meant Lord of the Mountain.

"When do the rites end?"

"His training is nearly done," she said. "He's already learned to speak with the beasts."

"That's a good skill for an emperor to have. The best."

She drew away, sitting up, her breasts swaggering in the darkness. "You're the most impious man. Perhaps you should never be responsible for Varius."

"If I was, I'd put a stop to those rituals."

"How can I love you?" she asked. "A man who has no idea of the invisible forces that guide us all."

* * *

I had no answer for her, as I had none for her mother. Fortunately, Julia Maesa was unconcerned with the manifestations of the god. If a more practical woman had been born to the province of Syria, I had not met her. Every day she rigged her pleasure dome with more delights, while she charged me with the defense of the city.

Fortifying Emesa to repel an attack or withstand a siege was useless against the legions. I spent most of my time recruiting archers and training them in tactics. Their finest skill—the ability to loose accurate volleys from horseback—was what would damage Roman troops in formation most. The arrows of their composite bows could nail a man's hand to his shield or his foot to the ground. The thumb-rings used to loose the arrows gave great speed in the release.

The effectiveness of the archers was limited by terrain. In open country, where the maneuverability of their mounts allowed them to loose arrow after arrow, and their bows could be fired even while riding away, they were superb. On difficult ground, where they could not easily wheel, they were less effective. They also had problems facing other mounted archers, like some of their clansmen from Emesa. Every garrison in Syria had a complement of Emesenes.

The men I trained had horses as fine as any, and if not, they were provided with better. They had all grown up with a bow in their hands and come to manhood hunting animals in the foothills. Bear, boar, wolves, deer, hyena, tigers, and lions could be found outside the city.

I wanted badly to hunt boar, but found no time for it. The date set for dedicating the pleasure dome was January 9th, the Agonalia, the feast to honor Janus, the god of new beginnings. Soldiers from Raphanae, Apamea and other garrisons would take their leisure in the city and relay tales of earthly delights back to their barracks.

I went to the temple early on the morning of that day, accompanied by Philomene, my Egyptian, to coordinate intelligence. Maesa had spent much time in the last months eliminating the frumentarii from Emesa. She had tracked their sources, bought or neutralized them, except for three men she used to feed false information back to their headquarters. The last had been my contribution. It was often more valuable to insert the wrong thing into the minds of the enemy than to have them arrive at an informed guess at the right thing.

I had another idea I wanted to put into effect, but Maesa, de facto ruler of the clan of Bassianus, was unsure of its application. "I see some value in what you say, Marcellus. Having a report come every day could prove useful."

"Then I don't see the problem. It's not my impression the princess objects to logic."

Maesa rolled her fingers as if touching strings. "Perhaps I do not have enough faith in the ability of this girl. In this direction, that is."

She might have a point, but did not think it should be made by a woman. Philomene's beauty was such she seemed to have been rendered rather than born. The Greeks of Pericles' time made sculptures like that, but only of men. Her face was Roman and Egyptian, so well-drawn in its lines it could detract from the body of even finer proportions. She was in no way large or gross, but from the fall of her long black hair to the tips of her painted toes, her silken garments clung like an invitation to explore.

"Philomene has a keen memory. She's learned to read and write Roman characters. Before long, she'll be able to collect and organize the reports we receive from the women and put them in writing. In the meantime, she'll summarize her findings directly to you."

Maesa's eyes seemed to doubt that, but she looked at Philomene for the first time as if she were more than a receptacle. "Girl, are you confident you can perform these duties?"

"Yes, mistress."

"I should have you recite the books of the Aeneid as a test."

"Yes, mistress."

When Maesa looked to me, I nodded. Philomene knew the enormous poem by heart, or as much of it as I had asked her to repeat.

"She'll report exactly what she hears. Determining the worth of the information is your job. Soldiers rarely know much of value in any part, but the whole, gathered from many detachments, could be significant."

Maesa smiled. "We should also be able to reverse the flow to our benefit."

"That will be harder. The women must be natural when planting information. The main thing the soldiers should take away from this place is gratitude toward the temple and its high priest, who will shortly be among them to share their burdens."

"Today," said Maesa. "At last. This will be our day."

* * *

At noon, the hour appointed for the high priest to appear at the ceremonies, I walked to the temple. The streets that had been vacant in the early morning were filled with people. Some made their way to the temple grounds, while others headed the opposite direction. It was as if the city had been attacked and the only rule was confusion.

I grabbed the first man not in full stride down the hill. "What happened?"

He tried to jerk away. "The beasts!" he said. "The wild beasts are loose!"

Subterranean pens outside the amphitheater kept the animals for the games that would begin later in the day; but I did not think he meant that. I would have asked him, but he already began to run toward the public baths.

Then a group of children appeared from the arcade above that overlooked the street before the entrance to the Temple of

El-Gabal. "The high priest!" they shrieked and beckoned. "He is come!"

I took the new marble steps to the front of the arcade, which was crowded with people, many of them children. After making my way to first rank, I displaced one of the smallest, a girl, and sat her around my neck, where we had a view of the procession.

Three horsemen led the way up the long road. Gannys sat on a bay mare in front. On his flanks were two outriders, young men by the way they held their mounts at a very slow gait. I thought that the skirling music of the flutes and drums at the rear was responsible for their horses' agitation; until I saw the golden chariot and the even younger man who stood alone in the car with reins in his hand.

Varius. He stood in the car taller than I remembered, wearing a purple tunic and a blue diadem beset with gems. Though impressive, he struggled hard with the reins as his chariot lurched fitfully, springing forward and almost stopping. At a parting in the crowd, I finally saw the animals. I recognized their long tails first, gathered in colored knots, their backs bedecked with ribbons, and their manes encrusted with pearls. At last I heard them roar.

The high priest of El-Gabal—the boy I had rescued to become a man—had been drawn to his investiture by two full-grown male lions.

* * *

I watched the ceremonies for the new high priest as a spectator. It was some time before I recalled that a child sat on my shoulders; and even later when I realized something should be done with her. As I swung her to the ground, the little one was angry to lose her perch. "Put me back!" she said. "Put me back the way I was!"

That could never be for any of us, especially Varius, who had arrived at his destiny. As the procession stopped before the steps to the temple, he descended from the chariot like a man with a purpose. His movements were graceful but thought out, each leading to the next in sequence. The only provocative thing he did was linger before the lions who had brought him to the temple of the sun. He passed them by but turned back as if he had forgotten a courtesy. Stepping into the maw of the beasts, he caressed them gently, stroking their manes.

It was terrifying. The lions were well fed, and they may have been stupefied with drugs, but the man who values his life does not put it close to the mouth and claws of an animal who has been forced to do the thing he loathes, which is to work in the traces for the benefit of another kind. A male lion will sometimes kill and eat his young, if his belly bids him.

Suddenly, Varius turned his back on them. He held, presenting his neck in the position that a stalking lion will make the most of every time. But nothing happened. When he resumed his course, the lions simply watched him. The one on the left, which seemed the most aggressive, opened his mouth and bared his teeth, but did not growl. He seemed to be yawning, telling the world that he regretted losing the company of such a fine young man.

That was the signal for the crowd to vent their pleasure. They chanted "*Barlaha!*" which meant Child of God. The drums, trumpets and flutes thumped and wailed in the strange mayhem of Syrian music. Though seemingly chaotic, it was a repetitive set of rhythms that worked at an ingenious level. Those caught by it could not but respond. Their blood hummed and their feet moved even if they stood in place. Every sense became focused on one object, which was the deity, and his representative.

On this day, the stench of the lions mixed with the music and drew it to a greater pitch. Varius reached the top of the stairs and the gates of the propylaea as he turned to the crowd. He assumed a strange position, one hand held up, palm open, the other held palm down. When he shuffled his feet, moving without seeming to move, dancing without seeming to dance, the crowd mirrored his movements, thrashing to and fro in one compressed wave. And when Varius turned into the inner precincts of the temple behind the walls, they followed, crying his name, which was the name of the deity: "El-Gabal! El-Gabal!"

The sun god's chief servant advanced. All these people were strangers except for the two soldiers of III Gallica standing at the edge of the crowd beyond the guard of archers. They were not dancing or shouting, and on any other day would have scorned this ceremony. Yet their right arms were outstretched, raised in a military salute, as if hailing Caesar.

SILPHIUM

From the quarters of the high priest, a small palace to itself, most of the city below the acropolis could be seen. The torches did not light the streets, but seemed to separate passages in the night, opening gaps that human beings parted on their rounds. The smoke from the houses and gardens rose thick, and the sounds of voices, too, along with laughter and singing and the wail of flutes and beating of tambourines.

The night was eerie. Looking right, I revisited the courtyard where those things had been done to honor the god. A fire which was never put out burned before the altar, flickering on the stone of El-Gabal that in its passage through the ether had absorbed the power of the sun.

The black rock of El-Gabal was said to be sentient. A balustrade before the stone kept the worshipers from touching him. Draperies and parasols kept the sun from touching him. Nothing must touch the god but the hand of his high priest. In niches along the walls stood statues of the priests of the Bassianus family, those men who were like small kings, but no sculpted image of the god was to be found.

That too was not permitted. The god of the black rock could only be contacted through ritual—ancient ones like the undeviating movements of the dance, or the pulse of the music, or through prayer, but best of all through the letting of blood.

The day had seen an enormous engorgement of blood. Varius had made sacrifice upon the vast altar, performing his offices with immense concentration. He began by offering a long curved knife above his head, displaying it to the crowd, then bringing it down slowly, until he turned and plunged it into the throat of a black ram before him. He held fast while the beast thrashed under him. He held until all life stopped, then he cut open the ram's chest, withdrew its heart, and held it up to the populace. It was meat now. The people would eat.

The boy I had known was drenched in the blood that blew like a spring from the earth. His priests and servants came up to wipe it away, but he gave no indication that he noticed their attentions. His face was as rigid as the stone of his god. His eyes were so fixed that I thought of drugs—and nothing else. He handed the knife to one of the priests, who replaced it with another equally sharp, as Varius turned and accepted the next beast to be slain at the altar. A calf. And the next. A goat. And the next.

The feasting had gone on all day in an orderly way. The sacrifices were parceled out to people who infrequently knew the flesh of animals. They accepted it, and the flesh of all the animals that were slaughtered upon the altar, as consecrated gifts from their god.

That was one way the high priest kept hold of the people. He had done so from time immemorial. Not even the rule of Rome changed things. In every major campaign in the east, the priest-kings of Emesa sided with Rome and enhanced our victories with their archers. All of Anatolia had fallen, Syria, Palestine, and with each victory, their power grew as their autonomy was preserved. No other place in the empire was so independent. No local king had as much power as the family Bassianus. That was true even before one of their daughters married the future emperor, Septimus Severus.

"You did well today, Varius."

He joined me on the balcony where the high priest displayed himself to his people. He dropped the embroidered linen cloth on which he had dried his hands. Almost before it reached the ground, the cloth was retrieved by a slave.

"If the ceremony was not perfect," he said, "then it was useless."

Varius spoke with an authority that was unrecognizable. Everything he had done was unrecognizable. Everything he said seemed to come from someone else. I reminded myself that he was fourteen. Although of the age when he was considered a man, he still had growing to do, a beard to cultivate, love to explore. He could do the latter in plenty. Even the male prostitutes of the pleasure dome, chosen for their beauty from all over the empire, did not exceed his.

"The ceremony seemed perfect to me. You've overcome your fear of blood in a very definite way."

"I came to realize its importance," he said, sitting in a leather chair. "This is the ancient land of Phoenicia, which abides by ancient ways. We were great sailors who lived in cities when Romans lived in small huts. We gave the alphabet to the world. We showed the way to the most distant places in the Middle Sea and beyond. Our rites are the most ancient—and the purest. In the days of our forefathers, we were not content with sacrificing animals. We sacrificed people when necessary."

"What would make that necessary?"

"A crisis," he said.

"How was it done?"

"Not with a knife, Marcellus. In those days, the objects chosen for sacrifice were usually children. They were bound in sacks and thrown from the propylaea to the stones below."

The propylaea was high, perhaps seventy-five feet above the courtyard of the temple. That gruesome image brought back the memory of Florianus, who had fallen from a lesser height and hit rock like mud. I could still hear the sound. I knew I would hear it all my days.

"Could you have done that sacrifice as high priest?"

"We did it," he said. "Perhaps we would do it still."

"Perhaps, but for Rome."

That gave him pause. The empire that Severus ruled was the same that had forbidden human sacrifice since the days of the Republic. Varius had been a Roman all his life, but the way he said *we* seemed as if he given something up. His past? All that he was? All that he could be?

"Rome does not rule men's souls," he said. "Rome counts them. All gods of all religions are accepted as long as they conform. Hence, all gods are worthless to Rome."

"That's logical, Varius. But not quite sane."

"Nor is religion," he said. "It does not depend on the processes of the counting house. Truth is found through revelation."

"What happened on the mountain, Varius? They told me you fell on your head. How hard was the blow?"

He smiled for the first time since his investure. "Hard enough. Though as I see it now, it was simply part of the progress."

"Toward revelation?"

"Yes."

"So it happened on the mountain."

"Inwardly," he said. "If I could tell you the things I saw, you'd be awed as I am."

I wanted to know his thoughts, and his experiences. I did not think I could know them as he did, but sharing was the first step.

"I've seen strange things in my life, Varius. Most can be explained without reference to the gods, but not all. My mother once appeared to me in a dream and said I must wear into battle the stone amulet she had given me before I left home. Place it next to your heart, she said. That day, I took an arrow and would have died but for her warning."

"Mothers are always with us," he said. "In fact, they are us as we are them. Was she still alive when she appeared to you?"

"No. She died two years before."

He nodded with the weight of his office. "One of the things I discovered is that there is no death. There is only a continuation. I'm happy to have this confidence from you, Marcellus. I think in time you could arrive at the things I've found. All men have the capacity to find it—if not the opportunity. I believe that's why men like us exist. We lay out the trail for others to follow. They must be led by servants of the god. It's the only way they can know him within the humdrum of their lives. In that sense, we're nothing more than instruments of the god's will."

"God," I said. "Singular."

"Forever."

I had no wish to undermine Varius' certainty. It seemed to be the source of the confidence that was so impressive. If he could translate it to the rule of government, Rome might have what it needed.

"I'm glad we understand each other, Varius. That should make the days to come easier. We must cooperate in everything and not question the reason for things that are necessary."

"In your sphere, you will be supreme," he said. "In mine, please do not interfere."

"Very well. Are you resigned to staying within the temple grounds until we have some sign of a change?"

"I will do what is asked," he said. "If I must, I will remain here the rest of my days."

"That shouldn't be necessary. But Macrinus tried once to end your life. He may try again."

He took my hand, holding tight. "I was told what you did. I know you suffered for our cause. You will know my gratitude, Marcellus."

"That you're well is my thanks. The only thing I'll caution you against is relying on anyone too much. You are your own man. Others will always want things for themselves."

"What do you want, Marcellus?"

I looked to the courtyard and the fiery illuminations of the god. It was said that he talked to those who understood him. It was also said that he granted wishes.

"My wish is that the prophecies of a crucified priest come true."

* * *

After I set the guard, I went to the room that had been reserved for me on the temple grounds. It was little more than a sleeping alcove with a couch and writing desk in which the presence of another person could not be hidden. The woman who awaited me, dressed richly but not in the garb of a functionary of the temple, had no desire to obscure her person or rank.

"Princess Mammea."

She rose from the chair before the desk as if she expected no courtesies. "We met in the courtyard," she said quietly. "You also met my son, Alexianus."

"A fine boy."

She accepted the compliment, knowing that her son was a scion of the Severan dynasty, but not the candidate. Alexianus was ten years of age and somewhat frail. He compared to Varius like a kitten to a lion. In the same fashion, Mammea compared to her sister, Soaemias. This princess was younger but seemed older; blonde but not brilliantly, fuller in figure but tighter in the eyes. They were brown and attractive, but in no way mysterious.

"I hope you'll excuse this visit," she said. "But I must speak of my son's placement. As you know, I was with him during the time he spent on the mountain."

I did not know where they had been, but heard she refused to leave her son alone. She was a loving mother with a streak of rectitude like the blaze she wore across her bosom. That of course made her trustworthy.

"Whatever concerns you have, feel free to voice them."

"What I will say does not speak to your competence. I know what you have done for us, and I know my mother, Princess Maesa, trusts you in all things. But—" She bowed her head as if composing an objection. "I do not like my son having to remain on the grounds of this temple."

"May I ask why?"

"If I may speak bluntly," she said meaning that she would do no other, "it's the atmosphere of degeneracy in this place."

"You're referring to the—" I waved my hand toward the house of sacred prostitution.

"That's what I mean," she said. "But more. I'm speaking of the man who inspired it. The eunuch."

It was as if she could not speak the name aloud. "Gannys, yes. But I didn't know he was the force behind the . . . annex."

"He's the force behind every foul thing done in the name of my mother," she said. "He has already corrupted Varius. I will not have the same thing happen to my son."

"But Varius seems to have come of age in good order."

"Yes," she said scornfully. "He walks like Gannys. He talks like Gannys. All the religious instruction he received came from the mind of a man who sees people as objects to be manipulated. The temple to him is nothing but a source of revenue. Our family is a means to his ends. Even that would be of little concern were he not so devious, but he has ways of controlling people that are vile. He's a doctor, which makes him a master of drugs. He's a priest, which makes him a master of primitive ways. His hold over Varius and my sister is unnatural."

I listened carefully to her accusations, as would any man who sensed the beginning of an alliance. Mammea's stiffness might not be useful in a lover, but as a weapon to wield against an adversary she could not have been more alluring. In this case it was Gannys, but who knew for the future?

"What would you like me to do, Princess?"

"I want that man's ambition curbed."

"Nothing would give me more pleasure, but if he's as powerful as you say, that may not happen quickly. I promise I will break his hold on Varius. As for your sister, I think she knows her own mind."

"She knows what Gannys tells her," said Mammea, again with scorn. "Their relationship is more than you suspect, and more than is healthy."

She had advanced the point as if presenting a challenge. She was telling me there were things I did not know—but must.

"What do you mean?"

"They have been lovers," she said. "Perhaps they still are."

Until she spoke those words, I thought Mammea was overwrought with worry for her child. But the strange tension in the women of the family seemed to have churned her mind past absurdity. Those feelings might have been reflected in my face.

"You must excuse me, Princess—"

"You are incredulous," she said as if anticipating it. "I do not know what you share with my sister. It must be good, because she seems happy, but believe me, she takes her pleasure where she will. She dislikes silphium on one hand, and pregnancy on the other."

"But a *eunuch*?"

"It's not as you think," she said in a way that closed a door. "And certainly not as most think. A eunuch has limitations. He cannot spend the seed he no longer possesses. But for the rest—"

"The rest?"

"For that, he is a man."

* * *

I spent the rest of that night in the kind of pain I thought I had left in prison. Regardless of the motives I might impute to Mammea, I knew what she said was true. I had sensed it from the first, and certainly from the time that Gannys walked into the bedroom of Soaemias like its owner. But what I sensed I had thought impossible. Or improbable. Or beneath contempt.

"Is that what I am to you—contemptible?"

"At the moment."

"And if it does not pass—"

Soaemias dared me to a break. That was the prerogative of a princess. She could not be threatened or made to conform. At her whim, I might be cast back into prison, or the desert. But none of those things would happen unless she was stupid.

"Tell me about it."

"And that will be all?" she said.

"That will be a foundation. With luck, it won't topple from the weight of lies."

She exposed the violet highlights of her eyes, and her contempt, as she looked away toward the hills that appeared from her terrace. Shrunk with distance and tamed by it, the hills were like green medallions of spring. I thought I sensed the past raveling within her, caught on a spool. Her eyes were simple blue, and her voice touched emotion.

"You were not raised in a palace," she said.

"I thought it was. Until I knew that it was a villa in Verona."

"Yes," she said. "Every child thinks his world *is* the world. You must imagine a place where that is true."

"I can't."

"But mine *was*. The world came to my door. It begged like a slave to be recognized. When I was young, I asked my mother, in the presence of my uncle, for a doll that could speak and cry. The next day my uncle, the emperor, sent me a dwarf from Spain. He spoke and cried, and had a cock, too."

"How old were you?"

"At the age of curiosity."

I knew if I asked my next question, the mood and more would be broken, but I could not stop. "Was he a eunuch?"

"Yes."

"Functional?"

"More than most."

"Perhaps I was mistaken in pursuing this."

She closed her eyes as if agreeing. "Then I will tell you we found out what he could and could not do. It was not as much as we liked but more than most could imagine. Peico was a living doll. We used to do such terrible things to him. Such monstrous things. Caracalla, too. He once set Peico afire so he might call him Smoky."

"Was he called that? Or Ashes?"

"Peico survived," she said quietly. "He never rebuked us. He could not. No one could. Not even our parents tried very hard. That's a terrible thing for a child to know. That there's no one in the world to restrain them."

I knew she was trying to tell me what she needed. Although I wanted to squeeze every particle of palace life from her body and mind, I took her in my arms. "Should I restrain you?"

"Marcellus, I think you must."

"Then I will. All you need do is let me do what I do best. First, I'll dismantle your toy. But don't worry, he'll still be functional in most ways."

* * *

It was important that Gannys retain most of his functions. The things he had done were done in the interests of the family he served, and perhaps at their orders. He had brought Varius back ready to assume his position as high priest; but until the eunuch appeared at the head of the procession, leading the chariot of lions, I had not seen him at all.

It was good that Gannys had not been present in Emesa when I was there. That proved he was not a fool. Nor did I think him a coward. He was, however, corrupt. Every man in the city carried a tale of money or goods paid to Gannys, who ran the civil affairs of Emesa to the last detail. No permits for public works was given without a bribe. No cases at law were argued without favor. No lotteries were won except by approved parties.

Though many liked the stability that sort of governance brought, I was never one. I liked the uncertainty that an honest man brought to the job.

"Gannys. A moment."

He stopped and turned as he walked from the offices of the city administrator, which lay in the same complex of buildings as the temple. The city treasury and mint were also there. Another eunuch, shaven to the skin, holding an abacus under his arm, accompanied his master.

"Marcellus Decimus. I hardly recognized you without a beard. When I first saw you at the ceremony, I took you for an Egyptian. Or a spy."

"There are no spies in Emesa. Our purpose is not to drive the legions off, but to welcome them, as many as possible, in a peaceful manner."

"Peaceful?"

"That's what I call it."

He seemed bemused, blinking like a toad in the sunlight. "We should speak about that some time. I'm afraid the judgment of Princess Maesa may be impaired on this matter."

"Perhaps you should tell her that."

"I do not tell my lady anything. I suggest."

But he was good at it. His voice, though high-pitched like all eunuchs, held the tones that touched the mind at a level where it usually resided in sleep. He used tricks with his voice and eyes, some of which he had taught to Varius. One of the things I discovered was how much he had taught to Varius in a short time.

"Gannys, this matter is going forward. You'll only damage yourself if you oppose it."

"I can't believe you approve," he said. "You know too well the nature of Roman power."

"Better than you, I think. But those months in jail made me reckless."

Gannys knew he stood on unsteady ground. As if he felt a tremor, he put his hand on the wooden pilaster that marked the bounds of the temple precinct. That hand was the only visible part of him that was not bald.

"You feel I betrayed you."

"I'm sure you betrayed me. I'd like to know whose idea it was, but I doubt I would have the truth."

"And if I said it was the woman whose bed you entered—"

"Do you say that? Or are you suggesting? I find the first unbelievable, and the second cowardly."

His answer was slow. "You must excuse my bewilderment. I'm trying to understand why you go out of your way to provoke me."

"Let's say I have no use for men whose balls are not all that should be taken."

He touched his naked chin with his hand. "Perhaps our differences arise from a misapprehension of our . . . duties."

"Princess Soaemias is no longer your duty." I held the index finger of my left hand up, as if I had a point to make. "The order of command has been revised. Consider everything that relates to the temple none of your concern. The rest of your duties will remain as they are as long as they do not prove corrupt. If you concentrate on them, you may still prosper."

The struggle between pride and greed showed in his face. I believe I know which vice would have won if his indecision had not suddenly come to an end.

I felt the missile pass me on the left side, a quick tunneling sound that might have been the last Gannys heard. He reacted late, flinching as the arrow buried itself in the pilaster inches from his heart. He was late stepping back a pace. In his first moment of coolness, he knew the finger I put in his face was a signal. The arrow still vibrated in the pilaster.

"But understand one thing." I began to raise my finger again, and then held back. "The archers are under my command."

* * *

Gannys' capitulation seemed to be complete. He did not involve himself in military matters, nor did he venture near his princess unless in a public place with witnesses present. He continued to administer the civil affairs of the city and to enrich himself, but made no attempt to dissuade Maesa from her main concern, which was the restoration of the Severan dynasty.

I could not imagine the huge sums spent to further her end, but my banker in Alexandria informed me that eight hundred thousand sesterces were deposited to my account. The archers were timely paid. On my recommendation, Maesa hired a Greek expert in fortification, two Syrians who had served with Macrinus' cavalry, and a Parthian armorer.

She gave special attention to the operation of the pleasure dome. That grand edifice had been a success from the first, but as the mild winter turned to a milder spring, its fame spread throughout the garrisons of the East. Soldiers came not only from Raphanae, but Apamea, and posts in Mesopotamia. Yes, they talked to the women. Information came piecemeal, and not all was accurate, but it came steadily. The portrait that obtained was of an army in disarray.

To what degree was the question. I hoped for an answer when on a day near the end of March I met Maesa in the quarters behind the whorehouse, next to the armory, where she had installed her secretaries and accountants. Philomene was at her side. That had become her station.

"We now know why Macrinus dallies in Antioch," said Maesa. "It's certainly because he is slothful, but it appears he has another reason to avoid Rome."

"Not the Parthians, I suppose."

"The Parthians, yes. But not in the way we had imagined." She turned to Philomene. "Girl."

My Egyptian, whose time had become less mine every day, bowed to her mistress. "All the information we have received is of the same kind," she said. "The battle with the Parthians went worse than we thought, and worse than the emperor told the people. Two legions were almost totally destroyed, according to an *optio* who was present that day."

"This has been confirmed by other men," said Maesa. "But never by an officer of that legion. Go on."

"What was formerly unknown were the actions of the emperor that day," she said. "It seems he had no plans to engage the Parthians. The two armies camped close together, and when a dispute broke out over the water supply, one legion attacked without orders. The rest of the army was thrown unprepared against the enemy. What began as a disadvantage grew to disaster. On the second day, when it seemed the Parthians might rout the legions, the emperor fled the field."

"*What?*"

Maesa smiled. "This is the second report of his cowardice. The first came from a Praetorian of the third cohort, who carried the battle standards that were nearly captured. But more telling information was gotten from one of Macrinus' baggage carriers. It seems the Parthians not only forced the emperor from the field, but entered his camp and almost took it."

That news was important. Macrinus could justify his actions to the people by saying he must protect his person at all costs, but it made little difference to his legions. He had run, leaving everything behind. That simple.

"So Macrinus remains in Syria because he cannot trust the legions to obey him."

"He pays the price of the usurper," said Maesa. "His only rest will come on the day he is deposed. His only sleep will be death."

* * *

Maesa's words were not as cheap as they seemed, for they were backed by hard currency, which was in short supply. The drain on the treasury caused by the swollen legions of the East, and the huge reparations sent to the Parthians, drew the coinage down again. I had it on good word—from the head of the mint—that the silver content of the denarius fell under Macrinus to less than fifty percent.

The legions knew because the moneychangers they dealt with knew it. They also knew the bonuses Macrinus promised had not been paid except to his Praetorians. While he took the measure of every fleshpot in Antioch, living in luxury, his soldiers made do with tents. Their only option to the life of the field was the pleasure dome.

The operation of the whorehouse went smoothly until Soaemias called me to her one day. A temporary condition due to a common circumstance had turned bizarre. She brought it to my attention because it had been brought to hers. As a priestess of Astarte, her expertise on sexual matters was often sought out.

"It occurred three days ago unexpectedly," she said as we sat in her bath. "It was like nothing in my experience, although I have heard of it happening at other temples. It can happen when women live in close quarters in a large group. They begin to have their cycle of blood at the same time."

"You mean, during the same period."

"I mean on the same day. It was the tenth of April exactly. Within twenty-four hours, all the women were awash in the blood of the moon."

I was out of my depth in speaking of menstruation, but I wondered, who could be within? "Can you explain how that happened?"

"The Syrians say it is the work of Astarte. For my part, I have no opinion that could be divulged to you. But I must say it's worked a hardship in servicing the men."

"Well, there's always your mother."

"She was willing. For the good of the cause. But the risk to the reputation of the sanctuary was too great."

"Are we serious about this?"

"Yes," she said. "All of it."

"She's too old. They won't pay for a grandmother."

"They seldom pay in any case."

"Then the temple will be impoverished."

"Not as long as mother makes up the difference, Not as long as Varius is high priest."

"Varius? Is he availing himself of the girls?"

"I'm afraid so. I've warned him several times of disease, but he seems heedless. Perhaps you could speak to him."

"I'll give him the benefit of my wisdom. In the meantime, what's being done to entertain the troops in the absence of one hundred and sixty beautiful women?"

"That's the point," she said. "The men have taken to the high priest of El-Gabal like a substitute for sex. Many of them go to watch Varius perform the daily sacrifices. They stare, enchanted. They say he looks like a god. Like the statues of Bacchus as a young man."

They were not far wrong. Varius' beauty, enhanced by his clothing and jewels, moved him from the everyday like a god. Even hard-bitten soldiers of the legion could be affected.

"Your mother must be happy to hear that."

"More," said Soaemias. "She has an idea."

"Does she mean to share it?"

"She left that to me."

Soaemias rose from the circulating tub, her flawless skin glowing in every part from the heat of the water. Slowly, she lowered herself into the steaming pool of water where I lay. Her legs searched for mine, found them, and wrapped.

"Mother's idea is this," she said. "We grew up in the palace together—all the children, as you know. As all the troops know. And as everyone knows, Caracalla was adventuresome to the point of madness, even as a young man."

"I concur."

"So if the rumor is circulated that Varius is the son of Antoninus, the soldiers, who miss his bonuses, would welcome the idea."

I found myself welcoming the idea not at all, or that she proposed it; but the decision was hers. There were no prohibitions against marriages between cousins. Alliances like those were encouraged. Only the usual strictures against adultery applied.

"Have you thought of the damage to your reputation?"

"My reputation does not equal my ambition for my son."

"But it's a long reach to that belief. Varius is much better looking. And he looks very different."

"He has the nose of a human being, not of a pig, like Caracalla," she said. "But otherwise, the family resemblance is in place."

"In the vicinity."

"Which is good enough. If the legions are as discontented as they seem, they will see in Varius what they want to see, which is the image on the coins they no longer have to spend."

"That's exactly what they'll see."

"It will provide them with the reason they need to foment a rebellion."

"It could provide an excuse."

She swam closer to me with one stroke, and lifted by the buoyancy of the water, seated herself on my lap. She held her hands outstretched as if to say no hands, until she found what she wanted on my body with her body.

"Is the plan brilliant, Marcellus?"

"It's incredible."

She came down slowly, everything inside her just below the temperature of the water, feeling her way, deprived of one sense but heightened in every other, until she enveloped me completely.

"But you believe it."

"Of course."

"Say it."

"I believe."

* * *

Until that time, I had made myself invisible in the town, never mixing with the troops or showing myself at the temple in daylight, which was the only time the rites were performed. But that changed when the identity of Varius' true father was revealed to the legions.

The temple became crowded with uniforms every day at sunrise, and again at the zenith. Some of the men were Syrians who worshiped the sun, others followed the god Mithras and worshiped the sun, but nothing could account for the number of soldiers who came to watch Varius burn incense, make sacrifice, and feed them on the flesh of the slaughtered animals. The devotion of these hard men seemed uncanny. It became clear they were not worshiping a strange and exotic stone, but the young man who should have been emperor.

Then of course they repaired to the pleasure dome to continue their devotions, which were supplied by the family of the deified Caracalla, who had taken such good care with their pay. Even the officers of the garrisons began to appear in Emesa, especially from Raphanae. By then, I had regrown my beard. I began to know the feelings of the men when I received salutes on the street. And when the officers of III Gallica sought me out, I told them they were welcome to share my home rather than put up at one of the inns when they visited the city.

Thus did my hilltop villa become a barracks, and a focal point of discontent. I did little to promote the condition. Usually, I slept in my room at the temple, or at the palace of Soaemias. The questions put to me were always the same sort.

"Is he really the son of Antoninus?"

"If I said yes, could I prove it?"

"You could say no."

"With the same assurance. Use your eyes, my friend. Let them speak to your heart."

The heart, fortunately, can be lied to. That was done from the beginning in a calculated way. Everything from Varius' appearance in a chariot drawn by lions was meant to recall Antoninus, known as Caracalla. He had lived as his army lived—dangerously. Not content to march alongside his legionnaires, he had drawn water and built fortifications with them. He had fought as a gladiator with beasts in the arena, which the soldiers applauded as manly.

Nor had he restrained himself with women. None who came near him were safe from his attention. To think he had made love to his beautiful cousin was believable.

And admirable. What mattered to the legions was that the man who had paid them so well, and lived so heedlessly, left someone to repeat his glory. That, as it happened, was Varius.

I had seen him almost every day since he assumed his position at the temple, but at times I found him hard to reason with. His certainty about every matter under the sun was not easy to deal with in a fourteen-year-old boy.

"I'd like you to come to my villa tonight to meet some of the officers. That is, if you can tear yourself away from your nightly devotions."

Varius smiled because he was still a boy. "Do you know what it's like to be the loving father of so many beautiful prostitutes?"

"I know what your mother thinks it's like."

"Marcellus, you don't understand."

"Give me some credit, Varius. I was your age once, but with less opportunity."

"Is that what you think I'm doing?"

"Yes."

"You would be wrong," he said. "I go to the women so I may discover all that can be known about the holiest act of my god."

"*Holy?*"

"What would you call it?"

"Necessary. The man who calls it something else will find himself in bondage."

"But I'm already in bondage," he said. "To El-Gabal."

I put my hand on his shoulder and squeezed hard. "Varius, forget everything Gannys told you. Think of one thing only. Do you want to be high priest of a temple in the hinterland of Syria? Or ruler of the Roman Empire?"

He took my hand from his shoulder and kept it in his hand. "Marcellus, listen. I know things few men are privileged to know.

The rest I'll learn. It was my destiny to become the high priest of El-Gabal. It's my destiny to be Caesar. I know one cannot happen without the other."

He was so sincere I believed him. "All right. But you can't talk to soldiers this way. You have to speak their language."

He shook his head. "I'll come to your villa tonight, Marcellus. I'll speak to the officers, and they will understand."

I could have stopped him.

* * *

My dining room jutted over the rim of the ravine, cascading into darkness that seemed of its own making. The air that came through the windows was fresh and cool. The tapers were lit and the table set with every fruit and viand found in the empire. The servants whisked each dish of six courses to and fro like silent machines. The musicians played their harps and pipes. The dancers, nine and one for each man, were chosen from the best of the temple. The *vomitorium* down the hallway came fully equipped, but it was easier to eject into the garden below.

Everything had been thought of and all things apportioned, even the spaces in the alcove set aside for each man's valet. It was the perfect time and place for a symposium of the gods, who often appeared in Roman uniform. Even the most loathsome sects, like Christians, often clothed the image of their savior in the breastplate of the legions. Everyone, it seemed, recognized power. Everyone, clearly, wanted more.

Verus, the commander of the garrison at Raphanae, who sat in the position of honor, had power, but not enough to suit his ambition. The two centurions of the second cohort, and the decurion of the third, who flanked him on the middle couch, knew too little rank and too much responsibility. One of the military tribunes of Raphanae, Gaius Dardanius, a late arrival, occupied the first couch, because his portion of power was political and mobile. The freedman paymaster Falx had none, but practiced its application in his work. The two Syrians at my table were without it and therefore the most effusive. The first, Comazon, was a friend of Varius and a spirited young man who had yet to learn his limits. The other, Aziz, was head of my archers.

"When do we see him?" asked Verus. "And will he dance?"

I smiled like Verus' greatest sympathizer. "He's promised to come, leaving his musicians and lions at home."

There was laughter, but nervous. The chief centurion of the legion, Gratus, ended it with reminiscence. "Do you know Antoninus had a lion he called Rapier? The damned big thing clawed off his tunic one day and scraped his arm. But if you think that put the beast in the arena against fifty javelins, you'd be wrong. Antoninus promoted him to centurion of the Guard and gave him a necklace of rubies."

"Style!" said the decurion, who was drunk. "Though he was a mere emperor, he had it for the ages."

"It would have been better for the future had he passed over Macrinus and made Rapier prefect of the Guard," said Comazon. "There's no substitute for intelligence."

"So you're saying our emperor is as slow in mind as he is fleet afoot to the rear in battle?"

"He talks like a hunchback looks," said the decurion. "I mean, he mumbles. He and Oclatinus made a perfect pair. The one speaks like a fart in a windstorm and the other writes his name by the smell."

"The frumentarii rule this empire!" shouted Comazon. "Torturers are our gods!"

"Your god is not of that kind. Nor is he hiding. He waits for his day to come."

The voice seemed to arrive from nowhere. I recognized it, but not the cadences. When I turned around on the couch, I saw Varius in his latest incarnation.

He stood at the entrance to the dining room like Bacchus on his feast day. On his feet he wore sandals, in his hair a crown of laurel, and on his body the same white tunic and broad belt worn by the officers at the table. But his cloak, draped over his shoulder, caused the room to fall into silence. It was purple. Not the usual shade, but the purple made from the shells of sea creatures that spawned on the eastern shore of the Middle Sea. The royal purple. An ordinary citizen, wearing a cloak of that color, would have his body fed to the wild beasts while he was still alive to watch the progress of the pieces that had once made him a man.

"Welcome Varius Avitus, son of Antoninus."

"Thank you, Marcellus Decimus. I know you served my grandfather, and my father, as well as any Caesar could ask. I know you refused by the dictates of your conscience to hold any position in the government of the usurper."

Varius had always been well-spoken, but now he held forth in a voice that carried. He cast his eyes slowly around the sides of my table, as if enumerating forever all who had come to this hilltop supper.

"These are good men, you say?"

"They are all friends of your father."

I did not know what Varius was doing, but I could see it worked well. The distance he created by the formality of his words, and the way he walked to the table and passed around it, took hold of the company. They were not comfortable with him trailing behind them as if examining the back of their heads, but they were silent.

"My first campaign, at the age of six, was in Britannia against the Caledonians," he said. "Did any of you share that time?"

"I, Marcellus Decimus, was there."

When no one else claimed that dubious honor, Varius seized the opportunity. "Do you recall the last words spoken by my grandfather, Septimus Severus?"

"No, young lord."

"As he lay dying, he admonished my father, Antoninus, to secure the pay and well-being of his legions." Varius paused as if listening to a distant voice. "The great Severus gave no other advice to his sons."

"And would *you* follow it?"

Varius came round to Verus, who had spoken. He was a man not of marble but granite. His skin was mottled and pockmarked, his nose as wide as a lion's, and his eyes alternated their heavy attention not quite in sequence. Varius confronted him mildly, taking his measure and more.

"When I am emperor, the legions will be paid what they are worth. On my ascension, I promise a *donativum* of four hundred sesterces for each man. Each year, base pay will also be raised in a like amount."

"Your word," said Verus.

"As I speak it."

"No offense," said Gratus, the centurion. "But we've heard promises like these before. Macrinus did nothing but hide them in his pockets."

"And enrich the Parthians," said Comazon.

Varius did not remind us that his family had always paid the legions, that the clan of Bassianus was incomparably rich, and that the table set with precious plate and rare food was the smallest part of their largess. Slowly, he let his cloak down from his shoulder.

The cloak was heavy by the way it hung, as if pressure built within it. Then suddenly, the purple folds were charged with gold. The gold became coins that slid onto the table, ringing like small bells onto the floor. They rang and rang as if from an inexhaustible source, brilliant and blinding. A small fortune. It was all that each man could do not to follow the coins down and grovel on the floor. Not to abandon the thing said to be most precious to a Roman—his dignity.

"I would have no one accept my word for more than it is," said Varius. "I would have every legion pay the closest attention to my deeds."

As if to demonstrate, Varius took a pear from a bowl of fruit on the table. He held it before his face as if he had never seen its like. "Syrian pears are the delight of the civilized world," he said. "The nectar of the sun."

He turned and walked back around the table as if strolling along a street. He took a bite from the pear, and stopping when he made the circle, lay the pear upon the table.

No one could take his eyes from it. Where the flesh had been removed from the fruit, a bright red spot appeared. It seemed liquid. It seemed to grow. When it welled up from the surface, the red spot, which looked like blood, widened and began to course onto the table.

"I know what I ask of the legions in return for their pay," said Varius. "It will be their blood that is shed."

Like our servant, Varius took two steps back and bowed low. He moved slowly to the entrance of the dining room, then turned his back and walked away. A coin fell from his cloak. Another. And another. It seemed we heard him long after he disappeared from sight.

* * *

"How did he do that?"

"You mean the pear?"

"What do you think I mean?" said Verus angrily. "That thing bled. I saw it."

"I saw it, too."

We had examined the pear. The thick red liquid was of the consistency of blood. It tasted like blood. It had stopped suppurating shortly after Varius left, but not entirely. Now that everyone had left, I picked it up again, but knew no more of its origin. The liquid had dried completely. It had dried quickly, like blood.

"We're dealing with a magician for an empire," said Verus. "I can't say I like that."

"A very wealthy magician. Those coins are real."

Verus looked at the stacks of gold on the table. Comazon had gone around after his friend left picking them up and apportioning them to each man; but the commander of Raphanae attained to a somewhat larger share. As was proper.

"He created a distraction with the coins," said Verus. "While we were all agog, he performed his trick."

"That's plausible."

"And when all is said and done, he buys a Roman garrison for a few gold pieces."

"More than a few."

"Still, he's gotten it cheap."

"If he has it. Does he?"

Verus smiled. "How much are you culling from this venture, Marcellus?"

"Expenses."

"They must be high. This is a fine villa. The food was fine. The women magnificent."

I shrugged.

"You don't bother to reckon accounts."

"Not unless we're speaking of figures."

"What do you imagine we're doing?"

One thing about Verus: he was direct. He was also corrupt, but circumstances made that handy. The legions would probably never be more discontented or disrupted. Macrinus could at any moment decide that the clan of Bassianus was worth his violent attention.

"Three million sesterces."

"Five," he said.

"If you deliver within the month."

Verus looked as if he had expected more haggling. He held his hand up as if he meant to count his fingers. "This is the month of the goddess Maia, good wife of Mars," he said. "I must say war seems appropriate."

THE BREACH

We left the city of Emesa on the Ides of May, the last day of Lemuria, the festival of the dead. As night fell, a comet that had been seen for the last three days appeared once more to sear the sky. Although that was a bad sign, among the worst, its intent fell against those in power. The appearance of a comet portended great change—and we were its agents.

Varius, Soaemias, Comazon, and twenty archers commanded by Aziz made the journey. The presence of Mammea and her son Alexianus had also been requested by Verus, but Maesa demurred, and so did I. Our reception, though well prepared, was not guaranteed. Alexianus might find himself the only surviving heir of the clan Bassianus.

The archers fanned out when we reached the crossroads leading to the garrison. We took the eastern fork, skirting the sprawl of buildings and huts that had grown up around Raphanae, as around every legion post. Here, the road narrowed. Our chariots descended single file, clattering on the cobblestones. Nothing could have been done about that. If we were betrayed, speed in retreat was far more important than silence in the approach.

We halted within sixty yards of the walls, near the first row of houses, where the amphitheater and baths stood. Soaemias got down from her car. In the darkness, I could not tell if she looked my way, but she slowed as she passed Varius' chariot. She spoke one word—"Conquer"—before passing into the first house on the left, where she would await our signal, or our failure.

At a walk, we brought our chariots under the walls before the triple ditch that ringed the garrison. Raphanae was approachable only by the main gate, where timbers spanned the ditches. When we reached the southernmost of the four gates—the one closest to the praetoria—I gave the signal to halt.

As I got down from the car, I still saw no sentries at the walls or before the double doors. I crossed the first two ditches, but no movement showed from the twin towers above, or from the siege ramparts spanning the space between. The moon at the quarter gave no useful light. The torches from the ramparts in the last hour before dawn threw mild shadows.

As I crossed the last ditch, one of the twin doors of the gates opened to the width of a man. I saw nothing in the shadows, but stopped and gave the password: "Men of Mercury!"

The door swung open on Gratus, the chief centurion. If I could have wished for one man, he was my choice. Gratus was the best soldier in III Gallica, as the chief centurion was in every legion. They had the respect of the men even more than the commander.

"Men of Mars," he said, drawing back his cloak and showing me his sword and dagger were at rest.

I was relieved, but could not afford to be convinced. If I meant to lure a man into a trap, this is the way I would do it.

"Is everything ready?"

"Verus awaits us in the strong-room."

"Where else would he be?"

Gratus followed me to my chariot, where we unbuckled the money chest from the car. Carrying it to the gate, we entered Raphanae with our burden. The door closed fast. Standing behind it was Gaius Dardanius, the tribune from the supper party.

"Payday."

"The first," I said. "But not the last."

Although the tribune was a political being from a high-ranking family, he shared the twin poles of the legion's fancy—women and money. He had been one of the most frequent visitors to the temple and its congenial annex. Smiling, he led the way down the Via Praetoria.

I knew my way around Raphanae as I would have known any Roman legion post at any time of day or night. Each garrison had four walls rounded at the corners, four gates in the middle of the walls, and two main streets that bisected them. Each barracks, granary, hospital and stable was located in the same place in Germania or Spain or Greece. The praetoria, or headquarters building, was always set near the center of the garrison at the junction of the streets. Each strong-room, where the garrison kept its cash, lay twelve steps down in the vault of the praetoria.

We found Verus there with a set of keys in his hand. His big blunt nose twitched when he saw us heave the money chest between us, and he seemed nervous. I was not sure if that was bad. The commander had put more on the line than anyone else in the garrison—his head—but he was being compensated for the risk.

He waited until the door was opened by his keys, the chest manhandled inside and placed on a table, and the tribune posted outside against intruders, before he spoke.

"Two million?"

I handed him another key from my belt. "There's quite a bit more. The rest will be distributed to the troops as needed."

He inserted the key and drew back the lid painted with the images of Phosphorus, the evening star, and Hesperus, the morning star, sharing quadrants of the same night sky. The interior was also divided into equal parts—the first with silver coins, the second with gold. Verus put both hands into the latter and sifted the round gold through his fingers.

"In this I trust," he said.

"You needn't worry about the *permutatio* either."

"How will I know that the rest of the money has gone into my account?"

"Have a word with your banker."

"I'm not going to Antioch today," he said. "It may be that none of us will be going to Antioch in this lifetime."

"Then the money will rot."

Verus laughed and clapped me on the back. "Perhaps we'll march on the city this day. Shall we call it incentive?"

It was always best to appeal to a Roman's balls instead of his mind. Not only were they bigger, they were what he gambled with. This was the greatest gamble of Verus' life. Would he hedge?

"You'll assemble the troops."

"I'll have them assembled," he said. "But I can't order them to proclaim that boy master of the world. That's your job."

True. I received the personnel roster from Verus and went through the lists of names. I knew some of them, and tried to gauge which were sympathetic and which might be trouble. All things had gone as planned to this point, where they would diverge into the lap of Fortune. To many Romans, she was the only goddess that mattered. She was luck. Where her wheel stopped was the fruit of every venture.

* * *

It was still dark when I fetched Varius within the walls, but the sun could be felt on the horizon. He did not seem disconcerted when we entered one of the guest rooms in the praetoria. The place said Verus had a taste for luxury. The mirror before which Varius stood as he changed his clothes was pure silver, carrying the length of the wall to the ceiling. Many of the furnishings were costly and imported from great distances.

To my surprise, Varius asked to see the troop roster before he finished dressing. He gave it close study, as if he knew what he was looking for in those many names that were unfamiliar to him. III Gallica was once composed of men from Gaul, but that had not been true for years. Now, there were as many Syrians as Gallic stock. Although a solid core remained, none spoke anything but bad Latin.

"The only one who needs your attention is Verus," I said. "He's left us to play our hand. He'll stand aside and see how the revolution progresses. If all goes well, he'll lend his backing. But we have to do the work. Do you think you can speak to the legion in the mass?"

Varius adjusted the folds of his golden tunic in the mirror so the purple stripes that ran down the shoulders were aligned. The idea was that he should dress as Caracalla had dressed, and emphasize every feature that recalled the memory of the assassinated Antoninus. Luckily, when Caracalla came east, he shaved his face and even his chin, like a boy. Varius could not have grown a good beard if his life depended on it.

"Have no fear, Marcellus. The god is with us."

I looked around for a presence in the shadows. The way Varius had taken to speaking breached common sense at every turn. "You must bring everything you have to bear in the next hours. You might even want to produce the bleeding pear again. Anything that will hold their attention and move them to act."

"I have no pears," he said. "Nor any special powers. It is the god who does all things."

"Pray to him then. And tell me where you would like to hold forth."

"The place does not matter," he said. "We are in the homeland. Here, the god is everywhere, but he appears at his most radiant with the dawn."

"Then the men should be turned out immediately. By the time we roust them from their beds, the sun will be rising."

"Yes," said Varius. "That is how it will happen. At dawn, I will go among the men, and they will know Him."

* * *

I was worried, my stomach churning bad milk, as we went outside. It was good strategy to call the men to assembly to meet the rising sun, since many of them worshiped it, and it was even better to present them with the image of Caracalla as he had never been in life; but the best work resided in the money chest, where I placed my faith.

That was not what Varius meant. His smile as he spoke of his god was like a big cat who follows an inexhaustible herd of prey. That look of inner communication did not disappear from his face all day, which was the most remarkable of his life.

It began with a flurry of confused movement. I helped Gratus carry a long plank table outside, where we placed it at the head of the parade ground in front of the praetoria. Comazon and Gaius Dardanius followed with the money chest. Only Verus was conspicuous by his absence. The two million sesterces that were his share had vanished beneath the lid of stars. The remainder would have to suffice for his legion.

The men began to pour out of the barracks shortly, summoned by the horns that called the first hour earlier than usual. Their numbers would be about five thousand, not counting the men on leave and contingents assigned to duty at other places in the area.

They scurried about in the chaos that preceded order, presenting themselves in the tunics and belts and hobnail sandals that were their normal garb. Only the centurions had swords and daggers. That was a cause for concern, but disarming the legion's battle leaders would have created suspicion. Although the men knew with the certainty of prey that something unusual would happen, they fell in quickly, as if it were any other day in their twenty years of service.

I wanted to make sure this day was nothing of the kind, but when I looked toward the praetoria, I could not locate the person who made the crucial difference. "Where's Varius?"

"He was in the fore-hall a minute ago," said Gratus. "Asking questions about the men."

I looked to Comazon, who shook his head. "I haven't seen him in the last minutes."

"Look around, friend Comazon, find our future emperor, and take him by the hand. Lead him here."

He turned to enter the praetoria, but stopped short. "I'm afraid that won't be necessary," he said in a voice that ascended to wonder. "Look!"

I followed his eyes, which moved higher than the parade ground. They stopped at the building behind. For a moment, I saw nothing strange, but just then the sun rose and like liquid poured into a vessel mounted the walls of the garrison. The cup did not fill with light, but at the lip, which was the roof of the granary, I saw the outline of a man. His arms were upraised, as if taking the first light of the day to himself and embracing it.

I guessed that the dark form was Varius, and when the rays of the sun struck him like a cymbal, I knew I was looking at him as he looked at his god. He wore something like a diadem on his head, and his body above the shoulders shimmered. The light seemed to lift him in its brilliance by his crown. The rest of his body wanted to follow but held back, glowing in a lesser shade of gold, which was his tunic.

Suddenly, Varius was not standing on the roof of the granary. He stood before it, balanced on the flag staff. He was twenty feet above us, but the height looked like more. His body seemed stretched, growing larger, glowing brighter, like a secondhand image of his god.

Finally, the legion knew it, too. Glancing at the ranks, I saw only the backs of their tunics, and their hair, the colors of which were as varied as the nations of the empire. Each man had turned to watch that brilliant apparition. The sounds they made, quietly but unanimously, married their many tongues to awe.

The figure pinned to the morning sky began to move. Slowly, Varius let his arms apart, swinging them wide like the wings of crucifixion. When they were parallel with his body, with an almost visible effort he stilled his arms.

"Lord, he's going to fly," said a low stupid voice from the front rank.

Varius dropped. One moment he stood on his narrow perch above us, and the next he was gone. He did not gather himself but simply stepped into space. It happened so quickly that my mind hung suspended on the roof when he struck the ground in front of the granary. I did not see him come to earth. The light above was bright, but below darkness consumed him.

The legion surged toward the granary. I still saw nothing as I made my way through the ranks, which were no longer tight but tumultuous. I recalled the training Varius had undergone—the falls from heights—but my faith in his skill meant nothing until I saw the large bags of grain that had been placed against the side of the granary. A brake. I heard voices from the front of the granary and from every side. They were cheering, "He's well! He lives! He is the son of Antoninus! He is the son of the sun!"

Varius stood unharmed amid the brute admiration of the legion. He stood out among those tanned and muscled men like a pale wraith. The diadem on his head was gone, demolished in the fall, but his blond hair shone brightly. His tunic was streaked with dust but still shot with gold thread. His face seemed transformed by the light he greeted so well. None of these soldiers ever had skin as pure, as luminous. None had eyes like the Greek sea. None had performed the ghost of a miracle since they breached from the bellies of their mothers.

It might have been a miracle. Varius must have struck the bags and tumbled, he must have practiced falls many times, but still—

"Are you well, my lord?"

As if on the next mountain top, Varius gave great voice. "I am among my legions," he said. "How could I not be well?"

"He looks like Antoninus," said one man.

"He speaks like Antoninus," said another.

Varius walked forward as if no one stood before him. Quickly, that became true as the mass of men parted, clearing a path for him.

"I've been told that these men, who served my father well, are being badly paid. Is that true, Marcellus Decimus?"

"It is true, Caesar."

Varius smiled as he heard the word that could transform him again, and for the greater. "I would have my legions recompensed in their back pay," he said in voice that carried beyond us. "I would have them enrolled with all the increases they were promised but did not receive. I would do this at once."

"Yes, Caesar!"

"Where is my war chest?"

"This way, Caesar!"

Varius knew where it was. He had never stopped moving forward, and the ranks never stopped parting as quickly as they closed. The legion listened to his words with an attention they rarely lent their officers in battle, and they relayed the best news of their lives faster than we found the front of the praetoria. By the time we reached the table with the money chest, the legion crowded close in our wake, buzzing and murmuring.

Varius lifted the lid from the chest. Slowly and deeply, he put his hand into the money. The silver coins slid from his hand in the same way as the gold had slid from Verus' hand; but this time a huge audience watched with total attention. That slippery sound brought down a hush on the legion. Even the morning birds that twittered from the trees, from their perches on the ramparts and flagstaff, observed the silence.

"Publius Caelius Assanius!" he said. "Step forward!"

That request took some shuffling of the mass, but finally a tall middle-aged centurion came forward to face him at the table. If I had not seen so many of his like in my eighteen years with the legions, I would have said that Publius Caelius was unique. His face and body were as rugged as the map of the empire—an Italian boot of a nose, a chin like all of Spain, shoulders as broad as the sweep of Anatolia, arms like archipelagos and legs like peninsulas, eyes as calm and brown as the trammeled earth of every continent he had known. As a centurion, he was used to being singled out in matters of discipline or urgent need, but seldom for an unknown reason, and never on a morning like this. Publius Caelius seemed puzzled, and his left hand was too close to his dagger.

"You are *princeps* of Legion III Gallica."

Publius Caelius' answer was not reticent. That would have sounded false coming from the second-ranking centurion of the legion. "Yes, lord. That is my position at Raphanae."

"You served Rome for nineteen years," said Varius as if counting his fingers and toes. "You fought at the battles of Issus and Lugdunum, which settled the succession for the Severan dynasty. You fought in Parthia and Caledonia in campaigns against the barbarians."

"In truth, lord."

Varius looked closely at the man, as if testing his recollection. It was a fine ploy to create a personal link between them. No one knew the information had been gotten from the rolls a few minutes before.

"Princeps, did we know each other in Britannia?"

Publius Caelius shook his head. "No, lord. But several times I observed you as you rode with the emperor."

"My grandfather, Septimus Severus."

Publius Caelius was unsure of the relationship, but not that it existed in some way. He nodded. "Yes, lord."

Varius dipped his hand into the money chest. As he turned back, he held up a fistful of coins to show the assembly as he moved close to Publius Caelius.

"The money you receive is for faithful service to the rightful dynasty of the empire."

Publius Caelius, stunned, held out his hand, both hands, as Varius released the money. The silver coins flowed from one to the other until they were filled. And when they could hold no more, the coins began to spill onto the hard dirt of the parade ground. They bounced and rolled. They continued to spill from Varius' hand and continued to fall. They continued to roll away. It was impossible that so many coins could have been gathered from the money chest by one hand, but it seemed to have happened.

Publius Caelius looked down at his feet, which were covered with coins to the laces of his sandals. There were hundreds. He said, "By the gods," but the coins continued to flow from Varius' hand. Coins rang one upon the other but still they came on—a torrent. They did not stop until Varius raised his hands to show that they were finally, unaccountably, empty.

"I do not think this levy of coins too much for a man who has given his life's blood in the service of Rome," said Varius. "I think it only proper."

The men listened, though they were murmuring and maneuvering to glimpse the bounty in silver. They watched hungrily as Publius Caelius retrieved his fortune, trying to maintain the dignity of his rank while clawing at the earth.

While he was still at the task, Varius moved away, looking over the heads of the legion and deep into their ranks. "Julius Lucius Ennodius!" he shouted to the throng. "Will you step forward?"

That soldier, though far within the ranks, advanced to the front immediately. He was of the third cohort, a standard bearer whose chest was so stout that he looked as if he wore a metal cuirass beneath his tunic. He was a perfect specimen of the Macedonian nation. The brown hair on his cheeks and chin descended without a break into the darker hair that rose like a pelt from his tunic. The plates of his knees were as big and round as loaves of bread. His thighs were as large as Varius' trunk. The right arm that could have felled big game at a blow shot out strong.

"Caesar!"

Varius nodded as if to say this day was a learning experience, and the first and most important lesson was the name he should bear. He waited until the lesson reached the last rank.

"Julius Lucius, you have served with this legion for seven years."

"Yes, Caesar. Six years, eleven months, and four days."

Varius agreed with the count. "I understand you have taken a wife, who has given you two children."

"Three, Caesar. A second boy came this month."

Varius inclined his head in wonder. "Rome stands in awe of your prowess, Julius Lucius. But I would ask if you knew that before my grandfather Septimus Severus came to the throne, no man in the legions was permitted to marry?"

"Caesar, I did not know."

"And why should you?" asked Varius, strolling before the assembled men, throwing his voice to the most distant ranks. "None of us should be chained to the past. What is bygone is best forgotten. Done." He turned forcefully on his captive standard bearer. "But I understand, Julius Lucius, that your wife is a native of the region. She is Syrian."

"Yes, Caesar."

"I wonder if you know that my father, the great and lamented Antoninus, gave the law that all freemen of the empire should enjoy the benefits of Roman citizenship. In other words, that your wife should become a citizen of Rome, as well as your children, and grandchildren, until the end of time."

"Caesar, I am aware. I think every man here knows the gift of life Antoninus gave us."

"And what has the usurper Macrinus given you?"

Varius leaned forward as if to gain an answer; but Julius the *signifer* was trapped, betrayed into an opinion, which was close to thought. The man who carried the battle standard used his head to steady the pole—and nothing else. In a pinch, he could blurt the first thing that came to his mind.

"Caesar, he has not kept his promises of better pay!"

"But he fulfilled his promises to the Parthians."

"That is what we hear, Caesar!"

"And to the Dacians."

"Yes, Caesar!"

"And the Armenians."

"Without a doubt, Caesar!"

"Because they *threatened* him," said Varius.

"That is correct, Caesar!"

Varius paused as he heard the voices of many others join in affirmation. The men in the front ranks pushed forward, they were almost pressing against us, and they began to find a common voice. When Varius knew that, he raised his over theirs.

"And when the Parthians did more than threaten—when they took the field against him—the usurper did not commit his legions! He refused to fight until he had no choice!"

Julius Lucius meant to answer, and perhaps did, but his words were engulfed by the roar of voices from the sides and behind.

"*Yes!*" said the legion. "*Yes!*"

Varius leaped atop the table that held the money chest in one dexterous bound. He pitched his voice far, gathering the strength of all those voices to his.

"And when battle was finally joined that day, Macrinus led the legions to slaughter!"

"*Yes!*"

"And when he saw that defeat was possible, he turned his back. He abandoned his camp to the enemy! He *ran!*"

"*Yes!*"

"He deserted the legions! He deserted *Rome*!"

"*Yes*!"

"And now I say Rome must desert him!" Varius raised his fist. "*We* are Rome!"

"*We are Rome*!"

Varius pumped his fist. "Down with Macrinus!"

"Down with Macrinus! Down with the usurper!" A thousand, two thousand right arms went up together, raised in salute. "Hail, Antoninus, son of Antoninus."

Varius raised his arm to return the salute. "Hail Legion III Gallica!"

"HAIL, CAESAR!"

* * *

"I find I like being guided by the wisdom of the people," said Varius as he sat at the table in the atrium of the praetoria. "When I'm emperor of more than a garrison, I shall take the name Marcus Aurelius Antoninus as my own."

A fine choice. Marcus Aurelius was the last great emperor of Rome. Antoninus was the last great emperor of the legions. This boy gave promise of equaling both.

"In the meantime, what shall I call you?"

"Varius will do." He laughed. "Or god."

He laughed again, like a boy. He was as giddy as any boy with a legion to call his own. The composure he had shown before the men modified, but I thought nothing of it. I thought it natural. If pressed, I would have said it was the most natural thing to happen that day.

"Varius, how did you pour a barrel of silver coins into that centurion's hands? I watched you at the money chest. You took a handful."

He shrugged. "I had nothing to do with that," he said. "I held my hand over his. The coins . . . multiplied."

"Money," I said, "does not grow except in banks. And at an orderly rate."

"I can't explain it," he said, curbing the smile on his face. "Believe me, I had no idea what would happen. I felt I should give that man his due, whatever it was. I thought something would make that happen." He held up his arms, as if to show that he had nothing up the sleeves of his tunic. "But the result I assure you was due solely to the will of the god. When I needed him, he came."

"A miracle, then."

"If you like."

He was serious. If Varius had absorbed every trick in the magician's canon from Gannys and the other priests of El-Gabal, he still could not have done what he did.

"Varius, what happened to you when your father died?"

He looked at me as if I might have touched something important—and secret—in his life. "When my father died," he said mildly, "I found my father."

"Is that the same as being hit on the head too hard?"

"Similar. Things happen inside me now. I have no control over them, but I can direct them. I think my purpose on earth is to discover the proper direction."

"Varius, I'll grant your god all the powers in this world, but the man who depends for his life on the intervention of the supernatural will find himself alone in that stinking latrine. And at the worst possible moment."

"That's why the god has given me Marcellus," he said. "You are my sword and shield. No matter what happens, we will be together to the end."

"I wish you a long life."

* * *

I set about guaranteeing that. In conference with Verus, who had been cooperative since his men determined his fate, we decided that Raphanae should be fortified against a siege. We could not lead an attack on the legions of the East, but from a defensive position we could hold until word of our rebellion spread. We were confident that elements of all the legions would declare for the cause of Marcus Aurelius Antoninus. If other legions joined us, we would have the means to overthrow Macrinus. We also knew it would have to be done quickly if it were to be done at all.

The legion set to work shoring up the ramparts, taking in supplies, stockpiling weapons and gathering their wives and children within the walls. Verus had not agreed readily to the latter, but he knew noncombatants were at grave risk if left without, and he understood, since his mistress lived in the town, that the men would fight better and longer if their loved ones were protected. The garrison had supplies for a week, and longer as more were taken in. Two wells within the walls guaranteed that III Gallica would not be brought to ruin by thirst.

We did not know how long we had to prepare for a response from the emperor. The entire garrison had gone over to us with no dissenting voices, but when the head count came, it showed thirty-eight men missing from guard duty and patrols in the area. We had to assume that some had deserted to the enemy. Though cavalry was sent out to hunt for the deserters, less than a dozen were found on the road to Antaradus. Five more were found on the road to Apamea. On the smaller roads that led south, north and west, none were discovered.

Word of the rebellion could reach Macrinus in a day. If he took the better part of a day to respond, we should have three to complete our preparations. Knowing Macrinus, we might have a week. His last decisive act had been the assassination of Caracalla.

Our luck was that word of the rebellion did not reach Macrinus first, but Ulpius Julianus, one of the two prefects of the Praetorian Guard. He had been detached from Antioch to the city of Tyre in southern Syria to quell a disturbance among the population, which he had done with the legion at his command. He was on his way back when the news of our rebellion reached him near Aradus. From there, it was a four-hour march to Raphanae. The horse archers who brought the news of his approach arrived in the afternoon about two o'clock.

"Julianus was on the high road at noon," said Aziz, who had donned the mailed battle dress of the Emesene archers. He seemed not to know whom to favor with his report—Verus, Soaemias, or myself—so he spoke to all. "He could be here in three hours."

"With one legion."

Aziz nodded.

"But he can gather reinforcements along the way," said Verus. "Small garrisons are at Aradus and Arca, and if he sent forward to Apamea, he can be joined by two more legions."

"Later," I said.

Verus nodded.

"I doubt if he has much in the way of siege weapons."

"Probably not."

Less them, his choices were limited. It would be hard to scale the garrison walls. Triple ditches meant that his casualties would be high. Even with artillery, ample munitions, and more ladders than he could carry on a punitive expedition, the prefect faced heavy going. He had one logical alternative.

"If he attacks, he'll concentrate his forces on the gates."

"He'll have archers," said Verus. "Fire arrows could keep us busy and give him the cover he needs."

"Then let's give him what he thinks he needs."

"What are you saying?"

"I say we give him the gates."

"*Our* gates?" said Verus.

"Not all of them, commander. Just the ones we'd like him to have."

* * *

Accompanied by the thunder of drums, Julianus' legion looked spirited as it came over the rise. They traveled light, without their baggage train. Scouts were deployed in the van but in contact with the main body. The pioneers who did the dogwork came next, followed by Julianus with his senior officers and bodyguard of cavalry.

In the middle of the column were the siege weapons I was most concerned with. They were nothing unusual: two cheiroballistras that could launch bolts but not stones of great size; two small catapults that could hammer the walls and barely reduce their height; and three battering rams. The last were Julianus' best hope, but our plan could make them our allies.

His legion would do its work as it was usually done—with the blood of its men. The rank and file who appeared behind the assault weapons were a full complement of five thousand—and perhaps more. I counted the centuries and came to a figure of about seven thousand. Julianus had clearly gathered reinforcements on his march. His horse-archers were Emesenes. That was good for us. They were the best at their trade, but would not eagerly embrace orders telling them to destroy the high priest of El-Gabal, the earthly factor of their god.

The infantry was another matter. They were the sinew of the legions, the highly trained cohorts that never varied in purpose or strength. Five thousand men of the legions had gone many times against twice the number of barbarians and come away the victor. Sometimes, the five thousand had gone against fifty thousand and not taken a backward step or ceased killing the enemy until they were so spent that they could not raise their swords above their knees.

And it seemed we had bad luck in this legion, for many of the men were African. They would fight for Macrinus as no other troops in his command.

Nor would Julianus hesitate to use them. He would spend their lives to subdue our rebellion and contain discontent in the legions. He had been one of the heads of the frumentarii before he became prefect, and he knew the situation in the garrisons of the East. He also knew that if he eliminated the heir to the Severan dynasty, the discontent no longer had a focus.

But there were things Julianus could not know, which were the things we had done to welcome him to Raphanae. I would not have tried to deceive an experienced legion commander with our ruse, but Julianus was a spymaster. Like Oclatinus, his skills lay in the administration of pain. Of military strategy I hoped he knew enough to bring himself down.

As his troops moved through the town outside the walls, I watched his banners. For several minutes, he and his mounted bodyguard vanished and did not reappear. Eventually, as his legion began to deploy in a battle line before the garrison walls, I saw figures come into view at the top of the amphitheater, where the gladiatorial games were held. I recognized Julianus, who wore the golden breastplate of a Prefect of the Praetorian Guard.

When they put up signal flags outlined against the sky above the amphitheater, I made a circuit along the ramparts of Raphanae. Julianus' Africans had formed up before the gates, as expected. They ignored the west gate, where the ground was sewn with man-traps that were easily visible. The legion massed before the north, south and east gates.

They had not stopped to rest after their march, nor had they been fed. It was clear they planned to carry Raphanae by frontal assault. They waited for the chieroballistras and catapults to be placed at the rear, and then brought the rams toward the ranks but not within reach of our archers. At that point, all activity stopped. Even the pounding of the drums stopped.

In the quiet, I heard the sound of ratchets cranking back the catapults. It was a long excruciating sound that also, after a time, stopped. At the top of the amphitheater, one of the signal standards came down. In response, both catapults released.

The machines were not so powerful that the missiles blurred in flight. I saw them as they overshot the ramparts by twenty yards. The first thumped against the wall of the hospital, while the second struck the roof of the easternmost barracks, and loosening some of the tiles, brought them down along with the dark round missile they had delivered.

I hurried down the stairs to the margin inside the walls, two hundred feet deep around the perimeter. I was sure what the objects were. Perhaps everyone in the garrison knew what they were. Not stones or incendiary balls. The missiles were soft, and so to speak, harmless.

I reached the wall before the hospital as a centurion of the third cohort unwrapped the first object. It was bound in a layer of cords, and a second of cloth. Both meant to preserve the integrity of the object, which emerged slowly but consecutively— the eyes, the lips, the bearded chin, and the beginning of a neck.

The centurion held up the head by the hair. It was that of a middle-aged man. "Do we know him?"

I would have said no, but Soaemias called from behind. "His name is Calvinus. He was the brother of my sister's husband, Gessius."

I turned to shield her from the grisly head of the man she knew as Mammea's brother-in-law; but Soaemias stepped around me. I believe she would have lashed out at me if I had moved to block her path again.

"You should not be here, lady."

"Where else should I be?" she said angrily. "At my *loom*?" Her eyes were of a different color than I had seen, a glowing crystalline blue, purely Roman and filled with hatred as pure. "Where is the other?"

It was being brought, uncovered, held by the hair, which was of longer and finer texture of a pale shade of red that seemed orange with the tint of the sun. The head was that of a woman whose identity I did not know but now could guess.

There were no tears in Soaemias' eyes when she saw the second head, nor anything but anger. Her voice did not alter. "This is Allia, the wife of Calvinus Marcianus, late of the city of Arca."

Almost before she finished speaking, two more dark objects soared over the wall. Both were smaller. Both struck the ground in front of the hospital, since their weight was less. They bounced and rolled nearly to Soaemias, who had the cords and cloth unbound so she might see the severed heads of the children of Allia and Calvinus Marcianus.

* * *

"A herald!"

I was halfway up the rampart stairs at the southern gate when the call came. Verus had already taken position on the rampart. He looked down at the man who stood on the road before the gate at a distance where signature of rank could be seen. The transverse crest of horsehair on his helmet marked him as an optio of the auxiliary cavalry. Expendable.

"You are commanded to lay down your arms!" he shouted. "All mutineers will be received like men of III Gallica as of this moment! But not one instant longer!"

"Kill him!"

Soaemias had mounted the stairs. I had not seen her take up the long dagger she held in her hand. The only thing the same was the tone of her voice.

Verus tried to put her off. "I'm afraid they'll be angry if we do."

"Isn't that what we *want*?" Without waiting for a reply, she turned to the squad of archers at the wall. "Kill him! That is the order of your princess! Kill that man now!"

The archers looked to me. I did not like bringing down a man who stood defenseless before the walls, but what she said was true. The death of Julianus' emissary would send a message that would be received with fury. And that was what we wanted.

When I nodded, four archers drew arrows from their bow cases. The way that Emesenes loaded was unconventional, the arrows placed to the right of the bow instead of the left. It was a quick release that should not have been able to reach its mark accurately; but I had seen them do it so many times I had become a believer.

The optio fell, hit four times.

* * *

I had Soaemias removed forcibly to the praetoria, where she joined her son under strong guard. I was sure Julianus' response to the killing of his emissary would be prompt and vigorous. I no longer saw him at the top of the amphitheater in the light of the afternoon sun that had begun to dim; but when I ordered more archers to the rampart walls, the standards at the top of the amphitheater flashed to signal the assault of his legion.

They came at the three gates simultaneously. We knew how they would come, and where, and what we wanted them to do, but even with forewarning the fury of the assault was a shock. The siege weapons no longer meant to terrorize but to batter and maim as they flung rocks and heavy bolts against the outer walls and into the garrison. Fire arrows quickly put two buildings in flames in the compound. Their archers, moving behind the screen of troops, darkened the sky with their arrows, and the rams were quickly brought forward.

The first line of Moors who came with the rams held doubled shields over their heads. They came fast and low, crouched beneath the shields of trebled oxhide that had been stretched across the rams. They did not waver. When a man went down, his place was filled. When bodies began to pile on the roadway and impede their progress toward the gate, those wounded men, some still alive, were blown harshly aside.

If we ever doubted that we faced Roman legions, we knew now. The shocks as the rams struck the gates shook the walls. They seemed to shake the entire garrison, as if we were a gigantic drum that would be beaten until it breached our most defenses. And that, we hoped, was true. That was the plan.

Our task was to keep them from the walls and funnel their charge through the gates. When the rams struck again, and again, the gates began to buckle, and the mass of their infantry readied the charge. That was when I ordered the ramparts to be fully manned. A quarter of our legion deployed in good order at the walls, archers to the fore; a quarter massed at the margins behind the three gates, archers to the fore; while the rest were held in reserve for what was always unanticipated.

With a blast from the trumpets and a mighty roar, the Moors came on. Each of their centuries carried long boards to span the ditches and eighty-step ladders to scale the walls. They were not so many, but enough if they could move us from the ramparts.

The Moors were the best in the legions with spears and lightest on their feet. When they ran toward us, the points of their weapons glistened in the sun like a machine with a thousand bristling spurs.

It was impossible to know the events at each gate, such was the confusion of noise and distortion of time, but when the Moors came within range of the archer's bows at the south gate, I gave the standards the signal: discharge in volleys, five volleys, then fire at will. At the same time, the Moors' three rams backed up for what they hoped was their last charge.

The ram struck the south gate where I stood as if the force could collapse it. At the same time the volleys of our archers struck the attackers. The first rank of Moors fell almost to a man, some from the impact and some from fear. Some would rejoin the battle, but others would never find the means.

Quickly, the third and fourth ranks were raked by volleys of archers in succession. Many fell nearly in unison, faltering with their ladders, dropping their ladders, becoming tangled in the ladders, cursing their burden. By the time our archers began to fire at their own pace, the bodies of the Moors were stacked high, snared on a bloody matrix of human limbs and boards.

That was when I gave the order for the gates to give way as we released the crossbars. That was the luck of our plan, and it was great. Never had I thought the attack of the entire legion would be directed to the gates—all the gates—at the same time. The impact of the rams meeting little resistance blew them through to the interior—on the north gate by twelve feet—and from that the Moors took heart. With their centurions leading the way through a barrage of arrows, they carried headlong into the garrison.

Into the pits. They had been dug fourteen feet deep, inset with sharpened stakes, twenty feet across and forty wide. The first wave could not stop their charge to the fore, so they died meanly, falling headlong until their bodies were impaled on the stakes. The next wave, which was like a continuation, brought themselves up short, but the concerted charge from the ranks behind drove them forward, so many of them fell onto the stakes, too.

The momentum of the assault stopped completely. The tremendous screaming made it so—the screams as the Moors fell into space that was anything but empty, and the screams of pain as their bodies were pierced and often pierced through.

The third wave of the assault tottered on the rim of the pit, knowing they could not go forward, and knowing there was nowhere to go. At their backs their comrades still came on. In front of the pits at the margins the first row of our archers knelt, and fired; the second row, standing, fired; and from every position inside the garrison where a man could stand and draw a bow, he fired.

I did not have to give the order for our infantry to charge, but because they were soldiers of the legion they looked to their centurions, who looked to me. I gave the order to the trumpets. Our line surged forward at once, planks down over the pit as our spears flew, swords up as they met the Moors' devastated front.

I was worried that if the first charge did not carry there would not be another, and our men would be stranded in the crossing. That did not happen. Using their shields like rams, the infantry charge blasted the Moors down, folding the rank like reeds. With nothing but momentum, they battered the enemy line back a full ten paces, making room for the oncoming cohort, which did not slow or stop. Which accelerated.

The carnage carried. Hundreds of men fell before the gates until the space was stanched by their bodies. I looked to the other gates, mired in dust and smoke from fires. The same scene was repeated. The attack had been broken. The men in the rear ranks had begun to turn and run, but many of those were being cut down by the archers at the walls.

The attackers did not retreat like men of the legions, carrying their wounded on their backs and withdrawing in formation, but like barbarians they fled, abandoning their weapons and shields. Many more were struck as they ran from the field. I was sure that in this heedless attack Julianus had lost a quarter of his army.

Our casualties, by the count, were light. We had twelve dead and thirty-four wounded, mostly from fighting at the walls. Those men had their women to attend them as darkness fell and as we cleared away the bodies of the enemy and rebuilt the gates against them.

* * *

"I could kill you," said Soaemias with an anger that had not diminished. "That was the most humiliating moment of my life."

"To kill me, you must be alive. That might not have been true if you stayed at the walls. You were not even properly protected."

She struck herself on the head. "So if I wore a helmet, I could fight alongside the men."

"And armor."

"I will have it made."

She rose immediately to her feet and walked from the room, clapping her hands and calling for the steward.

I did not stop her. Nor did I know what I could do but tie her hand and foot. And mouth.

"You don't understand her, do you?"

I looked across the room at Varius, who had spoken calmly. He had not been as unhappy as his mother at being deprived of martial glory. He made no protest when I confined him to the praetoria, nor did he try to escape his gilded prison. Tiled in red marble, the walls painted with scenes from Virgil, the room did not look like a Roman garrison, even in Syria.

"I understand your mother, Varius. Dealing with her is a different thing."

"She's a woman," he said. "Beat her."

"Is that what you father did?"

"When necessary."

"What did it avail him?"

"Very little."

"Very little is not the same as nothing."

Varius smiled like a man older and wiser. "It availed him one night of a knife wound in the groin."

"That's what I thought."

"But you needn't worry," he said. "As long as she thinks you're important to the cause, she'll obey you."

"And later?"

Varius shrugged. "She trusted Gannys, you know, because he wasn't quite a man. If you turn your back, she'll have him back."

"She'll have him back missing more than his soft parts," I said. "Nor should you concern yourself with him. If all goes well, you won't take orders from any man. Or woman."

"Even Mother?"

"Especially her."

That prospect did not sit as easily with Varius as most things. He went inside himself, perhaps to parley with his god. It was a strange thing to watch because it seemed so private and unconfirmed. It was the only way in which he was not qualified to be emperor, but who could protest after the events of the day?

"What will happen tomorrow, Marcellus?"

"I don't know. But you must be prepared. We may need your presence. We may even need your miracles."

"And if I have none?"

"Then we'll make do with our swords."

* * *

I went to sleep more comfortable with Varius the boy than Varius the god. It may have been for that reason I never really slept. Three hours after midnight, a centurion of the watch found me to say that Verus requested my presence at the north gate.

We had agreed to split shifts throughout the night as the gates were rebuilt. Taking advantage of their casualties and the disruption of their cohorts, we extended the perimeter beyond the ditches to within thirty yards of their camp.

Julianus let these things happen as if they were of no importance. Perhaps it was because he was a Prefect of the Praetorian Guard. His experience with fighting legions had been small, and he was probably loathe to consult the men on his staff who could correct his deficiencies. I thought change had taken place until I came to the gate.

"A deputation's come to see us," said Verus. "It seems they want to talk of the future."

"We're not in the oracle business."

"But we're in business," he said. "We should listen to any good proposal."

"What power do they have to bargain?"

"They're led by the military tribune who was in charge of the garrison at Arca. And the chief centurion of the Africans."

"Interesting."

"I thought you might agree."

Naturally, Verus thought it best if only one man met the enemy on neutral ground. The fact that we had killed one of their emissaries before the gates less than twelve hours ago might have had something to do with it. That was not anyone's notion of fair play.

The three men in uniform who stood in a tight circle at the outer edge of the perimeter had refused to give up their weapons or come within the walls. They refused to say what they wanted and would not talk to anyone unless he was their equal. Nor did they give their names until I tendered mine.

"I am Marcus Aemilius Cornelius," said the tribune. "This is Fulvius Belenus Crassus," he said, indicating the centurion on his left. "And Appius Afer Casca is with us as guarantor. His brother, Julius Afer, serves in III Gallica as a sergeant of cavalry."

"Is this your way of telling me we're engaged in civil war?"

The tribune inclined his head and the helmet he held in the crook of his arm, as if he had two of everything. "Can anything be worse?"

"A great many things, Tribune. This is a war of restoration, as you are aware."

"Possibly," he said. "But we've no way of knowing if the things we heard are true. We're told the son of Soaemias is the son of Antoninus. Is that what you say?"

"Your sources are correct."

"We're happy to have your word," said the tribune. "But the legion will need proof. There are many among us who regard the son of Antoninus as the true emperor of Rome. Were we satisfied in that, our allegiance could be made known at the proper time."

"Now is the proper time, Tribune."

He hesitated, looking left and right, where he was flanked by comrades. Finally, he nodded. "If we could see him."

"One of you may. That man will surrender his arms and submit to a search."

"I'll go," said the tribune. "I fought with Antoninus in Parthia. I'll know his son."

The tribune was conducted to the praetoria. While he was searched by the guards to his skin, I woke Varius and had him dress in the garb that best resembled Caracalla's. Though wearing the same clothes on any day in the same month was repugnant to him, Varius agreed to sacrifice for the cause.

"This is important," I said. "He'll report back to the others. They'll be guided by his impression of you."

"Are you sure this tribune's not acting alone? On impulse?"

"I'm sure of nothing, but if this is an impulse, it could cost him his life. For our part, we have nothing to lose as long as you conduct yourself like an emperor."

"You mean like Antoninus."

"Like an emperor."

I knew one day I would have to watch my tongue when I spoke to this boy who would be Caesar. He seemed to take the memory of his newest father seriously.

"I feel regal," he said. "We may proceed."

"Admit the tribune."

The guard at the door indicated that his search had been satisfied. He stepped aside as Marcus Aemelius Cornelius entered the room uncertainly. This was certainly his first close view of an emperor of Rome. He stopped at two paces and stared.

Varius returned the stare as if their roles were reversed, and the tribune the one whose lineage should be verified. It was a perfect performance with not one word said.

"Caesar, this is the tribune who requested an audience."

Varius tipped his head by the smallest measure. He turned to the right, as if to display his profile. In that pose, he indeed resembled Caracalla. The extreme fleshiness that was the difference in their noses all but vanished, and the chin, the hairline, and the eyes were so close a copy that I wondered if there was more than invention in the rumor. What did life in the palace of the emperor forbid? What restraints could be placed upon children who waited to inherit the world? What, in the waiting, did they not explore?

"What say you, tribune? Did my father's blood run into the desert sands there to expire?"

Marcus Aemelius did not answer. When it seemed that his mouth must open to save his silence and mortification, Varius let out his hand.

The tribune took two paces forward so quickly I became alarmed; but when he dropped to one knee as quickly, he accepted Varius' hand and kissed it.

"Caesar," he said.

* * *

On a cloudless morning, the sun rose on our remade garrison and Legion IV Scythica arrayed against us. Julianus' battle line had been drawn again, but the Moors who made the assault on the previous day were largely absent. In their place stood the men of IV Scythica, who were less ardent in their need to die. The tribune Marcus Aemilius Cornelius had been positive about that, and he promised to spread the word of the reincarnation of Antoninus. He also agreed to relay our guarantee that the legion's pay would be increased if they declared for the true heir to the throne of the Roman Empire.

The only thing he asked in return was for Varius to show himself to the legion from the ramparts. He could not be moved from that demand.

I agreed, though I had no liking for the idea. We had drawn a great many of our troops back inside the gates, but the battle line was close enough for a well-placed arrow to reach a target on the walls. The enemy had plenty of incentive to do that. Julianus knew the mood of his legion, and he might know that contact had been made within the walls. He might have sponsored the secret meeting himself. Although a poor battle commander, he was capable of ordering the thing he had done best in his life—assassination.

I tried hard to convince Varius it was best to show himself in armor, but he would not agree. "They want to see the son of Antoninus in the flesh. How will they know me if I look like everyone else?"

"I don't like stationary targets in my emperors."

"Then have my chariot drawn up," he said. "I'll ride a circuit of the walls."

I asked myself what strange fascination this young man had with danger in high places, but I admitted that he satisfied my objection in a way worthy of an emperor. I even conceded that talking to the beasts might have a basis. Varius had become a skillful charioteer. That was clear on our journey from Emesa. But I wondered if he could keep a horse—a team was out of the question—on the rampart when blank space yawned to the garrison side. The legions—theirs and ours—would love the show. Good pay was not the only reason they revered the memory of Caracalla. The ruler who lived with lions was the man who captured their hearts.

For this day, the ramparts of Raphanae were the towers of Illium, and Varius was Hector, tamer of horses. After the stallion had been drawn up in a sling, and the car was joined, Varius donned the purple cloak and stepped into the car, visible to those without the walls.

For moments longer than I wanted, he held the team steady and gazed upon the men of IV Scythica like their leader. His hair shone like white gold in the sun, his skin like the mother's milk they did not remember, his clean limbs and rich garments the stuff of their fantasies.

Then Varius snapped the reins and the chariot moved off slowly, cruising between the crenelations of the ramparts as if he were being transported by an invisible machine.

Cheers first arose from III Gallica. As soon as the men of IV Scythica knew what was happening, they began to shout. I could not hear what they said distinctly, but the same words, like a refrain, slowly came again and again.

"He is . . ."

By the time that Varius had covered half the distance from the north gate to the east, struggling with the reins, the voices from the ranks beyond the walls began to rise. Some of the men broke formation, ignoring the commands of their officers. They were milling about and shouting.

One trumpet, followed by a barrage of trumpets, signaled the legion to resume its battle line, but the calls were unheeded. When the sound of the trumpets died away, the voices of IV Scythica could be heard clearly.

He is . . . like a god.

He is . . . like the sun.

He is . . . the son of Antoninus.

Varius was nearly nothing but broken bones and blood, for as he neared the angle of the garrison where the north wall veered, he saw the turn was too sharp. I was about to tell him to rein in when he jumped off the car with a light step and landed upright on the ramparts.

The stallion, taking his head, bolted, charging upon the left angle. Without pause, he turned to the left, and with no restraint, veered too sharply. In an eerie pantomime of descent, he left the ramparts as if, like Pegasus, he could fly.

For a moment he did, but only until he crashed into the margin, screaming, and the car crashed atop him, its tongue pronged into the earth, the car flung halfway to the granary. Even before the car stopped, Varius climbed onto the crenelations and held his hands up to the men arrayed on the plain. He did not look back. The frantic sound of his finest steed seemed not to reach his ears. Nothing concerned him but the sight of his newest legion.

Standing like one of the finest targets ever made, looking down like the most concerned gods, Varius put his hands on his chest. His voice as given to him by his mother was not strong, but the sounds that he pulled up through his chest now were loud and brazen, flung as far as the most distant man gathered on the plain.

"Men of the legions, look upon me! Look! Tell me, who was my father?"

They roared: "Antoninus!"

"Men of the legions, who am I?"

The answer arrived in another roaring wave of different words in many tongues, but they all seemed to roll together into one booming phrase: "The son of Antoninus!"

"Men of the legions, who will I be?"

Again, the sounds began as many, inchoate, rambling, but coalesced into a single rising voice: "Caesar! Caesar!"

Varius waited until the din arose over the whole legion, traveling in a wave of acclamation. He held his hands high over his head until the clamor ended.

"Men of the legions, I ask you. Will you share the future with me?"

"Yes!"

"Will you join my forces?"

"Yes!"

"Will you follow me wherever we may go?"

"Yes!"

Varius turned back to the garrison. "Open the gates!"

I turned to Verus standing by me at the rampart. "Give the order to open the gates!"

He hesitated, looking out over the plain at the legion that numbered as many as ours. "We can't let them inside as long as they're armed."

"Order it!" I said. "Do it immediately!"

He turned on me like an enemy. "This is *my* legion!" he said. "These are *my* men!"

"Aziz!"

The commander of my archers instantly raised his hand. Six archers brought their bows to the target, which was Verus. They held.

"Order it!"

Verus saw no help for himself in the faces of his men. He gave a moment for his pride before he turned to the guard. "Open the gates!" he said. "Open them!"

Only then did I wonder if I done the right thing. If IV Scythica rallied to Julianus, were we consenting in our doom? Once inside, an equal number of legionnaires could create an equal number of casualties. All would be Roman soldiers.

The first ranks of Legion IV Scythica had already marched on the gates. They were calling to the rest of their cohorts to follow, and they were armed. I had a bad feeling as the vanguard reached the ditches and the gates swung open.

The first legionnaire who entered, a tall red-haired man of uncertain rank, had probably been recruited from the barbarian tribes north of the Euxine Sea. He took out his sword. He whirled it round his head as if to swing on the attack. As suddenly, he brought his sword down, kissed it, and flung it into the ditch.

All the men of Legion IV Scythica kissed their swords as they came upon the gates, and flung their weapons into the ditch. They entered the garrison of Raphanae as brothers under the standard of the Roman eagle.

We were no longer a legion.

We were an army.

THE WHEEL

We were twenty-five miles outside Antioch, near a village called Ba'al Geddete, when the first reports of contact with the enemy came from our scouts. They put Macrinus' forces at three legions with elements of a fourth. At least three cohorts of Praetorian Guards were also with him.

That meant we were outnumbered, though not overwhelmingly. We had begun the march north with two legions at full strength, but after III Gallica joined with IV Scythica, many more men rallied to us. They arrived daily at Raphanae from every garrison in Syria and points north and south, bringing their weapons and allegiance to the right and solvent cause. Along the march toward Antioch, we gathered contingents at almost every town of any size.

"When will their advance units reach the village?"

"Within minutes," said Dexion, the Ethiopian, the best of our scouts. He was also the most taciturn, never owning an opinion or venturing information until asked.

"Is the emperor with his legions?"

"Yes," said Dexion. "I saw his standards."

Varius, riding next to me, put the only question that seemed important to him. "Is his son Diadumenianus present?"

"Yes, Caesar. The boy rides with the baggage train."

"Excellent," said Varius with more zeal than sense. "The usurper and his whelp. Both heads on the line."

Now was not the time to inform Varius that the outcome of any battle was uncertain. He was confident, and it was best if he remained that way. His grandmother had given him a white Parthian stallion as big and aggressive as Bacchus. Varius rode along the line-of-march all the way from Raphanae, gathering the admiration of the troops.

He had been wild since we took the head of Julianus and sent it to Macrinus bound in cords. The emperor, anticipating a victory, had forsaken the pleasures of Antioch and come down to Apamea. There, he named his son joint Caesar, minted coins to commemorate the event, and ordered a banquet for the citizens of the town. At that point, Comazon, dressed in a courier's uniform, presented the head to Macrinus' court. Comazon somehow managed to leave before it was unbound. The emperor left when it was unbound, appalled by the sight of his disembodied prefect. He rode back to Antioch and called up his legions to meet what he finally saw as a threat.

We could have let him descend on Raphanae, and tried to beat back his legions again; but the longer we waited, the more troops Macrinus might gather, and the enthusiasm of ours wane. Our legions were in high spirits, but if they sat behind walls, congratulating themselves for having done the right thing, they might start to think they had done the worst thing, which was to put themselves against the will of the Senate and the wrath of Caesar.

But he was a strange Caesar. My conclusion about the cautious man I had known was that the long years of bowing to the will of a madman, and his reliance on the devices of the frumentarii, left their mark on his character. Fear had confirmed the servility of a man too old to change his ways. Macrinus was fifty-four, and the chief evidence of his vigor was the son he had sired very late. The young man would have to survive to an age when he could rule. He could not do that unless his father survived this day.

I gave orders for our cohorts to deploy for battle. III Gallica was to hold the pass before the village with IV Scythica in support. Although we could have marched out to meet them, the pass was a notch in the road less than fifty yards wide with no quick way around.

Macrinus' legions would have to meet us head-on. The narrow ascent could not help but make their assault harder, reducing their advantage in numbers. The same field, and the wooded terrain, would render our archers less effective and hinder our cavalry. I tried to be objective about the situation and calculate our chances, but could not arrive at an answer. We would meet at the mouth of an impasse and hope for a break in it.

So the battle for empire came down to this: two Roman armies of identical training and nearly identical composition facing the other with swords and spears. The winner, as always, would be the one with the best leadership and the greatest portion of luck.

* * *

We had hardly settled ranks when the Alban Legion came round the bend of the hill into the valley and began to deploy against our front. I would have liked more time to ready the men. I had sent aquarians to every cohort with fresh water, for the day was uncomfortably warm, but they had only made their way through the first ranks when the trumpets sounded Battle-Line.

We watched as the men of the Alban Legion sloughed their packs to the ground and girded their loins, binding their tunics around their crotches. With deliberation like arrogance, the process was meant to impress the enemy as he prepared for battle. Their swords and daggers remained sheathed, but their spears came ready behind their shields.

Everyone knew how the battle would proceed. When the order was given to advance, they would move within range, launch their spears at our front and charge. We would take casualties, but more damaging, the spears would bend on impact with the shields, designed so they could not be dislodged and thrown back. That meant our shields, burdened with ball-weighted spears that could not be removed, would be useless. How fast our ranks filled from behind, and how well, would do much to determine the outcome.

"It happens now!"

Two battle chariots drew up at my right, but I did not look to see who was within or who had spoken. Maesa and her daughter, Soaemias, had accompanied the army from Raphanae. I could not forbid the banker of our rebellion a place on the field. I made only one rule: no litters.

"You shouldn't come so close to the front. A battle has a way of moving about."

"Not if Verus holds," said Maesa. "Will he?"

The old woman was persistent. She wanted value. Verus' legion would take the brunt of the assault, and when their line broke or broke back, it would be in retreat or in the van. IV Scythica stood on the right flank.

"We'll know soon. The attack will come when their rear ranks close up."

I sent a runner to the cavalry on the left flank under the command of Comazon, telling him to hold his position unless there was a rout, in which case his men were to fall on the pursuers. I sent another to Gannys, telling him to speed his preparations. He had charge of setting up a hospital to care for the wounded. As far as I could see from the top of the hill, not enough had been accomplished.

I did not have an unimpeded line of sight to the enemy, but it was easy to see that his ranks had filled in. I made out the standards of three legions, and at last, taking up a position at the summit of a hill that was a near-mirror of mine, the imperial standards of Macrinus came into view. At the distance, which was close to a mile, I could not see individuals, but I fancied the purple cloak of the Emperor of Rome was visible among his body-guard. That was our target. Dislodged from the hill, Macrinus would be Caesar without an army.

Suddenly, I saw movement in his signal standards and runners fanning out along the hill, moving toward our battle line. The drums began a roll that built to a crescendo. When they stopped, the trumpets blew, relaying the order: "Forward!"

The lines of the two armies were forty-five yards apart when the enemy's shield-wall began to move ahead in one interlocking piece. The first rank leaped forward like one piece, and six long paces later, they reared back as one and their spears soared through the air.

The shock was immediate. Our line sagged a split second before impact. When the spears struck, the line buckled.

Our line should have closed up, the second rank should have come forward quickly, but the formation became tangled along the front. At the moment when it became seamless again, the spears of the enemy's second rank were loosed, and the line buckled again. Before our third rank could step up, the charge of the Alban Legion struck them like the impact of the lightning bolts painted on their shields.

The clash of shield on shield could be heard like rolling thunder along the front line. Wood, leather and metal met in that mighty boom and within it the sounds of hundreds of blades of steel. I had no idea how long I looked on the shifting landscape of battle, but I became aware that our line had almost disappeared under the onslaught. I found myself looking for some sign of resilience anywhere along our front.

I saw none. The first and second ranks of the Alban Legion pushed forward. Our line began to reel. Where was Verus? Where were his damned centurions?

"They falter!" screamed Varius. "God, let them hold!"

"Standards up!" I shouted. "IV Scythica to wheel!"

The signal standard went up telling IV Scythica to move its rear rank in support of the crumbling line of III Gallica. I sent a runner with the same orders in case the dust that had begun to rise thickly from the battlefield obscured their view.

My view of the line grew dim. I saw the Alban Legion had pushed forward, beginning to roll up the left flank of III Gallica, but the jumble of shields so much alike competed with the thick dust. This was the time in every engagement when the crush of numbers melded into a whole. On the field it was a contest of might, shield against shield, the strength of an entire army engaged like dray animals pushing and pushing until the other side yielded.

The attackers moved forward, stabbing with their swords, the defenders pushed back, stabbing, never slashing. The legions were trained not to go for the head of their enemy or his limbs or upper body. They went lower, thrusting for the softest parts of their enemy. A Roman battlefield quickly became a slippery mass of broken bowels, blood and piss. The men under attack were expected to hold their positions without relief for twenty minutes, at which time they were replaced by the next rank. Unless they died first. Or the line broke.

That was happening. Although I barely discerned direction in the movement of the mass of men, further toward the rear I saw the troops of Macrinus' second legion making for the front at a steady pace, as if nothing much was in their way. And I saw the rear ranks of IV Scythica, closer to my position than any, as in their wheel they came to a stop.

They stopped in confusion, their ranks in disorder. The reason was that the men of III Gallica had begun to retreat. They did not give ground step by disciplined step, each man covering his space, never allowing a gap to open. The legion was fleeing, destroying their formation and the converging formation of reinforcements from IV Scythica.

"No!" came the thundering voice from my side. "Stop!"

Varius had screamed, though I did not recognize his voice, which rose past anger to rage. He drew his sword—the one Alexander the Great carried into battle at Granicus—whirled it high above his head, and drove his horse down the slope.

I could not have stopped him. Perhaps I could have stopped the next thing, which was the two chariots that followed him down the hill. His grandmother Maesa and mother Soaemias ordered their charioteers into battle. The old woman actually beat her man across his shoulders with a whip, screaming, as she hung onto the careening car. Soaemias' chariot was at the front, clambering in the wake of her son.

I had no men to waste retrieving them. I sent a runner to the foot-archers with orders to fire at will into the enemy legions and not to trim their aim. It would be bad to lose men to our own arrows, but the survivors would thank me. The important thing was to stop the panic. The right flank had nearly been turned, bending to an envelopment. If it collapsed, the gap would be open to oncoming cohorts. The battle would be won by Macrinus, and quickly.

That was when Varius at the bottom of the hill turned his mount along a stone wall. He began to canter behind it where a peach orchard ended in a field of barley. Immediately behind him, the chariots of his mother and grandmother stopped.

The women leaped onto the ground. It was impossible to hear them, but I imagined their voices raised in anger. Yes, they were screaming at the men who vaulted the stone wall. Yes, Maesa was using her whip on them instead of her charioteer. And yes, Varius rode before them, herding the men back toward the line as they came over the wall, wielding the flat of his sword like Alexander.

I lost my angle on the wall when a message came from Verus confirming his situation. The flank had been turned. Disaster was next unless we were prepared to beg for mercy.

I was about to send the runner back telling him there was no such thing as mercy for rebels, but when I looked back to the field, I was shocked by what I did not see. The panic had subsided. No more men came over the wall. The two women stood atop the wall, arms upraised, fists upraised, exhorting the men. And Varius, gathering his mount in a circle to the rear, urged it forward, and in one incredible leap of faith, convinced his mount to fly.

The white stallion cleared the three foot fence with room to spare. I saw Varius snap forward and then back when he came to earth, nearly unhorsed. He dug forward in the saddle, riding as fast as he could for the ranks, which was very fast. The men who stood in his way went smashing to the turf, the quick ones stopped and stared, while others began to cheer. They raised their arms and fists like the women, and cheered.

And they began to turn back.

* * *

The actions of one man seldom carry a battle. In the history of the legions, and behind every day of a soldier's training, lay the idea that no man mattered more than another. In the legions, there was no such thing as single combat against an enemy. There was no such thing as a thrust of steel in a soldier's unguarded back. There was no enemy so brave he could not be defeated by a fighting unit that was cohesive and coordinated.

Yet Varius, assisted by two women of the most pampered tribe on earth, did that outside a village on the border of Syria Coele. When the men saw his white charger, and when they had been shamed by two women who went against the enemy in their place, they returned to the front they had abandoned, reclaimed the weapons they had thrown down, drove back against the enemy who had broken their ranks, and began to fight as they had not before.

As soon as the battle was rejoined, Fortune's wheel turned to us. The concentrated fire of the foot-archers took its toll, and IV Scythica moved into the gap to reinforce. The slow intolerable grind commenced, the fighting hand-to-hand, inch by inch. This was the declaration of territory. Slowly, then quickly, Macrinus' legions came to understand that they faced an enemy who was like them in every respect, as well-trained and determined, but fighting from better ground. As they began to yield precious inches under the counterattack, they caught glimpses of the future in the momentum of the wheel.

Still, the battle carried. Many times before, Roman legions had fought Roman legions shield to shield for days on end, stabbing the things that stood before them until there were no things left to kill. If they lost discipline, their centurion gave it back to them with his rod. If they lost blood, their wounds were stanched by their fellows, who knew exactly how much a soldier's body could stand. The only thing they could lose without replacement was the will to fight for their cause. For the enemy, that was the cause of the Emperor of Rome, whose name was Macrinus until he ran from the hill.

When I first became aware of his absence from the field, I did not believe it. The hilltop where he had placed his standards could not be seen through the dust, but word came from the scouts I had placed along the chain of hills to the west telling me that his standards were no longer in place.

"He's pulled back?"

"He's gone," said the scout. "There's no doubt. He rode off with a small number of his officers."

"I'd like to know where."

"There was no way to follow, lord. But he rode north."

Toward Antioch. It was the only place he had ever gone in his one year, one month and twenty-three days as emperor. If this report was accurate, his reign would not exceed those numbers.

"And the Praetorian Guard?"

"They remain in the field. They've taken off their scale armor and put aside their dished shields."

"Fleeing?"

"They come this way, lord. They've taken up battle shields."

It seemed out of character for the Guard to fight for an emperor who was no longer in the field, but they were under orders from their prefect, Nestor. He had the Guard remove their armor to improve their mobility, and exchange shields for better leverage in close combat. They would be formidable like that.

I was concerned with the strategy of their master. Macrinus seemed to have calculated that buying time with the lives of his Guard on the battlefield was better than retaining them for protection. If the battle were lost, his recourse was flight to Rome, where he could raise support in the Senate and among the uncommitted legions of the West.

I turned to my aide. "Send heralds along the line, as many as can be found. And trumpeters, too. Give the word that Macrinus has fled the field. Also say that those who lay down their arms may enter our service under an amnesty. No reprisals will be taken."

"Yes, lord."

"Now move! *Move!*"

A dozen heralds drove toward the lines with trumpeters. There were not many of the latter to be found, but enough to claim the attention of men who had been fighting for more than an hour. It was important that the offer be announced to the ranks before the Guard joined battle.

I saw the heralds reach the battle line and heard the trumpets sound, when at the same time I saw through the haze the three cohorts of Guards marching up the road. They were awesome in formation, tall and broad even without their scale armor and scorpion shields. Near the front I saw Thrax, who stood over eight feet high, as he led the first cohort.

It would be a shame to kill something that big, but we would do it. I thought that as a loud noise went up from the ranks on the right flank. There, the battle stopped so suddenly that it caused the noise to withdraw as into a tunnel. That made the trumpets all over the field sound loud and clear. The voices of the heralds rose above the trumpets, calling for surcease.

It was not happening everywhere, but seemed it could. I gave orders for the archers to move into the field behind the stone walls and direct their fire on command to the Guard who were just now reaching the enemy's rear ranks. At the same time, a wind blew across the battlefield, cleaving through the thick clouds of dust. Clarity came in an instant. I saw all the way to the hill-top where Macrinus had put down the imperial standards.

They were gone. I had not believed my scout. I could not believe that it had happened. Again.

If it meant so much to my eyes, it should mean as much to others. I ordered the three aides with me on the hill, and the runners who remained, to go down to the ranks: "Tell them to look to the hill! Tell them to find their emperor on the hill if they can! Ask them who they fight for!"

I rode down into the melee, amazed at how the battlefield had lost its coherence in my first time as commander-in-chief. The precision of the lines and the definition of color and posi-tion had given way to anarchy. Men lay dead, men lay bleeding, men lay on their shields awaiting succor. Fragments of weapons and armor, pieces of bodies, and gouts of horseflesh littered the ground. I saw one long white tail caparisoned with blue ribbons and thought of Varius. His giant Parthian steed could have left that severed member behind.

I did not see him or his mount. I rode along the left flank, pressing Bacchus against the rear ranks, pressing them forward, raising my voice loud. "Look to the hill! Where is the Lord of the World and Emperor of all the Romans?"

I sheared Bacchus along, pitching men forward under his powerful flank. "Look to the hill! Where are the imperial standards? Where is your emperor?"

I heard a voice from behind me, high up, too, calling the same thing, and I knew that it was Varius. "Where is bloody Macrinus? Do you see his standards or his back as he rides away? Where is the usurper? Where has he gone?"

Varius was still bolstering the line. He was still in the saddle, and his Parthian stallion was covered with blood from his withers to the tail that he once wore so well.

The sounds of combat died all along the line. It happened fast. The men of the Alban Legion turned to the hilltop where their emperor should have been. They saw nothing but green sward and a skeletal Guard.

The fighting declined everywhere, even in the center of the formations where the clash had been fiercest. I moved that way, watching the three cohorts of the Guard fight their way to the front. They were the only ones to give battle. The clash of swords and shields was loud as they threw themselves forward. The huge figure of Thrax loomed above them.

And I saw Gratus, the chief centurion of III Gallica, as he stood at the rear rank of the center, supporting the line with his sword and rod. His helmet was so deeply dented that it could not be brought down upon his head, and the left arm that held his rod hung loosely at his side.

"On command, part the ranks!" I said. "All centuries to part!"

He blinked and balked. "Let them *through*?"

"On my command!"

As I backed up my mount to the stone wall, Verus came at a gallop from the right center. "Are you *mad*?" he shrieked before he reined in. "We've beaten them! Now you want to give them the field?"

"As much of it as they can hold."

I turned as Varius rode up to us. His eyes were wild, his horse the next thing to dead. His sword had seen no blood, but the weapon that carried Alexander the Great to his destiny was still in his hand.

"Remove yourself behind the wall!"

"Marcellus—"

"*Now!*"

Varius moved his mount to the stone wall behind which the archers stood, but he made no attempt to coax the spent beast forward again. I was as glad to see that mark of sanity as I had been glad to see his insanity.

As Varius moved around the wall to safety, I turned and gave the signal to Gratus, who passed the order through the ranks. The entire formation swung away, the rear at quick time, the middle walking, the front pivoting. In two minutes, nothing remained between the stone wall and the front ranks of the Guard.

They charged ahead, heedless, until they realized with a slow slackening what had been done. These men who had discarded their scale armor looked directly into a double line of archers whose arrows could penetrate their shields. The shields, though they would have protected men of normal size, barely covered the torsos of the giants of the Guard.

The rest of Verus' legion had swung open on two sides in a solid wall of shields. Behind the Guard were the remnants of the legions that had once belonged to Macrinus but now held at a standstill. They refused to fight any longer for an emperor who had run from the field, and were willing to join an emperor who had not.

The Guard halted. Quickly, they swung around into the only defensive posture they could hold, which was the circle. I waited until they closed it around the figure of their prefect, Julianus Nestor.

"Do you yield?"

I received no answer. I could not see Nestor among the mass, but I looked at Thrax, who stood above the rest as if on the back of a wagon. I threw my challenge at him.

"Enough Roman blood has been lost on this field today! But if this is the place you choose to die, so be it!"

I raised my hand.

The archers drew down. They held.

"What are the terms?"

Thrax had spoken. His voice flailed the lowest register and no other.

"You will serve the true emperor of Rome!" I said, sweeping my hand to Varius astride his bloody mount. "This is the son of Antoninus! Look on him! Did he run from battle? Is he not the picture of his father?"

Those ranks of enormous men knew their day had ended. They would settle for what they could get, so they made a show of wonder as they looked at Varius. The ranks began to loosen and voices were raised, one, two, then in multiples.

". . . like Antoninus."

"The shade of Antoninus!"

"The image of his father!"

Then I heard the rattle of wheels. The Julias had taken to their chariots again. The old woman and my lover in their cars were like Nemesis and Victory, swaying with the aftershock, awaiting the resumption of their dynasty.

Soaemias' voice rise above the clamor, forcing down the exhortations of the men who would be the guardians of her son's life. "Bring me the head of Julianus Nestor!" she screamed. "When I receive the head of your prefect bound in cords, you will be received with honor!"

THE LAND OF THE BLIND

"Our greatest priority," said Gannys, "is to find Macrinus. He cannot under any circumstances be permitted to reach Rome."

It was hard to argue. Gannys had managed our administrative affairs since we decided to go against Raphanae. He had displayed skill, creating confusion in our enemy. Letters were sent to the Senate asking what kind of Caesar refused to meet a young boy in battle. He dispatched emissaries to every province in the East announcing a new government while the old still lived. His maneuvers created doubt about the center of power and told us who we could depend upon as allies. These things also returned him to influence in the family, especially since Macrinus took up the challenge and lost.

"A party of men has been sent ahead to Antioch," I said. "If Macrinus hesitates in leaving the city, we'll have him."

"We may assume his legs show more courage than his heart," said Soaemias. "The man runs well."

"But which route will he take?" asked Maesa. "There are ten ports in Syria where he might embark."

"I've taken the liberty of dealing with that," said Gannys respectfully. "Couriers have gone out to every city and town on the coast warning ships of the danger involved in receiving him on board."

"A good *precaution*," I said, using the word for Gannys' benefit. "But Macrinus won't risk a sea voyage from Syria when better routes are available."

Gannys looked at me askance. "You know his mind?"

"I know his needs. He must arrive at Rome as soon as possible—before news of his defeat reaches the streets. There's only one way to do that. He'll go overland to the Propontine Sea and make the short sea crossing to Europe. Once on the other side, he has good road all the way to Rome."

"That seems logical," said the eunuch.

"It will be inevitable unless we lay hands on him quickly."

"Then we should send couriers immediately to the Black Sea Fleet at Cyzicus," said the eunuch.

"He'll not go to Cyzicus *because* of the fleet. Bithynia is closer across the sea."

Gannys turned to Maesa. "Caecilius Aristo, the governor of Bithynia, has been our man from the outset. He'll be watchful on our behalf."

"He should be for what he's been paid," said Maesa. "You might tell him if Macrinus slips through, I'll have his head next to Nestor's on a pole."

Like candelabra. My eyes went from the garden where we sat to the front of the villa where the head of Macrinus' prefect was planted on a spear. No one had gotten around to binding it in cords. Nestor's countenance, which in life had been unwholesome, seemed transformed by death. He smiled, or nearly so. His eyes remarked the day with equanimity.

His repose made me feel better about his execution. A man who promises terms to the enemy does not like having them abrogated by a woman. That happened to me for the first time on the day of battle.

"I gave no orders for Macrinus' execution," I said. "The idea is to find him."

"Where he is destroyed makes no difference," said Soaemias. "An Emperor of Rome who still breathes can breathe life into his cause. There are many who hate us in this empire."

"We should also take steps to prevent Macrinus from reaching Rome across the Propontine Sea," said Maesa. "Marcellus, can you do that?"

"I can try."

"You must do more," said Maesa. "If Macrinus reaches Rome, all we have done will go as naught. Civil war will be a reality."

* * *

The princess was correct. Macrinus' flight from the field guaranteed he could remain a factor in the empire until he was eliminated. Gannys was told to write a letter to the Senate, rendering an account of the battle, but until he wrote another stating time of death the Senate would not be forced to recognize Marcus Aurelius Antoninus, his god, or his eunuch.

With a century of cavalry, I rode into Antioch that evening through roads littered with the ruins of Macrinus' baggage train. It had been attacked by local elements and relieved of everything valuable. As we neared the city, his defeat was everywhere. What troops were left had gone over to looting, carrying off any goods that could be stuffed in a sack. The citizens shut themselves up in their homes, refusing to trust the streets. At the palace, a bare watch of Praetorian Guards remained where my advance unit had left them. The Guard waited to find to whom they would surrender.

Macrinus was not at the palace. The head of my advance unit had searched the palace and grounds. He said that I might want to question one man—a centurion of the Guard named Arastos.

I had him brought to me in the same room where I had met Julia Domna more than a year before. He understood that upon his answers rested his life.

"When did the usurper flee?"

Arastos, a Spaniard, was shorter than most Guards. He seemed to like his dark head in its position. "Lord, he left the palace last night late on horseback. Several companions accompanied him, but none of the Guard save Vitellus. The emperor also took his Parthian dog."

"Only those he could trust, eh?"

"The emperor—pardon, the usurper—had shaved himself entirely, even to the hair on his chin, to prevent recognition. He wore a dark garment over his purple robe, and kept it close to his face. Truly, I would not have known him."

"Where has he gone?"

"I can't say, lord. In fact, I know not, but Vitellus is a native of Eribolon, from a family of fishermen at that place."

Eribolon was the port of the Bithynian capital. Lying on the Propontine Sea, it was a possible destination for a man who had to navigate those waters to regain an empire.

"What of Macrinus' son Diadumenianus?"

"He did not arrive with the usurper, lord. As I heard, the boy was sent to another place before they came to the palace. Epagathus and some others went with him."

"Where did they go?"

"I believe the boy was sent to Artabanus, king of the Parthians, to seek asylum."

Bad news. Macrinus had to be intercepted, but the son he named Caesar must be taken, too. An heir to the throne in Parthian hands was something Rome's enemies would appreciate to the fullest.

"By which route did they travel?"

"They went in the direction of Zeugma. At least that's what I heard from talk around the barracks."

Zeugma in Anatolia was a logical place to link with the Parthians. The destination of the emperor-designate might be an invention of the centurion's mind, but if so, it would be his last.

"You won't go back to the barracks, Arastos. You'll repair with Claudius Pollio to Zeugma. Find the boy and you find your future."

"Lord, he will be found."

* * *

We picked up Macrinus' trail on the third day by luck. Near Agae in Cilicia one of my centurions stopped at a blacksmith when his horse took a stone. He returned with the news that a man matching Macrinus' description had paid the blacksmith well to rig a cushioned seat in his carriage to comfort his aging bones.

This man was about fifty-five years of age and careworn. His face had been shaved to the skin in all parts that showed, but he did not wear the imperial purple. He had removed his robes of office for the uniform of a soldier—a *peregrini*. They acted as couriers for the frumentarii in all parts of the empire. In that way, if no other, Macrinus remained in character.

We were more than two days behind, but his advantage less-ened as we moved across Cappadocia and Galicia with hardly a stop for rest. When our horses fell from exhaustion, we exchanged them for fresh at the peregrini posts scattered at intervals along the roads. We rode in staggered relays across the length of the subcontinent in the driest of summer, eating dust with every meal and all the times between.

By the time we reached Bithynia, we reckoned we had made up most of a day. That should have put us behind Macrinus by hours. At Eribolon, the port that served the city of Nicomedia, we set out to scour the harbor for the man who would still be emperor.

I could have sent ahead to Caecilius Aristo, the provincial governor who had declared for our cause, but I trusted no one in this case, because no case was comparable. An emperor on the run will promise anything, including all the good things of the earth, to the people he needs to buy. If they believe his promises, the friend of yesterday was today's enemy.

While my men searched the boats at anchor, I went to the harbor master to find out which fishing vessel belonged to Nelius Vitellus. The Praetorian son would certainly consult his fisher-man father, and perhaps hire him to his doom.

"Vitellus the elder is a fisherman no more," said the harbor master. "Everyone tells me his son rose high in the Emperor's Guard. True or not, it made the old man into something more than a stinking piece of bait even the sharks liked to ignore. Five years ago, he bought himself a bigger boat with sail. He's been running a freight ferry to Chalcedon ever since."

Chalcedon was on the Asian side of the Propontine Sea, a mile or so across the water to Europe. For Macrinus, it was life renewed.

"Where's the elder Vitellus now?"

"Haven't seen him," said the harbor master, picking his teeth with a stick of the gum tree the natives here used for hygiene. "He usually runs a load about midmorning, but he was seen nowhere today. Someone said he put to sea with the dawn. I don't believe that, knowing what a lazy ass-chaser he is, but something got him out of bed and on the water."

"How long is the voyage to Chalcedon?"

"A good three hours. More like four with less than a perfect sea."

And they had a good three hours' head start. "This boat—can it cross the water to Europe under sail?"

"Chancy," he said. "You'd need a forty-man trireme to be sure of pulling through that current. The god of Fortune died a hard death there many times."

Once more would be necessary. I called off my men from the search that had produced no results. It was our lot that Fortune presented us with a bounty in the form of a sixty-oar military trireme that had put in at Eribolon after capturing a vessel filled with contraband. The captain, a Circassian from the Euxine Sea named Egon, needed little convincing to throw in his hand with the restored dynasty. We would be in Chalcedon in two and a half hours, he said, even if all his men fell at the oars.

Several did. More had to be taken from the posts where they sat, the skin of their hands left behind on their oars. Others left their blood on the benches and their puke on the deck, but we rowed on to the beat of the drum and the slip of the oars. I imagined that slick sound was a timepiece that notched away the life of an emperor.

We were lucky that the Propontine Sea was like a huge lake with no tide and few storms except when the ill-wind blew from the south. We made speed that would have been impossible on the Middle Sea or any other. It was nearly three hours to dark when we rounded the cape at the bluff of Dragos and began to skim along the shore of Asia. Across the water, easily visible but much harder to gain, lay the opposing continent of Europe.

Several boats were upon the sea, including two that might have been ferries, but Egon doubted they were our mark. "I know

Vitellus' boat. It's as ugly as two Greeks and would take all day long to work the passage across. I'll wager your man's put in at Chalcedon to hire a swift ship."

I did not tell our captain how large was our wager, or the identity of our fugitive. Egon was known in Chalcedon on the waterfront and with the maritime authorities, for whom he had done favors. Many times that consisted in looking the other way when illegal goods were offloaded, but for now his familiarity served us well. The weather began to blow our way, too, as dark clouds moved in from the north, pushing a strong wind before them and sending all boats toward shore.

Egon was on watch for Vitellus' ferry, but the port filled quickly with the coming storm. None of the vessels that put in matched the profile. To the north, three small ships headed off to other anchorage, and to the south two more put ashore out of our sight.

We did not identify any as the green-hulled vessel of Vitellus, nor did we see a sign of it at the docks at Chalcedon. It was obvious the vessel could have entered any of the coves on the Asian shore. A lot of time would be spent searching them.

"If they made it across before the storm, we've lost them," I said. "If they decided not to chance it, they could still be here."

Egon, a small man with shoulders that dwarfed the rest of his body, nodded as if he had thought of that. "It's not a small place, just a stupid one. Everyone with any sense lives on the other side in Byzantium. That's why they call Chalcedon the Land of the Blind."

I had never heard it called that, but saw no reason to argue with a man with close knowledge of the area. Chalcedon was a flat homely place with one tall hill several miles off rising like its spiteful obverse. The view of the water was fine. Looking at it and living off it were the compensation the inhabitants could call their own.

"You say Vitellus plies his ferry route as often as he can. Three or four times a week."

"I'd say three as an average."

"Does he go back in ballast to Eribolon?"

"I doubt that," said Egon. "Not unless he's stupider than the people who live here."

"Does he load his ship on the same day?"

"If he can find a cargo. Otherwise, he stays over until it's made."

"Where does he stay?"

Egon shrugged his great shoulders, displacing his tunic as if it was his mind. "I don't know. An inn?"

"He's been making this run for the past five years. He's a sailor, and this, for all its faults, is a port. I think he'd try to trim his expense and find something more comfortable than the slops of an inn."

"I see what you mean," said Egon. "A woman's man, which he is, could have a woman here. And I don't think it would matter if she was truly blind."

"Let's say we find her. A thousand sesterces for the man who does."

"She will be found if she exists, lord."

Egon's officers, and my own, set out with enthusiasm I hoped would translate to results. In the meantime, I contacted the proconsul of the province as he left his office for the day, wanting to clear the way for any action against Macrinus. He had an obliging attitude toward the representative of the new emperor and insisted on extending the usual hospitality. I hardly had time to extract myself from his office when Egon, who had gone out into the town himself, returned with news.

"She ain't blind, but she's got this webbing between her toes, like a duck. That's what the man at the tavern said. He knows, because she used to work for him until old Vitellus set her up in a place outside town."

"Any word of visitors?"

"None that I heard. And I asked."

We set out immediately for the House of the Duck in the Land of the Blind. It lay in the suburbs on the road to the chalcedony mines that had been worked until the stones the size of a shield diminished to the size of a thumb. Nowadays, all that was left were three shops selling chalcedony sculptures, and several whorehouses that serviced the reduced population of miners. The last house on the left, perchance, was the refuge the defeated Emperor of Rome had found.

But he did nothing to announce his presence. No sentries were posted and no horses or other conveyances stood in the small barn. As it was nearly dark, I decided to wait the few minutes until we could cloak ourselves completely. While we waited, I sent six men to infiltrate the woods at the rear to cut off retreat. For the front, well, the dog would have to die.

He seemed territorial, but aimlessly. Sniffing every flower and bush, he lifted his leg so many times he must have run dry. When that was apparent to him, he scratched up a dusty patch of earth near the walkway, curled into a ball, and settled in for the evening watch.

As the last light of dusk closed, an arrow through his chest pinned him to the earth. He yelped, but when the second arrow struck his neck, he made no more sounds. His collar was gold or a close second. He was barely more than a lap dog, but well fed. Parthian?

His death had been quiet, but not quiet enough. The front door swung open. The man who stormed into the early night was a Guard, Vitellus the Younger, with his sword drawn. We came up the walkway five strong, but he moved against us with no hesitation, lunging toward my centurion and bringing his sword down in a powerful arc.

Six and a half feet of leverage tore my centurion's cuirass apart and pierced his flesh to the bone, but Vitellus had left himself open. My thrust pierced his belly three inches below the heart. That should have been good enough. Not so. The blow produced nothing but a loud "Oomph" and a counter thrust by his dagger. Barely clearing myself from his blade, I stepped back, leaving my sword in his belly as the man on my right put another there.

Yet Vitellus did not go down. He threw the dagger at my heart and cleared his blade from the centurion as with a roar he came on again. He was hit again, this time on the shoulder near the neck. And again on the neck with a blow that produced a gout of blood. With his head nearly severed from his body, he turned completely around, his guts trailing like dirty clouds, and lunged at the men in the rear. Three blades from the men by my side entered his back and drove Vitellus to the ground. They pinned him like the dog to the earth, grinding and chopping and stabbing until he was completely still. Even that intense moment of surcease took longer than I imagined.

"He should have a decent burial."

"He should have several," said Egon, "when we collect the pieces."

"See to it."

The man who protected his emperor, knowing his mission would mean his death, was an honorable man. Vitellus had been unlucky in his choice of Macrinus.

From one of the men who had gone to the rear of the house, I had word of Macrinus as soon as I passed through the door. "Lord, he's in the bedroom. I told him to dress if he wanted to die proper, but he sits there like a stump."

They gathered up the others—Vitellus the Elder, his web-footed woman, and three docile men from the emperor's retinue. In five steps, I entered a mean bedroom meant for a meanly kept woman. There was little furniture except for a bed nailed together rather than joined. A wash stand stood by the bed with a basin that looked pissed in. In a rude chair of pine sat the Emperor of Rome in his nightclothes.

"Marcus Opellius Macrinus, you're under arrest."

He looked up as if he did not know me, and perhaps it was true, for I have never seen a man so exhausted in body and spirit. His eyes sat in his skull like stray eyes. His face had been clean shaven until he forgot his servants were no longer there to continue the work. The only thing that seemed the same was the hole in his African ear.

"How did you find me so quickly?"

"I should have found you on the field of battle, Marcus Opellius. Failing that, I followed a man and his prick. Old Vitellus."

Macrinus blinked away the tiredness that a week of unceasing travel had put into his face. "It's always the result, isn't it? Our vices show the way to our destruction even when they're not our own. I suppose I should account it a favor to be murdered by a man whose face I finally recognize."

"Later," I said. "You will not die in this place."

Macrinus smiled, or attempted to do that simple thing with a confused movement of his mouth. "Where will it be?"

"You'll be returned to the emperor."

"Oh, yes," he said meanly. "The Syrian catamount."

"He's an emperor and a priest. His god is more powerful than your luck."

"You have a point," he said, murmuring as if to himself. "We almost made it across the sea. We saw land and even some people on the shore. But suddenly the wind came up. It blew us back. Nothing we did with the sail made a difference. It was as if we were destined not to reach Europe."

"Clearly, you were so fated."

* * *

Did I believe that?

Perhaps, but I wanted Macrinus to believe it in his heart. A man in despair who feels that the favor of the gods is against him stands to be an acquiescent prisoner. We had a long return to Antioch.

I tried to make the journey comfortable for the man who had been emperor. I located his carriage set down the road in a draw, and put Macrinus' weary bones within like the tamest of men. I did not bind him or blind him before we set off.

Why is it that the road recently traveled seems so long? Is it like a woman we know too well, finding one night that we have done the most intimate things in exactly the way they were done before, complete in every detail of pleasure? Do we understand that knowing the way removes the wonder?

I was impatient to reach Antioch, but became more so as we neared Cappadocia. There, we received word that Macrinus' son Diadumenianus had been taken at Zeugma and executed. I tried to keep Macrinus from learning what had happened to his ten-year-old boy, though I might have tried harder. My mind held too hard the memory of how he tried to eliminate Varius, and the time I spent in prison. He had spared my life, but spared me no pain.

I'll never know how he learned of Diadumenianus' death, but I learned the result on a mountain road as we passed through the fairy chimneys of Cappadocia. Riding behind the death train, I saw a movement from the carriage that seemed like the figure of a man who leaned out to spit and simply kept going, his momentum tossing him into clear space. The figure struck the ground hard, nearly landing smash on his head. I knew at once that the man was Macrinus and that he had found the courage to force an action in a way he had never shown as emperor.

He seemed in pain as I knelt down to him at the side of the road among a mass of scattered white boulders with pointed brows. "That was a stupid thing to do, Marcus Opellius. What did you hope to accomplish?"

Macrinus answered slowly, holding his shoulder. "To escape. To find myself."

I suppose he meant he had tried to commit suicide by launching from the carriage onto the rocks. Macrinus had not landed properly on his head, however. As usual, he had not quite done what he should.

"I'll have the surgeon look at you."

"Take my life," he said. "Do it now."

I walked away as the surgeon attended him. The report he returned minutes later was bad. Macrinus' shoulder was broken and could be set. The treatment would work, but with the jostling of the carriage over mountain roads, the shoulder might not remain set.

"Does he have pain?"

"I'd say so, yes. Considerable. Nor will it lessen with the journey or the shoulder mend before we reach Antioch."

I turned to my centurion. "Take his head. He wants it no longer."

* * *

We left Macrinus' body at the side of the road and carried the worst of him back to Antioch, where his head joined a collection—Julianus Nestor, Diadumenianus, Fabius Agrippinus, the governor of Syria Coele who helped the enemy; and in due time Pica Caecillianus, the governor of Arabia who refused to declare allegiance to us; Claudius Attalus, the governor of Cyprus; and several high-ranking officers of the legions whose crime was their service to Macrinus.

We hung those heads before the ramparts of Antioch, our headquarters. The clan Bassianus reclaimed the rooms in the palace from which they had fled in the wake of Caracalla's assassination. In that city on the Orontes, they awaited the word from the Senate that his dynasty was officially restored.

That happened, though not promptly. The men of the Roman Senate, who fought hard to prevent Varius being emperor, finally rallied to the side of strength. They accepted him as the son of Caracalla without mentioning discrepancies in the process. To a man, they acclaimed him Emperor of All the Romans and Lord of the World, Marcus Aurelius Antoninus.

BITHYNIA

218–219

THE GREEK WAY

We wintered at Nicomedia. The city's location was supreme, monitoring access from Europe to Asia from its position on the Propontine Sea through the Bosporus to the Euxine Sea. The fertility of its hinterland was unmatched. The richness of its vineyards, orchards and fields supported a large population, and graciously, the court of Marcus Aurelius Antoninus.

I kept busy through the fall and winter dealing with rebellions that took place in Anatolia from Bithynia in the west to Cappadocia in the east. Shifting allegiances as one emperor fell to another created instability that some saw as opportunity. If women, a eunuch, and a boy could seize an empire, why not real men? Twice I went out to the provinces, so I barely spent more than a week in the city and mixed little in the life of the court.

I was sometimes sorry when I did. Varius proved something of a disappointment in administering an empire. The job naturally fell to the people around him—the women, and near-woman Gannys. The meeting I attended in early December was typical of the functions of the new order.

"You are needed in Galatia." Gannys put up his finger, as I had once put up a finger to demonstrate that life could depend on small things; in this case, however, he simply informed the freedman at his left hand to suspend transcription of our words. With another gesture, he gave the freedman to understand that his presence in the chamber was no longer required.

I waited until the man removed himself before I spoke. "May I ask what in Galatia requires my presence?"

"The governor," said Maesa.

"Has he not declared for us from the beginning?"

"He did," said Gannys, "and with alacrity. But it has come to our attention that he disguised his intentions." Gannys leaned forward, his pate reflecting the light from the table of green stone. "It is known that the governor recently caused likenesses of himself to be stamped and plated in gold. This is the first step in his rebellion, according to our sources. His next will be to invade Cappadocia."

"With what?"

"He has a legion at his command," said Gannys.

"He has local militia."

"Nevertheless—"

I found it difficult to listen to nonsense. "What do you want done with him?"

"He must be executed," said Gannys.

"Without being heard?"

"What reason can he give for usurping the coinage of the empire?" asked Gannys, as if there could be none, or any misstatement by his spies. "At this time, in this place, neither insubordination nor the smallest hint of usurpation can be tolerated."

"Will you go at once, Marcellus?"

I could have refused Maesa, whose money made all things possible, but I found myself locked at the center of power in ways I had wanted but not thought out. We had done what we did in spite of the odds. The mistakes we made—and there were some—would be forgiven.

"Does the emperor know of this?"

"Of course."

"Then I will go to Galatia. I will return the governor—"

"Valerianus Paetus," said Gannys.

"I will return Valerianus Paetus so you may add his head to the ramparts."

I had spoken to Gannys, telling him the blood was on his head, and that I had made a mistake in not removing his when I had the chance.

"Marcellus Decimus, do you resist the emperor when rebellion is afoot?"

"Gannys, I'm a soldier. Killing is my profession. It's not my reason for being."

I left knowing I was leaving behind an enemy whose strength would increase in my absence. Maesa was under his spell. Varius to some extent always had been. Of Soaemias, who could say? She seemed to draw away from her mother, but in what direction was unclear.

By chance, I saw the emperor as I walked to the stables. It was not a common occurrence to lay eyes on Varius at Nicomedia. Every day, he went to the races at the circus, and afterward drove his chariot around the city in company with young men who had nothing better to do than attend the Lord of the World. When he was not behind his horses, the emperor visited every theater and tavern that promised diversion, absconding from the palace and frequenting places Macrinus would have shunned. He was being a young man of his age in other words, but without noticing that those who accompanied him saw opportunity.

"Marcellus, I must speak to you."

"My lord."

Varius had changed recently. The age he had entered upon, and the late hours, brought a blotch of pimples to his fair skin. The courage he had shown on the battlefield seemed leached by debauchery. As he took me by the arm into the courtyard abutting the stables, I saw he was agitated, too.

"I must ask a favor," he said. "I find you are the only man I trust to understand. Or to whom I can entrust the mission."

"What mission, my lord?"

"To bring the god from his home in Emesa to be with me."

"The god," I said. "You mean his stone."

"Yes." He began to pace between the colonnades of marble as if constricted by them. "I find that my powers—" Varius paused as if embarrassed. "We spoke of them more than once."

"I recall."

"I find that they are not the same. They have to some extent deserted me."

"You mean, since we arrived here."

He seemed grateful I understood. "I've waited for their return. And in vain. But if the god is brought here, they will be restored."

"Does my lord really believe that his power lies not within him, but in a rock that fell from the sky?"

The emperor moved closer. "The stone, which is the god, fell from the heavens. In its passage it took to itself the power of the cosmos. I do not expect you to understand, Marcellus. But believe me, I need the god here. You must fetch him at once."

"Is my lord not aware I am to leave for Galatia immediately at the orders of the Lord Chamberlain?"

Anger came to his eyes as to any young man with a hangover. Clearly, he had not known of the order dispensed in his name. "Galatia," he said. "That's on the other side of hell."

"Close, my lord. But don't despair. Others can make the journey to Emesa. I'll find a trustworthy man for the job."

"But I want *you*, Marcellus! You *cannot* refuse!"

He had forgotten himself. I forgot myself as I placed my hand on the shoulder of the Emperor of Rome. "I'd be delighted if my lord tells me to follow his orders in preference to those of a eunuch. But he must do that. He must countermand the order."

His answer would tell me everything about his will, and the way of his empire; but his silence told me more. The emperor did not want to contradict Gannys. At length, he capitulated.

"This is an important matter of state you venture upon."

I refused to let him off easily. "Perhaps."

"Then you must go," he said quickly. "I will find others for the work."

"My lord."

* * *

I left that afternoon for the mountain fastnesses in the dead of winter. When I reached Galatia four days later, I found the governor, Valerianus Paetus, had indeed stamped likenesses of himself in gold, which he had given to his mistresses as ornaments to adorn their bodies. Apparently, he was one who liked to look at himself at all times, even the most intimate. Perhaps vice, when it is so stupid, should cause a man to forfeit his life.

I gave him the chance at suicide, which he accepted in company with his wife of twenty-five years. When they opened their veins in the baths of the palace, it was said to be the only thing they had shared in a decade.

I stayed longer than I wanted in Galatia seeing to the installation of a new governor and installing discipline into his legion of militia. By the time I left, the troops were sure of their allegiance and missing two lax centurions.

The letter I received at the same time bearing Maesa's seal was more disturbing. She had heard of Paetus' suicide and rebuked me for not delivering him to the court. She also instructed me to proceed at once to Cyzicus, where a mutiny in the fleet must be put down.

Another mutiny. In all these uprisings, the Senate encouraged the rebels, thinking that nothing could be worse for them than the family of Caracalla. The Senators were enraged about many things, but chiefly by the appointment of Comazon as Prefect of the Praetorian Guard. Traditionally, that post was held by a man on the verge of senility, like Macrinus. Comazon's youth and lack of background were detrimental, as well as the fact that no one knew him well enough to bribe him.

They had a point. Comazon should have spent his days in the saddle crossing Anatolia. I had done it so many times I thought of it as a launch to obscurity. I spent much of the day of my return to Nicomedia from Cyzicus preparing a report on my mission to that vital port where the Euxine Fleet was stationed. I had sent the scroll to the palace by slave when another appeared with a message from Comazon requesting an immediate meeting.

I was not surprised to receive the message. While we were at Antioch, Comazon had consulted me on how to deal with three cohorts of large dangerous Praetorian Guards. I gave him advice that could do no harm. Make Thrax a tribune, or decimate one cohort. Since Comazon had no liking for a method that required every tenth man, randomly chosen, to be beaten to death, he promoted the Thracian giant with good results.

I had planned to rest at my villa, with which I had small acquaintance, and renew my acquaintance with Philomene, my

Egyptian. She did everything well, including those things for which she had been intended. We did them as often as my presence permitted, and as much as Soaemias allowed, though my affection for my slave was a strain on our relationship. That also meant the princess was a jealous woman who probably had a spy in my household. I would have to deal with the problem at some point.

"Will you return for dinner?"

"Unless I'm delayed."

"Then you will not eat."

Philomene had a way of answering her own questions. I had found her talent for gathering information did not cease when she left Emesa.

"What prompts you to predict the future this time?"

"I'd rather not say, lord. The Prefect of the Guard will certainly tell you his mind. He sent round to this house the last three days inquiring of your return."

"Then perhaps I will not eat. But I will return tonight."

I left for Comazon's office in the legate's palace, now the residence of the emperor, as it had been the seat of the kings of Nicomedia, who were always called Nicomedes. The last of the line, a Nicomedes so old and infirm that he no longer wished to defend his lands, made out a will that left his crossroads kingdom to Rome. He received nothing in return but the arch of Roman power to extend over his people. They were a mixture of local tribes with an overlay of Greek expertise, like most provinces of Asia.

That meant I had to make my way through two sets of Praetorian Guards at the gates, and three sets of eunuchs within, before I found Comazon in an office before the antechamber of the emperor. When he saw me at the door, he called "Marcellus," shot from his chair, and passed by two secretaries to take me by the arm. "How was the journey?"

"Too long, but productive."

"And the mutiny of the Euxine Fleet?"

"Concluded."

"You crucified them all?"

"I hanged the Greek freedman who was stealing their pay."

Comazon smiled with teeth so even and bright they seemed to precede his lustrous beard. It was as if only the specter of violence, meted out quickly, could please him. But instead of inviting me into his office, which was, like all the rooms in the palace, lavishly appointed, he steered me into the corridor.

"You're just the man to root out corruption," he said. "Hanging Greeks must be better than a week in the pleasure dome."

"Prefect, you seem harried."

"Not a bit," he said, urging me down the vaulted corridor toward the west side of the palace where the gardens lay. "Not a bit," he said again.

"The Guard. They're restive?"

"Of course, but that's not the problem." He corrected himself. "Not the real problem."

"The Senate has refused your appointment."

"They didn't dare."

"Then what?"

His pace slowed when we reached the doors inset with colored panes of glass. They opened at our approach, carried by enormous hinges and two eunuchs. Their bows brought a frown to Comazon's handsome face like the crescent moon that was the symbol of Bithynia. The prominent brown eyes that were the oldest part of him seemed rimmed by pain. The chin that was prominent but heart-shaped moved aggressively to emphasize his words.

"I don't know who else to talk to," he said as we passed a lane of mulberry trees to a ramp planted with sculpted yews above a rank of fountains. "What I mean is, I have no other *man* to talk to."

"Then I'm yours."

"You'll learn not to say that, Marcellus, if you spend much time here. You've been lucky in that respect. I know this looks like a fool's paradise with all these sexless creatures, but believe me, it's the foulest place on earth. Scratch your ass in the latrine, and the next morning—sitting on your night table—is a jar of

Greek powder to cure your itch. It might come from Varius, or his mother, or from some Aegean cocksucker in the Council. You never know. You want to, but you can't."

"This is your first exposure to court life."

"To insanity," he said. "You know, my mother was an actress before she married my father. She played so many parts when I was growing up I thought everyone talked in bad rhyme. I thought false tears were her milk. I thought Terrence and Plautus were consuls. But this—" He threw his arm in an arc that included the fountains, which were tinted a peculiar shade of orange, the yews, which were ornamented with colored glass balls, and the walks, the stones of which were painted in scenes from the Trojan Wars. "This is completely—"

"Artificial."

"Degenerate," he said as if he had found the word. "My Guards, you know, are mostly from the frontier. Men, in other words. They don't understand these people. The tailor comes to take their measurements for the new uniforms that look like steel flowers, and while he's doing them up, he fondles their privates. They throw him out the window on the second floor. I have them flogged, because the eunuch who runs this empire says it must be done."

Comazon hit himself with the flat of his hand. "I don't sleep at the camp any more. I refuse to because those men are angry. They won't even listen to Thrax, which means they won't back down from an elephant." He sat hard on a marble bench where two cheeks had been hollowed from green Boetian marble. "Tell me what to do. Quickly."

"You're having trouble with Gannys, I take it."

Comazon's face underwent changes below the skin. His cheekbones flattened and the line of his jaw filled. "That bastard grows more arrogant every day. The men who oppose him grow weaker every day. Basically, it's because there're less of them. You remember Castinus, who served Caracalla so well."

"Yes."

Comazon looked around the garden to make sure no one overheard his words, but still they were spoken low. "While you were away, Castinus was sent to Emesa to retrieve the emperor's god. The rock. He brought it along well enough, but while they're in the mountains, the carriage hauling the god overturns. But it's just a stone falling onto frozen mud and none the worse for wear. So Castinus loads it up like a good pagan. He makes nothing of it. He's been told the thing walks and talks and likes to be tucked in every night, but he doesn't believe it. He fetches it here to the palace and puts the parasol back over its head and thinks he's done his job."

"Wrong."

"Dead wrong," said Comazon. "It happens the god doesn't like it here for some reason. The emperor says it doesn't, and the emperor knows. Then Gannys discovers the reason, which was the jarring fall Castinus allowed to happen. He tells the emperor. That's how Castinus lost his life. They pulled him into four pieces with chariots at the circus."

A man of Castinus' rank should never have been executed in that way. A beheading perhaps, or suicide. And, of course, it could have been me who dropped the god.

"I don't understand the sentence. It isn't right."

"The reason given was religious sacrilege," said Comazon. "That's how Gannys proposed it, and the emperor agreed. Anything can be done to a man who violates the sanctity of the god."

"That still doesn't sound like Varius. Nor quite like Gannys."

"It might not sound like the men you knew," said Comazon. "Gannys is the same, but the scale is altered. It's worth noting that when Castinus came here from Antioch, he locked up the olive oil concession for his syndicate in Rome. Somehow, after his death, Gannys came to control the concession through several upstanding citizens of Bithynia. Greeks like him. Some have balls, though they're not what we'd call men. You'd know what I mean if you went to the baths in Nicomedia. All these fellows go to look at the ass, and it's not mixed bathing. Greeks know all about men's asses. It's the come in their beards that gives them away."

"Gannys was always mercenary," I said. "It's strange. Men like to pile up their fortune for their children. I wonder what moves a man who has no one to follow him."

"It may be just that," said Comazon. "No hope of tomorrow. You won't find the other eunuchs giving away money either. They spend and spend, trying to impress each other while there's time in this life. They're connoisseurs. They love everything unnatural, which means they love themselves best. When they look in the mirror, they see perfection. A woman's taste in a man's body."

"The good thing is we'll be leaving here soon. The first of spring, I'm told."

"I'm looking forward to it more than you know," he said. "The problem is, Gannys will be coming with us."

I would have said a eunuch could not thrive in Rome at the highest levels, but Caracalla had disproved the idea. His eunuch Rufus had ruled the city until he displeased his master.

"Sempronius Rufus was convicted of embezzlement, wasn't he?"

"I wouldn't say convicted. Caracalla waved his hand and a twenty-foot stake went up the eunuch's ass." A light came to Comazon's eyes. "You aren't thinking of that, are you?"

"Not yet. I want to speak to the emperor first."

"Be prepared," said Comazon.

"For what?"

"A lot's happened since you've been away. I mean changes." Comazon lifted his eyes like dark stones fallen from heaven. "But see for yourself. Yonder arrives the Messenger of the Sun."

I had never heard the name applied to Varius before. The term seemed localized to Nicomedia, where it died the death it deserved. How many other things died in this place I would not be able to say.

Marcus Aurelius Antoninus emerged from his apartments in the west wing of the palace at the head of a dozen men and women dressed in the most lavish costumes the mind and hand of the East could devise. Every color of the spectrum was present, each garment a flowing creation in silk, each more Greek than Roman, and more effete than either.

Indeed, I could discern no difference between the men and women. Both sexes wore chitons that broke above the knee. The garments were embroidered in motifs in silver and gold thread that could have retold all of Homer. Beneath the chitons, loose trousers billowed above dainty linen shoes set with sparkling gems. Look at us, they seemed to say, are we Roman citizens, or the most magnificent barbarians ever seen in this garden?

They chattered like barbarians, thronging the figure of their emperor, who was the most magnificent of all. Varius had obviously set the fashion for the dress of his entourage. He was arrayed in gold, the color of his god, with a diadem, chiton, trousers and slippers. Purple, the color of Caesar, was evident, but at the margins—in the stripe on his shoulders, in the stripe that ran down each leg of his trousers, and at the center of a large object hanging from his neck. It looked like an amulet. I could only assume it was of importance to fashion, or to the god.

"You'll never guess what's inside that thing," said Comazon. "Never."

"Before they tore Castinus apart, they plucked out his eyes, which were boiled in oil. The effect is uncanny, like the brightest of gems. But it can be grisly if you know the source."

I found it hard to think of Castinus as a source, like a bear for fur. He had not been the best man of his time, but I had no problems with him save the obvious. Like most Romans, he thought the role of conquerors was to pillage. Losers were simply that, and he never considered himself one. To think he had survived Caracalla to be extinguished by a greedy man like Gannys, and a gentle one like Varius, was ironic. To think of the light of his avaricious blue eyes dangling at Varius' breast was more.

Then the emperor saw me as I rose from the bench. "Marcellus," he said, raising his hand and voice. "We heard you had returned in triumph again."

I could not tell if Varius employed the imperial we, or assumed the role as spokesman for his coterie. I stepped to the mosaic walk in front of the pool to meet his imperial progress.

"Intact, my lord. Hardly in triumph."

"He puns like a Roman," said Caesar to his court. "He conquers like a Roman. Now if we could teach him to fuck like a Bithynian."

If I was shocked by the greeting, I did not show it to the court. They were laughing at the wit of Caesar. In other circumstances, I might have joined them; but it was my bones on which Varius built his derision, and it was my blood that might have been spilled on his behalf at Galatia and Cyzicus. I said nothing. I recognized the rapport the emperor and I shared was a useless thing for the moment.

He seemed to know he had been unkind. "Marcellus Decimus is our greatest warrior," he said to the coterie. "If he becomes too much like us, what use will he be?"

I did not heed the titters of the crowd. I gave my answer respectfully. "The use to which my lord puts me is my only purpose. He knows this, I trust."

Varius might have answered if another young man had not stepped between us. He was, if I read protocol correctly, the favorite of the court who stood at the right hand of the emperor. Short, red-haired, soft in his belly and as soft in his limbs, he seemed to carry them on loan from someone else. In his left hand he held a long-stemmed quizzing-glass with a green lens. When he came within arm's length, he put the magnifying device on me, gazing in sea-tints at a specimen of humanity he seemed not to fathom. When he had run the quizzing-glass up and down, he pulled it aside, turned to Caesar and spoke lightly.

"This Decimus is known to my lord, therefore I cannot comment on his merits. But it seems he slept too close to his horse, or the beasts of the field."

As he put the glass to one nostril, the entourage, like one being, roared with laughter. I watched to see if the emperor did, too. Not quite. He smiled. He was watching me.

I used the opportunity to strip the quizzing-glass from the hand of the sycophant. I spun him around, took him by the seat of his loose trousers, and with gathering force, threw him headlong into the pool.

It seemed like the thing to do, but the act was unplanned and dangerous, for the pool was not deep. Limbs flailing, the young man screamed as he hit the water. He submerged for a moment and seemed to die, then arose, thrashing and gagging with his forehead bleeding from a large gash. The fine silks clung to his body like wet leaves in morbid colors. What he heard belatedly, as the water cleared his ears, was the laughter of the imperial party, more heartfelt than it had been before.

I turned my back on my enemy for life, knowing it would be the last time I could do that. I waited until the laughter ebbed and I was sure my words could be heard.

"Some men require tasters for their food. I find I must have a substitute for my bath. This young man, fortunately, volunteered."

More laughter issued in precise sheets, and it was within the laughter I first noticed the lack of an upper register. The laughter of women was absent. It was as if there were no women among the group. I put the quizzing-glass on them. They immediately came closer, and though distorted by the lens, were bigger. Their flaws were bigger, and it seemed incredible I had not recognized the one that would change my life.

The women in the party were too big by a little, too muscular by the drape of their clothing, and although their hair was piled high on their heads, swept up in spires of curls, swept back in buns, and gathered in plaits, the hair was too lank. All these women wore wigs. They were all heavily made-up, painted in white lead and antimony, but that could not obscure the shadows of beards under the cosmetics. I realized at last there were no women at all among the party. There were men, and there were men who dressed like women.

I heard Comazon's voice behind me. "Yes," he said, as if he knew the exact moment when I knew what I had never wanted to know.

I dropped the glass as the emperor spoke to the silence that descended on the imperial party. "We do not recall Marcellus Decimus as being so droll. We do understand that he is a man of action. Nor would we have him otherwise."

"My lord is also a man of action," I said. "He has proven himself on the field of battle. Perhaps he would agree to accompany a hunting party with his humble servant. We could find some boar."

Varius smiled, and I knew him as he had been. Not a freak. Not a reprobate. Because he was intelligent, he would know that my object was to detach him from his coterie. His answer would be the gauge of his mind.

"Will you promise me a boar?"

"I promise my lord the useful exercise of his limbs. These things, I perceive, are neglected due to the rigors of his high office, and the many demands put upon him."

"I shall consult with my chamberlain," he said, giving Gannys a title instead of half a name. "You will have our answer."

"My lord."

Varius understood I was disappointed in him. Apparently, he could not decide upon a chance at real sport without the consent of a eunuch. He took his leave with a hand raised in blessing, but as he walked by me at the head of his court of deviants, I noted his face at closer range. He, too, was painted with lead and antimony. He did not look like an emperor, or a Syrian god, but more like a drawn and unseemly ghost.

* * *

"Now you know."

I said I did as the imperial dross descended from the walk to the ramp leading to the stables. Would they go out in their chariots, or perform unspeakable acts upon dumb animals? I felt stripped of something, as if the future had been taken away like a missing ladder.

"It's not his fault," said Comazon. "What can we expect when he's surrounded by such creatures?"

"Who allowed this to happen?"

"No one *allowed* it, Marcellus. The emperor of Rome does what he wishes for as long as he wishes. Gannys is happy with the arrangement. As long as Caesar's playing with dolls, no one can tell his eunuch how to run the empire."

"Yes, I see that now."

"What will you do?"

I did not answer. I had no answer.

"It's up to you, Marcellus. No one else can break that bastard's hold."

He was wrong. The Praetorian Guard had done worse, assassinating emperors, including the last legitimate one, Caracalla. Comazon was saying he was not willing to take on the task of rearranging the government.

But he was an ambitious young man who could be ruthless. He had been responsible for one of the heads that hung from the walls of Antioch. Attalus, the legate to Cyprus, had done Comazon a disservice while they served together in Thrace. So he died of a personal grievance. But this matter was political, and the violence would have to come from within.

Comazon did want to risk that for himself or Rome. He wanted someone else to do it.

I wondered why it should be me.

* * *

I still had no answer when another eunuch bade me follow him to the quarters of Soaemias. She occupied a wing of the palace that once housed the concubines, male and female, of the various Nicomedes. The windows and doors of the rooms were screens of latticework that divided spaces into barriers shot with shining lozenges. The feeling was cloistered, assisted by the boldly colored marbles on the floors and walls, the frescoes and statues, and the hangings chased in silver.

She seemed at one with her quarters, sitting on a couch draped with Tyrian tapestry that ended in a fringe of gold as thick as ship's lines. The servant attending her had finished dressing her hair, which was done in the style of her son's coterie. Golden ringlets fell across her brow, curls mounted in rows along the crown and fell into a bun at the nape of her neck. More dramatic was the elemental line of her cleavage. Not that of a typical Roman matron, it was deep, revealing flawless white skin nearly to the nipples.

"Marcellus, I missed you so much."

"As I missed much, Soaemias."

She heard the tone of my voice and dismissed her servants as if she wanted to be alone with me. She served with her hands unwatered Chian wine spiced with nutmeg and another substance I could not identify.

Inviting me to occupy the space beside her on the couch, she used her hands to weave a mood and recall the things that had passed between us, which was itself a powerful aphrodisiac. Is memory always that way between lovers?

The wine came to my head like soft drums. My body seemed to vibrate with power that passed without stopping to all the seats of pleasure. The chief one is the center in a man and the only one I had ever known. It sprang from its place like a centurion's rod.

I was amazed I could make love at that moment, when my world had been so damaged, but without the slightest pause I found myself tearing the silk from her body and entering her like the last man in a hundred. Only when she cried out did I pull back, and when I did she said no, please, do it exactly like that.

I did it, hearing her rising voice that spoke in no tongue, feeling her legs wrap my legs, urging me deeper, wanting to be violated in the way I wanted to violate, knowing the reason was none I could name. When I came to climax, it was as if I had accomplished a victory that would never be repeated.

* * *

"That was the first time you made love to me like a soldier."

"I thought you might say a savage."

"Let's say a man in touch with his needs. Something caused you to make love like that."

"Perhaps it was the wine."

"Perhaps not," she said quickly. "In wine there is truth, but never a truth that was previously unknown."

"So you welcome the animal."

She put her tongue in my navel, working it in slow delicious increments. "I liked his impatience, which spoke of love in the most primitive way. It was like a problem that demanded an answer."

"If there is something wrong, Soaemias, we would know it."

"Some games I do not like, Marcellus. Say what you mean."

I had always thought of myself as direct within limits. Now the limits surrounded every word. Perhaps the things that had happened to Varius would not have happened if I had been at his side in the last months, but was that true? Could I have affected a young man's lust or the direction it had taken?

"I saw your son today. Caesar, that is."

"Was he—"

"In high state. With his friends."

"I see," she said, but nothing more.

"You wrote me in Galatia. You wrote me at Cyzicus. Never a mention of this—" I searched for the word to match my feelings. "*Travesty.*"

She took offense, but what did she see when she looked upon the menagerie that her son commanded with no regard for his office? "You're referring to his tastes."

"In men."

"And you find that a travesty."

"I find it disturbing."

"Why?"

"Because it's unnatural," I said, regretting those words. "The gods did not create man and woman for the species to die out."

"The gods," she said. "So you think that the order of love is foreordained."

"That's obvious."

"And what if the love of men for men is also foreordained?"

"I don't understand that."

"You might try," she said with less patience. "Do you think men like my son have a choice in what they want? Do you think beatings at the proper time would change their mind about whom they love?"

"It might."

"Yet I can tell you that harsh treatment does not effect a change," she said with authority. "I'm a priestess of Astarte. Many times I've been consulted by fathers and mothers who wish with all their hearts to change the desires of their male children. Never have I known a method of punishment or inducement to work for long, or for the better, which is to say the usual. The best that can be obtained is duty toward women. Their first love—for men—never varies."

"Never?"

She moved her head slowly. "Do you find that hard to accept?"

"I find it a waste."

"There's no such thing as waste in love," she said. "What mother since the beginning of time could think that? What mother of an emperor would care?"

If she was right, she was too disingenuous. I felt that my service to her family had been misspent, and that she had been a vehicle of subterfuge.

"When did you become aware of the emperor's . . . preference?"

"Recently," she said. "The atmosphere in this place seemed to promote what was previously hidden. Or previously unexplored."

"We are not speaking of a journey to the frontier, Soaemias. This is a swamp that must be skirted."

"You did not think so tonight," she said. "You defiled me like a woman you found in a mud hut."

So I was called to payment already. The drums of the wine that called me did not exist. The woman who called me did not exist except as the mother of the emperor. She knew every lesson of love and the ways to apply them. She had.

"I apologize for my behavior. Perhaps your son will apologize for his."

"I'm afraid that neither the emperor, or his god, agree with you."

"His god. You mean Gannys."

"That's blasphemous," she said, suddenly flushed. "You do not understand the basis of our religion."

That was true, nor had I ever thought of it as hers; but I understood, at last, that I should. "Are you telling me that lust is the basis of your religion?"

"*All* acts of love!" she said. "Of which *none* is perverted!"

"Is that what Gannys says?"

"He—" She stopped before she embarked on his defense. "I think you should not slander a man who has been valuable to our family."

"I think his value has come to end ingloriously."

She paused and took a breath. "And what would you propose as a solution?"

"An island in the Mediterranean all to himself. Or a post on the frontier in Germany."

"I thought you might say death."

"Then death," I said.

"Very well. I marked your opinion."

"I give it with all due respect, Soaemias. He's an able administrator, but many others of the kind exist."

"You may be right," she said. "But you must clear your mind. You should think seriously of how you can serve an emperor who does not command your respect."

"Perhaps I will learn."

I slipped from the couch, knowing I had promised something I did not believe. Soaemias never looked better. Her skin was chafed with mellow highlights that the most beautiful silks of her son's entourage could not match. Anger put red rose with the heart of white, and might keep it there each time we met.

"I hate to part like this, Soaemias."

"Then don't," she said.

I did not want to. I reached to her table and drank the wine again. I listened for the drums, which began at once.

* * *

I arrived home very late, but my dinner awaited as always. As I partook of it, I was surprised, again, by the nature of my appetite. The food made by the cook Philomene had engaged was said to be better than the emperor's staff could offer, but I had never found it necessary to attest to his skill. That night I consumed every morsel, never doubting it was the finest to be had.

When the meal ended with fig pastries wrapped in twenty-seven layers of dough each as thin as a membrane, I went to my office, where every surface was covered in a layer of dust as thick as the pastry. I was glad my orders had been followed. The desk unto the drawers, and the chests in every compartment, had not been disturbed. She was obedient, my Egyptian.

I called for her to know her mind on one important subject. Though available twenty-four hours a day like all slaves, she always contrived to appear in the freshest clothing and spirit. Before she made ready for sleep, she wore the silken garments I had brought from Antioch.

"Tell me something, Philomene. You knew about Varius—the emperor—before I went to the palace today."

"Knew what, my lord?"

"That he had declared himself."

She understood, and for longer than I thought. That was clear. "Yes, my lord."

"When did you first know?"

"At Emesa."

"How did you know?"

"When the emperor took himself to the male prostitutes."

That was simply put, but the import was no less. "Did he always take himself to them?"

"In the beginning, no. But afterward—"

"Did he go to them often?"

"Yes, my lord."

"Did his mother know?"

"I believe so."

"Yet you did not tell me."

"No," she said. "My lord, you did not ask."

Philomene never lied to me outright. It might have something to do with our intimacy and the trust that I had given her, but her honesty had preceded it. I did not understand what could change it.

"You say that it could be, but wasn't. Then why did you not tell me?"

"It was the wish of his mother," she said.

* * *

The mood I felt may have been due to Philomene's words, or the wine that finally left my body. In its wake, nothing prospered. I spent the next two hours composing a letter to Princess Maesa stating my desire to be released from the service of her grandson. The letter never grew to more than three brief sentences, but it was the most difficult to which I have ever subscribed. My mind and hand performed the work, but my heart failed at each word.

I might be signing my life away. One did not quit the service of the emperor for better employment. He decided the time and method of departure. He determined if the retirement was honorable or a terminal breach of faith.

I called for Philomene again. "This will be delivered to the palace in the morning."

She accepted the scroll as if made by the hand of a leper. "For the Mother Augusta?"

I said, "Yes," though I was not used to thinking of Maesa with that title. She had been awarded it by the Senate at her request after her grandson was confirmed as emperor. The man who delivered it to the august body of Conscript Fathers had been a mere centurion whose virtue resided in his voice, which was loud, and his manner, which was arrogant. The insult to Senate had been deliberate, the requests orders.

I found there were reasons for everything now.

THE HOLLOW

I waited a day for a reply to my letter. I spent the time ordering my affairs, making out my will and devising a document that would upon my death manumit my slave Philomene. I settled a sum on her, while the rest went to my sister in Verona.

I knew the reply would tell me much about the true state of affairs of the Roman Empire. Would Varius order the death of the man who had saved his life, or would his mother, his grandmother, or his eunuch, do it? When would I hear the sound of troops in the street?

The answer arrived in a prodigious litter. Preceded by a dozen Praetorian Guards, borne by slaves who were all blond, of identical height and clothed in blue tunics, the Mother Augusta of Rome, Julia Maesa, alighted from her conveyance like a goddess made of suet and silk, stepping onto the back of a slave and thence to the good earth of Bithynia. Two parasols bloomed over her head. A streamer of carpet rolled out at her feet. I neither saw nor heard trumpets.

Nor Gannys. I had the Mother Augusta conducted to my garden, which opened onto a lazy view of the Propontine Sea. It was a beautiful day that could never pass for winter in more northerly climates, the sun pouring soft light on the vertical hills of Nicomedia. The headlands jutted into the sea like knuckles in a glove. The ships in the harbor at Eribolon lifted their cruciform masts and yards into the air, seeming to hover and yearn, like us all, for the center, for Europe, for Rome.

"Mother, welcome to my home."

Maesa nodded but did not return the greeting. She sat in a large chair sculpted from stone, sampling the honey cakes my servants put out, drinking sips of water from Palmys that was as sweet. She did it without a taster, showing she trusted me with her life.

"Did you know I chose this house for you?" she asked without expecting a reply. "No finer vista can be found in Nicomedia. I thought what you needed was perspective."

"Most of all," I said, sitting on the marble bench facing her.

"But it seems you have not acquired it. The curse of power is that we can bestow material gifts but not those of the spirit. In those, until now, we had never thought you lacking."

"We?"

"Shall we say my grandson and his mother, whom you have grievously wounded. They care for you more than you know or they can say. Soaemias especially you have behaved badly toward. I do not like seeing my daughter weep over a man who has no regard for her love."

"That is not the case."

"Then we must speak to the case," she said. "What I would like to know is what you think you are doing by submitting that ridiculous document to the court of Marcus Aurelius Antoninus." She looked at me as if I were her greatest puzzle. "I understand from my daughter that you two disagreed about the ways you could serve the emperor. Yet how this translates to not serving him at all is beyond my comprehension."

I wondered why she insisted on that. If I had not spoken to Philomene, I would never have known the depth of the subterfuge and would never have written the letter. What else lay hidden in this family?

"Mother, let's say I find it hard to keep up with the emperor's *changes*."

She looked at me from within her layers of fat as if from a carapace. The look was cold but curious. "That's a polite way of putting a trying circumstance. I should deny your accusation, but I find I cannot lie to you as I would like." She bit into the honey cake again, savoring it. "You have a very good cook in your household."

"I'm told he's the best."

"I'm inclined to agree, but I suppose that's a matter of taste. In much the same vein, I wonder if you know my grandson is not the first Emperor of Rome to display the tastes he has shown? The list would begin with the first Caesar, whose name was Julius.

When he arrived in Bithynia one summer, he become the lover of King Nicomedes."

"A rumor, I think."

"Then I will continue with less ambiguity," she said. "In order, there were the Emperors Nero, Caligula, Titus, Domitian, and lest we forget the man whose name my grandson bears—the indomitable Marcus Aurelius."

"Yes, but they did not flaunt their love publicly."

"The Emperor Hadrian did not?" she asked. "I'm sorry to disturb your sense of decorum, but when his lover Antinous fell from a boat into the Nile and drowned, Hadrian built a city there and named it after him—a city that still lives. He erected statues all over the empire to Antinous. Yet this emperor, this *man* who loved *men*, is thought of as one of the greatest Caesars."

"Perhaps."

"You can't keep saying that."

She was right. My expectations of her grandson caused the problem. Romans never exalted the love of other men as did Greeks, but it was tolerated. Any man could practice love for another as long as he did not practice submission. Dominance was all. A Roman did not abase himself. A Roman emperor took what he wanted even if it was unnatural.

"Have you thought of the problem in terms of an heir?"

"Of course," she said.

"Has Varius?"

"I'm confident he will do what is expected."

"But are you sure?"

"An heir will be produced," she said. "Never fear."

"But I do, Mother. As long as Gannys holds sway in his court, I'm afraid the emperor will never be encouraged to his duty. A wife who could move her husband to abandon his god—and other men—is a threat. A child who might brighten the future of his dynasty—" I held up my hands. "Well, who could say? It might convince your grandson to rule his empire."

"Perhaps."

"You can't keep saying that, Mother."

"So you think Gannys' head on a stake would right all that."

"It would allow the possibility."

"And that is your price?"

I was always amazed at her directness. Though she was bargaining, and under no obligation to honor the bargain, she advanced the idea without qualms. Gannys' head in exchange for what? There was something I did not know about this visit.

"Mother, if you ask, I will forgo my resignation and serve the emperor. Gannys' head would be a bonus."

"Then in the best of all worlds, you would not demand it."

"I'm sorry if I've given you that impression, Mother. I have no wish to see Gannys end his life in this place. You might send him to Emesa to look after civil affairs as he did before."

"That's impossible," she said. "I can't have *him* at my back, too."

Too? Maesa knew she had said too much. She applied to her glass bowl and drank of the best water of Bithynia, but before the bowl was refilled by my kitchen slave, she returned to the question.

"I propose this: I will inform Gannys that he is charged with curbing the excesses of the emperor. If he does not succeed, then his head will be yours when you return."

When I returned. Now I knew I would hear what she wanted. I did not trust her to rid the empire of the eunuch; but I trusted her demands.

"Where am I going, Mother?"

"Syria," she said. "We have just had word that Verus is in revolt. He has taken Legion III Gallica, which you know well, and gone to set up government in Tyre. He has declared himself the new Emperor of Rome."

* * *

I arranged for six triremes, along with three transports, to sail from Nicomedia for Tyre, and half the Euxine Fleet to rendezvous. None of the captains took the orders well, fearing winter voyages above all things—unless it was the displeasure of an emperor so close at hand. With luck, the fleets would appear off the Syrian Coast at the same time as my two legions.

Although Verus commanded only one legion, he was a threat. We had begun our revolt with one legion—the same III Gallica. My task was to ensure he remained one, and in that I had an advantage. Verus' claim to the empire had no legitimacy except what he commanded in the field. His blood did not connect with dynasties past or present. His politics consisted of no more than ambition. His only currency was greed.

Verus' choice of a base of operations was a gauge of his defects. The city of Tyre lay on an island close off the coast of Syria, which made it easy to defend and difficult to assault. But Verus would be isolated once our ships moved to blockade. If he did not come out and give battle, he would wither through a siege.

That was not the preferred method. Once it was clear a revolt had begun against our emperor of six months, disorder might spread throughout the East. Judea lay south of Tyre. Egypt with her vast population was next. That elementary fact of geography was not hard to grasp. Even the Mother Augusta, her eunuch, and her grandson, saw the danger when we met secretly at the palace. The room was small and unadorned, a sealed chamber of state.

"Besiege if you must," said Gannys, "but by all means have it done by spring. We cannot afford to tarry longer in the East."

"Why not?"

The emperor spoke in a dull tone. Varius had been uninterested in the council from the moment he left his friends at the door. In the airless room, his paint had decayed, marking his face with sweat and releasing an attar of roses. He toyed with the amulet at his breast, putting it to his mouth from time to time, as if sucking the essence of Castinus.

"My lord must arrive at Rome soon," I said. "He cannot repeat the mistake of Macrinus. The Senate must be brought to heel and the affection of the people won."

"Macrinus' chief mistake was having a hole in his head." Varius tapped his ear. "I saw it."

He looked around the table to see if we appreciated his wit, but his lack of seriousness caused the faces of Gannys and Maesa to grow grimmer. Spanking an emperor was out of the question, so Gannys, who had warmed to his role as enforcer, pounced with harsh words.

"Perhaps the emperor should take instruction from the carcass of Macrinus he took the time to observe in the wilderness. The man who lived in it plumbed every whore in the city of Antioch when he should have been listening to the advice of his counselors."

"And taking to the field," said Maesa.

"Is that what you want me to do? Go to Syria with Marcellus? Well, I'm all for it. May I take my playthings with me?"

"You'll remain in Nicomedia until winter recedes," said his grandmother. "Your first task, and the only one for which you are suited, will be to pose for a portrait to be sent to the Senate of Rome. If they cannot have you, they must know you at a distance. For this portrait, you will sit in one place and wear the toga."

The emperor looked at the Mother Augusta as if he had seen her before but could not recall the circumstances. "I find your suggestion worthy of my time." He placed his hands flat on the table. "But I will wear the vestments of my god for the portrait. The people of Rome will see the glory that awaits them in the worship of El-Gabal."

Before the Mother Augusta or her eunuch could protest, Varius walked to the door. He swung it open, and in violation of the sealed chamber, spoke to the world at large.

"You will suppress this rebellion, Marcellus. I have full confidence in you and you have my full support."

"My lord."

"Whatever it takes, old friend."

* * *

I departed as soon as I mustered the legions. I had obtained more than I hoped for from Caesar and wanted no conditions on his words. Clearly, neither Maesa or Gannys controlled his whims, but they interpreted his commands as they pleased.

I even managed to talk Comazon into lending me a full-strength cohort of his Praetorian Guard. The mark of the emperor must be visible on this campaign, I said. He believed me because it was true.

The Praetorians were bad campaigners, mostly men from Thrace and Pannonia and the Germanies who thought the long ground was covered best, and only, by horse. Accustomed to living at court, they looked upon duty in the field as a betrayal of their purpose. Our rapid pace on the march caused grumbling in the ranks that began before we cleared Bithynia, and quickened as we crossed Asia. We had not quite reached Cilicia when one day at noon I received a deputation of the Guard led by the giant Thrax.

He was the only man to approach within twenty feet, though his mates waited at that distance. We were the same height because I was ahorse. His voice, so broad that it seemed as big as his body, carried the respect he gave to the normal run of men.

"Commander, the Guard asks me to speak for them."

"Speak clearly, Thrax."

"They say, Commander, that they will spend their bodies and risk their lives for the welfare of the emperor, but not as beasts of the field."

"I'm not interested in their interpretation of their duty, Thrax. The Guard are engaged to protect the lives of the emperor *and* his family. You may tell them that is the task they have embarked upon."

Thrax seemed daunted, but only in mind. "Commander, we see no Caesar here."

"In three days, when we reach Emesa, you will be given the job of safeguarding the lives of Princess Mammea and her son, Alexianus. Now, is your duty clear?"

Thrax hesitated, but nodded.

"Then fall in," I said. "We have ten miles more to march today."

We made those miles every day until we reached Syria, where we made them faster although we gathered more troops along the way. At Apamea, the greater portion of Legion II Parthica had wintered. We joined the nearly three thousand troops to ours quickly, because the commander, Frontinus, was a staunch supporter of the family. From Apamea, we went directly to Emesa, bypassing Raphanae and the troops Verus had left in garrison.

I had not lied to Thrax about his duties. When I suggested relocating Alexianus and his mother to Maesa, she agreed; but she assumed I would retrieve them after taking Tyre. That was not my intention. I wanted members of the royal family in my army when we met Verus. That would show the legions what he lacked.

I expected some resistance from Princess Mammea when we reached Emesa, but she surprised me with her decisiveness. She met me in the atrium of her home, listened to my words, and asked only one question.

"What is the danger?"

"The risk can be controlled. Alexianus will never be exposed in the forefront of battle. In any case, the Guard will protect him with their lives, and so will I."

"I believe you," she said, "if not them."

That was all she said. Mammea assembled her baggage and the minimum of servants, along with her son, whom she put on a horse. We set off to join the main body of troops at dusk, and before the moon was high, found them encamped on the shore of the ancient lake south of the city. Fed by the Orontes, it was forty square miles long with farms to supply ample provender for the army on the last leg of the march.

We took some immediately. With Mammea and Alexianus, I shared an evening meal of duck shot on the wing, mounted on baked polenta layered with sweet cheese in a sour cherry sauce. My cook and the weather were the chief advantages of campaigning in Syria. I could see that Mammea, whom nothing impressed, treated the food as if it were acceptable.

Alexianus had matured since I saw him last. For a boy of eleven, he had an even temper unusual in most and unheard of in his family. Not as tall as Varius, he displayed a moderation of character reflected in the strong line of his chin. Although he had been trained by the priests of El-Gabal, the experience had not touched his life as it had his cousin's. That was due to the influence of his mother. Mammea was no priestess of Astarte and never seemed to have known the acquaintance of carnal love. Her speech was succinct and her questions clearly put.

"How goes my nephew, Emperor of All the Romans?"

"I wish I could answer directly, Princess, but I've little contact with him lately."

"We have heard strange things in Emesa," she said. "Rumors."

"Of what sort?"

"The disturbing sort," she said. "It's said Caesar does not attend his realm. They say the rituals of *ka'aba*, which are usually confined to the temple, are practiced openly by him."

"*Ka'aba*. I'm sorry."

"I'd explain them if I could. The word means *he-she*. If it means anything."

"He-she," I said. "Man and woman. That's basic, isn't it?"

"Man and woman, yes. But for the ritual, both reside in one body."

"At . . . the same time."

"We were told it was possible," said Alexianus with detachment. "The priests said the man who maintained that essence would rule the world."

"But your cousin already does," I said. "Rule the world."

"All worlds," said Alexianus. "We're not simply speaking of Rome, Parthia—"

"Then of what do we speak?"

Alexianus looked at his mother for permission, which was given. "The idea is combination. According to the priests, the man who masters *ka'aba* holds within him the past and future as it combines in the present. Only he can meld the essence into one. Only he can direct the flow of the sun into one vessel. One religion. One god."

"That would be El-Gabal."

"Yes." Alexianus was certain of that, but not of its sanity. That promised much for him.

"So if the emperor practices *ka'aba*, this would not be preference, but a religious act."

"Perhaps both," said Mammea.

Yes, both.

* * *

Finally, I understood no more of Syrian religion than I did the day I set foot in the province. What was most remarkable about it was the convenience. Any manner of behavior could be excused, and exalted, if the god was also exalted. All it required was belief.

I understood more of Syrian banking. Aurelius Eubulus, one of my military tribunes, had been detached to ride ahead to Antioch two days before. I was pleased when he caught up to our army and reported on his mission before I went to sleep late that night.

"Verus' funds are frozen," he said. "No payments will be made to him or his troops."

"Are you sure?"

"I had his monies transferred to the mint," he said.

"They agreed to release them so easily?"

"They agreed after I executed the head of the banking syndicate," he said. "His son was only too happy to comply. I believe he was also happy to be rid of his father, though he made it seem otherwise."

"You took the old man's head?"

"On the floor of his counting house," said Eubulus. "All the bankers on the Street of Mercury noticed, as it's staked to the altar at the crossroads. No one will send money to Verus."

Then the rebel was cut off from a source of legitimacy—his only one. I was sorry that Eubulus' mission had been accomplished violently, but I had told him what must be done and left it to him to do it. He was an Emesene of mixed Arab and Roman blood, a volatile combination, and a favorite of Soaemias for that reason. The desecration of an altar at a sensitive place like a crossroads was something I did not want to contemplate. It seemed what civil wars did best was violate comity.

In the morning, our legions began the march south down one of the longest valleys in the East. It was called Coele ("Hollow") Syria, for it seemed scooped from solid rock. To the west toward the sea stood the Lebanon Mountains, while in the east rose the Anti-Lebanon, broad-backed, equally rugged. Both were brushed by snow, and the plain that lay between was fertile and rich, ten miles wide and often wider, watered by the Litani River that emptied into the sea near Tyre one hundred and fifty miles downstream. We would be at the gates of the city in less than three days unless we were met in the field beforehand.

I had hopes of the latter. I detached most of our cavalry to ride for Damascus, then wheel around the mountains and halt near the town of Philippi. Although their route was longer, they would precede our arrival by a day and be in position to observe troops moving up the Hollow. If Verus took the bait, he might come into the field to meet us.

He would have scouts in every direction, and spies along the way, but I was confident he had none in Emesa that could be relied upon. It was unlikely that he would learn of the cavalry moving behind the mountains or know our numbers. The thing he would know first was that his funds were cut off. That would make him desperate for assistance from any direction. He might settle for any promise of help.

The day before at Apamea, I had sent a centurion disguised as an emissary to Verus at Tyre. He was to say he carried a message from II Parthica, which Verus had contacted ten days ago, asking them to join the rebellion. Their answer, given by their commander, Servius Frontinus, had been a quick "no." Frontinus had been the one who sent word to Nicomedia describing Verus' treachery.

But what if II Parthica had a new commander? What if they now wanted to join in the revolt? Then Verus' plan might see a resurrection.

That was the bait my centurion held out. II Parthica had shed its commander, who was now willing to join Verus but could not stand alone before the emperor's army. In the meantime, II Parthica had marched south through Syria, trying to stay ahead of the oncoming force that the emperor had sent to quell the rebellion.

The best deception is one that cannot be proven a lie. II Parthica did march down the Hollow, but under my command. We were now three legions with maximized cavalry and a cohort of Guards. If Verus could be lured from Tyre, he would meet superior numbers in the Hollow. The cavalry that appeared at his back would cut off his line of retreat to the city. He might fight his way through, since no cavalry could completely block a legion on foot, but they would harass every step and our horse-archers would inflict heavy damage in open country.

We camped that night near the city of Heliopolis, whose temple of the sun was as rich as its sister at Emesa. II Parthica, my straw dog, made camp on the southern end of the city. A portion of the other legions were housed in the enormous pre-cincts of the temple, while the remainder went into a smokeless camp on the outskirts of the city.

Verus might send an emissary to II Parthica in return, and I did not care if he sent scouts, too. The people south of Heliopolis could tell them nothing except they had seen troops moving into the city. If the scouts ventured north, they would not return. I was concerned about my centurion, but he knew his family would be cared for in the event of his death. Probably, Verus would hold him hostage until he was put up for trade.

That was the advantage in dealing with greed. A man like Verus was bold at the onset, like any gambler. I was sure he would continue to move at full speed. His revolt had to grow or die. I had to convince him he was correct in his assumptions.

One of the first things I did at Heliopolis was call for the temple artist to come to my tent. He was a Greek who had fashioned most of the statues, paintings and wax images in the sacred precincts of Ba'albek. It was fortunate that the god, once Syrian, had been Romanized. The central temple was dedicated to Jupiter, which meant that Dexippus had great experience in creating lifelike images.

"A head must be made quickly." I pointed to Frontinus, commander of II Parthica, who sat in a camp chair at the table. "That man's."

Dexippus seemed to have imagined every possibility except his presence in my tent. "How quickly, lord?"

"Tonight."

"Impossible."

"Let me put it this way. I will have a waxen head of Servius Frontinus expertly made in four hours. Or I will have yours from your shoulders."

Dexippus had not thought of his commission in those terms. His large brown eyes grew larger. His left hand flapped as if he thought with it, as he did. "Not a work of art, then."

"A work from life. All that's important is it looks good for the next few hours."

"The paint cannot dry that fast."

"The head will be staked high on a pole. If it is seen tonight, it will be seen in torch light. By morning, the paint should dry."

"The torches will aid the drying," said Dexippus. "But you must not place them too close to the head. Wax melts easily."

"Noted."

"I can't promise much," said Dexippus, as he took in his subject with a different eye, "but it will help that he's bald."

* * *

Three hours before dawn, four officers from III Gallica, accompanied by cavalry, arrived by the main road to meet with the staff of II Parthica. The two tribunes and two senior centurions reached our headquarters without seeing much of the city or the camp; but they did not fail to observe the head of Servius Frontinus mounted between the legion's standards.

I kept out of sight, inserting Aurelius Eubulus as my agent. He was unknown to Verus' staff and had the advantage of looking like a Parthian. All the Parthian Legions had retained their identity, having been created by Septimus Severus for campaigns in the East.

More negotiating was done than seemed likely. The meeting lasted two hours. The main point of contention was the location of the legions under my command. The officers of II Parthica guaranteed that their scouts had seen no more than two legions encamped at the lake of Emesa; after which they headed down the Hollow. The officers of III Gallica did not believe a march from Bithynia could be made so fast, or with minimal cavalry. They could not be convinced until two captured "enemy" scouts were produced, who verified the information under torture.

They were two of my best men, who had volunteered for the work. One, Dexion the Ethiopian, died under the hand of the Gaius Dardanius, whom I had first seen that magical night at my villa in Emesa. That made up my mind about one thing. I had never asked the emperor or his grandmother what was to be done with III Gallica after they were subdued. Now I knew.

Just before dawn, Verus' emissaries rode back to Tyre, convinced that II Parthica had committed to their cause, and that immediate assistance was necessary if the legion were to survive. II Parthica would continue its march south until met by Verus' army, or until they reached the city. Either way, victory could be ours.

Gaius Dardanius was left behind by his companions as a hostage and liaison. He knew what had happened to him when the trumpets sounded and troops poured from the grounds of the temple to assemble. He knew his fate when his sword and dagger were taken. But he did not know how badly he had been gulled until he saw me approach with Frontinus.

"Gaius Dardanius, you killed my best scout in a foul way."

The tribune did not focus on his greatest danger. His eyes shuttled from the wax effigy staked between the standards to the living model who stopped before him. In the growing dawn, the discrepancy between the two seemed obvious.

"You mean the black," he said.

"All bodies take on the same color after they hang from a cross for a time."

Dardanius focused on that image, which should never be his. He seemed to sink by one shoulder, resembling the man who with Comazon had carried the money chest from the praetoria to the parade ground at Raphanae on that morning less than a year ago. Slowly, he continued to sink to one knee.

"I appeal to you," he said.

"Your appeal is accepted on one condition. You will be questioned. You will answer with all the information you have on the disposition of Verus' troops, his intentions, and the current fortifications at Tyre. Do these things and you will know a quick death."

"An exchange," he said, pleading.

"You will not be exchanged."

* * *

We marched from Heliopolis down the eastern side of the Hollow as the Litani River drifted west and drew close to the foothills of the mountains. By noon, we had begun to move abreast of Mount Hermon, the biggest in the chain and its southern terminus. We were in contact with the cavalry that had ridden from Damascus to reach the terminus. They waited southeast of the Litani and west of the town of Caesarea.

I did not alter their orders. The information we had received from Dardanius indicated that it would take great persuasion to move his master from Tyre. Nothing less, he thought, than the keys to the kingdom. But that was what we offered in the gift of II Parthica.

I kept that legion in front, separated at a distance of three miles, but in close contact with the legions that followed. I would not have done it if there was a danger of ambush, but Verus could not enter the valley with a large body of troops without being seen by my cavalry scouts.

I still had no idea what he planned until mid-afternoon, when at five-minute intervals riders arrived from my cavalry—and from Verus. The first informed me that III Gallica had been seen marching north ten miles from Tyre. The second, a cavalry squadron led by an optio of Verus' auxiliaries, told II Parthica's officers much the same thing, while wanting to know the latest on the emperor's forces.

They learned nothing of that and everything about captivity. Without much convincing, the optio told us that Verus had committed his entire force, including the contingents of local militia he had been training for the last two months. Approximately three thousand men, they had few horse and fewer archers.

We continued our march south. II Parthica stayed in the van, but the legions in the rear marked double-time. As we approached the bend in the river, where the Litani turned sharply west, the mountains ceased and the valley floor became hilly. Directly ahead was a shield of rock broken only by the passage of the river, and beyond that the road to Tyre.

The day would be decided in the next few minutes, so I left the baggage train and our siege weapons and drove the legions hard through the pass. The trail was rocky with the river gaping on one side and a high cliff on the other. More than one man fell to his death in the water below. Many more fell to the ground exhausted.

We came down from the shield onto ground made for us. To the north lay the river. To the west was the floodplain that rimmed the watercourse. There, I placed II Parthica to make the welcome and the fighting front. To the south lay a range of hills, low and wooded. There, I set the two legions that had come all the way from Bithynia. They found enough cover to hide their movements and enough distance to allow them to close quickly.

I sent a rider to our cavalry with new orders as one of our scouts came up, driving his mount so hard that it collapsed as he reached the command post. Even before he got to his feet, pointing to the west, I saw the haze that rose from the plain as if from a fiery source.

Verus. His dust.

* * *

When Roman legions find themselves surrounded by a superior force, they draw up in a defensive square, presenting a solid wall of shields, solid rows of swords and spears, and moving parts several lines deep. The formation can be impenetrable and has often been. When Verus knew that he was trapped, he gave orders to form the square.

He had begun to suspect a ruse when his cavalry squadron did not return from their mission, but by then he was too far along to turn back on suspicion. He had to know, as all men who rolled dice had to see the eyes of the bones fall from their hand.

I held my three legions a hundred yards out and sent the cavalry, all Emesene archers, against the auxiliaries on the west side of Verus' square. Most of the native troops were untested and poorly armored, but even if they had been the first line, they would have suffered heavily by the attack. That was what I wanted III Gallica to see.

The Emesenes rode at full speed on the open plain, attacking in full numbers. They were able to wheel and skid-turn, maintaining their fire without losing their mounts. They were able to back off quickly, simulating flight, then fire while riding away. They could attack in tiers, the rear ranks firing in parabolas, raining arrows down on the heads of the auxiliaries, while the front ranks fired low as they held the manes of their horses, taking the auxiliaries down at their legs. They were able to fire continuously with their quick-release bows. And they were resupplied continuously from the baggage train I had brought through the pass.

In twenty minutes, half the auxiliaries fell. More took to the river, flailing in the water. The ones who stood and fought did so from the shelter of their comrades' bodies. They became aware as never before that arrows do not blow men's bones apart or sever limbs or carry heads from shoulders but kill by slowly drawing the life's blood from a body through deep cuts. They began to be aware of how long that took. And they knew there was no end to it.

Three legions awaited them if they attempted to break out, but Verus made no move forward. He was a gambler and subject to the curse of gamblers when they think luck has deserted them. I had seen that reaction the morning he tried to keep IV Scythica from entering the walls of Raphanae. He committed himself, but always kept something in his pocket.

It was my task to see he died rich. I called off the archers before Verus' auxiliaries were completely destroyed. They were no longer a fighting force but a screaming mass of men humping the ground, cowering beneath their shields.

When they knew our arrows no longer sought their flesh, they still did not stand but for one man gone mad. Rising from the dead, he ran toward our lines. He stopped halfway very suddenly, dropped to his knees, and picked up a mound of dung that had been dropped by one of the horses. He shredded it with his hands and stuffed rank steaming shit into his mouth as if it were the means of his salvation. We watched, all of us, until at the command, one of the horse-archers dismounted and put him down.

Still Verus did not move from his square. He refused to send against us the little cavalry he had. He put his archers to the fore, causing some casualties among our horse, but not seriously affecting their barrages. Perhaps he meant to keep his horse and archers back to hinder us in his retreat. It would be dark in less than two hours.

I could not allow him the chance. Verus' inaction had given us time to work the siege weapons through the pass. I set them up conspicuously on the hill two hundred yards to the south. I brought up the heavy cavalry and put them before Verus' front. They were heavier than Rome had ever known, horse and rider mailed from head to foot, each man carrying a ten-foot lance that was fastened to the front and rear of his massive Parthian mount. Used like that—like a razor-sharp ram—the lance would be driven three men deep in a charge.

Last, I brought up Mammea and her son. I put them on the back of the wagon that carried their baggage from Emesa. Mammea wore a white stola, Alexianus a toga rimmed with purple bands. Standing on the wagon draped in golden cloth, they looked like a dynasty restored. I parted the ranks before them, revealing the representatives of the emperor to both armies.

The cheers came slowly, but they carried strong, rolling along the front in a wave of sound, rising and gathering force until our whole army shouted their praise.

The cheering did not stop with them. It passed like an echo to the ranks of Verus' men, who lifted up the same words in nearly the same voice. For those men, the sound of acclamation was now the sound of hope.

I sent forth heralds and trumpets, telling the men of III Gallica that their lives would be spared on surrender, but saying nothing of their leaders.

COMMUNIQUÉ

To Marcellus Decimus, also known as Tyricus
From your servant Comazon

I received your letter detailing the destruction of Verus' legion and the new order that has arisen in the East. I was convinced you had lost the use of your limbs in battle, accounting for the lack of information we had; but the latest product of your mind reassures. All the court is in awe of your exploits, which must rank among the first in history. Alexander the Great spent months in siege before the city of Tyre, which you conquered in a day. Lucullus broke the bodies of his men and all his mind thrashing about the East. Only Pompey (also known as the Great) could claim a more complete victory, if not as quick.

Know I am also in receipt of my cohort of Guards, including Thrax, who arrived on two mules lashed together. They delivered Mammea and her son, young Alexianus, at the same time, none the worse for their journey.

All on the surface may be said to be well, but I think you will want to know that not every noble personage was happy to see the arrival of these two family members. Soaemias, for one, beheld in the young boy what no one else had the power to see: a rival. She was heard to curse the name of her sister, and the name of her mother, and last, your own.

My friend, how could you leave so little impression on a woman that she seems to want your blood rather than your attentions? Such a gentle thing she is, too.

It's hard to believe she and Mammea share the same mother. I believe the reason for Soaemias' fury was the courtesy Mammea extended to you. She spoke so highly of your conduct in the campaign that Soaemias could only wonder what had passed between you two. Mammea especially praised your leniency toward the rank and file of III Gallica. I concur. Disbanding the legion instead of slaughtering it showed foresight.

I should tell you that my opinion is not shared by all. Grumbling was heard when the news arrived, chiefly from those who know nothing of the world outside this court. It was said you had set loose upon the land five thousand men whose only training is warfare. I spoke on your behalf, explaining to these fools that the men of III Gallica lost everything when their legion was disbanded, including their pensions and the only work for which they were suited. The best will end their days as gladiators in the arena, the worst as beggars on the road; but our legions will have a living example of the fate that awaits every rebel against this Caesar. Perchance we will have no more revolts to divert our attention from the business of the empire.

We have already had another of which you should be aware. Small in compass but not insignificant, it's the reason for this hurried letter. I know you will welcome the news that Gannys is no longer with us. He passed to the bosom of his ancestors two days ago after a knife was inserted into the back of his neck, severing his powerful brain from the spine that was never used for any purpose. The murder was accomplished at night as he sat at a desk in his office in the palace. It was done in silence, so he did not emit a cry, or alarm the watch, or do anything but soil with his blood the decree upon which he labored.

That document would have named him regent with full powers to function in the emperor's name. It lacked only a signature—the emperor's—and the countersignature, his grandmother's. The irony is that if it had gone into effect, Gannys would have been entitled to a century of Praetorian Guards for his protection. As it happened, none were about that night except the sentry in the south corridor. He saw nothing.

I examined the scene, but found not the slightest evidence to point to the killer. Gannys' private office, as you know, lay on the second floor of the palace, accessible by only one door from the corridor. The windows, which were open when I entered the room, vent directly onto the garden. The wall could only have been scaled by a nimble man with special skills—a professional gymnast or the like. He would also in my opinion have to be a professional assassin to do the job as it was neatly done. Unless a man can be found to answer these descriptions, I believe the murder could only have been committed by someone with access to all the palace apartments.

That gathers under suspicion the palace staff, as well as the permanent residents. I had Gannys' eunuchs thoroughly questioned, and his slaves tortured, but to no avail. I also offered a reward for information, which produced the same result. None of my Guard own to having anything to do with the deed or having heard anything about it. That circumstance obtained even after I had the sentry on duty executed as an example to the others.

If the truth be told, never was murder greeted with such unanimous approval in so many quarters. Intense mourning was decreed by the Mother Augusta, but no one could mistake the joy that reigned throughout the palace. And perhaps among the denizens of the underworld, too, as they took one of their own into the fold. Gannys had been one of theirs, I suspect, since the day his balls were dedicated to the dogs of the streets.

The emperor in all this held himself aloof. He observed mourning, ordering sacrifices to El-Gabal for his fallen servant, but true inner peace cannot be disguised. The attempts Gannys made to restrain Caesar's behavior were not appreciated. The increasing power Gannys assumed did not go unnoticed. What further steps might have been taken by him to consolidate his power will never be known, but if the document found on his desk is an indication, his grasping nature had not yet found its natural end. Or found one that only death could satisfy.

Thus ends the tale of murder with mystery. Everyone who knew the man had motive(s) for killing him. Nearly everyone in the palace had opportunity. I wish the man who had once been Urban Prefect of Lugdunum was among us to practice his skill, and apply his unmatched knowledge of the human heart, but even he might be daunted, since those with the most reason to kill Gannys are beyond the reach of law. I'm afraid we find ourselves faced with a crime where not even a signed confession of guilt would bring a resolution in justice.

I'm sorry you have been detained in Syria, but the decision to remove the title of *metropolis* was not taken lightly. Removing the seat of government to Sidon must have caused you inconvenience as well as a dislocation of time. Ensuring the loyalty of such inflamed legions would try the patience of Augustus. Of all the great men you resemble, to that man, or god, you are no kin.

But do not lose heart. I hear you will be made Prefect of the City when we finally locate our persons in the capital of this empire. Another possibility sees you as joint Consul next year, sharing the title with the emperor. Perhaps you will be awarded a triumph. Imagine gliding through the streets of Rome in a gilded chariot, a golden crown held above your head, while a dim-witted fellow whispers in your ear that all fame is fleeting.

In the meantime, you must settle for my words. I hope to see you before we set out for Rome. We are preparing apace and should be ready to proceed by the end of next week. I can only say I shall be glad to leave Nicomedia behind. This place is a crossroads, a bridge between East and West, but its Lares, and all the things it names as spirits, are grim. Nothing good has happened here. Whatever awaits us in Rome must be for the better.

Until then—

ROME

219–222

THE PALATINE

By the vagaries of Fortune, I did not arrive at Rome until the fall of the year 219. My departure was delayed by continuing problems with the military and civil affairs of Syria, and by a fever I contracted while at Tyre, a most unhealthy place. It's no mystery why the Phoenicians left that fetid island to cross the Middle Sea and found a better city on the north shore of Africa called Carthage.

The strength of Rome lies in her seven hills. They hug the River Tiber, allowing little space for flatlands. Each hill is defensible against enemies that come upriver, or from any direction overland. Each hill is a step toward the heavens, lifting its people from the vapors spreading disease in the valleys below.

The greatest of these hills is the Palatine. It hovers like a cloud in marble, red-roofed and glowing, above all of the city that matters. The sweep of the eastern flank that faces the river is a congregation of vaults, arches and columns, shining white in the sun and glowing like crystal in moonlight.

The patrician families who ruled the city built their homes on the Palatine, sending their orders to the Senate, their sons to the forum, their daughters to their neighbor's sons, and their slaves to market; but that was during the Republic, before Julius Caesar reached for the crown and Augustus took it. In a gradual displacement of power, the Emperors of Rome claimed the Palatine as their own. The grand purview of the patricians in almost every way was gone.

The only thing the old families of Rome hoarded like the waxen heads of their ancestors were the names descended from the days when Romulus and Remus were suckled by a she-wolf. Some traced their lineage to the founding twins, while others named the beast as their ancestor. Among the latter were the clan of the Julii. One of their number, Julia Cornelia Paula, had been chosen as the bride of Marcus Aurelius Antoninus, the most eligible bachelor in Rome.

I wondered if the women of the family asked Varius' opinion of his bride. Their first order of business, once the imperial party arrived in the city, was to consult the patrician directory, then the astrologers, for the proper alignment of blood and time. When it was decided which virgin would best serve the needs of the dynasty (the Julii had never failed to produce a male heir in six hundred years), the answer took on all the flaws of the inevitable.

"Is she comely?"

"I never thought of that," said Caesar. "But I'll be better able to tell once she shaves."

"Her face?"

"Everywhere, I hope. Roman women are nothing like Bithynians. They're uncivilized. They have hair all over their arms and legs—to say nothing of their money-makers."

The emperor took my arm, leading me like a goat, as we walked the quiet grounds of the hippodrome. The place was not a stadium, as its name implied, but a carefully tended garden where the flora of the empire had been gathered in trophy. The trees of Egypt, Britannia and Germany, the bushes of Spain, Bithynia, and Gaul, were all represented within the walls enclosed by twin stories of arches and colonnades. The twin fountains at each end of the rectangle splashed like the pulse of an old but virile man.

"She's thrilled of course," said the emperor, or Varius, as he seemed this day. "She could have been let out to some old lecher with a wooden prick."

"I'm sure she's happy and anxious to please."

Varius smiled in his old way. "Would she die, do you think, if I asked it?"

"Doubtless. Of course she's doing that in a way. Many women do not survive childbirth. And that seems the purpose of this exercise."

"I'm glad to be informed," he said. "I thought it had no aim but to discommode the Emperor of All the Romans. That's not a good idea, do you think? Especially when we have Alexianus tucked safely in the closet."

"You should let him out to play, my lord."

"He doesn't know how," said the emperor. "That boy is so serious I can't bear to have him at my table. We do release him for festivals. We *force* him to enjoy himself, but we're not always successful. If he casts a pall at my wedding games, I'll have him beaten. They will be glorious, glorious games."

"Yes, my lord. Fifty tigers are waiting to be sacrificed."

"Nero did fifty," he said. "I require fifty-one."

"I can see to it."

"These will be the grandest games that Rome has ever known," he said, sweeping his arms around his tame wilderness. "You'll make certain of that, Marcellus."

"If my lord wishes."

"I want you to take over the preparations from Eubulus. He's a moron."

"Yes, my lord."

"Yes, you will? Or yes, he is?"

"To both, yes."

"But he's mother's moron, is that what you're saying?"

"I'm saying it's difficult to tell whose moron wants replacing."

The emperor laughed like a man trying to hold up the folds of his toga, although he was not dressed as a Roman. He still affected the garments of the East, the chiton and silk trousers and linen shoes. He never dressed any other way in the city, and no one seemed to mind. It was part of the honeymoon every new ruler enjoyed with his people. But I thought it was good he had stopped painting his face.

"That's excellent, Marcellus. Your sense of humor is what I've always loved about you."

"Was I being funny?"

He looked at me as if he wondered. "I know what you're saying. I pay too little mind to the administration of this empire. But that condition will not last. When I've done the things I must, I'll turn my attention to the governor of Pannonia Inferior more than he'd like."

"These are the things of the god you must do first."

"They are many. You've seen the Elagaballium on the north spur of the hill?"

"The temple? I saw its foundation."

"It will be the finest in Rome!" he said with enthusiasm. "In all the *world*! I'm building another—a companion—on Caelian Hill. It's to be part of a complex dedicated to the god. The palace will have gardens everywhere, and baths, and a theater, and a race course as large as the Circus Maximus."

I wondered if Caesar realized what he said. The Circus Maximus in the valley between the Palatine and the Aventine was the largest structure in Rome, exhausting a fifth of the total space in the area fronting the river.

"My lord, perhaps you should make it ten feet shorter."

"You think my plan presumptuous."

"I think Caelian Hill is not as convenient as it might be to the people. It's they you must please, Caesar."

"Then ten feet shorter it is."

"A wise decision."

"Grandmother will be glad to hear of my wisdom. It will mean a few hundred thousand sesterces less for construction, and she counts the coins these days. We have a bargain, you see. She allows me my toys, I allow her to collect her heads."

"For the time being."

"Now you understand," he said, squeezing my arm. "And you must understand I have a purpose. You know because you were there when that man spoke the truth of god in the praetoria of Septimus Severus."

I wondered when we would rid ourselves of the specter of the Blue Man in far Caledonia. It seemed impossible. The more time passed, the more his prophecy resonated.

"Yes, my lord. I recall very well."

"It's my work to unite the religions of the East and West," he said. "That *will* be done. The governor of Pannonia Inferior is not privy to my thoughts, nor would he understand them. But you do, Marcellus."

"I understand when you're serious, my lord."

"Then you know more than most. They think I'm crazy."

* * *

Everyone thought the emperor was not quite sixteen, and they wanted to join him in a celebration of youth and beauty. His bride, as young as him, did not conform to the sad creature he described, but was a lovely specimen of the Roman upper class. Julia Cornelia Paula seemed dazzled by the honor done her, and willing to do whatever her husband wanted.

And that seemed to be everything. Although the wedding games could not be given in the Coliseum that had been so destroyed by the wrath of Vulcan, every other venue in Rome took its place. The forum was decked with banks of flowers, the vast palace complex draped in banners and bunting, and a titanic statue of Marcus Aurelius Antoninus, rendered in gold, crowned the imperial box in the Circus Maximus.

In the greatest of all stadia, where more than four hundred thousand people could be entertained, the emperor formed his bond with the people. He had his fifty-one tigers, his thirty-three elephants, and so many leopards (including two whites), panthers, ostriches, bull, bear, antelope, rhinoceros, and hippopotamus that the mind failed at the count. The only thing stinted on were the gladiatorial contests. Human blood still offended the emperor's sensibilities, as if men, the cheapest of animals, were less worthy to die in his honor.

The flaw was hardly noticed except by members of the Senate. Banquerius, the most famous hunter of his time, slew thirteen tigers armed with only a spear. Helix, our greatest athlete, won the wrestling and the pancratium, a feat never before accomplished. The chariot races for which the Circus Maximus was famous were the most exciting in memory, as Gordius added to his laurels, becoming by his seven victories the greatest charioteer of all time.

Team Green dominated, taking from the Red, Blue and White nearly every race that was offered, which was as many as twenty-five a day. When on the last day the emperor appeared in the imperial box clad not in a toga, or the sensuous materials of his god, but in the colors of the Green, wearing the boots, tight trousers and banded tunic of a charioteer, garments that only a young man or athlete could wear, the cheers of nearly a half million of his subjects rose high. With inspiration that must have come from his god, the emperor left his box and leaped onto the track. Taking the reins of a full *quadriga*, he lashed the team of four matched stallions twice around the race course.

It was an image come down from Olympus. Every man in the circus thought as they watched him lay on, his blond hair streaming in the draft of his team's headlong charge, that the emperor would take his bride to her wedding chamber; that like those hard-charging steeds at the fore, he would go willingly to stud and give them this night an heir to the throne.

* * *

"They slept in the same room is all I can tell you," said Comazon. "It wasn't noisy, so we can't call it rape."

"I would have found even that encouraging."

"You're a barbarian. No wonder Soaemias turned you out."

"We need results, Prefect. If he can't manage, snuff the candles and call a substitute."

"You should be careful of your tongue," said Comazon, as a slave in a yellow tunic passed us in the hall outside the *lararium*. "We have three factions reporting to their masters—the emperor, the mother of the emperor, and the grandmother of the emperor. Now that Mammea has come to stay, we'll have a fourth."

"That must complicate your life."

"It will complicate yours, too. The Mother Augusta is the de facto regent. Follow her orders in every administrative matter and you'll be clear. But all religious matters are dealt with by the emperor, and Soaemias as she speaks in his name. Follow their direction and you'll be clear. The problem arises when the lines of jurisdiction, so to speak, overlap."

"What happens then?"

"I close my eyes and hope my head's attached to my body when the dust settles."

"I see where problems might arise. You have to be dexterous."

Comazon smiled. "You, too, friend. They've made you Chancellor of the Italian Departments because they can't think what else to do with a competent man. They may be hoping you stumble so they can send you out to the East again."

"And if I don't stumble?"

"You'll be urban prefect next year. But if you do too well, they'll make you Lord High Cup-Bearer to the god. That could ruin a man's career. I tell you I yearn for the days of Gannys. He kept the hatreds simple."

"Were you able to learn more about who killed him?"

"Nothing at all," he said.

I was interested in hearing how Comazon spoke those words, which was rather quickly. The man who had executed the guard on duty in the corridor that night—the only person in a position to know more—could have learned the real circumstances surrounding Gannys' death. He should have, even if it told him to look in another place.

"Well, the empire doesn't seem to notice that he's gone to find the rest of him. Nor does the emperor."

"Yes, he's been remarkably well-behaved," said Comazon. "Let's hope it continues."

* * *

And it did as I settled into the job of administering the Italian Departments, which had greatly expanded when citizenship was granted throughout the empire. Assisted by a cohort of freedmen and slaves, I shuttled from my office in the Severan addition of the palace on the south side of the Palatine to my apartments in the Domus Tiberiana. Built by Tiberius Caesar, it was a series of courtyards, living space and baths that dominated its portion of the hill. The view from my windows, overlooking the fora and the streets that led to the Tiber, was grand. It was the rampart of power, where I had always imagined myself.

To aid my dream, I enlisted Philomene, who set about buying and training slaves to serve my household. I trusted her for that and all my needs. Nor was I disappointed. If something could be done, she did it well. If something could be known, she knew it first.

"What do you hear of the young couple?"

"Has someone been married?"

"I thought you would have noticed."

She liked to tease, especially with her tongue, but those things were always subtle and well designed. Nothing about her was unobservant. Only the things she decided not to notice occasionally rankled.

"I observed a ceremony performed in the Roman fashion," she said with malice, "after two strangers had been joined in the Roman fashion."

"You prefer a love match."

"Doesn't everyone?"

"It's unnecessary. The empress comes from the best stock."

"So in your mind Roman women are like cows. Perhaps I agree, though it's not my place to do so."

"So critical. You really have taken this to heart."

"Was ever a marriage so important?"

Perhaps not. Philomene sat up in the plush bed she had bought in one of the catastrophically expensive shops in the Horrea Agrippiana. She crossed her sleek legs and settled her arms on her knees as if sitting around a hearth fire in her village along the River Nile; as if there was no difference in the life that she had led and the one she had been sold into.

"I wonder," she said quietly. "Why do Romans ignore the things that matter? Why leave a marriage to chance? That girl should have been chosen for her beauty and trained from birth to give pleasure to a man. Then there would be no problem."

"And you think there is. A problem."

"I can't say. The women responsible for the emperor's bed clothes claim to have found evidence of some activity."

"Blood?"

"On the first night, yes."

"Semen?"

"That is more uncertain."

But it was good news. I was glad I had sent Philomene ahead from Bithynia to set up the apartments and give her time to put her lines into the palace in a quiet way. Slaves had the best information about their masters. They were wary of talking to outsiders, but less to one of their own, even if she had been recently manumitted. Everyone, it seemed, talked to this one.

"What else do you hear?"

"On that score?"

"On any."

"It is known that the emperor sometimes stays in his room through the night."

That, too, was good news, though I didn't like the way she said it. She seemed to want to draw my attention to what was true—and different—part of the time.

"Are you telling me, in your less-than-obvious way, that the emperor has the habit of *not* spending the night in his room."

"That's what I heard."

"Where does he spend the time when he should be sleeping?"

"In low places," she said.

"What do you mean? Any place below the Palatine is low."

"Let's say on the Viminal, and sometimes in the Subura."

At night. In the worst places in the city. I was surprised I had not heard of this before, or that no one else seemed aware of it. "That's too much of a surprise. I think your sources must be defective—or malicious."

"Possibly," she said. "But these sources are close to the emperor. They say he goes out at night dressed in a dark wig and the garments of the most common of his subjects. He goes to places he could never go in the light of day."

"What places?"

"Taverns. Brothels."

"Brothels of what sort?"

"Where there are women."

"Praise the gods."

Philomene did not seem to share my relief. She spoke analytically. "But his behavior in these places is peculiar. He does not generally engage the prostitutes for their bodies."

"Then there would seem to be no point."

Philomene laid down her words like a mason with bricks. "The emperor, it is said, talks to the women."

"He *talks*? To prostitutes?"

"To many, yes. It seems he questions them about their techniques. All the things they do to please their clients."

"That is peculiar."

"I thought so," she said, "and for some time. Until I found out he once paid a visit to Numantia. This woman is often called the Queen of the Subura. You may know her. She numbers among her clients some of the richest men in the empire, including the senators Pomponius Bassus and Dio Cassius."

"She must be very expensive."

"No doubt. But I was lucky to discover she frequents the Temple of Isis, the goddess of Egypt who's the patron of the prostitutes in this city. At the temple, I heard from Numantia's lips that the emperor had given her a hundred thousand sesterces for an evening of her time. It seemed he wanted to talk. And he wanted demonstrations."

"Demonstrations in what?"

"Techniques, again," she said. "All the things that in her vast experience she has learned. All the thing that relate to pleasing a man."

"A man?"

I did not know I had spoken aloud. I heard Philomene rise from the bed, slipping from the sheets. "Perhaps it is innocent," she said. "And all our worries are for nothing."

* * *

But I had it in mind the next day when I was summoned to Princess Soaemias. I did not know what to expect from that quarter. Since my return, she had not put out signals to indicate that my presence was necessary to her. Rather, she made it seem as if I were another in a list of lovers best left to pine.

She knew my needs were met by others. The needs she had should be filled by the trappings of power around her. Always, she was attended by a retinue that dwarfed her son's and mother's. She never held forth to less than a public audience—in this case, the basilica adjoining the throne room—the most gorgeous area in the palace.

Eighteen columns of yellow Numidian marble led like pillars of the sun to an apse where she sat in an ivory-plated chair. The walls behind were sheathed in polished marble that reflected every image. Eight Praetorian Guards stood at the entrance, a dozen servants, as many freedmen, and ten priests draped in silken garments and waiting. For what? I did not know how to speak to such an audience.

"We wanted to thank you for making the wedding games of my son so perfect," she said. "All Rome shares our happiness."

"Perhaps Rome will be happier at this time next year. I wonder how the cries of children will sound within these walls."

"We shall live to see it," she said. "This dynasty will be the last Rome ever knows."

"The gods willing."

"The gods have nothing to do with it," she said, her tone instantly colder. "The gods in their many names are antiquated. Roman religion is as dry as a bone and more brittle. It makes contracts with its gods—bargains where goods and services are exchanged—yet never do we hear the mention of salvation. All over this city are monuments to its irrelevance called temples. I would have them shut down if it were necessary."

I was aware of the concerted attention of the priests. None looked at Soaemias. It seemed change was in the air and these men were its agents. What nonsense they had poured into her ear I did not know, but it was the kind she wished to hear. Salvation. Transcendence. Ecstasy in the god.

"The princess is wise to ignore things that are irrelevant. But closing temples that have existed since the founding of Rome is bound to provoke anger among the people."

"The temples will stand," she said imperiously, "but as pillars to support the one true god. They have no existence except to serve El-Gabal. The people will come to understand that."

I wondered why I was surprised to hear her speak like this when she had always spoken like this. What was different was that each word held the force of absolute power. Clearly, she had assumed it like a cloak, and believed it her duty to wear it.

"I understand."

"Then I command you thus," she said. "Go at once to the residence of the Pontifex Maximus. Have him tender to you the records and accouterments of his office."

I could not speak for being stunned. The Pontifex Maximus was the supreme religious authority in Rome. Of all the offices of state, his was the most ancient. Even his name, which meant Great Bridge Builder, was sacred. Without his authority, Rome could never have extended its reach across the Tiber.

"Is the princess saying she means to dissolve the office of the Pontifex Maximus?"

"Let the name, like the temples, stand," she said. "And like them, let it be an empty shell. The high priest of this empire is the high priest of El-Gabal. In time, the Pontifex Maximus will be no more than a memory of the past."

"Does the princess speak for the emperor in this?"

"I speak for the god," she said. "And my son, who is his chief servant."

* * *

Where the Palatine overlooked the forum at its closest point, a break marked the cliff. Below lay the Temple of Vesta, a domed structure symbolizing the never-ending power of Rome and the never-ending cycles of nature. The holiest place in Rome, it was the hearth of the empire where an eternal flame was kept by the virgins who served the goddess.

The virgins, who were always six, and always chaste, had their quarters in the House of the Vestals on the Sacred Way behind the temple. There, they kept the wills of the important people of Rome, along with secret books pertaining to all aspects of religion descended from the beginnings of the city. These books were guarded by the only man permitted to live within the walls of the Atrium Vestae—the Pontifex Maximus.

The man who held that office was Domitius Curtius. I had met him when he served as Legate to Upper Germany and I Prefect of Lugdunum. He was a good governor and a throwback to upright times. Destined for an office that would measure his worth, Caracalla gave him the job of reconstructing the Atrium Vestae, work that had begun under Septimus Severus after a consuming fire. When two years later the regnant Pontifex Maximus died, Curtius assumed his office, making his home the building he brought back to life. He installed new Vestals, working to restore dignity to the one institution that in the centuries of its existence, in spite of scandals, always had it in plenty.

Was he happy here, ruling women? The vapors in the lowland were unhealthy, the noise great at all hours of the day and night, and the responsibility, too; but the House of the Vestals was the most centrally located in the city, the Pontifex Maximus was the most respected figure outside the court, and the new Atrium Vestae was the finest version of a building that had always been one of the best in Rome.

My summons at the bronze door was answered by a female slave, who gave way to a female freedman, who gave way to a Vestal. She was too old to be an apprentice and too young to be senior. An active virgin, she was one of two servants of the goddess who performed the ceremonial tasks that called for grace. She was beautiful, her delicate face with a flaring nose framed by the mantle at her shoulders and the banded headdress worn by all Vestals. The *infula* swept from her forehead like a diadem of fresh snow. It could have spoken of devotion or chastity, but not many other things.

"Marcellus Decimus, from the Emperor Marcus Aurelius Antoninus. I am here for the Pontifex Maximus."

She bowed from the waist. "I am Aquila Severa, servant of the goddess. Will my lord follow me?"

I trailed her steps at a distance, daunted by such archaic modesty in a woman. We passed through a vaulted atrium that gave way to a long rectangle lofted in three floors gathered round in a courtyard of surpassing peace and beauty.

"If you will wait here," she said in a voice that repeated light and shadow from the sky.

"I can think of no better place."

She meant to smile, but could not impeach her vows so wantonly. Gathering the folds of her white stola, she moved to the stairs at the end of the courtyard and climbed to the upper floor.

And left me to wonder at the richness of her cloistered life. Although I saw no graven images of the goddess, whose essence could never be captured, statues of past Vestals, rendered in white marble, graced the verges of three stately ponds. Water circulated quietly, below the threshold of hearing but not without touching every sense. Servants, all women dressed in white, passed to and fro, carrying ewers of liquids that must be blessed by the Vestals if this city and this empire were to prosper.

Superstition? The gods and goddesses of Rome never promised salvation. The sum of their worth was the way they cleared a path to the future for anyone who could grasp it.

Curtius understood that if he understood nothing else. He was a tall man whose dark hair was shot with white, which he kept by force of will. He carried a toga bordered in scarlet on his body and in his arms, hoisting it as he trundled down the stairs from the apartments on the second floor. The toga was not the only burden of his office. He could have dressed like a man of the city, but chose to assume his bundle of discomfort as another link to the past.

"Marcellus Decimus. Welcome."

"Thank you, Curtius, but I can't return your greeting in kind. This is a visit of state."

"You come from the palace."

"Directly," I said. "Reluctantly."

"It's that bad?"

Nothing I could say would soften my orders. "The new emperor has definite ideas about the direction religion should take. Even the oldest."

"Direction?" he asked. "The roots of Rome are in this place. They are immutable."

"I'm afraid the palace thinks you're nearly correct. Your office is seen as an impediment to change."

The Pontifex Maximus blinked as if standing in the sun when nothing but broken rays of light penetrated the lower courtyard. The trees and bushes that stood by the ponds required endless attention to bring them to leaf and blossom. He looked at one, a lotus tree with long strands of hair in various colors hung from the branches. That was the hair of the six Vestal Virgins, which was shorn when they entered the service of the goddess.

"Remarkable," he said. "And the emperor is of what age?"

"That is irrelevant. Others of greater years are committed to his course."

"You speak of the mother."

"For one."

"I met her the night of the wedding banquet," he said. "Never have I had such a terrible premonition. When she smiled, I felt bitten. That woman is a fanatic. She will have the Orontes flow into the Tiber. Every good thing this city stands for will be washed away."

"Let's hope you're wrong."

He shifted his head by grave increments. His hand went to his eyes as if to cover them, but instead capped his fleshy nose. "Well, what's the verdict?" he said, sweeping his hand away and slapping it against his side. "*Damno?*"

"You're guilty of nothing, Curtius. I'm charged with the duty of receiving the insignia of your office, and the records kept by you."

"Not the books," he said. "Not the Pontifical Books."

"Those most of all."

"The wills?"

"*In toto.*"

"So they will have in their hands the means to destroy every important family in Rome."

"They have that already."

"Of course," he said. "But now they will know exactly how to go about it."

"There's been little of that, Curtius. For a civil war, casualties were light. As the emperor grows to the fullness of his age, I'm confident the toll will cease. He's not bloody-minded."

"He's not old enough to know what he is," said Curtius. "Insanity lives in that family like a curse declared. I served Severus, knowing he was a ruthless man, but strong. The rest have the blood of Syria. Antoninus was a monster who grew more monstrous every year. Can anyone believe his son—or cousin— will be different?"

"We can pray."

"I should tell you what to do with that prayer, but you are my guest." Curtius squared his shoulders. "I *refuse* to deliver the things I am charged with my life to protect."

"Then they will be taken."

"Not while I guard them," he said. "You may have the life of this Pontifex Maximus. I ask only that I am permitted to say good-bye to my wife."

"Of course."

He took a moment more than necessary to look away from me—to turn and walk under the colonnades toward the stairway— but he wanted me to know there were Romans who would resist power. It was a gesture, only that, but all that was left of honor.

The office of the Pontifex Maximus was a lifetime appointment. Domitius Curtius could not be relieved of his duty except by death. He had told me he would meet it as a Roman until suddenly, as he reached the top of the stairway, he told me when that would happen.

He halted at the corridor that led to the upper apartments. Although the stop was full, I sensed it was more. A beginning. I knew what he would do the moment he began to move again, but there was nothing I could do to stop him. Nor would I. In two steps he reached the marble bench that rested in the corridor against the gap in the colonnades. Curtius was at a run when he stepped onto the bench and vaulted.

The drop from the second floor was not great. A man landing on his feet would have suffered little. But the Pontifex Maximus dove to his death. He went headlong over the low railing, and by some tremendous act of will kept his head down, the tangled folds of his toga flown up over his arms and shoulders.

He struck the base of one of the statues of the Vestals with his skull. There was no sound except the noise of his bowels as they released. His arms, thrown outward as he fell, seemed to hug the statue. His blood began to flow into the holy waters.

THE SIGN OF TANIT

I expected a foul reaction to the death of the Pontifex Maximus. Soaemias was not displeased at the result, but the Mother Augusta was angry. The Pontifex Maximus was in her eyes a political figure who should have been dealt with as a political problem. The princess had exceeded her authority in her orders, and I displayed poor judgment in following them.

The Mother Augusta's verdict was unfortunate for my career, which, I was given to understand, would be lucky to stagnate. She was influenced in her thinking by the riot that ensued on the following day, as news of the suicide of the empire's religious leader spread throughout the city. Although the disturbance in the forum was quelled by the Praetorian Guard, the power structure had been shaken by the first sign of public disapproval of the new regime.

An official inquiry into the cause of the riot was held, chaired by the emperor. Throughout the proceedings, Varius conducted himself with dignity. He questioned the witnesses, which consisted of the slave who admitted me, the Vestal Aquila Severa, and myself. The woman who had issued the order—his mother—did not attend. Thus the inquiry came to the result for which it was intended—none. A new Pontifex Maximus was appointed. No further raids were made upon the insignia of his office, or the wills stored in the Atrium Vestae.

The same could not be said for the Pontifical Books. Those ancient documents, which were written in an archaic Latin few understood, had been spirited away to the palace. At the time, I was unaware of the theft because of the confusion surrounding Curtius' death. Not until winter had passed, and spring began to show in the trees, did I learn the truth. That happened when I received a summons to attend the emperor. He awaited me in the imperial library.

I was lucky to find him alone, an uncommon condition. The emperor was usually surrounded by priests, not only the minions of his god, but all the religious leaders who arrived at his summons and stayed at his will. Even the galli of the Great Mother, whose ranks we once thinned, came to pay obeisance. They were some of the most frequent visitors, since the Temple of Cybele stood within the imperial compound not far from my apartments. Clearly, Varius had decided to gather the wisdom of the ages to his side, though in narrow sense.

The library was vast, with thousands of scrolls kept in cupboards that rose in three tiers to the ceiling. I found the emperor seated at a long table engaged in the arcane study of the mystic sciences—the cope of the night sky laid out on a spangled chart of the stars. The heavenly bodies and their paths were not compounded on a scroll, but etched into a sheet of copper.

He looked up at me with eyes that were at times his mother's—changeable to earth-tones, tending toward the purple it was his destiny to wear. He seemed startled by my presence.

"Have you calculated our course into the future, my lord?"

"Yes, but the data is contradictory. This man Sarpedon, the Chaldean adept. I've come to doubt the usefulness of his methods."

"Your grandfather Severus placed great faith in the movement of the stars."

Varius looked up from the chart. "I'm glad you brought up his name," he said, shifting aside a mound of scrolls. "Grandfather was a perceptive man. He never discounted the power of the gods or the men who were their servants. Tell me, when we were at Nicomedia, did you visit the shrine he erected to Hannibal at Libyssa? The great warrior died there, you know."

"My lord, I was too often absent from Bithynia."

"And lucky for us," he said. "Had I not been so bored by the place, I might have neglected to visit that monument myself. But I did one day. I was moved by the sight of the altar of Hannibal. He was the greatest general who ever went against Rome. A Carthaginian. African like grandfather. And adaptable in the extreme. He fought more often than not with mercenary troops. He worshiped the gods of Phoenicia transplanted to Africa. They were the same gods under different names. What

would have happened, do you think, if he had finally and con-
clusively defeated us?"

"We would be speaking Punic, my lord."

He smiled. "It was close for us, you know. Only the timely
intervention of the Great Mother saved our way of life."

"The legions may have had something to do with it."

"The legions had been beaten for fifteen years by Hannibal,"
he said. "Defeat after defeat. Only when the Great Mother's stone
was brought to Rome from Asia did the tide turn."

I did not disagree with the legend the emperor embraced.
His chosen role was to believe that invisible forces ruled our world.

"No one knew what to do," he said. "Hannibal had beaten
us over the length and breadth of Italy. Beaten us on our soil!
The Senate in desperation consulted the Sibylline Books. Poetry,
mind you. These prophecies told them Cybele's stone must be
brought to Rome and worshiped as one of the deities of our city.
That day marked the turning point. And that, more or less, is
the sort of work I've been doing in this time of crisis."

"Crisis, my lord?"

"Religious crisis," he said, as if that was clear. "A most serious one. This empire yearns for salvation. Cults proliferate every
day. Mithras, Bacchus, Isis, the Great Mother, the Christ. This
confusion demands to be made into a coherent whole. And I
have tried. Do you know every day I have the Senate and all the
Equestrian Order gathered at the Elagaballium? The priests and
dancers assist me in sacrifices. Every ritual of the god is carried
out to perfection. Yet there is no issue. They laugh behind my
back. Look at that deranged boy, they say, prancing before the
altar. Look at the massive slaughter of cattle and sheep. Look at
the *waste*!"

That was exactly what they said, but it did not stop them
from lining up in the exact ranks that were awarded them. That
did not stop harsh words from flying if one man edged ahead of
another in the order of precedence. The monumental sacrifices
to El-Gabal were the scorn of every fashionable table in Rome,
but the sacrifices were fashionable nonetheless.

"I'm puzzled, my lord. What do you expect from shallow people? Or from yourself?"

"You saw," he said. "You saw what I could do. At your villa. At Raphanae."

I searched for the proper word, but found only one. "The miracles."

"If only I could perform them now. What joy I would bring to the world!"

"But I thought when the stone was brought from Emesa, your powers were restored."

"That did not happen," he said. "Taking the stone from its home did *nothing*!"

Having drawn closer, I saw his eyes were bloodshot, and the lashes crusted with a pale substance, as if they had not known the sun that was his god in days. How long had he been shut up in this library? How happy was his fractious court to have him here?

"I see the problem. My lord studies these documents to find a way to regain the power."

"The Pontifical Books," he said, turning his hand to the mass of scrolls on the table. "The Sibylline Books. Do you know what it's like having to know everything? By day I must learn the names of the Chaldean demons, of whom there are seventy-three! By night I pour over the manuscripts of Stoics to see what sense may be discovered in them. This is to say nothing of the temple incubation of Isis, or the rituals of the Great Mother, all of which I must *know*!"

He had gotten to his feet, his hands strummed the air, and his eyes were like a bird of night. Suddenly, he swept the desk clear, strewing the scrolls to the floor. They were all old. Ancient. And obscure even to their makers.

"My lord, who tells you that you *must* do these things? Who may order Caesar to ruin himself in study?"

"*Ruin*?" he said, peeping over the word at me. "This is an act of *creation*."

"What are you creating?"

"Order," he said.

"From religious studies."

He nodded.

"When you know, and as you once told me, that the basis of religion is irrational."

"Yes, yes," he said impatiently. "But in all of it is a thread. A thread that in its end never varies. Each piece of rant—" He cast his arm at the scrolls. "Each monument to incoherence has its private method of coming at the truth, but in everyone there is an equation. All deal with opposites."

To emphasize his point, he reached to the table. With vehemence, he flung the chart of the heavens across the room. The thin sheet of copper took sail and gathered purpose, teetering through the air until it struck the thick shaft of a candle with its base on the floor. There, it stuck briefly, until it slid with a faint clash, like cymbals, onto the tile.

"The stone of Emesa embodies the power of the sun," he said. "Now tell me, what is its opposite?"

"The power of the moon."

"Day," he said.

"Night."

"Male."

"Female."

"Logical, eh?"

"Quite."

"And if I were to say there's another stone of great power?" he said. "An opposite. A stone of the moon. Of the feminine gender. This stone is descended of the very same Syrian ba'als. Legend says it was carried by the ancient Phoenicians across the Middle Sea to its home in Africa—to the city of Carthage—where it was worshiped above all other gods. Even when our legions with the assistance of the Great Mother defeated the city and sowed its lands with salt, the stone in the form of a statue was preserved. Even now it resides in the Temple of Juno-Caelestis. Or if you prefer her Phoenician name—Astarte. Or her Punic name—Tanit."

"I believe I understand. My lord means to combine the gods of Carthage and Rome. In effect, East and West."

"Exactly."

Exactly as the Blue Man had predicted as he stood on the threshold of death in the praetoria of Septimus Severus, the emperor from Africa.

"I will marry these gods, Marcellus. They will be one. The power of the heavens will be combined in me, in this city, and this empire, forever."

* * *

"He wishes you to retrieve the rock?"

"Yes, Mother."

Maesa sighed like an aggrieved tree in the wind. She enveloped the chair where she sat, so nothing of it was visible. She seemed merged in a sitting position between two green marble columns, as if someone with no regard for the laws of nature had hung her there. On her left stood young Alexianus, dressed in a short tunic. He might have been exercising with the Guard, or come from the gymnasium, but he was often found at his grandmother's side.

"I suppose he has his reasons," she said.

"He means to marry the sun and moon, Mother. Nor will he be dissuaded from trying."

"It would be better if he applied the same effort to his wife," she said. "It's five months with no sign of an heir. I'm beginning to think the sun and moon—as distant as they are—have more chance to succeed in marriage."

"These things can take time, Mother."

"They take a man," she said. "That's all."

"Perhaps the empress—"

"There's nothing wrong with her except that her hips are a bit narrow," said the Mother Augusta. "But they are within tolerance. I measured them myself. No, it is my grandson who lacks the proper equipment. All that dancing before the altar weakens his loins."

"The dance is important to the god," said Alexianus. "Within its rhythms he is reached."

"The emperor is all-important to his empire," said the Mother Augusta. "Remember that. Forget the rest."

Alexianus nodded as if he would be glad to.

"Now for the Carthaginian matter," she said. "You must present this in a way that honors them. Tell them their goddess will be the goddess not of a city, but an empire. Say Severus, an African himself, wanted it. Tell them any lies you wish, but do not upset their rituals. Above all, do not allow their high priest to jump from a high place onto his head."

"The emperor wishes me to leave at once."

"Do that," she said. "Perhaps the advent of this stone woman will stimulate him to observe all his duties."

* * *

I set sail from Ostia two days later in a trireme with twenty-seven men of the Alban Legion who had accompanied me from the East. They were picked troops I had trained in civilian maneuvers like quelling disturbances in the streets and preventing looting—things the legions disdained. They did not ask why they should embark on a voyage when winter was a keen memory, or why they were necessary on a peaceful embassy to a city that had been a model Roman colony since Great Augustus raised it from the ashes two hundred years ago.

I neglected to say that our mission might not be peaceful. While the Emperor of Rome could command anything of his subjects, ordering the surrender of the chief cult object of a city fell beyond the normal bounds. My mission could easily place me between the emperor, who demanded the statue of Tanit, and his grandmother, who demanded calm.

We had anything but that when we entered upon the seas, which were boisterous. Heavy winds and rain were our companions as we angled down the coast of Italy. I cursed myself for not taking the overland route by the Via Domitiana to Rhegium at the toe of the boot, but in that I bowed to superstition. The family of Domitius Curtius had built that road.

We passed Rhegium, then crawled along the coast of Sicily until one morning we were blown bare pole into a storm. We were lucky to put in three days later at the old Carthaginian city of Motya, where we waited out the gales before making the last leg of our voyage across open water to the African Coast.

There I learned about the nature of the goddess whose statue I was sent to confiscate. We spent several days in the city making sure the ship was seaworthy, so I had time to explore. Beyond the southern limit of the city was an ancient necropolis. The oldest tombs were Phoenician, going back nearly a thousand years. The later ones were Carthaginian.

"You see how big they are and how rich they were," said my guide, a gladiator from my squad named Frugius. A native of Sicily, he had fought his way to the peak of his profession over the bodies of many men. If he had learned to keep his hands off precious things, Frugius could have conquered Rome as the Carthaginians never had.

"It's all here in these graves, lord. Carthage controlled the west of the island and the Greeks the east. They fought over this place for hundreds of years. Until we won."

By "we" he meant Rome, though Frugius was barely Roman. His hooked nose and hair was Carthaginian, his lips Greek, but his awesome frame, especially his shoulders, spoke of barbarian forms. Not many years from bondage, his blood mixed the nations of the slaves who had worked this island for centuries.

"Have the tombs all been looted?"

"Most," he said. "The Carthaginian more so. They buried their dead with jewels and coins. The only ones the looters didn't touch are the urns with the Sign of Tanit."

"The Sign of Tanit?"

"Over here, lord. Look."

I could not account for my feelings as Frugius led me deeper into the necropolis. We moved past towering monuments with bilingual inscriptions, weatherworn statues that spoke of the hard men who were the models, and family crypts the size of small houses.

We stopped before a group of stelai that rose like swords near an earthen mound. Mingled with them were square urns of ancient origin. If the hair did not stand on my neck, it was because the light rain off the water kept it close. My unease increased when Frugius stopped before one of the steles and an uncovered urn that seemed to make a pair.

"The Sign of Tanit is a stick figure of a woman," he said. "It's what's inside the urns that will send you to the vomitorium as fast as your legs can move."

"Not jewels or coins."

"Children," he said in a voice as soft as the rain. "Usually three or four years old, but they could be five or six. None of them died naturally."

I knew what he was going to say, so I said it for him. "The children were sacrificed."

"And not just anything thrown into the pot," he said. "They were the children of the rich. Sometimes they'd buy a good specimen from a poor family, but usually they put up their own. They couldn't offer the lame, the halt or the blind either. The children had to be well formed and in good health. Tanit wanted nothing less. The sacrifice must be worthy."

If that made sense, I could not imagine it. "For what purpose was the sacrifice done?"

"Who knows? It might be a plague, or famine, or our legions at their walls. That's when they called on the goddess and slew their children."

"How were they killed?"

Frugius looked at me as he could not decide if I were obtuse, or a connoisseur. "Sometimes they were thrown down from high places. Sometimes their throats were slit at the altar, and sometimes, as bad as it seems, they were put into the flames alive. No matter how the ancients made sacrifice, that's the end in those urns." He pointed again with his blunt finger. "Little bones. Ashes."

* * *

We landed at Carthage near the mouth of the River Bagradas without incident. The city sat on a peninsula like a delta, backed against the Lake of Tunis and joined by a strip of land to the mainland on the south. In its grid-like streets and buildings, Carthage resembled every Roman city. Baths, gardens, theaters, amphitheater, circus—all conformed in the familiar way.

But the *Byrsa*—the Oxhide—was the ancient citadel of Carthage that Queen Dido, its founder, laid out. When she arrived from Phoenicia, the local king told her she could have as much land as she could cover with the hide of an ox. So she cut one into thin strips, tied them together and ringed the hill. Thus was the city founded on a woman's cunning. The richest empire of the time grew up around the Byrsa. The focal point of the city, it was converted after the destruction of Carthage into a master-piece of Roman engineering—a gigantic terrace of concrete and massive arched vaults rising two hundred feet above the lower city.

The new Byrsa gave the citizens of Carthage a sense of what had been but could only continue under our aegis. This was not the seat of an enemy who had fought Rome for centuries. Its people were as mixed in blood as Frugius. The colonists sent out long ago from Italy intermarried with local stock as their gods intermarried. The Temple of Jupiter dominated the forum. The Temple of Juno-Caelestis stood on its right hand.

I saw both from the quarters of the Proconsul on the second floor of his palace. Atius Cimber was an African of Roman blood with a rapacious nose, a rudder jaw, and keen blue eyes that spanned the difference. He owed his rise to the Severan dynasty. The Proconsul had served Macrinus, too, which meant he was a politician of some skill.

"So you've come all the way from Rome to pay your respects to our goddess. She'll be delighted."

"I hope so."

"You must stay a while," said Cimber with a smile that seemed practiced but odd. "Apply yourself to the rituals of the temple. It takes the best part of a week, but the Oracle of Juno-Caelestis is guaranteed to a heartbeat."

"Juno-Caelestis. You mean Tanit."

"Local usage," he said. "It's not the name, but the heart of the supplicant that matters."

"And here I thought it was blood."

Cimber spoke quickly. "Not under Rome. I know of what you speak, but those were ancient rituals. Discarded. Under Severus, the gods of Africa climbed into the light. We expect that under his heir they will be ascendant."

"I'm sure you're right, Proconsul. But my stay in your city must of necessity be brief."

"You'll come to the banquet," he said. "You must. I'm planning on tomorrow night. All the city will honor you. We seldom have visitors direct from the emperor's court."

"I'll be back on my ship tomorrow night. The emperor's orders leave no room for delay. And as much as I hate to impose, I'd like to speak to the high priest of the temple soon."

Cimber was disappointed at the loss of a social occasion, and even more in the chance to discover the real purpose of my visit. His response was unguarded and friendly to a fault.

"Make that the high priestess," he said. "And good luck with her. I never had any."

"Hard to approach?"

"That depends on how you make the approach," he said seriously. "The last man who tried it was forced to put his hand into a hole in a wall and wait for a nest of deadly snakes to make him their meal. I had to approve the sentence. Laying hands on the Boudon of the temple is punishable by any torment."

"I'll be sure to keep my hands in the light."

"And if you need anything—"

* * *

I would be sure to call. I went to sleep that night knowing Maesa's calm would prevail until I delivered the emperor's orders to the high priestess of Tanit's temple. I knew that Cimber could not be counted on for anything good. The man who would voice a threat, however casual, against Caesar's representative, was more secure in his position than he had any right to be. Or more afraid.

Of what? The high priestess? The Boudon? A strange name. A strange place, draped in the trappings of Roman power, yet hiding, like a rampart, the wild continent that lay beyond.

I fell asleep on land for the first time in weeks thinking of the Boudon, and the rituals of her goddess that were said to be discarded. I wondered what had replaced them. Apparently, it was something that caused the chief Roman official of Africa Province to shy from the smallest offense to her dignity.

* * *

In the morning I set out upon the Byrsa dressed in the banded toga of a plenipotentiary. I did not renew my respects to the proconsul, who sent word that I would be received by the high priestess. I ordered my troops to filter by twos and threes across the forum and stand by at the entrances to the Temple of Juno-Caelestis. I detached four of the boldest—all ex-gladiators—to bracket the chambers of the high priestess, which lay adjacent to the sanctuary.

Two eunuchs seven feet tall, as black as the African night and as mute, guarded her door, one with a sword and the other a mace. Seeing my archaic garb and my escort, they waited as I announced myself before they stepped aside. One immediately left to fetch his mistress.

I passed through her atrium, entered a small but more elaborate chamber, and sat in the chair I thought was hers. I had seen nothing like this claustrophobic yet infinite room since campaigning with Septimus Severus. The domed ceiling was covered with a replica of the heavens on the clearest night of the year with no star omitted. The rugs repeated the motifs of the sun and moon, the tapestries bore the signs of the houses of the zodiac, and the symbols of the infinite reposed as statuettes, candleholders, cups and bowls. This was the abode of a woman obsessed, or an office that must carry out obsession as its charge.

She did not look like that. Of middle age, her skin as dark as brier and her eyes as bright as obsidian, the high priestess seemed utterly controlled and open to unannounced visitors. Her smile was slow but incandescent. Her robes were ornate and brightly colored, tightly bound to display a body of which I had never seen a better. She hesitated when she saw me in her chair, but only to show she had noticed. Like a queen of the night, she came closer, and putting out her hand, took mine. At once, I felt the heat.

"I bid you welcome. My name is Virgilia, Boudon of the Temple of Juno-Caelestis."

I still held her hand. On her wrist was a tattooed stick figure of a woman—the Sign of Tanit. "Marcellus Decimus. Special ambassador from the Court of Marcus Aurelius Antoninus. Please, sit."

She smiled at my impertinence and took the chair opposite, as if to say that she knew I outranked her on this day; but the way she filled it made me think the condition would not last. She drew down her heavily-lidded eyes sensuously, as befit a priestess of fertility. All her features showed beneath the sheer taut cloth, even the smallest variation in the shape of her nipples and the delta between her legs.

"May I offer you something?"

"Your cooperation," I said. "I don't expect this interview to please you or your temple, but it will go easier if you choose the most peaceful way."

"You come with soldiers."

"I have what I need." I withdrew from my toga the scroll I had carried from Rome. "You recognize the seal of the emperor."

"Of course."

I handed her the scroll, which she opened. As she read, the Boudon did not reveal her feelings. In time, she put the scroll aside on the table between us. She studied her hands, the nails of which were painted blue, and her tattoo, also blue, before speaking.

"The emperor wishes to possess our goddess."

"He will possess it, Boudon."

"Yet it seems possession is not enough. He demands the gold of our temple."

I had not known about that order, of which I should have been informed; but it would be awkward to admit ignorance. "I'm afraid that's true."

"For what purpose, do you think?"

Since she seemed more curious than hostile, I gave the truth as I understood it. "The emperor, as you know, is the high priest of El-Gabal. His knowledge of the hidden world leads him to believe that a combination of god and goddess is necessary. His first concern, always, is the spiritual well-being of his people."

She nodded, closing her painted eyelids. "A *hieros-gamos*. A marriage of gods. The gold of this temple is her dowry."

"That's the idea, yes. I'm glad you see the necessity."

She seemed to accept it, or take it to a place where it could be consumed. She leaned forward, exposing her breasts to the verge of those nipples until it seemed they would spill into my hands. I felt my hands stir in spite of the effort to still them.

"I did not say I agree to the necessity, Ambassador. Or the wisdom. But for days I have been expecting a manifestation of some sort."

"Is the Boudon prescient?"

"Perhaps," she said. "I know one thing about the gods that few understand."

"Which is—"

"They have no power to shape our events," she said. "Men— and our Great Mother the Earth—do that. The only thing the gods do is lend us their eyes from time to time."

"To see forward."

"Yes."

Her answer was short, but left more things unsaid. Like all people who had power within their sphere, the Boudon hoarded hers. She wanted me to come within it.

"The emperor is an adept at the mystic arts. Perhaps he'll keep you apprised."

The Boudon smiled. "I would like to tell him what I know."

"You wish me to carry a message to the emperor?"

"Yes," she said. "I want you to tell him that his idea will succeed."

"I'll relay your words. I'm sure he'll be happy to hear them from a colleague."

"Would you like to hear the rest?"

"If you wish to share it."

"His idea will succeed," she said. "But he will not. A forced marriage of the gods can never come to any good. What he proposes is akin to rape. The goddess has no wish to leave her home. She has no wish to be forced to share the bed of another god, no matter his origins. The man who thinks he will tame her is the man who will go deeper into violence than any other. He will abide in blood. And he will die a violent death."

This woman had a gift for rhetoric. Her voice was deep and her words charged with the cadences of the march like all good Latin. "Boudon, I have no wish to impugn your prophecy, but many emperors of Rome have died violently. The event is regrettably common."

"This will be different." Her voice shuddered like an echo in stone. "It's the quality of things that matter. Every man knows he will die. But the man who places his arm into a dark hole knowing he will but not when or how, that man suffers in a few seconds more than anyone can say."

"Is that what you wish me to convey to the Emperor of All the Romans?"

"No. That is for you, Marcellus Decimus."

* * *

I confined the Boudon, her guards, priests and priestesses, to the sanctuary while the rape of her temple advanced. The hatred in her veil-of-night eyes was palpable, but she did not make the protest that proved her impotence. The will of Caesar cannot be resisted, least of all by his servants. Gold of whatever value may be replaced. Not so, perhaps, for the most venerated cult object of temple, but even the sacred seemed fungible in the end.

The stone was large enough to be a mate for the heavenly body of El-Gabal. Where the latter rose to a point, like a phallus, Tanit's stone was concave, like a womb. Cleft from a bed of golden marble, the goddess of Carthage provided a fine contrast to the darkness of the Emesene god. Though not a statue in the usual sense, it was easy to see by the twin mounds of her breasts and hips that the stone meant to be a woman. It was easy to see everything but hard to imagine a conjunction. At three hundred and fifty pounds, the lady outweighed her spouse. This marriage wanted more than a ceremony. It demanded engineers.

I had brought none. Frugius, the strongest of my gladiators, lifted the stone, but could not carry it more than a step. Not wanting to exhaust the day transporting the lady, I sent for an ox cart while we fetched the gold of the temple to the ramp at the sanctuary in the rear.

The goods we confiscated were plentiful, for the temple was richly adorned. I had the loot—the dowry—cataloged to prevent pilferage. My freedman Bato set to work with his tablet, tallying the candelabra, amulets, receptacles and the many statuettes. We were well along with the count when Frugius and Adranos called us to the storage rooms below.

The lowest level of the temple was poorly lit. Though fifteen feet below the surface, it stood above the raised ground of the Byrsa. The three rooms at the end of the long planked passage held items used infrequently for ceremonial purposes. Not all were of value, but the exception was so striking that it made up the difference.

Standing on two pedestals of porphyry, more brazen than the sun, were two bull calves rendered in solid gold. They were twins, nearly as big as life, created by the hand of a master. I did not know their worth, or any way to determine it, so I had the approximate weight, which was the value in bulk, written down.

"What do you think, Frugius?"

"One hundred and fifty," he said, holding the statue in his arms fondly. Stealing something like it had made him a gladiator. "No more than one hundred and sixty by any reckoning."

"We'll accept the word of a master. One hundred and fifty-five."

I nodded to the freedman clerk, Bato, who made the note on his tablet. I watched him inscribe the amount when the long dark shape dropped from above. It fell on Bato's shoulder, hitting heavily, and when he drew back in panic, dropping his tablet, the snake struck his arm.

The strike came so fast I had no time to react. It was a large, dark, hooded snake, and deadly. An asp.

Bato screamed and jumped back, he jumped again, and each time he seemed not to touch the ground. I searched the folds of my toga for a weapon, thinking that sandals were the worst things to wear, when Frugius spilled the golden calf to the floor and unleashed his sword. With a flailing stroke, he severed the snake in two as it lunged toward me.

I watched the halves of its body writhe, listened to the screams of a man who thought he was dying, and understood that we were under attack. The Boudon would not allow her temple to be pillaged without taking revenge. Somehow, she had fed that thing down here.

"There'll be more," I said. "Take the calves. Follow me at two paces."

I pushed Bato ahead toward the passage. I should have looked up. Before we reached the passage, another snake dropped, falling to the left of Bato and rearing into its stance immediately. I swung my sword and cleaved its head cleanly, throwing that dark hooded thing with the open mouth and incredibly keen eyes against the wall, where it lodged on a wooden shelf, looking back as if it could not believe it had failed in its work.

I wished I had the Boudon. I would use her as bait to make our way through the passage to the surface. We needed a shield. All we had was a bitten man who could not be treated.

"Move!" I said to Bato, who had stopped as if choosing a place to die. It was a bad thing to excite his blood by walking, but if we got out quickly, he could receive attention.

Feeling the effects of the venom, Bato turned and lurched into the passage. I followed him closely, the sword held so tight that my hand began to cramp. I saw now that the snakes had dropped through the holes of the ventilation screens in the ceiling. They had no intelligence, or purpose, but it seemed as if they must. More. It seemed they were directed by a single mind.

They were a weapon. I imagined that vengeful bitch loosing the asps and willing them to the kill. How many did she keep? Was there enough light to see by in the long passage ahead?

Barely. There were two more, but visible. The first asp landed in front of Bato, falling to the planks with a splat of flesh, like something dead but unkillable. The second fell between us, grappling down from the ventilator as if in pieces. I lashed my sword at him twice, but with bad light and no clearance for the blade, I missed twice.

What saved me was his defensiveness. The asp scuttled into a ball, coiling against the side of the passage, rearing and making a profile. With more instinct than sense, I lunged with the tip of the sword, aiming for his widest part, which was the broad fan that had swelled in his neck below his head.

I caught him low but well, penetrating his hood. His fangs struck for the only thing he could reach—the sword blade. When they hit, and hit again, I pinned him to the ground and crushed his head under my sandals.

And looked ahead. I saw a scene chiseled into a stern medium, like a tableau. Bato had stopped with a motionless that was complete. The asp was not more than three feet from him, coiled, his hood extended, head swaying in a dance. I had seen sights like this in the streets of Antioch, when the piper called his snake to perform for the crowd. I wondered why the asps never struck at the music, or the musician, until the man put down his instrument and challenged them with darting movements of his hand. They were not pets, he told me. The asp was an aggressive snake.

It would strike anything, and being a meat eater would attack and eat its own.

I did not think that Bato could survive another strike. I reached down, and in spite of every instinct, took the dead asp by the tail. Swinging it for leverage, I flung the corpse at his mate.

He struck as the four-foot length of meat came at him. Quickly. Very quickly. With no curiosity but the kill. Just as quickly, he reared back into his upright pose, hissing, spreading his hood to its full span.

I swung my sword backhanded, certain that I would take another head, but as the blade came forward, the asp struck again. I felt him hit me. I felt the fangs fan my toga. He drew back so fast that I could not move for surprise, but I was thinking his fangs might not penetrate the thick folds of the wool, and for the first time in my life I was grateful to those Romans who had devised such an inconvenient garment as a toga. I swung my sword backhanded again.

And caught him. The blade did not sever his long length, but took him most of the way to his end. He was caught on the side of my sword, his neck held by the flesh below his hood.

Like that, I smashed him against the wall. He still hissed. He could not strike again, but he tried. I smashed him again and again, hearing the hiss until it seemed he carried that sound all the way to the place he was going.

* * *

By the time we made our way back to the upper level of the temple, the cart had arrived. While the temple physician tended to Bato, we loaded the goddess into the back of the cart. Although it strained the backs of the men, I made sure she was treated with the respect befitting her role as the consort of El-Gabal. To keep prying eyes away, I draped her in a swatch of sacking. The objects of gold we loaded next, also hidden by sacking.

Word of our raid would spread among the people of Carthage, but I hoped we were clear for a quick exit. If we could pass to the ship in safety, the rest was in the hands of Fortune and the gods of the Middle Sea.

The first indication that things would not go well came when we opened the gate at the bottom of the ramp. A crowd of thirty people stood outside the apron of the ramp. One look spoke their mood. They were sullen and angry, but not yet demonstrative.

Something like this was the reason I had come in daylight. The sun made it easier to see us, but my concern was how well I saw what was coming. A theft like this could not be hidden, nor was there any way to keep word from spreading through the city. The functionaries of the temple would see to it no matter how well they were guarded. And it was clear they had.

"Bring that bitch to me!"

Frugius and Adranos went off eagerly. They saw mayhem in the streets, which was as good as the sand of the arena. I wondered if the Boudon would arrive intact.

I sent another man with a message to the Proconsul, saying that on my order he was to convene the City Assembly. To that body he would deliver the news that their goddess had been honored above all deities as the mate of El-Gabal. The elevation of the Province of Africa, begun by their native son Severus, would find its conclusion in a marriage of equal gods.

My man had already crossed the forum to the Proconsul's palace when the Boudon appeared with Frugius and Adranos. Her look said she would have killed me if she were a snake.

"Into the cart."

She did not move.

"Cut off one of her fingers and put her in the cart."

She stepped onto the seat beside me before Frugius drew his dagger. I took her hand but did not release it. I held those lovely fingers until my thumb touched her Sign of Tanit.

"A wise decision, Boudon. Now listen. You'll stand as we pass through the city. Your arms will be crossed over your chest, as if praying to the goddess. Your face will wear a look of contentment. Not a smile. But of happiness surpassing words."

"That will convince no one," she said.

"Your concern should be to convince me." I motioned for Frugius to sit on the other side next to the Boudon. "Or this man will kill you."

She said nothing, but when we set out down the ramp and rumbled through the gate, the wagon bed so low to the ground that it scraped cobblestones, the Boudon of Juno-Caelestis stood in the cart and played to the people of Carthage. She lay her beautiful hands across her extraordinary breasts. Her look of bliss lacked sincerity, but that would not matter at a distance.

The guard that preceded the cart, and flanked it, and the double guard bringing up the rear, guaranteed that no one would come within twenty feet without risking harm. I hoped our numbers sufficed for crowd control. Angry civilians were exactly that. No matter how angry they became, going against armed soldiers brought second thoughts. My main concern was of missiles thrown our way. Having the Boudon with us in plain view was protection.

That worked well for the first half mile. We cleared the Byrsa and descended the broad road leading north to the port. The crowd at the gate followed us silently, but as we passed the flower market an entire tavern turned out to join the throng. Worse, in the same block, I saw one of the black eunuchs from the temple. No coincidence. He lingered at the edge of the crowd, which now numbered a hundred, leading an enormous mastiff by a spiked collar.

The crowd grew rowdy, louder, talking among themselves and lifting scattered voices in challenge. That made it a mob. At the same time, we came to the old part of the city, where the Roman grid gave way to narrower, more crowded streets. Here the smells were grosser and the people poorer, buildings with rotting plaster overhung the street, and the cobblestones were loose upon the ground. We were a quarter mile from the dock, but it seemed like a long way.

Only the gods can hurry oxen, but we tried. I had sent a man ahead to tell the captain of the ship to be ready to take us aboard and quickly load our booty, but I was not optimistic about the mood of the mob. It had darkened as fast as it had grown. At

every tavern and gymnasium, every school and factory, and at the crossroads of every street, it added numbers. Every portion of it grew bolder, edging closer to our guard, venting their emotions with calls and jeers and spittle. When the first rocks flew through the air, striking one of our men in the back of his helmet and clashing against the shield of another, time had run out. The mob understood where we were headed, and that made for a destination.

I gave orders for the men in front to wheel back along the sides to support the line. The rear I told to stand and hold, meeting whatever came with passive force. That gave pause to the mob. It hesitated, reeling back and opening a path on the street. Several men pulled up paving stones, and several more were urged on by the eunuch with his dog. Belatedly, I saw the second tall black eunuch, also with a mastiff. If the mob concerted a charge, our line could be breached and our journey go for nothing.

Then at the top of the hill to the rear I saw the litter moving toward us carried by two slaves in saffron tunics. That was Bato lying upon it. I had asked the physician to send him on after he had done his best. I wanted no one left behind to experience the wrath of the temple, the Senate, or the mob.

I did that as an afterthought, but it now seemed like the thing that could move us home within the Mother Augusta's mandate. I sent another man at a run for the ship with instructions for the captain. I had the guard advance into the mob, shields locked, to clear a path for the litter.

* * *

In ten minutes, the dock was in sight. The crowd grew bolder against our line when they realized we did not respond with lethal force. Young men hurled themselves against our shields as if they had found a game with limits they could test. Some had weapons—pieces of timber and daggers and swords—which they used to effect. My men began to fray, their tempers mounting at the pressure and the blood—their own—that had already been spilled.

Matters grew worse when the eunuchs unleashed the mastiffs. Those huge dogs, trained to attack, ran under the shields to take meat in their mouths. They ripped the legs of several of my men until I gave orders to cut them down. We got one before the other fled. That pleased my men, but enraged the mob as nothing else had. They began to push hard, buckling our line in three different places. The air filled with pottery, roofing tiles and stones.

We were lucky the ship had berthed at the military slip set along the river, where forty men of the Third Augustan Legion were billeted. I had not wanted to turn them out and loose real bloodshed, but when the crowd charged in a mass as we turned down the hill to the river, I saw no choice. My men were trained in riot control. The legions were not. They were trained to advance and kill.

I gave the order for the detachment to block access to the dock and cordon a passage for us. Their swords were out and the ranks went forward, shields raised against the missiles from the crowd, as they advanced in a *testudo*. The shields made up the shell of the turtle, but no denizen of the sea came on with a three-foot sword aimed at his enemy's vitals.

The mob backed off, screaming, trampling their fellows in retreat. I heard the second great dog cry for his life as he ended it fighting from broken legs. I saw two men go down without moving, bleeding where they lay, but the legion did not give chase to continue the rout.

When the mob realized the charge of the soldiers had stopped, the barrage of stones and every putrid leaving on the gutter came thicker and faster. I was hit in the chest by stones and a stake, for which my toga proved little defense. The Boudon had been hit and bled from a wound on her forehead. The sight only added to the rage of the mob.

We passed through the cordon, the oxcart first, the flanking guards following, and last, the rear guard with the litter. It was the man sick with snakebite I wanted the mob to see. Bato was dying. His breathing was shallow and his face so white it seemed to settle on bone. His sweat came in sheets. His mouth spewed a yellow substance that had not one thing whole in it.

When I was sure Bato had passed beyond the sight of every man in the mob (and there were women, too, many women), I gave the signal to the captain of our vessel. At once, Dolabella ran up the black flag.

The riot diminished, not in every part and not at long range, but the barrage of missiles gradually slackened. The citizens of Carthage quieted to a roar, then to a mouse. We were already on board the ship, and the goods were being loaded by the crew, when the silence of those hundreds of people fell like night upon the day.

The mob realized when they saw the black flag, and when they remembered that feverish man on the physician's litter, that what they were chasing, and what they wanted so badly to destroy, and what they clambered so furiously to board, was a plague ship.

VESTAL

The Stone of Tanit was cursed from this day forward.

The curse could not be lifted by any devices of man.

Suffer the wrath of the goddess.

The Boudon told me those things when I put her ashore on an abandoned island off the coast of Sardinia, where we had been forced by contrary winds and an unusually strong current that drew us toward the Pillars of Hercules.

I might not have left her there if Bato had survived, but he died on the first day of our voyage in great agony. The Boudon might survive exile with the help of her goddess, though she did not seem confident of it. I took her warning as a reflection of her anger when I might have been better advised to heed it.

We were plagued by mishap for the rest of the voyage. Nearly every piece of equipment on the vessel broke, from the mast that snapped like dried meat in a squall of wind, to the rudder that split from what seemed like tension on defective stock, to the oars that were destroyed along one side when we struck a shoal of rock off Campania.

When we finally put in at Portus, we had been absent five weeks on a voyage that could have been made in a fortnight. I was anxious to relieve the vessel of her cargo before she sank at the jetty, and I may have been guilty of hurrying the slaves at their work.

While they were winching the goddess from the ship to the dock with a crane, the cable snapped. The stone, cradled like a four-hundred-pound infant in its net, broke loose and breached to starboard. Smashing the ship's railing, it took away part of the hull and killed a galley slave before toppling into water as if into sleep.

The harbor master came instantly to the jetty, or as fast as he could move from his office overlooking the inner harbor. He had seen the grotesque size of the goddess borne aloft and sent a runner telling us we should wait until a bigger crane was brought up. When he appeared in the flesh, he was angry. After noting the location where the goddess went down, he turned to me with an old mariner's eye—the unluckiest of all things.

"I've got a half dozen divers, but I don't know how they'll be able to get that stone up. The water's so dirty they won't be able to see a thing, and they'll have a wretched time getting a rope under it even if they do."

"When they do."

"You're in a hurry."

"The emperor's in a hurry. If the goddess is not brought up immediately, you may receive a visit from Caesar himself."

He put his hardest eye on me again, and this time I saw that he had sight in only the left one. Yes, it was a grim visage. Yes, that's what Marcellus Decimus must look like to the rest of the world.

"A damned rock," he said.

"A goddess."

"Well, that makes all the difference."

"Believe it and you'll prosper."

"I hope you know you can't order this like a cheese," he said. "Not with darkness coming on. I can promise you some of my men will die if they go down there now."

"They'll die if they don't."

* * *

None did, though a Cyrenian slave came close. The goddess finally saw the moon, her symbol, when it was three-quarters full several hours after dark. A net had been laid on the bottom with strong hooks attached, so she could be brought along the bottom and raised to the surface. Several striations had been gouged into her buttocks by the hooks, however, and her time with Neptune had darkened her golden color to a muddy brown.

But who knew what the goddess should look like? I could have inserted a piece of volcanic tufa in her place, and carved it to suit, but just then the watch sounded the alert. It was one hour past midnight.

Adranos came in the door of the warehouse, where I had put the goddess to cure. "The Guard approaches, sir."

I was not surprised. I had sent a message to the palace announcing the safe arrival of the stone when I was sure it was reasonably true. I had hoped to have the chance to clean the bitch before she was presented to Caesar, but that obviously could not be.

Preceded by a dozen Praetorian Guards, royalty appeared dressed in the fiery red silk of a holocaust. Not the emperor, but his mother, Princess Soaemias. Like a creature of night, she appeared more radiant in the absence of the sun. She saw me and stopped as if the light of her eyes had found its source.

"So this is Juno-Caelestis. The soul of the moon."

"That's what the people of Carthage believe."

She was immensely pleased, and perhaps with me. "And you, Marcellus? Is that what you think?"

"I withhold judgment pending miracles, Soaemias. It's possible we may have them."

She smiled as if recalling palmier days in a palmy place where we were all exiles. "You *are* the perfect Roman. You do what is asked, which is everything possible. If the gods get in your way, you bargain them down."

"Not this one. She has a mind of her own."

"I'm sure."

Soaemias strolled luxuriously around the Stone of Tanit, which sat on a pallet that her mass had somewhat dented. What the mother and new owner saw in the perspective bride I could not say, but it was fraught with wonder, and in the end, a hint of criticism.

"It's larger than I expected."

"As befits her station."

"These markings on her backside—"

"Will be turned to the wall."

"But her color," said Soaemias. "It's dark. I was given to understand that she held within her the tints of the moon."

"She will lighten, I'm sure. Unfortunately, the stone fell into the harbor while it was being offloaded."

"*Fell?*"

I tried again. "An accident occurred while she was winched from the ship by the dock hands. The goddess fell in the water. But there's nothing to worry about. She's drying nicely."

Soaemias completed her circuit of the goddess. She continued to gaze upon the great stone with different eyes. These were the ones that glowed in the dark.

"Who's responsible for this *accident*?"

"No one really. The goddess is large. The crane was too small."

"Nothing just *happens*," she said with grave certainty. "Every event concerning the god has meaning. If the meaning is detrimental, it must be corrected."

"So it was, Princess. We retrieved the goddess for good delivery."

"That is not enough to offset the insult. Those men should be crucified."

"Soaemias—"

"This is sacrilege," she said. "It must not go unpunished."

I did not protest because I did not believe what she had said. Soaemias was beyond seriousness. The sentence she passed was unthinking and incapable of being thought. A reflex.

"Do you hear me?"

"I hear the voice of someone I hardly know."

She turned to me and seemed to see the things that made me a man, her equal, her lover. Perhaps her eyes softened. "You don't understand, Marcellus. You never have. To you, this is a matter of shifting weight in cargo that came a long way at great expense. It's only a matter of obeying the whim of a boy who is your lord and master. You can't see what we do will change the world. You can't accept the truth because your mind is bound by what your eyes convey. Vision is what you will never know. True vision, which lies beyond mere things."

"I do not see visions. That gift I have never had."

She nodded as if her theories were confirmed in me. She spoke like a pedant to a pupil. "You understand that even the feeble gods of Rome demand the blood of the pig, the blood of the lamb."

"Custom," I said.

"Custom that's lost its meaning, yes. That's what will be restored to Rome in the goddess. This empire and its people will come to appreciate the meaning of sacrifice. When that happens, the glory of heaven will reign on earth."

"And the dock hands—"

"Never mind," she said. "I'll have the Guard do it."

* * *

With some effort I talked Soaemias into executing only one man—the leader of the crew that unloaded the stone, thinking he might have been guilty of negligence. She insisted on having him scourged with the lash before he was hung from a lonely cross at the end of the jetty looking across the sea to the south— and Carthage. By that means, his soul, which in the doctrine of the ba'al lived beyond his death, became consecrated to the goddess. In that sacrifice lay the beginnings of new life for himself and others.

Soaemias did not remain in Portus to watch the process mature. Its effects were invisible in any case, even by the glow of the lighthouse, and she was bound to see the Stone of Tanit, as well as the dowry, to its proper place. The twin golden calves she found especially pleasing. They would be ensconced in the temple as soon as we reached the city, a journey which we set out upon at once.

We should have gone by the canal cut across to the Tiber River, but Soaemias did not want to chance another desecration of the goddess. In spite of the slow progress of the carts and her litter on the Via Portuensis, we would arrive shortly after day-break.

"They'll occupy a place of honor in proximity to the goddess," she said as if nothing more were on her mind. "We'll do nothing further to insult her and everything to exalt her."

"So you think she's appeased for the moment."

"I am not her high priest, so I cannot answer with confidence. But we will continue to offer sacrifice."

"Animals, I hope."

"Blameless animals," she said. "The men who desecrated the goddess were hardly that."

Now was not the time to tell this woman that I had annihilated the temple snakes, slaughtered the temple dogs, kidnapped the high priestess and confined her to an island to die. Or that her blessed stone was cursed.

"The Elagaballium must be a fair sight by this time. Has the work been completed?"

"It stands as the greatest in Rome," she said. "It can be no less. But I will have the goddess and those calves of gold installed at the Astartium. With the emperor's consent."

I wondered about their relationship. Nothing like the link between mother and son existed on earth; but the link between the Emperor of Rome and his mother went beyond that. Several Caesars had made their first task of office the elimination of that relationship by exile or death. Soaemias seemed to have skirted the dangers by allying herself closely with her son's concerns. If anything, she led the charge into the future. I had never seen the Astartium, which was under construction on Caelian Hill in the suburbs of the city, but it was known to be her preserve more than the emperor's.

"Is the Astartium also near completion?"

"The temple will be done when it must be. In July."

"Is there a reason for the date?"

"The reason would not be understood by most," she said. "At that time, the Dog Star climaxes. When it reaches maximum intensity, El-Gabal will ambulate."

"El-Gabal. You mean his stone will . . . walk?"

"The stone will not walk as such," she said. "But it will guide the way, telling his high priest where to go. And that will be to the Astartium. There, the god will be joined to his mate."

"In the hieros-gamos."

"So you've learned the terms," she said. "It would please me if you accepted the spirit as well."

"We can only play the roles we're assigned to play. Perhaps you'll find some other way for me to please you."

Like the owner, she put her hand on my knee. "I'd like nothing better, Marcellus. I've missed you very much. The time we spent together is my fondest memory."

Her eyes shifted beyond me to the grating in the window. The perforations in the sheets of gold allowed a passage of air in this summer season. When her gaze returned to the violet tones I loved, she took my hand. Her touch brought back the past as if borne on a net. It seemed as if we hovered above the surface of the road. The sounds of traffic clambering to enter Rome before first light, the exhortations of the drovers, the rumbling of the wheels of so many laden carts, the crack of the lash and braying of animals, seemed now to be orchestrated.

"In the new temple, I will be the high priestess of Astarte, the goddess of love. Do you understand what that means?"

"I'd like to say yes."

"It means I can never again dedicate my love to one man," she said in a whisper. "As high priestess, I must personally conduct the rites of the temple. I will lead the prayers, burn the incense, draw the blood of animals, and when needed, prostitute myself to the goddess."

Suddenly, I saw the snake again, the swollen fan of his hood, the strike. I should have been protected by my toga, but wore none. His fangs entered my flesh. The venom traveled my body. My only defense was not to breathe. The mother of Caesar. A whore.

"Well, it should be cooler out there in summer."

"Yes, Marcellus. That is the reason."

* * *

We arrived in the city two hours later, laboring through its far precincts, drawing curious stares, for no carts or public conveyances were allowed on the streets of Rome in daylight. Vehicles on government business could skirt the rule; and the carriages of the Vestal Virgins, too. They were allowed to pass anywhere, anytime.

As we came to the head of the forum, a hooded carriage with white curtains moved from the stables of the Atrium Vestae onto the Sacred Way. It was preceded by two squads of Praetorian Guards. Two more brought up the rear. The carriage and its escort moved up the hill to the Palatine. Coincidence, I thought.

We could not keep their pace, but I saw the carriage and Guards turn right into the street that led past the Elagaballium to the Area Palatina. I did not know they had stopped at the temple until after we rounded the corner into the street minutes later. The Vestal carriage and most of the Guard stood outside the walls that surrounded the temple, sealing the entrance. Nearly every day of the week, hundreds of Senators and Knights, along with their wives and attendants, thronged the entrance, jostling for the best vantage to attend sacrifices to the god, or, at this hour, returning homeward to the city. Today, there were none.

Soaemias called a halt before the temple. After telling me to stand by the goddess, she went inside the gates. I knew there were things I was not being told, but wanted to end the day with Philomene rather than hanging on a cross. I did what Soaemias said until Thrax, who commanded the Guard at the entrance, saw me.

The giant Praetorian came forward like a man on stilts but broader. If I was emperor, the first thing I would do is chop three feet off him and put what was left on wheels. He could then talk to the rest of humankind without going to his knees, which he never did.

"Marcellus Decimus," he said in the deep voice that had not lost the accents of his Thracian home. "I'm happy you have returned."

"Why?"

Thrax was a blunt man who did not appreciate bluntness in return. "That story needs a long time to tell," he said. "But I'd like you to consider my request for a transfer to your staff, if it can be arranged."

"Do you read and write?"

"No," he said.

"What diplomatic skills do you possess?"

"None," he said. "But I will need none. Nor will you."

I hated looking at a man's chest when I spoke to him. I stepped onto the cart, looking from a better angle at the torques on the front of Thrax's uniform. Strange. Usually, when the Guard went into the city, they dressed in civilian clothing so they did not alarm the populace.

"It's not like you to speak in cryptic phrases, Thrax. What do you know that I don't?"

He raised the eyebrows that held more hair than some men's heads. "Last night, the Prefect of the City, Fabius Leo, was called to the palace to receive the emperor's orders. When Leo heard them, he declined. The emperor then told Leo he would be replaced as Prefect. Leo said he would like that. And the emperor said very well, I have someone in mind."

"Myself."

"It is so," said Thrax. "I heard the emperor say the words to Prefect Comazon. He knew you had returned from Africa. Those two boys know when they need a man."

"A pliant man."

"That is their wish. The best man would be someone to tell them what fools they are. Prefect Comazon was given the orders that Prefect Leo refused. He carried them out unwillingly, but they were done."

"What were the orders?"

"We were told to go to the Atrium Vestae, men as we are, and remove one of the virgins from her home."

"You were told to kidnap a *Vestal*?"

Thrax nodded. "And bring her here."

I now understood why Leo, a pliant man, refused his orders. In all the empire, almost nothing of the old ways, or respect for them, remained. The exception, shared by every Roman, was the Vestals. They were the spirit of Rome. They were its purity, if that thing still existed. The persons of the Vestals were inviolate.

The man who touched one of the virgins with evil intent would be scourged until the flesh fell from his bones and the last of his blood left his body.

"What do they want from the Vestal?"

"They did not tell me," he said. "Perhaps they do not know themselves."

"Which of the virgins did you take?"

"The beautiful one," he said.

"Aquila Severa?"

"Yes."

She had testified before the emperor at the hearing on the death of the Pontifex Maximus. Of course he saw her afterward. The Vestals presided over many important functions in the city, even the games. Was it possible Varius had fallen in love with her? What perversity caused him to be infatuated with the one woman in the world he could not have?

"Why bring her here?"

"I can't say what's on that boy's mind. Or the mother's. All I know is they take blood in there."

"The blood of animals."

"Thus far," he said.

"Thrax, your imagination is sick."

"The man who will be Prefect of this City had better share the same mind," he said. "The people will be angry at this."

So they would. It was the Prefect's job to see they behaved in spite of provocation. He had charge of the Urban Cohorts—the police, the courts, and much of the body politic. Theoretically, his office was the most powerful in Rome. On this day it was the riskiest, too.

"Thrax, do you see that stone in back of the cart?"

"The boulder," he said.

It was that, but looked better. Tanit's stone had dried to its natural shade of bright gold. No one would mistake it for a cross-roads marker now.

"Do you think you can carry it?"

Thrax did not hesitate. He nodded.

"Then pick it up and follow me."

As I got down from the the cart, Thrax moved to assume his superhuman burden.

"One more thing."

"Yes, lord."

"Don't drop it."

* * *

When we entered the Elagaballium, I was glad to see the altar at the southern side of the temple—the place of sacrifice—did no business. That meant the emperor and Soaemias were inside, meeting in seclusion. Thrax would have to mount twelve marble steps with large risers while carrying the Stone of Tanit. He did that.

The groom—the Stone of El-Gabal—which is said to bear the imprint of the sun, ruled from a pedestal in the middle of the closed temple. The priests of El-Gabal stood in ranks two rows deep, spreading incense from golden censors. The teenage Emperor of Rome, dressed in the same vestments but richer, stood at the right hand of his god with his mother on the left. They were fiercely concentrated on a third figure, the Vestal Aquila Severa.

The beautiful one, said Thrax. Nor was he mistaken. Severa's infula had been taken from her face. The absence of the thing that defined the Vestals—that so wonderfully framed their faces and set out their grace—did no harm to her features. Her long red-blonde hair fell to her shoulders explosively. Her blue-green eyes gathered light and shadow in another shock of explosion. The flaring nose seemed more pronounced, giving her a look of unpracticed wantonness that only virgins can display. Where else but in the imagination can the forbidden be fully explored? Was she still chaste?

"My lord, the stone of Juno-Caelestis."

Only the virgin noticed our approach, for only she yearned for salvation. The emperor and his mother turned when they heard my words. Their looks said they were annoyed. I believe they would have ordered me to leave if I had not advanced so quickly.

"I beg my lord's pardon, but I neglected to tell your mother what the Boudon of Juno-Caelestis said. Her words concerned instructions for the placement of the stone of the goddess. She said it must at all times reside within six feet of the god." I turned to Thrax, who had followed with his burden. I pointed to the marble floor near the dark meteorite. "Just there."

Thrax stepped forward and put the stone down in its place. He did it so easily I was sorry I rushed our entrance. Soaemias looked at me impatiently. Her son was merely puzzled.

"The Boudon," he said. "Who is she?"

"The high priestess of the Temple of Juno-Caelestis. She was a learned woman of great passion and skill."

"And she told you that?"

"She said more, my lord. With her dying breath, she gave a message for your ears only."

Wanting to hear those words, he took two steps toward me, but the Emperor of Rome seemed to vie with the high priest of El-Gabal within the body of a boy. I had not thought of him in that way in a while. Seeing him grow by miracles and maturation was a process of days following weeks; but the words of Thrax brought reality back. Marcus Aurelius Antoninus was sixteen years old. The ornate bejeweled raiment he usually wore obscured the fact. The aura of Caesar in his court obliterated it. Now we would have to come to terms with it.

"What did she say before she died?"

"The Boudon, who had the gift of prescience, said my lord's idea would succeed."

"She did?"

"Absolutely."

He nodded. "And that's all she said?"

"If there had been more, I would recall it, Caesar."

"But it's good," he said eagerly. "You said she was learned."

"A student of the stars, my lord, the greatest in all of Africa Colony. I brought her with me on the return voyage because she wished with her own eyes to see the marriage of the gods. She wanted desperately to meet their sponsor in marriage. But she took sick when we were two days out."

"And died."

"Slowly, my lord."

"You were right to bring her out of Africa, Marcellus. But how I would have liked to speak with her. The knowledge she possessed is not easily come by."

"Did my lord seek the advice of the stars on this venture?"

The emperor turned to look at the Vestal as if he had forgotten her. But he smiled cheerfully at the reprise. "She's exquisite, don't you think?"

"Quite. And a Vestal."

"Virgin," he said. "Possibly the only one of the kind in Rome."

"My lord has made a study of the subject?"

I would have been pleased if he had said yes, but the emperor did not take his eyes from Aquila Severa. He spoke with rancor. "Your lord paid a handsome price to purchase a bride who was the best to be had in Rome. Impeccable lineage. Patrician manner. A very patrician nose. But I was cheated. Marcellus, you could have run a quadriga between her legs. The first night I drew blood, you know, but that was because I beat her."

"Your disappointment must have been great."

"It was not *she* who lost her innocence that night," he said. "I had been promised an upstanding specimen of Roman womanhood, guaranteed by omens, but the first time I looked beneath the sheets, I found a birthmark on her body the size of a pisspot. I tell you the whores at the pleasure dome were far more pure in body and spirit."

"Then my lord had every reason to reject his wife."

"I did that," he said. "I divorced her and sent her home without a slave—or a pisspot. But I did not do it lightly, Marcellus. Or without thought. I mean to have better."

The emperor waved his hand, a strange rolling motion, but with a purpose. Immediately, two priests of El-Gabal sprung forward like a team, laid hands on the Vestal, and stripped her stola from her shoulders. The white garment fell free, bunching at her hips.

I looked away immediately, but like a fissure in my mind I saw the perfect body of the holy Vestal. The shoulders that seemed carved from the finest Luna marble. Her lush pendant breasts. The nipples that did nothing to darken her form. The virginal swell of her belly. That was all, yet it was enough to be damned for eternity.

"Nothing like the other one," said the emperor. "I knew it."

I kept my eyes on the emperor. I spoke to him. "Does my lord mean to take her to his bedchamber?"

"Are you mad?" he said. "She is not like other women. Nor will she be treated as other women. Aquila Severa will be my wife."

THE BATHHOUSE

"The idea is to have the stones of the male and female deities unite in marriage, and at the same time unite the high priestess of the old religion with the high priest of the new. In that way, the bond will be unbreakable."

"Is he mad?" asked the Mother Augusta with a disturbing lack of expression in her voice. "Has my grandson finally lost his mind?"

"That's hard to say, Mother. I think what fascinates him—and most young men—is the forbidden. Unfortunately, nothing is forbidden to the Emperor of Rome."

"His mother encourages his fantasies," said Mammea, in whose quarters we met. "*She* is the problem. Her wish is to show all the traditions of Rome are hollow. And replace them with outrageous, bloody things."

"That girl was always a problem," said Julia Maesa, making a confession. "I thought her husband would master her, but he proved a disappointment. The trouble with men these days is they aren't dutiful husbands. They dally with slave women and let their wives to run rampant." She looked at me. "Why is that, Marcellus?"

"It's easier."

"And that's what there is to life—ease?"

"That's what there is to home life. And that's why the Vestals are so revered. They're a symbol of all that used to be."

"The things that used to be but never were are the most powerful myths," said Maesa. "That's why the things the emperor and his mother do are dangerous. They threaten our rule."

"My sister has another idea that may prove as dangerous," said Mammea. "She means to convene a women's Senate."

"A *what*?"

"An alternative to the Senate of Rome. No women are permitted there. In the Women's Senate, no men will be permitted."

That was very much a surprise to me. The Senate would find it more so. Their legislative club was the last bastion of the patrician male.

"You're right, daughter. It *is* revolution she proposes. Nothing will enrage the Togas like that." She clapped her hands too hard, as if she couldn't decide to strike something or applaud. "What a diabolical child! And to think I could have exiled her to an island."

The Mother Augusta rose, relieving the chair of its burden. She moved like a bullock to the window that overlooked the double level of gardens in the courtyard of the Domus Augustana. Mammea's quarters were on the northwest side of the quadrangle of buildings and maze-like rooms. The emperor's were opposite.

"Marcellus, I understand my grandson has offered you the post of Prefect of the City."

"Yes, Mother."

"Did you accept?"

"Of course."

She turned back from the window, planting her fists on her hips, or in that area. "No one blames you for wanting the position," she said. "But you must understand that the man who accepts it will be subject to great pressure and greater abuse."

"I'm sure. A marriage between the emperor and the Vestal will not sit well with the patricians, the knights, or the plebs."

"And you have already been involved in a serious incident with the Pontifex Maximus."

"This will not be the last of the emperor's escapades," said Mammea. "He's surrounded himself with the worst elements in the city. They applaud his actions. The more lunatic they are, the louder they respond."

"But he seems to have fixed his gaze on the opposite sex. That's welcome."

Mammea regarded me with forbearance. She sighed like half her mother. "Would you be happier, Marcellus, if he had raped the Vestal?"

"I believe I would be."

"So would I," said the Mother Augusta. She moved across the room and sat in the chair again. "But it's not the emperor's tastes that worry me. It's his stability. While you were gone so long, and we thought you were lost at sea, he tried to put a man of his choosing in your place as head of the Italian Departments. This creature's only qualification for the office was that he had played the part of a palace administrator in a comedy at the theater."

"Not a bad choice when you think of it."

She smiled with no feeling. "Comedy has its place, Marcellus. So does good sense. I'd like to make a suggestion. Call it a request. See if you can find a replacement for your post in the Italian Departments—a man both you and I can work with."

"That might call for a tragic actor."

"I know what I'm asking," she said. "But you'll not have to serve two masters. Do what the emperor orders. As I will. We have no choice but to bide our time for the present."

For the present? What the Mother Augusta had *not* said held repercussions for the empire. Had she put a limit on the reign of her grandson? And what event would be the trigger?

"Until when, Mother?"

She looked at Mammea when she spoke. "Until Alexianus comes of age."

* * *

That was more than a year. Many things might change in the meantime. It was even possible the boy I had known as Varius would regain the portion of his life that had been taken "on the mountain."

I had come to look on those days in Emesa as the time when Varius lost his way. I saw now his mother kept him from me. Even the intimacy we shared was a form of manipulation. All the things for which I had blamed Gannys were better shifted to her.

I still had questions concerning that man's death. Since one of my functions as Prefect of the City was the investigation of crimes, I had the resources to inquire into the matter. I sent one of my best investigators, Canidius Piso, who was known more for his brains than his skill as a torturer, on a mission to Bithynia. With him went Frugius, the man in my command who was best equipped to speak the language of professional assassins, since he had been one.

I hoped they might find out who killed Gannys. All the people who could have ordered the murder were beyond punishment, including Comazon. That young man was not only Prefect of the Praetorian Guard, but had been appointed consul jointly with the emperor for this year. Though his new office was not as it had been during the Republic, when it was the highest of all, the title added to his prestige.

The means by which he had acquired these and other favors surprised me when I learned of them not long after I settled in at my job as Urban Prefect. The information came from a special department within my office called the Bathhouse. Its function was to compile the secrets of the city, especially those of its most important citizens, and particularly to their habits when disrobed. Due to the heavy volume, the records of the Bathhouse were purged every three years. That period, however, spanned the reign of Marcus Aurelius Antoninus from the first day to the last.

Was I surprised to learn that Consul Comazon was said to be the lover of Princess Julia Soaemias? Yes.

The man who had written the report, a jaundiced informant, credited the charms of that handsome young man with every honor that had come his way. Known to be a womanizer, he kept an apartment for trysts between the Palatine and Caelian Hills. The traffic passing through those rooms seemed inexhaustible and subject to change by the day.

Virtually the only woman who repeated was Soaemias. She had been seen five times at the apartment for periods of time that were long enough to bring an eager woman to consummation. The report did not consider the liaison anything but sexual, since meetings for political purposes would have taken longer. It speculated that the affair seemed not to have preceded their arrival in Rome. There were indications it had begun about the time I left for Carthage.

Was that better? Or worse? Had she taken advantage of my absence? Was she simply lonely? One thing seemed clear: Comazon exploited the timing. My disgrace and her disappointment gave them common cause. And that was political.

The report dilated on Comazon's influence with the emperor. The consul's mother had been an actress, but his father, whom he did not mention, was a juggler. So Comazon grew up in a household of quick hands and professional subterfuge. His contacts with that world had never been withdrawn. Even now, the acquaintances and friends of the emperor were drawn to an unwholesome degree from the world of the stage. The inhabitants were of many specialties, of all persuasions and sexes, and all beholden in some degree to Comazon.

I reread the report, but saw nothing that could be done with it. Comazon and his lover had accumulated great power in a short time. They would continue to exercise it into the future, or until they overreached. That was what the Mother Augusta had told me in her way.

It seemed we would all have to wait.

* * *

We were not bored in the meantime. The emperor's behavior that summer and fall veered from the outrageous to the fantastic. As promised, he ambulated the god at the climax of the Dog Star; but instead of a stately procession in daylight, the citizens of Rome witnessed a scene of tumultuous celebration that began in the dead of night.

Moving out from Palatine Hill, the god, installed in a chariot of gold, ornamented with golden disks that shone in torch light like the midnight sun, led the way to his new home. The reins of a quadriga were fastened to the stone, as if it were sentient. His high priest preceded the chariot, facing the god, moving backward at a trot, holding the bridles of the four horses and interpreting the will of heaven as it arrived in his hands. All the way to Caelian Hill the streets were strewn with fine sand, flower petals and gold dust, so the emperor, if he tripped and fell, would not harm his holy person.

The crowd at all stages of the journey was huge, as thousands of people from every part of the city and every walk of life turned out, even the children. They seemed not to care that their emperor had kidnapped a Vestal and meant to marry her, as he announced in a letter to the Senate. They seemed not to care that his god was born of the sun yet traveled by night. They cheered him in the name of El-Gabal, showering the procession with bouquets of flowers and wreaths of laurel and yew.

The closer the procession came to Caelian Hill, the greater the numbers of spectators grew. For many citizens, the evening was a chance to see their handsome young emperor at close range, and for most it was their first view of the complex known as the Horti Variani—the Gardens of Varius—with its magnificent new temple.

The last was something new for Rome, which valued fashion above most things, and the fashion of the court above all. It was an Oriental temple enclosed by high walls with small sanctuaries along its borders. The underground part of the temple was as elaborate as the visible, but that night all the people saw was the grand facade of the entrance. A monumental propylaea of black marble, adorned with the magical symbols of the East, it was crowned by twin towers that rose seventy-five feet from the ground.

There, as the crowd gathered before the entrance, trouble began. My good fortune was that I was not responsible for security. With the emperor's person so exposed, the Praetorian Prefect, Comazon, had called out his foot Guard, and the cavalry, too. They escorted the emperor throughout the long procession, but nervously, unaccustomed to large crowds moving pell-mell through the streets, shouting and cheering, throwing garlands and carrying torches.

Yet no serious incidents occurred along the way. The people and the Guard conducted themselves well until they reached the temple, where both sides began to grow restive while the emperor carried out the ceremonies to install El-Gabal beside his consort, Juno-Caelestis. The sounds of cymbals, tambourines and flutes, accompanied by Syrian chants, could be heard like the murmur of a summer mystery from a distant grove. The smell of blood from the massive sacrifice of animals wafted over the walls. The people began to think they would have meat, and perhaps drink at the public table. The anticipation of a feast was high. Their disappointment at the length of the ceremonies was obvious.

When the first of the crowd began to leave, meandering down the suburban streets, the emperor realized his mistake. He suddenly appeared on the ramparts atop the propylaea in his finest jewels and vestments, rearing high like a god of the Eastern night. In his hands, he held the ceremonial vessels that had received the blood of the sacrificial animals. Offering them with chants and exhortations, he flung them down from the heights into the crowd.

The cups were gold and silver. When their worth become known, scuffling broke out as each man tried to make the vessels his. As they contended for the precious goods, more gifts came down from the propylaea—plate and chalices, clothing of the richest silk and linen, jeweled shoes, amulets and necklaces, and last, live animals.

The havoc that followed was predictable. Men and women fell on each other's throats, weapons came out, and the crowd, panicking at the violence and the chance for sudden wealth, surged toward the entrance.

The Guard, set one rank deep, gave way under the crush. Instantly, the second rank came up with swords at the ready. They began to use their weapons, jabbing at the unprotected bodies of the people in the vanguard, but that did not stop the momentum. The Guard's line gave way. When they were nearly overwhelmed, the last rank closed from behind and the cavalry charged from the flanks.

Though countermanding orders may have been shouted by their officers, the Guard was under no one's control. Men, women and children went down under the horsemen. The crowd gave

way in every direction, running and thrashing about and screaming, flinging their torches aside and adding the panic of fire to
the confusion.

When the foot Guard regrouped and charged, panic gave way
to worse. Bodies were trampled wholesale. The streets of the suburb ran with blood. When the mass finally broke loose and fled
for their lives, the Guard, enraged at the attack, continued the
chase down the streets, hacking and stabbing. Some people ran
into the enclosure of the new race course (ten feet shorter than
the Circus Maximus), where they were cornered and butchered.

Before the riot ended, one hundred and forty-seven people
were killed, and thousands wounded on the night the gods were
joined in marriage. The toll would have been higher if my First
Cohort had not arrived from the barracks to stop the killing.

When order had been restored, I had the bodies brought inside
the circus where they could be claimed by relatives and kept from
the dogs. I counted the corpses and brought the tally to the
emperor, who waited in the temple.

He had screamed helplessly at his Guard as they swept forward, and then wept helplessly for his people from atop the
propylaea, but now he stood quietly before the sacrificial altar of
the god. Comazon was by his side. The fire burned bright in the
well. It was eternal, it was said.

"A hundred and forty-seven," he said. "I would have thought
more. The Guard seemed to spare no one."

"They spared no one they could reach, my lord."

"They overreacted," said Comazon quickly. "But they are
trained to respond to any threat to the emperor's person."

"*Trained?*" said the emperor.

"Daily," said Comazon. "As my lord is aware."

"You will double their training," said the emperor in a tone
that should have meant the prefect's head on a spear. "You will
also inform the Guard I am giving five hundred sesterces to the
families of each person slain this night. The money will come
from their pockets."

Comazon's mind moved fast as he calculated how much the shortfall would cost him; and how many of the emperor's wishes he could discount between Soaemias' sheets. The answer he gave might have expressed too much confidence in his ability as a lover.

"Does my lord think it wise to cheat the men who protect his life?"

"*Cheat?*" said the emperor. "If necessary, I'll replace them with a troupe of gladiators. Or a gaggle of *monkeys*! It is the god who has been cheated this night. His marriage has been made a mockery! All our preparations have gone for naught!"

Comazon's tongue was as bold as his ambition. He spoke before the emperor's words ceased. "The marriage of the god was consecrated with the blood of his people. Men are more than animals. The bond will be stronger."

Strangely, the emperor seemed to weigh those words. He stared at his consul, then turned his face to the sacrificial fire. The closer he moved to the flames, the higher his shadow pitched against the wall. He moved so close that his whole form glowed.

"The blood of innocents," he said. "Yes."

* * *

Comazon did not escape the debacle unscathed. It was understood that his first term as consul would be his last. Only by the length of his storied member did he retain control of the Praetorian Guard. Those men, who were never popular with the people, became the focus of hatred in the city. They did not dare go into the streets in uniform for fear of being attacked. They dressed like everyone else, or lived within the walls of the palace, or in their camp on the outskirts of the city. That made their mood ugly.

Surprisingly, the emperor, who planned to marry his Vestal on the day following the ambulation of the god, put off the event in deference to the suffering of his people; but a month later, in the early autumn, he took Aquila Severa as his wife in a ceremony celebrated throughout the Roman world.

As if to prove his mind was elsewhere, the emperor went before the Senate to inform the Togas that the union "between a sacred priestess and a sacred priest" would result in the production of "godlike children." Paintings and statues of the celestial couple were commissioned and coins struck in their images. To pay for these expressions of the divine, the emperor invoked a tax on the people of Italy, who were made to contribute to the dowry of the celestial marriage.

I was glad that I no longer administered the Italian Departments, which were already strapped by taxes. The building program on Caelian Hill, the repairs to the Coliseum, the completion of the Baths of Caracalla, the vast sums granted to Syria to exalt its place as the home of the dynasty, the gifts to the army and the people, and the extravagance of the court, made heavy inroads on the treasury. The quality of the currency declined again. Good coin vanished from circulation, as people hoarded what they had against a better day.

"There's a fantastic market in Egyptian hounds," said Philomene. "The Salukis are said to have a nose for gold and silver no matter how deep it's buried. Thieves have bought so many of the dogs that not one can be found. No courtyard or garden in the city is safe from them. Nor any villa in the country."

"If you said they had a nose for mutton or beef, I'd believe you."

Ceremoniously but with grace, Philomene laid the corn cake sweetened with butter and honey on the table. It was coarse food, campaign food, but I had a liking for polenta. Perhaps she was willing to please because she missed me. I spent my days at headquarters on Viminal Hill and many nights, too. Our lavish apartment on the Palatine went largely to waste, though it was still the best place for gossip.

"The Pharaohs of Egypt had all the blood drained from their bodies when they died," she said as if it were a family trade. "As mummies, they were buried in secret chambers deep within the earth. Yet the grave robbers found the burial grounds. They found all the gold and riches of Pharaoh's tombs, revealed to them by their dogs."

"So riches have a smell. I always suspected that."

"It's the same as the smell of death," she said. "To a Saluki."

"I've never known you to be so morbid. Or to scorn money. The bills I get from the shops are amazing. How much are you putting away for yourself?"

"Ten percent," she said. "And most of that is spent in bribes."

"Has the money been well disposed?"

"That depends. Does my lord not receive value?"

"I have no complaints."

"That's good to know."

Her short answer gave me to know that it was best to change the subject. "So tell me, what do you hear of the new newlyweds?"

"Approximately the same as the old newlyweds."

"Does the emperor still conduct his nocturnal excursions?"

"Yes, but now he has company. He doesn't hide when he goes out into the city at night. Everyone thinks he goes to the houses of friends, but that's true only part of the time. For the other part, he goes to the same places he always did. Even the actors and athletes who make up his circle are uncomfortable in those places."

"Are we likely to get an heir out of any of them?"

"No," she said. "Nor in the other place. The new empress, I understand, is still consecrated to her goddess."

"Still a *virgin*?"

Philomene nodded.

"But I don't understand. If she remains chaste, there was no point."

"Perhaps there is one," said Philomene with a pause as loud as a gong. "If that—from the first—was his intention."

* * *

It was unnecessary to tell Philomene to cultivate her sources and keep me apprised. She did that as naturally as she doffed her sandals and plied our palatial rooms in her bare feet. As it happened, her contribution was made redundant by fate. I was in the emperor's presence when the seminal event of his reign took place. That was the day he met Hierocles.

He rode for the Green. Hierocles was a young man of about twenty-five, and a favorite of the great charioteer Gordius, whose entries in the reports of the Bath House made up volumes. Gordius kept a stable of handsome young men who did anything to please. The lower their station in life, the more they did. Hierocles was a Carian slave who had been sold to Gordius by his first master, a building contractor.

The young slave began his career as the object of the contractor's attentions, if not his love. As Hierocles grew older, he demonstrated his erotic talents in a way that caused his master to put aside his feelings and place the slave in business as a prostitute. Hierocles' haunts were the private bathhouses, particularly those on the Campus Martius where many charioteers repaired each day from the faction stables.

Advertising himself by the hair that ran past his shoulders as fetchingly as a woman's, Hierocles prospered. One day, his master, who supplied the room where Hierocles serviced his clients, discovered that his precocious slave had been three times in one week with Gordius, who wanted a fourth and more. He wanted the young man for his own.

The offer the great charioteer made could not be refused. Gordius was a wealthy man, but his fame made him fearsome. The mania surrounding the circus was like nothing else in the empire. Although no one in a generation had thrown himself onto the funeral pyre of his favorite charioteer, preferring death to a life without the light of his fantasies, the fanatics who followed the races would have killed at Gordius' word. If the offer had been rejected, Hierocles' master could have died by the sharpest of blades or the stealthiest of poisons.

But good sense prevailed as it rarely did in the circus. Gordius took Hierocles into his home—a grand palace on the Carinae. The young slave was so good at what he did that Gordius set him free. Once free, Hierocles taunted his master with his independence, taking other lovers, while depriving Gordius of those many varieties of novelty and pleasure.

Finally, Gordius succumbed to his former slave's demand: that he should be trained as a charioteer. Thus, by the use of his body, Hierocles gained the means to transform himself into one of the icons of Rome. He ceased fellating horses for a fee, and began to thrash them around the vast track of the Circus Maximus, while a half million people urged him on.

Hierocles was not as successful in that arena as others, yet even a bad charioteer was a skilled athlete in excellent physical condition, and this young man had one of the finest bodies in the four factions. Standing in his chariot with his leggings wrapped tightly around his thighs, his tunic wrapped tightly around his torso, his long reins around his waist and his quick-release dagger in hand, he was the portrait of a champion. The only thing that marred his image was the charioteer's helmet on his head, and one day he found a way to rid himself of it.

What happened that afternoon, which was one of the first full day of races at the Circus Variani, the race course on Caelian Hill where so many people had been murdered, was said to be an accident. Perhaps it was.

In the third race—a quadriga—the chariots came round the turning post into the straightaway tightly bunched. It was the second lap around the course, and none of the charioteers had created enough space to maneuver. A dangerous situation. In the turnings, most of the accidents occurred.

When one of the Whites veered wide, the Green behind him, who was Hierocles, could not keep his angle on the field. His team brushed the wheels of the White. He should have driven inside, and taking the head of the White, challenged for the lead. Instead, he veered wider. When the two stallions at the head of his team bolted for open ground, the two mares followed, barely under control.

Hierocles struggled to keep his team in hand. As the chariot approached the straightaway, the stallion on the left broke out of his traces. The mares bolted that way, attempting to follow, and as they did the chariot whipped like a sling toward the barrier. The car tipped and tottered. When it seemed it would roll, Hierocles spilled to the ground. Quickly, before the team could drag him, he cut the reins free with his dagger.

And lost his helmet. As his team charged back into the race, dragging the car behind, Hierocles stood. Shaking out his long blond hair, he looked to the imperial box.

He had landed in front of the emperor's court. Most of the party got to their feet, concerned for the charioteer. When we saw he was unharmed, we took our seats. All but one.

The emperor remained standing. It was as if no other people were in the stadium; as if the race had not continued; as if those two young men were alone in their contemplation.

A loud cheer went up from the crowd as the White took the lead decisively at the far turn. Hierocles looked around at the race like a spectator. He shrugged before turning back and moving toward the starting gates.

The emperor motioned to Comazon, who came instantly to his side. The consul bent to receive his orders, then quickly hurried off toward the gates.

The emperor was still standing. He watched Hierocles pass from the race course and disappear behind the gates. A few minutes later, Marcus Aurelius Antoninus left the *pulvinar*, and the stadium, something he rarely did early in the day. He did not return to the circus that day, or the next, or the next.

Nor did Hierocles for the Green.

A WIFE

"It is as my lord fears. The emperor has given himself to this man completely."

Philomene's words destroyed the remnant of hope I retained for Varius. She could have said many things in different ways about the emperor and the charioteer, but she had put their relationship in terms of surrender.

"They're lovers?"

"Openly."

"How bad is it?"

"Very little is hidden," she said, opening her hand. "They're constant companions. Hierocles has the suite next to the emperor's in the Caelian palace. They walk arm in arm in the gardens. They go to the theater together, where they behave like man and wife."

My voice arrived late. "Which part does the emperor play?"

"I'm afraid that news is more unfortunate," she said. "The emperor seems very much the wife of Hierocles."

"You're certain."

Philomene took my hand as if leading me. "You should not be disheartened. The emperor is a still very young. This is an infatuation. It will pass."

"Into *what*? This time a charioteer. His next lover may be a *slave*!"

"Perhaps," she said quietly. "Slaves are often chosen for their beauty. And they are capable of love."

Clearly, Philomene meant more than she said. "I fail to see the point. You're speaking of natural relationships. A man who can't rule himself—or his lovers—can't rule an empire."

"That's what Romans think."

"That's what Romans *know*. They understand power because they're born to it. A man can love another man, but he can't *be* a woman. If he's the Lord of All the World, he doesn't go to his knees for any reason. Unless it would get him an heir."

"Perhaps it will—after a fashion."

"After what fashion? Do we have word on that?"

"I doubt you'll find it welcome," she said. "Last night, the emperor gave a party for his friends. They harnessed the four most beautiful female prostitutes in Rome to a chariot and raced them around the circus against four of the most handsome male prostitutes."

"Who won?"

"The women. They were given a great deal of money. The men got no money, but instead took the empress as their prize."

"The *Vestal*?"

Philomene nodded. "The male prostitutes are for hire to the richest women of the city. They were gathered by the charioteer, who commanded them like a general. He had them make love to the Vestal. Or they raped her. The accounts are unclear. She was heard to scream, but the nature of the screams are uncertain."

"You're telling me that the virgin was deliberately *defiled*?"

"That's your word as a Roman. Aquila Severa is a woman, a married woman, and of course the emperor's servant."

* * *

Nor was that the end of blasphemy. The reports I received from Philomene and my departments made a catalog of dissolution that pointed to Hierocles and the expanding summer residence on Caelian Hill, which now had its own circus, theater, gardens and baths. The baths and gardens were another name for indoor and outdoor whorehouses. The circus featured races between every beast on earth, including elephants, tigers, and zebras. The theater was more degenerate, dissolving the line between fantasy and reality. The things that were the usual province of drama, such as women being beaten and ravished, were at this theater acted out. Nothing was left to the imagination.

When winter set in, the court moved back to the Palatine, but the suburban complex was not abandoned. One day in early fall I saw the emperor and Hierocles driving twin chariots by the gate of the Castra Peregrini, the frumentarii's headquarters. They moved east, dressed in the colors of the Green. They looked like a matched pair except the emperor had whitened his face with makeup and painted his lips. And he had seen me.

"Hail, Marcellus Decimus!"

"Hail, Caesar!"

They sheared their chariots dangerously close to Bacchus, who shied and nearly broke. The ten mounted Praetorian Guard who followed came to a halt so close that I was afraid Bacchus would try to assert himself with the mares.

"Will you race us to the baths?" asked the emperor. "I've always wanted to see that horse challenged."

"He's no match for your team, my lord. Or your companion's."

"Parthian," said Hierocles like a genealogist. "Strong as a brick but short-winded. You are right in having no chance."

I thought he was trying to say more, but could not credit him with so much wit. His tunic was open to the waist, exposing the hair to his navel. His trousers were so tight every muscle made its relief.

"Bacchus was bred to a purpose. He's a war horse trained to ride men down. There's nothing else he knows."

"Well, don't point him this way," said the emperor. "We have use for all our bodily parts."

"My lord knows that Bacchus is directed only toward the enemies of Rome." I looked pointedly at Hierocles. "If the emperor sees one, he must tell me. One word, and I'll give the Parthian his orders."

"Always like that," said the emperor, laughing, to Hierocles. "We have no need for the Guard when Marcellus is near."

Hierocles reached across the car to the emperor as if to touch him, but the distance was too great. "We have no need for anyone, Great Caesar. Even the wind cannot catch us."

I thought Marcus Aurelius Antoninus would melt at those words. His hand trembled as he reached across his car to touch the tips of Hierocles' fingers. He might have done that if the charioteer had not drawn his hand back, teasing, as he put the lash to his team.

He cried: "For the spoils of the empire!"

And they were off, Hierocles swinging to the lead, the emperor flogging his team, calling to his lover "Hold, please hold," and the Guard following in disdain.

It was not hard to see the emperor was being led in the direction an unscrupulous whore willed. He was the wife Philomene had described—a woman who would do anything to please her man—and what the Emperor of Rome could not do for pleasure has yet to be thought of. I tried not to be surprised when on the following morning I received a report of an incident at the theater by the summer palace. Two lions were crucified on stage for having eaten criminals in the arena, which was their job. Somehow, they broke loose from their crosses and mangled several members of the audience.

When any foul thing lit the minds of the emperor and his lover, they repaired to Caelian Hill to enact their wants, where they were safe from observation, particularly by the Mother Augusta. Her impatience with her grandson grew daily. They were at odds about everything, and it was not clear who would win. The emperor, for all his faults, was still popular with the people because of his generosity in the dole, and the games he constantly gave.

"There's no money left to pay for his fantasies," said the Mother Augusta as we walked the long colonnades of the balcony overlooking the Circus Maximus from the palace. She threw her arm toward the valley below, where so many races and hunts took place.

"Do you know four thousand beasts were slaughtered every day in the Plebeian Games? If we hadn't been able to sell the kills to the meat market, the *fiscus* would be bankrupt by now."

The fiscus was the emperor's private treasury. Often depleted, in the past it was replenished by citizens who owed it money. Varius, in an attempt to curry favor, had destroyed the records of the public indebtedness. It took weeks to burn all the records in the forum.

"How will the difference be made up, Mother?"

"We've been forced to increase the crown gold tax," she said. "And it has been made permanent rather than temporary."

"Now if the tax could be enforced—"

"Aurelius Eubulus has been appointed to administer the fiscus," she said. "His vast experience with bankers recommended him to the emperor."

"His experience is in taking their heads."

"That may be necessary for the work," she said. "Appealing to the patriotism of bankers is a hopeless occupation."

Eubulus had been a compromise choice between the Mother Augusta and the emperor. I listened while she reviewed the recent appointments the emperor had made. A baker had been given administration of the *annona*, the corn dole that kept the people of Rome from starvation. A charioteer—a friend of Hierocles—took over the operation of the Pedagogium, the training school for imperial slaves. The actor who had been slated to be the head of the Italian Departments was now overseer of the highways. A wrestler was given charge of the all-important aqueducts and sewers.

"If nothing else, Mother, we may finally have proof that men do not matter. Only the gods can affect the course of events."

"He says the god instructs him in choosing his servants." The Mother Augusta farted once, loud, like a horse before a race, but did not stop walking. "My grandson has confused the god with that creature he loves so dearly. The first is made of stone, the other has it chiefly in his head."

"Has the emperor agreed to any sane appointments?"

"One," she said. "Ulpian will be joint prefect of the Guard for judicial matters. Comazon has no idea of how to do it, and never will. His only talent lies between his legs."

"It's unfortunate he still has the emperor's ear. Or should I say, Soaemias' ear."

"You can say it, Marcellus. If anyone has the right, it's you. Ever since you stopped being friends, Soaemias has grown bolder. Whatever madness her son proposes, she does her best to fulfill." The Mother Augusta stopped as we came to the odalisque that marked the rear entrance to the Pedagogium. "Have you heard what happened to the Vestal?"

"That she was accosted, yes."

"She was fucked until her body collapsed and her mind surrendered to numbers," said the Mother Augusta. "Regardless of what most men think, that is not an enviable experience."

"I hope she recovered."

Maesa shook her head. "I doubt she'll ever be recovered in the sense that she will return to what she was. Those men are good at their trade."

"Hierocles chose them, I understand."

"Perhaps, but my daughter made sure of their accomplishments. She is, as you know, a priestess of love. I was told she sampled the wares of those satyrs. And to think some were rejected on the basis of their performance."

Rejected? The word struck hard. I would have liked to further the conversation with glib words, but had none. I was not surprised by what Maesa said. Soaemias had told me as much, or as much as she wanted me to know. I wondered how much she told Comazon.

"You're quiet, Marcellus. Is it because your heart rebels?"

"I believe so."

"Then it may help you to know that my daughter had a purpose in all she did."

"Perhaps I should ask what it is."

"Perhaps," said the Mother Augusta. "You're a brave man."

"Is that a requirement?"

"More than you think," she said. "My daughter is a priestess of the moon. She was given the license by Severus, who saw no harm in having his niece be a student of the mystic arts. Later, she was encouraged by her cousin, Antoninus. He liked even more having a sacred harlot in his family. He liked that almost as much as he liked having her for his own."

That was another hard strike at my pride through the past. I always wondered why Caracalla was so concerned with Varius' health that day in the Alps. Here was an answer.

"Then the idea that he was Varius' father—"

"May be true," she said. "Perhaps not even Soaemias knows. She was already with child when we found a Syrian male of equestrian rank willing to lend his name to the product of her youthful enthusiasm. All I can tell you is that her cousin, the future emperor, was not the first to have her. That's a question for the alphabet."

"But if the child was the son of Antoninus, that explains the emperor's eccentricities."

The Mother Augusta looked at me kindly. "I'm afraid we don't have to look far for my grandson's aberrations. His mother's temperament is enough. Let's say she had an inclination to the irrational at an early age. It was never given up. Instead, we tried to harness it by putting her with the masters of the occult. First, she studied with the galli of the Great Mother, then with the priests of Apollo at Delphi, and last, for a long while, with the devotees of Astarte. All this has its culmination now. She has acquired knowledge that not many men or women possess. She knows how the moon and tides react with our lives. She knows how the cycles of the seasons meet in Hades and plan their return. And she knows the time of the month it's best for a woman to conceive."

"Are you telling me that's possible?"

"I'm telling you it happened one night not long ago on Caelian Hill. The Vestal lay on a silver bed with silken coverlets, like meat from the circus, in order to produce an heir from her body. No thought was given to the rank of the father. No thought of propriety. It was a mathematical calculation made by a woman who has lost her heart."

The Mother Augusta turned away. Tears fell down her cheeks. It might have been the first time I had seen her eyes released from heavy makeup. The true color was blue with purple highlights, like most of her family.

"I should have exposed that child on a dunghill the day she was born," she said, her voice breaking. "I should have known she would die there."

"Mother, you don't mean that."

"I do," she said angrily. "The worst thing is to think I might have approved her project if it had been successful. If it gave us an heir. What does that say about where we are? What does it say about who we are?"

* * *

The project had been unsuccessful, the event having taken place nearly three months past. That, I was informed, was the time when some result would have accrued. And that was the reason the Mother Augusta waited exactly that long to speak to me about it.

The desperation to produce an heir was shared by everyone, most of all Soaemias. She must have been grossly disappointed when her attempt to generate said item from a lottery failed. I wondered what she would devise next. Her ruthlessness had assumed a life of its own.

I was still thinking of that two weeks later when Frugius and Canidius Piso returned from Bithynia. They entered my office like a team. Piso was an investigator with the rank of military tribune in our Third Cohort. Physically unimpressive, with small bones and thick eyebrows, he looked capable of carrying Frugius' leg armor into the arena, but no more.

His voice was also unimpressive, high-pitched, with consonants meticulously set forth. "Prefect, we have acquired the information you requested. I would like to stress that we shared it with no one."

I looked from Piso to Frugius for a better reading of what lay behind those words. His demon eyes said he was frightened. The man had once faced three Thracians in the arena in a single afternoon. What could be worse?

"In other words, you adhered to your orders."

"Faithfully," said Frugius. "Our job would have been easier if we had not been quiet. We would have returned quicker."

"Understood."

Piso looked to Frugius nervously. "We traveled first to Nicomedia, where we examined the crime scene. Our conclusion agrees with Prefect Comazon's. Unless the Praetorian Guard had been corrupted at three separate posts in the palace, it was impossible to pass unnoticed to the Lord Chamberlain's office. We did not consider it an option. Such things cannot be kept secret when many people have to be bribed. Since only one Guard was executed, we assumed only he was involved. Or that he was a convenience."

"So you think the assassin entered from without."

"Yes, but he need not be a gymnast. Any nimble man could have climbed the wall and with help scaled the side of the building. If a device of some sort were placed in the room by an accomplice, the job required no great effort."

"A rope, say."

"Or a hook," said Piso. "The man could have carried his own rope. We found evidence of a hole drilled into the mortar beneath the window. Any man with access to the room could have inserted a device. But it would require a man who knew he would not be discovered to remove it safely."

Perhaps the investigator himself. "I see."

"We thought we should look for a nimble man, expert with a large dagger or short sword, but not of the common type. We also thought he would have to be very bold. Experienced, but bold."

I looked to Frugius. "A gladiator?"

"We went to all the contractors in Bithynia, lord. One named Gaius Gavros had been a *murmillo* himself until he saw more money in hiring them out to the arenas. He was helpful after his fashion."

"You didn't kill him."

"Not quite, lord."

"I knew you were a diplomat born."

"In my lord's service, I would be anything. I think since Gavros did not know the purpose of our questions, he could take away nothing useful from our meeting."

"Excellent."

"He knew only two men who could combine the skills we sought," said Piso. "One died recently in the arena. That did not mean he was free of blame, but we felt the assassin was well paid. It was not likely he'd put himself in the arena against men—or animals—if he had money to keep himself from harm."

"Animals?"

"Yes, Prefect. The man suggested by Gavros was an elephant hunter. A hamstringer."

I wondered what Frugius had done to elicit the information. Probably, he had taken a *falcata*, the long curved knife elephant hunters used, and put it under the man's neck. He would have applied some pressure, but not enough to sever the vessels necessary to life.

The hamstringer's occupation was as indirect. He dodged around the elephants when they were set loose in the arena, coming upon them from behind, and with his long blade severed the cords of muscle that bore the weight on their rear legs. It was a dangerous occupation requiring a bold and nimble man. After the hamstringer did his work, the hunters moved in for the kill on the immobilized animal. He was taken down, piece by piece, a colossus who could no longer apply his force against his enemies.

"What is this man's name and where is he?"

"We found him, Prefect, which is what caused us to be absent so long. He had retired from the arena as we suspected, but kept his contacts with friends in the business. Frugius traced him through the College of Gladiators. The man, whose name was Zeno, had moved to Antioch, where he set himself up under a new name. He did no work and had no clients, but lived well. He grew a long beard and married a Syrian woman. His villa in the suburb of Daphne was secure. He hired two gladiators to guard his property and kept a kennel of dogs on patrol. It took some doing to extract him."

"But you succeeded."

"Not without wounding him, my lord," said Frugius. "He was quick. And he had not forgotten how to use the falcata. We went at him for three days with questions, until the wound that was festering went to his head. At that point, he was like any other man. Afraid to die."

"What did he confide to you as he faced the gods?"

"He faced only one, Prefect."

I waited for Frugius or Piso to continue, but they had said what they wanted. Their opinion seemed identical with their fear.

"Can I assume that Zeno, once rehabilitated in Antioch, did not become a Christian?"

"He did not, Prefect."

"Can I assume that he worshiped a Syrian god?"

"Yes, lord."

"El-Gabal?"

"No, Prefect. Astarte. And Zeno was more than an adherent of her temple. He performed as a functionary in the sacrifices."

"A practiced cutter."

"Yes, Prefect. This is not work that can be done by anyone. He would have had to be an adherent of the goddess for some time. A man does not come to the position overnight."

"So he was completely at the bidding of the temple."

"And its high priestess."

They still had not spoken the name. Frugius had seen the dock hand crucified at Portus. Piso, an investigator, knew that and more. And at last, so did I.

"Thank you for your work. Do you wish to be exiled to an island for your safety?"

Piso looked to Frugius before he spoke. "If the Prefect guarantees this information will not find its way into the records of his office, I would like to stay and serve."

Frugius nodded. "Likewise, lord."

"So be it."

* * *

She needed a eunuch, so she took a eunuch.
She needed a warrior, so she took a warrior.
She needed a bodyguard, so she took a Praetorian Prefect.

When she needed an assassin, she found one to unite with her prefect against her eunuch while her warrior was away. The warrior had been manipulated by her prefect into thinking her eunuch was responsible for all the ugly things that happened at court. In reality, only one thing happened: the power of Soaemias had been threatened by a eunuch who wished to be regent of the Roman Empire.

Her plan was logical. It was intelligent. It was everything but human, which of course the god was not. He was a stone. She was a stone.

* * *

Three weeks after I spoke with Frugius and Piso—and two days after the Ides of March—I received what was apparently a routine request from the palace. The message had been signed by the emperor's secretary, but the tone did not sound like his master.

I was told to investigate a man accused of asking questions of the palace staff. I did not consider the matter of great importance, except as it was distinguished by its source. I assigned the investigation to Piso, who had returned to duty after taking leave with his family. I gave him three days to break the culprit, but Piso reported back later the same day.

"This man Esdras was a slave but now a freedman. He's also a client of a Senator—Silius Messalla. He admitted he asked the questions, but would not own it was done at the direction of his master. When I informed him that investigating the emperor's personal life is a capital crime, and the punishment in his case would be crucifixion, he furnished Messalla's name."

So a criminal matter had become political. Messalla was an important member of the Senate who had opposed the restoration of the dynasty. While we were at Antioch, he had been summoned from Rome so the case for legitimacy could be put to him. That gesture gave him a false sense of importance. Or else he thought his rank and wealth would shield him.

"This is a delicate matter, Piso. What did Messalla hope to accomplish by prying into the emperor's life?"

"Esdras said his mission was prompted by the influence the charioteer Hierocles has over the emperor. It is, according to Esdras and his master, common knowledge that the emperor no longer rules. They say he shares his throne with the dregs of the circus. Quite a bit more was said in unflattering ways."

"That's unfortunate for everyone, but particularly for Esdras. Confine him to an isolation cell. Tell him that if he speaks to anyone of these matters, he *will* be crucified."

"At once, Prefect. Though there's another matter of which you should be aware. Esdras in his haste to share the blame implicated a second man in the plot. Another Senator. Pomponius Bassus."

A second high ranking man. Extremely wealthy. I was angry at the arrogance of these patricians, which amounted to stupidity. This affair had grown into a scandal quickly.

"Anything else, Piso?"

"No, Prefect."

"Arrest Messalla. I'll deal with Bassus."

* * *

It was something less than a courtesy that caused me to cross the city to the house of Pomponius Bassus. His wife was my cousin. Four years ago in Syria, I received the announcement of her wedding. That broke the part of my heart that had survived service in the legions.

I had known Annia Faustina since she was a child, and our families at one point spoke of marriage between us. The contract would have been suitable to me, for she was a vivacious girl of high birth, descended of the emperor Marcus Aurelius on one side and Claudius Severus on the other. She was also a girl who had grown into a lovely woman.

That turn of nature moved her into the marriage bed of Pomponius Bassus. My fortune was nothing compared to his, and that was the way most Roman marriages were made. Faustina had birth and beauty. Bassus had the money to compensate for the wanton ways of her father, who had squandered the family fortune until all he had left was some property at Verona.

I had not seen her since I returned to Rome, though the chance presented itself. Twice, Faustina sent invitations to dinner, which I refused with polite demurrals. I had no wish to revisit my feelings toward her, or disturb my memories, or deal with her husband, who was not only vastly rich, but a meddler.

Bassus had been sent by Caracalla into exile on an island off the Greek Coast only to be returned to Rome by Macrinus on the wings of the most awesome bribe in history. Even that incredible sum did not harm his fortune or reduce his scheming. He continued to imagine himself a rival of Caesar, and through marriage, of better blood. His house, one of the only patrician homes left on Palatine Hill, exhausted a block of the most precious real estate on earth.

I dropped the bronze dolphin on his door, and when a black slave answered, I asked for the wife of Pomponius Bassus. "The Prefect of the City would like to speak to her."

"I will inform the lady, Marcellus Decimus."

I had not given my name, but he knew it as if he had compiled the patrician directory. Plainly, he was educated. Probably, he had heard my name used in the house.

I waited impatiently. At mid-afternoon, Faustina would have risen from her bed, have dressed and made up, received visits from her friends, and planned her evening. It was my duty to shatter that routine, and my wish to see what the years had done to her.

"Marcellus."

I saw her in the hallway, I absorbed the lines of her face and body, but could not make that image match the past. This was a different woman, so changed I looked to the name etched on the back of the dolphin. Yes, this was the residence of Pomponius Bassus. This was the dark-haired girl I had played children's games with, and chased down the streets looking for the inventive places where she had hidden, never suspecting that what she had hidden best was what she would become—the most beautiful woman of her kind.

The Roman kind. It was the beauty of a great bird when that bird was a predator. Her high-bridged aquiline nose, her high, precisely defined cheek bones, the sweep of her brown eyes, the complexion that did not share the sun but competed with it, were all every Roman was said to want in beauty. Was he mistaken? How often did he see in the flesh the portrait that had been promised by the poets of his language?

"Faustina. The Fortunate."

She smiled, remembering our play with names, and how she had fulfilled the meaning of hers. "Perhaps I am. And perhaps the title of Prefect of the City suits you better than any. I always knew you would do great things, Marcellus."

"Not today, I think, though I would like to."

"What can stop you?"

"Duty," I said. "Where is your husband?"

She looked behind her, as if Bassus were hidden by the folds of her stola. "Not here, I'm afraid. But if it's him you want to see—"

"He's who I want to talk about. May I come in?"

When she stepped back, I passed close by her, inhaling a fragrance so subtle it closed the distance between us to nothing. Her shoulders were bare, her cleavage deep. I stared.

"We used to take baths together, Marcellus, do you remember?"

"No, Faustina. And I would."

Her laughter snagged every register of memory. "I'm disappointed. What are cousins for if not to recall our innocence?"

She was telling me she was no longer that. This was a woman of the highest society in imperial Rome. She presided at legion-strength parties over the most sophisticated entertainment available in a decadent age. What had she not seen? Was there anything she had not done?

"Do you love your husband?"

She stopped at the threshold of the atrium. The ceiling rose sky-high, sunlight entered like dew, and the objects it touched were the best of their kind. I examined the room as if it were important—the furnishings of citrus wood, the interlocked marble in the floor, the plants that thrived on the fountain rising from the mouth of Neptune.

"I haven't seen you in six years," she said. "*Years*. I send invitations to dinners given in your honor, and I receive notes that sound like they come from a schoolmaster. My cousin is a powerful official in a city that worships power, yet he shares nothing with the people he knows. He sits in the Tiberiana and passes his nights in the company of an Egyptian harlot. I saw her at the market. She's beautiful beyond words. More beautiful than any woman who's borne two children. And no doubt more accomplished in many ways."

"Do you love your husband?"

She blinked to set out the grounds of my impertinence. I could have counted her eyelashes, so carefully were they defined. Yet her mood lasted only until pride pushed it aside.

"What right do you have to ask me that? Or should I say— what purpose?"

"Bassus is in danger."

She nodded as if the condition were common. "He's an intelligent man who does stupid things. The luck of great wealth is that it never seems to matter."

"It does this time."

She looked at me to reclaim her memory of what was serious in life, and the past told her volumes. "Only one thing can change a life like his," she said. "The palace is involved. What has he done?"

"Your husband and Messalla sent a clumsy man to inquire into the emperor's conduct. Perhaps they did not know their action could result in their deaths."

The news almost broke her reserve; but she had been brought up in the old ways, and she lived at the pinnacle of this city, which was devoted to the new. Those things brought her back. She spoke like a descendant of the most storied family in Rome.

"But you did not come for my husband. You came for me."

"It may not be possible for Bassus to save himself. You must face that."

"I am," she said.

"You have two options, one of which is the better. You may warn Bassus. I'm sure I won't be able to find him before morning. He may be able to make his way to safety. He'll be hunted, but there are places where his wealth can buy a new life. Having been exiled before, he might have prepared an escape route for a time like this. He'd be wise if he had."

She nodded as if that were a possibility. "And the second?"

"You know what that is, Faustina. It's the only way he can preserve his wealth and property for his children."

She looked around the atrium that was the pivot of her life. All this, and much more, her husband could ensure if he opened his veins, or fell on the sword he had seldom in his life used. Suicide was the only offensive weapon against the will of Caesar. The man who chose it lodged his protest and guaranteed his family and name would survive.

"Thank you for coming to my house, Marcellus. I owe you a great debt."

* * *

I thought of Faustina as I rode to my apartments, and wondered if she could convince Bassus to do what was right. I wondered if she would join him. Selfishly, I hoped she would bid him good-bye with a kiss. Seeing her had touched so many places in my heart that I dreaded the loss. She had two children, a boy and a girl: that would keep her from it.

But soon after I arrived home I found everything I had done for my cousin was futile. I had my bath and had dressed for dinner when Piso arrived. He did not seem apologetic at interrupting my home life. His voice, for once, was strong.

"I came to you as soon as I could, Prefect. I knew you searched for Bassus and would be pleased to hear he had been apprehended. We found him in the company of Messalla."

That was something I had not expected, but conspirators conspired. They did everything but sleep together, and who knew about that? "Where are they?"

"On their way here, Prefect. I thought you'd want to question them before taking them to the palace."

"The palace?"

Piso's voice weakened. "I informed the palace of the arrest. I thought—"

Telling a man you wanted to kill that he had done well was hard, but I did it. I set Piso at the door to watch for Bassus and Messalla, then called Philomene.

"Do you know Annia Faustina, the wife of Pomponius Bassus?"

"Yes," said Philomene with more understanding than I would have guessed.

"Go to her house. Say her husband has been arrested and will be taken to the palace."

* * *

Senators Bassus and Messalla arrived shortly afterward under guard but unbound, as befit their station. I had them put in separate rooms on the second floor with windows onto the court-yard, if they were inclined to use the drop to best advantage.

Both were models of their type. Messalla was tall, dark-haired and portly, Bassus shorter, red-haired and portly. The arrogance they displayed would have caused panic in their slaves, their mistresses, and the grain markets. Their finger rings could have ransomed provinces and their ermine-fur capes, too. Their tunics were shot with the best grades of linen and gold thread. The only thing missing were their patrician togas. Those garments were unnecessary in the high-priced whorehouse where they had been found.

I did not want to speak with Bassus, not in this life. Not on the lives of his children. I went into the room where Messalla stood like a conqueror, staring out the window. It was dark. He could see nothing.

"The emperor paved the walks in porphyry. I thought you might like to know what you voted for." Messalla turned from the window, speaking in the sonorous voice with which he addressed the Senate on many occasions. "He rapes the Treasury. He rapes the Vestals. No barbarian has brought more harm to Rome than this Syrian bastard."

"His ancestry is not the issue, Messalla. I'd like to know what you were doing by sending that oaf to sniff around the palace like a dog that had been neutered for brains? Did you plan to bring Caesar before the Senate on charges of sexual misconduct?"

"And if I said yes?"

"You might be forced to explain the exercise you sought in that bordello this afternoon."

Messalla was not tall, but long-waisted. When he took a bundle of cloth and his cock in his hand, he reached for the grip. "I used *this* to plumb the loins of a woman who not only resembled Venus, but had her name. I *took* her until she pleaded for more, or for mercy, I know not which, nor was she paid to cause me to wonder. But I tell you now, Marcellus Decimus, I did not bend over, I did not bow down, I did not spread the cheeks of my ass to accept the filthy member of an ex-slave who until three months ago was the joke of every stable in the Campus Martius. That wretched excuse for a man has been known to fertilize a mare with the contents of his mouth after he transferred the essence of the stallion he had just sucked dry."

Messalla let go of his cock and put his hands on his chest, where the folds of his toga usually depended. "Still, that cretin does what he must to survive. Compared to the emperor, he's a hero. This Caesar is not a man, or even a woman, but some putrid combination of the two."

"But still Caesar."

"For the moment," he said. "I may not be here to mark the change, but Rome will rid herself of his plague. There are many more like me in the Senate—and the army."

"But just now only two."

"One. Bassus had nothing to do with this. He knew what I was doing, but took no part."

I did not tell him that knowledge of the crime was as fatal as its planning. I did not question if his assertion was true. Messalla's state of mind might permit him to do one good thing.

"Would you put your signature to those words?"

"And no other."

"I'll send in a scribe."

* * *

Shortly after, orders came from the Domus Augustana to proceed to the quarters of the emperor. I had not been there in some time, but knew extensive alterations had been made to the suites of rooms while the court tarried on Caelian Hill. Yet I had no idea how the imagination of a young man, combined with unlimited funds, could convert elegance into a wet dream.

Imagine a hexagonal audience hall that moved entirely by invisible gears. The petitioners and wastrels who filled the space were never forced to look at the same vista, the same paintings, or the same neighbors, as they traveled in the round. The chairs and couches moved with them, circulating about tables laden with fruits and sweetmeats. If they felt a need to contemplate their surroundings, they could cast their eyes to the ceiling, the panels of which were mirrored.

The Praetorian Guards, who wore uniforms once described by Comazon as steel flowers, looked seasick from constant motion. They passed me through to a room where separate apartments had been combined into one. This place was cavernous and multilayered, set out in tiers like an immense bed, presided over by a golden sun suspended from the ceiling.

The guests, who numbered hundreds, were shelved like serpents on rocks. Yet they did not suffer. All the surfaces were covered in costly fabrics colored with rare dyes. All of Asia must have been shorn to to stuff the pillows and bolsters that kept the bare asses of the emperor's intimate friends from discomfort.

For they were nude, or nearly so. Lit by candelabra, the walls of polished marble crawled with so many faces, so much hair, so many cheeks and members that only a man gifted in exaggeration could enumerate them. Tall or short, standing or lolling on their backs, they displayed such grotesque proportions that I thought the mirrors of glass and marble distorted them.

What could be said of a woman with breasts as formidable as the tusks of an elephant? Or a man with a penis so big it should be carried separately? Another had three balls in his sac. Another as clearly sported not only a penis but ample breasts. Yet another had hair on every portion of his body, including his palms. It was as if the whole empire had been culled for the trauma that the gods inflicted on men in the name of sex.

That clearly was the goal of the gathering. The orchestra was heavy in pipes and horns, and the air redolent of so many exotic scents I could not separate them. The servants, naked and oiled, passed among the guests with platters of viands that were each an offering to Bacchus. Forcemeats molded into shapes and faces, cakes decorated in every motif of the animal kingdom, pies and savories pickled, jellied and iced, and the delicacies—hummingbird tongues, oysters of peacock, mullet's beards, sow's udders, camel's heels, and the brains of every fowl of four continents. To slake the thirst of the revelers, a fountain stood before the emperor's dais, gushing red wine and white, the former from the groin of a female statue, the latter from a priapic male.

I knew not the protocol of an orgy, but thought a man fully dressed would claim the attention of the emperor. Hierocles, who fondled a monkey with black and white fur, lifted one finger in my direction. The emperor appeared over a bank of cane-striped cushions. He looked out. He saw. He waved.

I made my way across the room through naked bodies to the emperor and his whore who were also naked. The Lord of the World wore makeup of white lead, and a hairnet, like a good wife, while his lover had mounted on his groin a penis sheathe of beaten gold.

"My lord."

The emperor held his hand out, flounced the air, and the sounds of the orchestra diminished. He lay that hand, and latterly his head, on the charioteer's breast.

"Marcellus Decimus, you know my husband."

Vaguely, I looked Hierocles' way, which was so much the emperor's way. He nodded. We understood each other completely.

"Marcellus is the investigative arm of my government," said the emperor in a soft voice that begged the attention of his spouse. "His vigilance guards us from treason."

Hierocles snorted. "There's a shithill of it around. Enough to keep him busy."

"Marcellus has no time of his own. His only concern is our welfare. Thrice he went against rebellions and thrice they were crushed." The emperor held up a finger, as if he had forgotten a vital point. "And he fetched my goddess from Carthage, where she was unappreciated."

"I neglected to inquire of my lord after the stone. Does it meet his needs?"

"Yes, admirably. El-Gabal and Tanit are united. They cohabit, and if the truth were known, are very much in love."

"Then all is well."

"Look around," said Hierocles. "The streets of Rome are paved with their offspring."

The emperor laughed at the wit of his whore. Another man, who was more like a boy of twelve years, sitting at the left hand of the all-powerful, tittered mildly, as perhaps was his role. Mine I could not understand, or the way in which I was to fulfill it.

"I'm glad my lord has experienced no disappointment in the marriage. His powers must surely have returned."

I had made a mistake by the emperor's eyes, which shifted instantly. He was drugged, yes, and drunk, but more potent was the anger that had been touched.

"For an investigator, Marcellus, you have always shown a lack of understanding of the sublime. The god is happy. His wife is ecstatic. The emperor is content. That is all that should concern you."

I thought by his words that something had gone wrong with the god and his consort. Rarely had he spoken like that to me. "My lord knows his servant's deficiencies in these matters. Perhaps he would turn to other matters more at my level of competence."

"Of course." The emperor sat up. "We must be informed of every aspect in the war of love. This conflict is not, as most think, between man and woman, but between the adventuresome and the hidebound." He waved his hand at his menagerie. "This the battlefield, and these are my warriors. Now what of the insurrectionists? That is, the reactionaries. The losers."

"This affair hardly forms a serious conspiracy, my lord. One man made inquiries into the habits of your court. He implicated his master as the guiding spirit behind the intrusion. He is Senator Messalla."

"Messalla," said Hierocles. "Pig of pigs."

"The Senator is aware of his mistake. He knows the penalty he must pay."

"And what of the other?" asked Hierocles. "We understood two pigs were in this rut."

I did not like the way Hierocles used the "we," as if he asserted the imperial prerogative as his own. Could Messalla have been right about that? Was Hierocles Caesar?

"Messalla was arrested in company with another Senator, Pomponius Bassus. We first thought his involvement was plain, but now it seems he knew nothing of the attempt to dishonor the person of my lord."

"His *person*?" Hierocles rose, and removing his penis sheathe, waved it in my face. "It's the imperial *staff* that's been dishonored!"

The boy on the left laughed. The emperor smiled as he looked at the unsheathed member. It was large but circumcised. The emperor, too, was circumcised. I realized belatedly that every man in this circus had submitted to the disfigurement of Eastern custom. But what other direction existed? The court of Marcus Aurelius Antoninus could not be distinguished from that of Parthia, or Bithynia, or any effeminate empire of the sun.

The emperor looked at me from the far place where he had gone to abdicate his throne. "Marcellus," he said, "you have my ear."

"It's my belief Bassus is innocent, lord. I have a statement from Senator Messalla attesting to that." I took the statement from my belt and placed it on the low table before the emperor. "I recommend Bassus be released from custody."

I thought he would take it up. The emperor's fingers stirred from the goblet he held in two hands; but Hierocles' quicker hand swiped the document away. With disdain, the charioteer put it between the cheeks of his buttocks, where so many things were wont to find their way, then he dropped it with a smell of shit back onto the table.

"Look this way," said Hierocles.

I had not done that. I found it hard to focus on the equestrian whore.

"I want the head of Messalla on this plate." Hierocles tapped the penis sheathe on the silver platter before him. "And the other, the Bassett, too."

I looked at him long enough to shame any naked man, but not this rank bitch. Hierocles, hands on hips, awaited my compliance. I turned to the emperor, hoping he would assert himself.

"My lord, I do not receive orders from a charioteer."

The emperor was interested, but not focused. He looked from me to his lover. His gaze rambled. What he saw was perfectly developed from the shapely legs to the tuck of his waist at the hips and the finely articulated muscles of his chest. And that did not account for the rest.

"Would you be happy if *I* gave the order?"

"My lord, it must be so. This as an important matter of state. Not an entertainment."

The emperor looked at me with a thought of sadness, but only that. "Prefect, I find I cannot go against my husband in this matter."

I wanted to shake him until the stupor fled by my hand. I had known him since he was a boy. He was still a boy. He was the Lord of the World who had no force.

"You must order it, my lord. Only the emperor may execute men of Senatorial rank."

"Two heads," said Hierocles.

The emperor lay back on the cushions and tugged at his lover's leg to draw him down. "Take the heads. Just don't bring them in here."

* * *

I have no memory of passing from the dinner party, through the dressing room and the rotary antechamber. My mind was intent on the act of killing. Hierocles was nothing but a color signaling a bet in the circus, his only relevance the appetite of Caesar, yet I thought of nothing but his head falling at my feet until I entered the passage outside the emperor's quarters. In the courtyard below, I saw, lit by several hundred flambeau, Annia Faustina.

The widow Annia Faustina. How could I tell her that?

I still had no idea after I descended the stairs. I took her hand. She said nothing. She had known what would happen since I told her that her husband had done the one thing sure to bring a patrician to ruin.

"Faustina—"

"You have seen the emperor?"

"Yes."

"And does he see my husband as a threat to his reign?"

"I'm afraid that Caesar no longer rules himself. Prepare yourself, Faustina. Bassus will die. His property will be confiscated."

"There is no hope?"

"None. If you believe I tried to prevent it, I'll be happy."

She did not hear me. Her eyes were like those of men in battle. "There's another way, Marcellus. I'm a member of the Senaculum—the women's Senate. I have the acquaintance of Soaemias, who presides over us. I will go to her and beg help."

I could not say why Faustina's words struck me as they did. What she proposed was logical. More, her appeal might have a small chance at success. But suddenly all the premonitions that in my life I had never had came alive.

"Please, don't go to her, Faustina. It seems the best thing, but it will be much the hardest. Believe me if we ever knew each other."

"Perhaps we never did."

"That's not true."

She knew it. She kissed me as if she had known it longer than I. "Farewell, Marcellus."

* * *

She had shed no tears. Like a true Roman wife, she would only do that to create an effect when she reached the place where it would do the most good. I saw her last as she entered the corridor leading to Soaemias' quarters. Faustina's expanding shadow was thrown against the waters of the multileveled pool until it disappeared, blasted by torch light.

I waited for her to reappear, or my orders to be countermanded. I sent a written appeal to Caesar, who had retired to Caelian Hill following his banquet of freaks and imbeciles. He gave no reply. I dispatched a horseman to the Mother Augusta in Tivoli, where she had gone for a cure. Finally, when the night bled away and I could delay no longer, I sent for the headsman.

Bassus died with the morning sun. He died alone with his head on the block. I sent to Faustina's house to notify her of the time, so she could be with him, but my servant returned with no answer. No one had answered her door. No servants were about. I went to the house to have those facts confirmed. Her children, said a neighbor, had been taken away in the morning hours. They had gone to the palace. Where else did one go under escort by the Praetorian Guard?

I did not see Faustina for three weeks. Nor did anyone beyond the Domus Augustana. When she emerged from the palace at length, she was no longer a private citizen with a life of her own. Annia Faustina, a woman of great beauty, of proven blood and fertility, had become the third wife of Marcus Aurelius Antoninus.

The Empress of Rome.

INK

"It's a sham. Like all his marriages, this one is meant to hide the fact that the emperor is a woman."

Princess Mammea sipped like medicine the glass of Falnerian wine I had poured. She had not come to the small apartment I kept on Quirnal Hill to gossip of things I already knew. She had come from the palace on foot, dressed in a plain stola that did not mark her as a person of importance. If my slave had not known her when she drew her wrap aside, Mammea would have been turned from the door.

"I confess to being confused, Princess. I don't understand why my cousin agreed to serve as empress. Or why her service is necessary."

"She agreed because her children were taken." Mammea looked at me as if I were deficient. "Any woman can be coerced if her children are the means of compliance. As for why it should be done—" She shook her head with slow vehemence and moved closer to me.

"My sister is a monster. She will do anything to keep her power. The only thing she cannot do is convince her son to make love to a woman. And perhaps he would if she were not at his side. I believe the emperor sees in all women the image of Soaemias. He grew up with a volatile, promiscuous mother. What the child learns first is that he must please a woman who cannot be pleased. He knows in his heart that she hates men. He knows that she hates him, because he is a man. So in small ways, she passes on her poison. He absorbs it like the milk he never knew from her. And when he chooses his love, he takes someone who seems so different that she bears no resemblance to her. Someone who is as beautiful in body as she is. Someone who can resist her. Or the idea of her."

"My information is somewhat different, Princess. Your sister and Hierocles work in tandem, I'm told."

"When the charioteer was uncertain of his hold on Varius, that was true. But no longer."

"They're at odds?"

"They vie for power," she said as if she knew what she was talking about. "Each is a prostitute. They understand what it is to sell oneself. They understand the rate varies."

Only one question remained: what was Mammea's price? I had no authority to act at the palace as Prefect of the City. My cousin Faustina was the empress of a zoo. Was that it?

"Princess, are you saying that you and the Mother Augusta have no one you can trust close to the emperor?"

"That's largely correct."

"Relations are that bad."

"Worse. The prostitutes have replaced every man of sense in the government with one of their own. The emperor ignores everything but the god and his own pleasure."

"So you think that Faustina—the empress—could provide you with an ally."

"That depends on the kind of woman she is," said the princess. "Even to speak of the weather with the emperor these days demands enormous tact. But if she seems to be tolerant of his excesses, and devoted to his rule, she could be useful to us."

"I've only seen her once—briefly—since she was married."

"But you could see her as often as she likes."

"Perhaps."

The purple appeared in Mammea's eyes, as it did eventually in all the women of the family. She was the least strange, but the secret in her eyes was the most hidden. "Are you angry with your cousin, Marcellus?"

"Disappointed. I don't know how any woman of character can exist in that atmosphere."

"Don't show your disappointment," she said. "She'll need your help. Especially when the emperor tires of her."

"Will she be safe at that point?"

Mammea shrugged. "We know the emperor has never murdered any of his wives. But he grows increasingly unstable."

Perhaps she was stating the obvious, or overestimating the danger to jog my feelings. She did not know how deeply they ran, but could guess. As a woman with a son who might ascend to the throne one day, her instincts could be no keener.

"Am I to assume the Mother Augusta's timetable is still in effect?"

"That has not changed," she said. "In spite of the devices of my sister, the emperor will produce no heir. Alexianus will be appointed consul on his birthday in three months. He will be of age to assume the throne. All that remains is to guarantee he is worthy of the honor."

"How will that be done?"

"I'm careful of his education," she said. "I've put him with Greek and Latin scholars of the highest character. His mind is being developed, but his body and martial skills want honing."

"I can recommend someone for the work."

"I do not want someone," she said. "I want the best that can be found."

"Be sure I will find that man."

"He cannot simply be a swords-master," she said. "Or a fine athlete. He must be someone who will teach my son to apply good judgment. And convert it to action."

"That's more difficult."

Mammea looked at me with a challenge that in any other woman could be mistaken for lust. "I've found the man I want. Your term as Prefect expires soon. You will not be reappointed. Instead of becoming legate to Moesia, which I understand is the post you will be offered, I ask you, I beg you, to assume the most important job in this empire."

"The training of your son."

"I require more," she said. "I want you to make him a man."

"My lady—"

"You will be Alexianus' guardian as long as he lives," she said. "There is no position of greater responsibility. When he is Caesar, there will be no position of greater scope. I will be Mother of the Camp. You will be Alexianus' regent."

* * *

I did not tell Mammea what she wanted for her son was seldom done quickly. I believed she knew what she asked. The manhood of her son was an issue even if the emperor woke up one morning and decided that a stone was a stone and a whore a whore. Though that was unlikely, stranger things had happened in the rarefied world of the Domus Augustana.

I was not as sure how to approach the empress. At our one meeting, I gauged Faustina's mood, which was worried, and extended an invitation to visit me at her pleasure. When I came home to the Tiberiana two days after the visit of Mammea, I found that Faustina had finally accepted the invitation. I made my way through five Praetorian Guards and several sets of attendants to find that Philomene had made the empress at home. They sat on the side balcony overlooking the Temple of Cybele, taking watered wine and roe, engaged in conversation.

Should I mind that the two women who knew me best were in conference? Did they pass secrets? Exchange thoughts on how to cope with the beast? My uneasiness did not quite disappear when Philomene so gracefully did.

"You look well, Faustina."

"Well enough," she said. "There are advantages to being empress. The service is one."

"Are there others?"

"Most things are infinite at the palace," she said, smiling. "But I sometimes find it difficult to navigate the crowds in my bedroom and bath, or when I'm with the children."

"Does the emperor like being a father?"

"Very much," she said with the same strained smile. "He sees the children every day. And he's gentle with them. He doesn't even correct Marcellus when the child pulls his beard."

I knew that her boy, who was two years old, had been named Marcellus. Nothing was surprising in the name, which had been in our family for three hundred years. It was more surprising that the emperor had allowed his beard to grow. That was a masculine statement at odds with what he had become.

"So the emperor enjoys his role as pater familias."

Faustina made an amused but distressed sound. "He's the head of a tribe, of that we can be sure."

That note of criticism was heartening. I closed the door to the balcony. Some months before, when I became aware that intimate matters had found their way to the palace from my apartment, I had the adjoining balcony blocked, the roof truncated, and the ground below planted in thistle and rose. Then I purged my household staff.

"You may speak freely, Faustina. Nothing we say will be overheard."

Her relief was audible as she made that amused but breathless sound again. I imagine she had seldom made it before the last month of her life, but it had since become a quiet manifestation of her unquiet emotions.

"If I could tell you, Marcellus, what's happened to me—" She paused, censoring her words. "But the truth is nothing. I live in the palace, I watch the comings and goings of the most incredible human beings ever seen on this earth, but *nothing* has happened."

"Between the emperor and you."

"That is so."

I should have been disheartened at the news that had come twice before, but this time I was happy to hear it. In spite of the neglect by her husband, Faustina looked as fresh as the sun. The cooking at the palace had put more flesh on her bones, which was flattering.

"That's the emperor's pattern. He marries, but like a collector of fine things. The object and its beauty are what he appreciates."

"And his wives are discarded."

"To date."

"There's one thing I don't understand. Am I to welcome the event or dread it?"

I wanted to answer, but could not how I wished. "I'm afraid the emperor has created a new class of women. His ex-wives. The average length of marriage is six months. The usual procedure when it ends is to claim their dowry and return them to their homes without honors. It's a shameful business, but no one has been seriously harmed. The process allows him to finance his pleasures and pass off his shortcomings. If it happens again, you'll have your children unless he plans to keep them as heirs to the throne."

"Can he do that?"

"He can do anything he likes. But I doubt he will. The children are not his blood. If it comes to adoption, there's always Alexianus."

"And if there is another alternative?"

"Another?"

Faustina slowly put her hands to her belly. She used both hands and held them there. There. Where life begins.

"But how?"

"It's Bassus' child—of that you can be sure. Of that the emperor can be sure."

I heard her words from a distance. My mind accelerated through many possibilities that jumbled like counters in a sack. Only one question seemed relevant in the end.

"Who knows this?"

"The emperor now. Soaemias from the beginning."

"You told her *that*?"

"On the first night I went to her, yes. She asked many questions, but most concerned my ability to bear children. When she found out I was pregnant, she seemed content."

"You're not far along then."

"Nearly three months."

The magic number. The Vestal had been discarded at three and a replacement found. This child would arrive close enough in time to be presented as the legitimate offspring of Marcus Aurelius Antoninus. No doubt the name had already been chosen.

"You say that Soaemias was interested in your pregnancy?"

"That's nearly all she asked about," said Faustina. "I promised her I'd do anything she asked if she interceded in behalf of my husband. And I have honored my promise."

"What did she promise you?"

"That she would attempt to save Bassus."

"Did she?"

"She went to see the emperor, yes."

"How long was she gone that night?"

"About an hour. Less. It seemed like more."

It would have been impossible for Soaemias to go to Caelian Hill and return to the palace in that time. It would have been hard for a man on a fast horse.

"Faustina, I don't know how to say this, but you've been lied to. Your marriage is more a mockery than you think. She wants the baby. That was her only thought—and still is."

Faustina touched her belly again as if protecting it. Slowly, the panic in her eyes locked into a decision. "This child belongs to Bassus. The emperor knows that if anyone does."

"The baby belongs to your husband. That's the law."

Faustina did not want to believe the truth. It was easier to live the fantasy she had entered. A pregnant woman has that right.

"They can't have done it," she said. "Not like *that*."

I would have said anything to ease her mind. If I had not received a visit from Mammea, I could have. "They do everything like that, Faustina. Power is the only principle in the palace. The people who live outside *want* it, but they don't understand what it is to *have* it. And what things must be done to *keep* it."

"But this is murder," she said. "Worse. The father is killed like meat. The child will be taken like meat."

"To Soaemias the child is the most precious thing in the world—the savior of her son."

Faustina put her hands to her belly again, but this time her grip was heavy. "It's only a child to me. A child who has no father."

"I'd not make that widely known, Faustina."

"That's because you're a man," she said. "You're not the mother of the savior."

* * *

I was unhappy with the way the visit ended, but when Faustina left she seemed like the woman she had always been. She gave money to my servants, as custom demanded, and said good-bye to Philomene. I waved from the steps like a man in a crowd.

Before she left, Faustina told me how to contact her secretly. The go-between would be her children's tutor, a Greek named Crysogones. The arrangement worked well in the following days as I neared the end of my one-year term as Prefect of the City. My appointment could not be legally extended, nor would it.

The empress came twice more to my home. She and Philomene struck up a warm but businesslike friendship. The information from Philomene's network, combined with Faustina's, provided a picture of insanity at the court that was almost too lifelike.

The only place those networks could not penetrate were the goings-on at the temple on Caelian Hill. That fair weather retreat had become a year-round residence, and the chief avenue of approach to the god. Soaemias and her son shut themselves in its precincts for days on end. The stories that emerged seemed like the products of fetid imaginations. Monkeys, it was said, were the current fascination. The emperor sacrificed great quantities of those harmless beasts in an attempt to stimulate the workings of the stone—or stones.

The most curious thing about these practices was that the Vestal took a leading part. Although discarded as the empress when she failed to produce an heir, Aquila Severa made herself useful as a servant of the temple. The emperor, who had never found value in her body, found it in her mind. She was said not to shrink from the bloodiest sacrifices, and to dine upon the gonads of monkeys like goose liver.

"They also say she serves as a prostitute to Astarte."

"The Vestal?"

"Yes," said Philomene. "I spoke to a man who had been with her. He said she came to the exercise like an athlete."

"I find that hard to believe. Not on her part, but the other. Laying with a Vestal guarantees bad luck as long as a man lives. Those who believe in the bad luck make it so."

"Yet some do not shrink from sacrilege," she said. "The young men who clamor for the emperor's favor will do anything to have it, even if it means having her luck."

"It's a good thing Faustina carries the savior. The child will keep her from harm."

"She knows that," said Philomene. "For the most part, she takes care of herself. Except for drinking wine."

"Watered wine."

"In any form, it's not good for the child."

"This opinion comes from your vast knowledge of birthing and rearing."

"My mother was a midwife," she said.

"But perhaps not the best at her trade. Or you would not have been sold into slavery."

Philomene usually reacted when I said something cruel, but this time she said nothing. That meant she was hurt. I tried for the rest of the evening, and the week, to make up for my loss of temper. Finally, she forgave me when I told the truth. The empress meant more to me than a cousin, and more than a savior. She was my innocence.

The place we usually met promoted the feeling of a sheltered time. In the gymnasium where the palace children, including Alexianus, took their lessons, I often felt a subtle shift on the temporal plane that brought back my youth as through the mouth of a tunnel. First darkness, then the warmth of memory. At Faustina's suggestion, I set up a class on Wednesdays, where military applications filled two hours. The children liked the practice with Greek pikes, Emesene bows and Balearic slings, especially the girls, who were by far the more aggressive.

I did not favor Alexianus in the curriculum. Indeed, I was harder on him than the rest. Frugius, to whom I delegated instruction with killing weapons, made him work harder still. Although the emperor's cousin demonstrated no great fighting skills, he was more attentive to those matters than his cousin. Nor did he complain.

Clearly, his mother had instilled in him a sense of what he could become. The difference between Alexianus and his cousin was that the younger had not succumbed to the influence of the priests. Alexianus had undergone the same training "on the mountain," but since only one male of the clan could be high priest, he did not complete the last phase—"the passage." That ritual, lasting a month, made the difference in his cousin's mind, which is to say, his life.

"He was changed by it," said Alexianus as we sat in the bath being scraped by slaves with a strigil. It was the only Roman ritual both healthy and good, and it came at the end of a training session where the boy had succeeded in getting inside Frugius' guard with a short sword. He had done very well.

"Just how were these changes accomplished?"

Alexianus waited until the slave left, and we walked backed toward the cold room. "My cousin was required to fast and practice the dance until he was beyond exhaustion. That and partaking of soma brought about his vision, which he was required to have."

"A vision of the future?"

"Can a vision be of the past?"

"Not typically. But this is far from typical. Your cousin began by coining money from his mind, but he's graduated to monkeys. I understand the Macellum Magnum—and the other meat markets on the Caelian—do a booming business in their parts."

"Monkeys." Alexianus seemed surprised to hear the news, but not baffled at its import. "That's logical. They're the closest to man. Their sacrifice would be more meaningful. It's important to heighten the letting of blood. Just as the fasting is heightened by the soma."

"The soma. It's a drug?"

"A powerful one."

"I've heard of it, but usually no drug has a lasting effect unless repeated."

"I believe he does repeat it," said Alexianus. "No one tells him he can't, least of all the priests. Nor his mother. But in doing it, and trying to reach the god, it's the dancing that matters most. The movements are always the same. They are precise. That's why the music is played in the same rhythm. The only way it varies is by growing louder and faster."

"Building to a climax."

"In the dancer, too," he said. "The important thing is that the movements are known but unthought. They must be part of the priest, as he is part of them."

The important thing about mysticism was that it must always be obscure. One thing was always part of another, unless it was part of the whole, in which case it was everything.

I did not blame Alexianus for his vague words, as they were the words of the priests. It was a mark of his good sense that he did not put the lessons into practice. The misfortune of the empire was that the emperor did little else. His dancing had become manic. He danced at every ceremony of the god, and lately he shuffled in that crazed way everywhere. When he announced to the Senate that he would divorce the Vestal and marry my cousin, the emperor danced as he spoke to that august and hostile body. It was as if he could not still his feet or hands.

"There must be something to this, Alexianus. When we were in Syria, I saw the emperor do incredible things. I can't explain them. They were, for lack of a better word, miracles."

"I was told what happened," said Alexianus. "The priests extolled the wonders of the god and his high priest. But it seems Varius' miracles did not survive the passage from Syria."

"So you think they were local miracles."

Alexianus shrugged. "The god is a local god. What if he was always meant to be?"

"Not to be exported, you think?"

"Possibly."

That was one way of looking at it. The emperor's ability to link with the cosmic on demand did not seem to survive those early days in Syria. Not the stone of Emesa transported to Bithynia, nor the stone of Tanit brought to Rome as its mate, restored those mysterious powers.

"If you were in the emperor's place, would you have exported the god?"

Alexianus' grew pensive. He usually hesitated in making decisions. Nothing he did was impulsive. That made him in most ways the opposite of the emperor. And as many were coming to think, it made him an antidote.

"I would extol the sun that is everywhere to be seen," he said. "I would not worship a stone, no matter what its origin. Nor would I scorn the gods of Rome."

"Well said."

* * *

The subject of our conversation was accidental, but had been prompted by the emperor's latest rampage against traditional religions. One morning in the preceding week, he had his priests repair to the Temple of Cybele, where they extracted from the statue of the Great Mother the stone that had been brought from Pessinus during the Carthaginian War. The stone comprised her head. She now had none.

The emperor next confiscated the Shields of Mars from the temple of that god, who was the patron and protector of the city. When asked what would happen to an empire bereft of the favor of the god of war, the emperor replied that he wanted nothing to do with violence. "It's enough that you call me Pius and Felix," he said.

Next, his agents raided the Temples of Isis and Serapis for cult objects sacred to the Nile gods. That incursion enraged Philomene, as well as the substantial Egyptian colony in Rome. And last, the emperor returned to the place that was his special fascination, the Temple of Vesta, where he seized the Palladium.

The theft of that object created a furor in the city, for the Palladium was the most important vestige of Roman religion. The oldest and most sacred cult object in Rome, it was a statue of Pallas-Athene said to have been rescued from the burning city of Troy by Lord Aeneas and brought to Italy. Made of wood, blackened by age and the catastrophes that had visited the city, the Palladium was hidden in a secret room in the Temple of the Vestals.

No man knew how to open the room, nor was any man allowed in it. Yet that happened. I was less puzzled by the burglary than most, for I knew Aquila Severa served the emperor ardently. She must have given him the key to the secret room, though I could not understand how she countenanced the sacrilege against the goddess she had served most of her life.

Legend had it that anyone who moved the idol from its place suffered a hideous fate. The Pontifex Caecilius Mettelus had been struck blind when he removed the statue in order to save it during a fire four hundred years ago. During another fire that swept the city in the reign of Septimus Severus, a worse fate had befallen another Pontifex who sickened and died with a fever and grotesque sores within three days after he, too, moved the idol from its place.

Those men had known the dangers. Never would they have touched Pallas except to protect her. They died miserably nonetheless. Think what would happen to a man who abducted the sacred idol and put it to his own uses. Nothing could protect him from the wrath of Athena.

So the superstitious of Rome, which was everyone, waited for the retribution that must come. The Palladium was stolen Tuesday evening.

Thursday morning, the empress miscarried.

* * *

Although deep mourning was declared, that, too, was a sham in every quarter of the palace but one. Soaemias took the news hard. She entered the empress' bedchamber with blood on the sheets, and was still within when I arrived. Her voice could be heard, loud and accusatory. Before I made my way past the Praetorian Guards, the bronze door blew open.

I barely recognized her face distorted with fury. Her hair was wild, bursting from her headband. Her eyes were preternaturally bright and her voice came from the same region.

"What accounts for this?" she asked, looking at me.

"Nothing, Princess."

"I thought you might say a wooden idol. I thought you might be like the rest, but you never were." She looked at me as if I had raped the Vestal to no result. "You don't believe in anything. Not even your own kin."

"This is not a question of belief—but of nature. The empress saw her husband taken from her never to return. She has been under great strain. Nothing should be worse for a pregnancy."

The fury in Soaemias' face found its voice. "The woman is weak! Her blood is bad! And it's *your* blood, Marcellus! I've given her the best care, the best physicians, the best of everything! And they tell me I have nothing in return!"

"Not everything can be controlled, Soaemias."

"If I want to hear platitudes, I'll call a damned Greek. I go now to the quarters of my son to tell him that his child no longer exists! When I return, you'll wish I had not! All of you!"

She swept her hand around her, including the palace, which was the world. Turning away, moving down the hall, carrying the folds of her stola in her hand, I heard her call for her Guard. They clattered to arms, storming from the palace and summoning their horse. In a matter of moments, Soaemias was off to Caelian Hill to commune with her son.

The door to the empress' quarters was open. The physicians, such as they were, gathered at the entrance in an academic mode, as if deciding on their spokesman. They were Greeks to a man. Perhaps they affected not to hear the princess' words. Hysteria was one of the constants of their trade. Surely, they were used to such threats from their employers.

One man put himself forward, but gingerly. He was Philocrates, chief physician to the imperial family. About fifty years, of florid complexion and speech, he bowed low. "Prefect."

"How is the empress?"

"Recovering." He posed his hand into his beard. "In general, I would say she survived her ordeal in good condition. But it's difficult to say how she will fare. The womb wanders in women. Indeed, the organ is rarely found in the same place twice. When pregnancy is upon them, the movement becomes more fluid. And traumatic. A failed pregnancy is the worst thing for their nature. Hysteria can result. In fact, it is often the result."

I did not question his verdict, which seemed like nonsense but could have been wisdom. None of the many doctors who attended the court were of the stature of Galen, or even Gannys.

"Will she be able to bear children again?"

"I see no reason why not."

"Was it possible to tell the sex of the child?"

He shook his head. "It was too early. But fortunate for the empress. The risk to the mother's health increases each day past three months. Yes, she was lucky."

A bit more luck and she would be dead. When I entered her bedchamber, I saw the change that Faustina's miscarriage had wrought. The extra weight that filled her face now hung heavily from her jaw, like a gorget. The color in her complexion was embers. If she had no fever, she never would. If she lasted the night, she might live a long time. That I knew from the battlefield, where every physician should spend his apprenticeship.

"It's Marcellus, my lady."

She had seen me enter the room, but gave no sign of recognition. Now she blinked her eyes as she lay upon the silk pillow. The dark lashes with an effort fluttered free.

"Cousin."

"I came as soon as I heard of your loss."

"Loss." She seized the word. "What has never been born cannot be lost."

She might be delirious. What she said to me, she said to the attendants still in the room. The bane of royalty was worse in intimate moments. Faustina had experienced pain and torment of body and mind in full view of servants, doctors, and guards. They were of no account, but were always present, always listening, always conveying the things they heard. I found it hard to speak to her and to them.

"My lady knows best. The doctors feel this incident has not impaired her ability to bear more children."

"So I will have another chance at a savior."

"It seems."

"But where will I find the seed?"

Not in her husband. Not in this palace. "I believe you, least of all women, should be concerned with that. Your life and health mean everything to your people."

She looked to the door where the convocation of doctors had reconvened. "What do the people know? How are they different from Greeks? When Pallas calls, we answer. She is the goddess of vengeance. She demands—always—the most of women."

"And if I said that was superstition—"

"You would be lying."

She was right. Superstition caused men—and women—to think of that thing first rather than consult good sense. Though I fought off the curse of Pallas with all my heart, I could not help thinking of it with my heart.

"You should rest. The goddess does not share her mind with us. And never with me."

"My cousin does not know," she said. "Which means no one can know."

* * *

I left the bedchamber feeling that something beyond the obvious was wrong. It was not Faustina's state of health or mind. Hysteria was one thing, a wandering womb another. Was I so long away from my cousin that I knew nothing of her?

When Lady Ursula left the empress' chamber, stepping into the hallway, I called to her. She was a friend of Faustina's who had left her patrician life to become one of the empress' close attendants in the palace. Tall, with brown hair piled in tight curls, she looked at most men on equal footing. Only her jewelry, from the looping earrings to the pendant of pearl and the many rings, pointed to her station as Handmaiden to the Empress. That, and the length of her nose.

"Prefect."

"Ursula, I've spoken to the empress' physician. He thinks she'll be well. But I'd like your opinion. Somehow, it seems more valuable."

She gave a smile that suited the moment. "I can't pretend to a learned opinion. But the empress' constitution is strong. I've never known her to be ill, even when she was pregnant with Viviana and Marcellus."

"And lately?"

"Nothing to remark," she said. "But perhaps you should speak with the *obstetrices*."

"Not Philocrates?"

"He has seen her of course. At least five different physicians have seen her. But her usual choice is Prenestina."

I was glad to hear a Roman name for the midwife. "I'd like to speak with her."

"Follow me."

Prenestina's room was a small chamber down the hall where three beds had been placed in a close row for the sleep the empress' physicians could acquire. Prenestina awakened when we entered the room, sitting up on her bed. She was an older woman with stiff gray hair and a broad nose with small nostrils that collapsed quickly. Her brown eyes were keen and gave every appearance of quickened attention.

"Prenestina, the Prefect of the City would speak with you."

Ursula did not leave us, but withdrew to the doorway of the room, as if guarding it. That made me uncomfortable, so I asked her to leave. She might be the eyes and ears of her mistress, but the palace had enough.

I sat on the bed opposite Prenestina. "I understand you were here last night and this morning. Did you observe the empress' miscarriage?"

"Yes, Prefect. I was here on this bed, but when called, I went to the empress' side."

No one would say less to the Prefect of the City, but I thought Prenestina was honest. Her manner, unlike Greek physicians, was not unctuous or condescending. She might be able to explain what had happened in layman's terms.

"What did you observe about the event, Prenestina?"

"When I came to her, the empress had already passed fluid. It was pale, watery. Shortly afterward, she passed a sanguineous fluid." Prenestina paused. "That means like water if meat has been washed in it."

"Thank you."

She nodded. "Next, there was a flow of blood. Bright blood. Then a thicker clot of blood in the ghostly shape of flesh."

"Are miscarriages always like that in your experience?"

"Not exactly," she said. "But nearly. The thing that varies are the reactions in the aftermath of the event."

"How so?"

"Differences in women cause the fluctuations. And there are some differences if the event is a miscarriage or an abortion."

The obstetrices had tried to tell me something that was not obvious. She did not say it directly in spite of her directness. I assumed it might have echoes if not confined to this room.

"You seem to have given me a choice. Which of the two events was it?"

"I can't say. Even Soranus in his book on gynecology could not say without doubt."

"Still—"

She lowered her eyes as if to turn their light inward. "There are a variety of symptoms a woman experiences in miscarriage," she said. "Her breasts may shrink, her loins may cool. It's as if nature is saying the trial is over."

"But otherwise—"

"Abortion can be induced," she said mildly. "The results are sometimes different. The patient may experience a fever, chills, cramps, sweats. That's usually the result of a foreign substance that has been introduced to interrupt the natural process."

"A poison."

"We don't call it that."

"What do you call it?"

She closed her eyes. "Ink."

"Ink?"

She opened her eyes as if all she saw in me was a man. "It's for the name that will never be written."

"I see. But do you think some substance was given to the empress?"

"It's possible, based on her symptoms. But complications can occur in a natural event. The same symptoms, in fact. Fever, chills, cramps. That's also the way the body reacts to some poisons. If I could tell you without hesitation, I would. It's not my goal to lose children."

* * *

I spent longer with Prenestina gathering facts about the nature of Ink, and the sources where the abortifacient could be purchased. When I left, I took her hand in thanks without saying more and moved silently to the door.

Ursula did not jump when I appeared at a distance of three inches, but she started like any woman who has been caught. I gave her a chance to reclaim her dignity before I took her to task.

"Has there been any change with the empress?"

"No, no," she said as if speaking from a balcony. "She's as well as she can be."

"And her tasters? Do they enjoy good health?"

Ursula blinked but responded. "You may see for yourself. They're in the next room."

I saw for myself, though Ursula accompanied me to the taster's quarters. The room was cramped with a window onto the latrines. She excused herself after introducing me.

They were three. Each was a physical type. The Gaul was slim, red-haired and rawboned; the Caucasian blonde, meaty and squat, the Numidian dark, heavily muscled, tall but shapely. All were slaves. All, based on their appearance, had not been given a poison that acted with any speed.

They had tasted the food at the three meals the empress had eaten yesterday, each a portion from each batch. Faustina had ingested no supplements or medications except the watered wine that she drank before she retired last night. That, too, had been tasted immediately after being poured.

"Were you aware of anything odd about the wine?"

"No," said the Caucasian, who had been on duty all night. "It seemed the usual."

"She took it every night?"

"Most nights."

"Did she drink it quickly last night?"

"When she went to it. After she waited for it to cool."

"Where was it placed to cool?"

"On the stand beside her bed."

"How long did it remain there?"

The Caucasian bethought herself. She was terrified, as were the other two. If anything were remotely wrong, or suspected of being wrong, all three would be tortured until they died. That was the procedure with palace slaves.

"Not long," she said. "Not a quarter of an hour. Less, I'm sure."

"Did anyone touch the glass?"

"Only the empress, as I saw."

I thought she was too frightened to lie, but not confident that torture produced veracity. Slaves had been known to lie to escape pain. Many innocent people have been convicted with forced evidence.

"Who else was in the room while the wine was on the stand?"

"The three Guards at the door," said the Caucasian. "Lady Ursula. And myself."

"Were you absent from the room at any time?"

"Only for a moment," she said. "The empress sent me to fetch her children."

"How long were you gone?"

"Not long," she said. "The children were still awake. I brought them to her and she bade them goodnight."

"Was that her habit?"

"Not often. Most nights, she went to them."

"Did you notice anything else unusual? What was her manner? How did she behave with the children?"

"I thought she talked to the children more than her wont, but saw nothing odd in that."

"Did you return the children to their room?"

"No. The empress did. She liked to tuck them in."

So Ursula had been the only one alone with the empress and her wine. I drew no conclusions. There were several suspects, but no crime that could be verified. And I was sure I would not learn much more from Ursula.

She was the empress' friend, and the only member of her circle chosen to follow her to the palace. Which meant Faustina trusted her. More, it meant Ursula was sophisticated enough to survive this environment. Question: was she sophisticated but incorruptible?

"I'm going now," I said to her. "When Soaemias returns, promising to take the heads of everyone in sight, refer her to me."

"You were satisfied with the interviews?"

"Yes, but for one matter. I'd like to know who chose the tasters."

"Prefect Comazon. He sent them to us after they were examined for health and loyalty."

I wondered how he tested slaves who would be tasters for loyalty. With torture? With a wand? "That's unfortunate under the circumstances, Ursula."

"Is it?"

"The empress should have been provided with tasters who were pregnant."

"Why is that necessary?"

It seemed to me that she should have known, unless she saw her duties as mainly social. "Healthy women would not be affected by a drug used to induce abortion. Unless they were also with child."

Ursula's complexion was pale, her cosmetics made it paler, but I thought she blanched, too. "Then it *was* an oversight."

"Yes, but I wouldn't expect Prefect Comazon to think of that. Perhaps you or the empress should have."

"Hindsight is not the most gracious gift that a man can possess," said Ursula with an anger she gathered in the pause.

"It's not a gift. More like a job."

That gave her something to think about while I went to my apartments, where I found Piso, whom I had sent for, and Philomene. Prenestina had given me the names of six people known to traffic in Ink. Three were midwives of uncertain reputation and three others unemployed—which meant they were professionals. Poison had been the preferred weapon of domestic assassination in Rome for centuries, and the reason Romulus and Remus were suckled by a she-wolf.

"Philomene will go to the midwives," I said. "Piso to the poisoners. Tell them that it's known they supplied the means of destroying Caesar's heir. Try to be sly about it. Say you've come to warn them for a price. You won't make much money, but if they're guilty, they'll react quickly. It's doubtful if they know the magnitude of the thing they've done. When they discover it, they'll run."

Philomene spoke first. "What do they have to fear but the person who bought the Ink?"

"Torture. Tell them it's certain. The confiscation of their property, too. After that, crucifixion. You can display conviction when you say these things. They are, or will be, true."

Philomene seemed to have difficulty believing what was said by the man she had known for three years. I gave her no reason to doubt it. Piso never doubted it for an instant.

"We'll have men waiting to follow?"

"To seize them, yes."

Piso made his objection. "There may be more than one who answers the call, Prefect. It could be that all the suspects will run."

"That's cumbersome but acceptable. They'll be brought—one or all—to headquarters."

* * *

I wanted to go down to the city, but that would introduce an uncontrolled element into the investigation. I did not want outright panic in the fraternity of poisoners, who were a skittish lot.

Nor did I want to leave the palace yet. If word got out that I had begun to investigate the empress' miscarriage, the two competing parties would react quickly. I thought I had fifteen minutes to wait for their move, but that estimate was off a bit. More than half an hour passed before the Mother Augusta appeared at the door with a double guard of Praetorians. It was the first time she visited my rooms in the two years I had occupied them.

"Mother, to what do I owe this honor?"

"You're free to be artful, Marcellus, but some other time. You know why I'm here."

She directed her massive body to my sitting room, where no chair could be found large enough to house her. I had the servants fetch my weapon's chest from the armory and place it on the balcony overlooking the Temple of Cybele, where the Mother Augusta sat like a small but mighty temple of her own construction.

"You may speak freely, Mother. Nothing we say will be overheard."

"Not even the gods should witness to this conversation. Even the Great Mother."

"She's lost her head in any case."

"That's the least funny thing you've ever said, Marcellus. I believe in nothing but this family, but some things should never be overthrown. There are many people who believe in Cybele, Isis, and Pallas. Now, literally, they've lost their moorings. Everything from their dreams to their stomachs are upset. My cooks complain that their eggs have two and three yolks, that the livers of calves have turned blue, and that eagles fall from the sky as if shot on the wing." She held out her hand as if the world balanced upon it. "I saw one of the yolks. It vanquished my appetite. It looked like the map of Syria in provinces."

"And the remedy for these anomalies—"

"We know what it is," she said like an executioner. "Now that your cousin no longer carries the hope of the empire, my grandson has nowhere to turn to divert the attention of the people from his folly. He will agree to Alexianus as consul. With luck, he will agree to have his cousin as Caesar, too."

That was an escalation. If the emperor accepted the proposal, he would also promote the end of his reign. "You seem to have everything calculated well, Mother."

"Not quite everything," she said. "I understand you've been investigating the empress' illness."

"I wouldn't call it an investigation. There are some indications that my cousin's miscarriage was . . . unusual."

The Mother Augusta stared at me without relief for ten seconds. "Marcellus, I'll tell you truthfully: I had nothing to do with your cousin's misfortune. If you investigate, you'll come to that conclusion."

"I've come to no conclusions, Mother. I'm not even sure a crime was committed."

"But what if you develop evidence of a crime?"

I saw her problem. The only suspects were in her camp. Only they had motive. But for Faustina, her camp was my camp. "If evidence develops, Mother, I'll keep it to myself. And I'll keep the punishment private."

"What does that mean?"

"If someone prompted the empress' miscarriage, I'll see them to their graves. Quietly."

"Very quietly. I want no suspicion to attach to Alexianus—or those around him."

"Then we understand each other."

"Marcellus, we always have."

* * *

That conversation did not elevate my spirits, but gave me the freedom to carry out the investigation. Maesa had never broken her word in any bargain. Her chief virtue was that she recognized efficiency, which was rare in government. The barbers, cooks and charioteers that her grandson had appointed were looting the treasury at an unprecedented rate. Several provinces were at the point of rebellion due to the tax burden and the rapacity of their legates. The only thing that kept the people of Rome from outright revolt were the extravagant games that the emperor continued to give.

While the Mother Augusta and I sat on the balcony, I had heard in the distance trumpets announce the emperor's return to the palace. Perhaps he had come to see his female wife, and I supposed, after waiting a decent interval, that I should, too.

I made my way to the palace anticipating a confrontation, but the scene I discovered as I entered Faustina's quarters was bare of the attendants that marked the emperor's presence. Instead, Philocrates, the Greek physician, sat alone on the bench along the outer walls. His hand covered his face as if he were deep in thought. When I came closer, I saw he was weeping.

"What happened?"

Philocrates looked up through blurred eyes. "What can I do? What can anyone do?"

"What has happened to the empress, man?"

He blinked. "She's well. Resting comfortably. She may be the only well person here."

Then he burst into tears, putting his hands to his face and woofing like a dog. Greeks. Was there nothing manly in their make-up? The Guards at the door to the inner chamber looked at him like beasts at bloody meat.

"Philocrates, control yourself. Then tell me what's upset you."

The physician did not control himself, but he lowered his hands and spoke again through his tears. "The emperor came here. He told me—he insisted—that I should make upon his body an incision."

"He wanted you to cut him?"

"Yes!" he cried. "In the midst of blood and disaster, he insisted on more. He was very emotional. He was angry. He was—"

I knew the word he wanted, but did not say it. The emperor was insane.

"What sort of incision did he want you to make?"

The physician put his hands to his groin. "Here. The emperor wished me to make him a woman. He demanded I make for him a vagina."

"A womb?"

"It's natural, I suppose. With the failure of the empress' pregnancy. He wishes to bear his own children."

"Natural, yes."

"But it cannot be done," he said. "No physician on earth can give him what he wants. A man's body can only perform the reproductive function for which it was intended."

I could imagine the emperor's desperation. I could imagine everything but the lunatic he had become. "Go to your library, Philocrates. Find the books that illustrate the bodies of men and women. Take them to the emperor when he is calm, and explain that what he seeks is medically unsound."

The Greek ceased weeping. "Do you think he will respond?"

"He likes pictures. All children do."

* * *

I left the palace wondering how the Mother Augusta would cope with her grandson. The volatility of the situation was incredible. If the emperor was as deranged as he seemed, forging an agreement might be difficult. He had nowhere to turn for an heir.

I did not want my investigation to impede an agreement. With shifting emotions I received a message from Piso two hours after midnight telling me the strategy we had applied to the poisoners worked. Two of the suspects bolted, carrying with them a significant amount of their portable goods, including ample currency of the older, harder sort. One, the poisoner, was far the richer. The fortune of the midwife did not impress, but it was all she had.

I arrived as quickly as darkness and traffic in the city permitted, finding the two best spies I knew—Piso and Philomene—waiting and ready. "We'll take the poisoner first. Then we'll know if we should question the midwife."

"She's a hard one," said Piso. "When I came to her shop, knowing what she was, she offered me a glass of spring water. She laughed like a hyena when I hesitated. Her shop sells baby clothing, if you can believe that."

"Offer her a glass of the same," said Philomene, who had ignored my order to go home. "Put a measure of mineral salt in the glass and make her drink it."

Piso looked at Philomene with admiration. "She'll think it's poison. That's very good."

I was always impressed when a woman measured another for harm. Some of the greatest fights in the arena took place between female gladiators. The things that were lacking in strength were made up by an absolute lack of pity. Philomene had dropped every inhibition when she went to the people who sold the poison that threatened the empress. Only retribution was on her mind.

"Weren't some of her poisons found when she was arrested?"

"Yes," said Piso. "A number of unknown substances in small boxes."

"Put one of them on the table, too."

My best interrogator looked at me as if disappointed in the subtlety of my mind.

"It's her way out, Piso."

He nodded, satisfied. "Yes, Prefect."

* * *

Those things were already done when I entered the room where Claudia Tuomina sat in disarray. She had not been harmed, but her clothing had been removed and replaced with sacking, the front of which was blotched by the water she had been made to drink. She had been kept moving, shifted from cell to cell, none of which were lit. She had not been spoken to. These things were done to make her know that she had entered the land of the dead.

That did not seem like a large step. Tuomina the Sepsis was a middle-aged woman with a face that spoke a record of every death she had caused. Not that she was completely unattractive. Her eyes were wide-spaced and predatory. Her nose was bold and bony, mirroring the planes of her face that were raked at severe angles. The man who liked an element of conflict in his bed, an edge of violence, would like her very well.

"You've had five husbands."

"Six," she said as if the count mattered. "The fifth, Xanthus, was a slave, but I put him in the tally."

Her voice was surprisingly youthful, indicating the demonic energy she drew upon. The teeth were not as good, but seemed adequate for most animal purposes.

"Did you kill them all?"

"I would not kill a man unless he was unfaithful."

That answered the question. I could not ask about her casual lovers while the Senate was in session.

"I'm interested in hearing your account of an individual who recently purchased one of your palliatives." I took up the metal box that had been placed on the table—a handsome little *pyxis* done in turquoise and obsidian with a silver base. "The substance I'm interested in is called Ink. You know it well. The mixture contains parts of silphium, black hellbore, rue, and several other ingredients."

"I was told that population control was an aim of this government," she said with a smile. "We've had no wars with the barbarians in years."

"Our emperor does not believe in war. He does, however, believe in the necessity of generating an heir to his throne."

"You don't find that up a man's ass," she said.

Although she seemed habitually bold, an insult like that was suicidal. It probably meant she had made up her mind to die. Looking for a quick way out of prison was what she had left.

"This can be made easy." I shook the small metal box in her face. "I will let you go to your infernal gods by your own hand if you supply the information I request."

She stared at the pyxis without emotion, but for a while. "Most of those are slow," she said at last.

"You have choices, Claudia Tuomina. You can be allowed to choose from the box something that's quick and painless."

"There is no such thing as painless, Prefect. This is not painless. All this damned talk."

"I'm glad you know who I am. You should also know that the empress is my cousin."

She did not seem to. The fear that settled in her eyes traveled a long way before it lay shelved in her harsh gaze.

"The empress and I grew up together, Tuomina. You may remember someone from your childhood who seems to embody the good things in life. When you look at them, or recall their names, you see the last light of day high on the Temple of Venus, you smell the bakery that used to awaken you in the morning when you were a child, you feel as if you're touching something just out of reach. It's something ordinary—but divine."

"What do you want?"

"A name."

"I have none to give. I do not deal in names."

"Then describe the person who purchased the Ink."

Until then, I did not know with certainty if I were dealing with a crime, or even a current criminal. When Tuomina spoke, truth lodged like poison in the bitterness of her words.

"She was highborn. Her shoes were silk with pearls sewn into the seams. She had rings on every finger, and little silver bells dangling from her earrings. She hadn't been to my shop in the Subura before, and she made it plain she'd never return. The blacksmith's wife, who wants to rid herself of that ugly bear of a husband, puts up her money without looking you in the face.

There's some shame, you know. But the ones that come down from the Palatine, they're buying a service. It's only money, and they've got it along with the gall they were born to. They always say, as she did, that they're buying it for a friend. They look down on you, all the way from the life you never had, and this one looked down a long way. Tall and thin she was. A nose like a dagger. Brown hair."

"Long hair?"

She nodded. "Lots of curls. Not what she was born with, I'd say, unless you count the locks gotten off her slaves."

"A pale complexion."

"Yes, and it could be paler soon."

"Why do you say that?"

"I sold her a second palliative," said Tuomina, liking the word. "Let's call it an adult palliative. She paid a good price because it was fitted in a golden brooch with a face of onyx."

"Poison?"

She nodded.

"Fatal?"

"But not so quick." She smiled like night. "I didn't care for her."

I left the room after placing the pyxis on the table for the use of Claudia Tuomina. I wondered which poison she would choose, and how quick it would be, but not for whom she cared.

* * *

"Ursula. I'd like you to meet Canidius Piso."

"Tribune," she said.

"Piso will conduct a search of your quarters. He's skilled in these matters and will disturb nothing that should not be disturbed. Please, step into the garden."

"You can't do this," she said. "Not in the palace."

I took her by the arm with force. "Would you rather accompany me to headquarters?"

Ursula did not want to go to a place from which some did not return and others were sorry to. She led the way into the peristyle garden of cut stone at the perimeter and early summer blossoms for the rest. Nervously, she touched the tips of the fingers to the temple bells that hung from her earrings. She had not worn them yesterday, and it seemed odd that she would repeat her jewelry more than once a month. Perhaps they were heirlooms and had sentimental value.

"I've just spoken to a woman who had no children but six husbands."

"At the same time?"

"In consecutive order, I believe."

As if trying to make me ill at ease, Ursula forged ahead on the walk with her long stride. "Bravo!" she said.

"You might not be enthusiastic if you knew her."

"Don't be too sure."

"Some of her clients believe that they know her. They buy her products with confidence, thinking they'll do exactly what she says. Sometimes, they're correct, but if they're not the buyer is seldom in a position to complain. The poison in the onyx brooch, for instance, is not what you expect. It's slow and painful."

Ursula continued walking, but with a step so stiff it was perfectly measured. "I don't know what you're talking about, but it sounds interesting. Dramatic."

But she did know. Her voice had recovered for the last syllables. The rest were weak. "I'm saying I spent the night talking to Claudia Tuomina."

"I'm afraid I don't know the name."

"That's not important. She knows you. She remembers who bought the poison the empress drank with her wine."

Ursula's reaction was not what I expected. She did not stop walking. She did not show anger or resignation. The only emotion I could detect was akin to sadness.

"If I told you, Prefect, that you don't know what you are doing, would you stop?"

"I have stopped."

"Very well," she said, coming to a stop on the walk. "I bought the poison of Claudia Tuomina."

That's when I knew Ursula was not the killer.

* * *

An accomplice, yes. When Piso came from her quarters after completing his search, I was certain. He had found the pyxis that once held the Ink, but of the brooch that held the poison he discovered nothing.

Ursula admitted she had bought Ink, but only that. Nothing would move her to say more. She could have been made to talk, but that would risk the ruin of the Mother Augusta's plans.

I had been Prefect of the City of Lugdunum for almost five years, and Rome for eleven months, but I knew of only one case where a suspect behaved as Ursula did. A young Gaul had confessed to murdering his mother by driving a bone needle, used for threading hides, through her ear into her brain. He was as stoic as most Gauls when facing death, but more so. I was troubled as much by his resignation as the method. A needle did not suit a man. Only after he was executed did we discover that his daughter, who was demented and living with an aunt in the country, had committed the crime.

I left Piso with Ursula while I went to the empress, who was in her quarters but not her bedchamber. She was in her reception room, orphaned among a swarm of servants and physicians, sitting on a couch before a window overlooking the courtyard.

The mass of blossoms and waterworks appeared startlingly bright as they accepted the strongest sun of the year. The water in the two pools glittered like snow. The four fountains, matching the corners of the empire, sent plumes of water aloft. Fish and other sea creatures, chosen for their fetching shapes and fantastic colors, plied the waters like messages in a dream.

"It's a beautiful day, don't you think?"

"Yes, cousin."

"How is it treating you?"

Faustina's smile rode the gentle curve of her lips like song. She did not seem to recognize the magnitude of what had happened. "Very well," she said. "I think I would have never known what happened if the physicians hadn't told me."

"And your husband?"

"I think he's more upset than me. And more disappointed. Have you heard what he has in mind? He wants to have his own baby. Conceived by himself. Delivered by his god."

"So I was told."

"I wish him well. I'm sure he cannot have less success than his wife had."

"Or more pain."

"I have no pain," she said like a child. "I feel like myself. The physicians say I could not be doing better. They're very pleased."

"Physicians are paid to be pleased."

She turned from me and looked out the window. "You don't believe them?"

"I believe the things I see."

"Which are?"

I walked to the back of her chair. I reached to the back of her neck and undid the clasp that held the gold chain around her neck. That was not as easy as it should have been. It never is with men's hands on fine jewelry. The empress did not resist as I drew the halves of the chain before her face and raised from the folds of silk at her bosom the golden brooch set with an onyx stone.

"I don't like you having this, my lady. It doesn't suit you, and there will never be an occasion for it."

"Never?"

"You have my word."

THE FALSE ANTONINUS

It was ironic that Marcus Aurelius Antoninus, who had been made emperor by two women, was brought to his knees by another. Faustina knew what she was doing when she destroyed the unborn heir to the Severan dynasty. Her sacrifice, which was greater than any the emperor performed to El-Gabal, affected her mind. She seemed to drift into a world where only she exerted control.

The balance of power in the palace shifted. The Mother Augusta recognized her advantage and pressed it vigorously. By the end of the third week in June 221, she had fashioned the agreement she wanted, and more. Alexianus was appointed co-consul to serve with his cousin on July 1st.

Perhaps the emperor did not realize he had furnished a standard around which those disaffected with his regime could rally. He put the best face on capitulation. Going before the Senate with Soaemias on his right hand and the Mother Augusta on his left, he informed the patrician fathers that he had decided to adopt Alexianus.

The emperor danced as he spoke, shuffling his feet and cradling his hands to hold the heavens. He invoked his god, saying El-Gabal ordered him to do this. The Senators, cowed by the executions of Messalla and Bassus, ratified the adoption on the spot. The session ended in laughter when the emperor said he should be congratulated for siring a child so large.

He took comfort in the knowledge that he had secured an heir from his own family. He managed at the insistence of his mother to have Comazon appointed Prefect of the City. That created a problem for me. During my last weeks in office, I purged the files that my replacement should never see. I made last-minute personnel transfers. Frugius and Thrax, who shared command of the civil disturbance unit, came with me to the palace with the rest of the squad. Piso asked to be reassigned, but I convinced him to stay on as my ears at headquarters.

Foreknowledge could be all-important in the future. I had finally succeeded in inserting a man within the emperor's circle. He was a young but dedicated rake named Haterius who had gone so far in debt keeping up with court life that his creditors threatened violence. Through a friend of Frugius, Haterius came to believe the threat, and through a friend of Philomene's, his debts were paid. In return, he understood that information was required.

The initial return on my investment was small. Haterius produced information, mostly accurate, during the summer months as the emperor settled into debauchery on Caelian Hill. The Mother Augusta, as part of their arrangement, discovered and released new monies to his court. That kept the banquets, sacrifices and games flowing. Not until September did an interesting item come from the man I code-named the Mede. Haterius was an Easterner, like many of the emperor's friends. His contact was another Easterner—Philomene.

"The empress will be divorced," she said one warm evening as we sat on the balcony overlooking the Temple of Cybele. "The Mede guarantees it."

"That's been a long time coming. Faustina should hear the news first. She may be able to safeguard some of her property by putting it with Bassus' clients."

"She'll want to even if it's risky," said Philomene, who still kept good relations with the empress. "In spite of her abstraction, she's always concerned for the welfare of her children."

"Do you think she's improving?"

"Possibly," said Philomene. "Yesterday, we spoke of what might happen if she was forced to leave the palace. She seemed more animated. The thought of leaving was a tonic. I believe the reality will be better."

"I hope so. But we have to wonder what substitute the emperor's found this time."

"I hear that the new empress has already been chosen," said Philomene. "In fact, she's the old empress."

"Which old empress?"

"The Vestal."

"But why? Is she pregnant?"

"Not visibly," said Philomene. "Her outstanding virtue is that she's utterly devoted to the emperor. She has no choice in that, of course. If she leaves him, her safety becomes a matter of chance. Many in the city feel she should have chosen suicide rather than submit to the emperor's wants."

"That's true. But Aquila Severa was devoted to her goddess, too. Correct me if I'm wrong, but aren't they all the same? Isn't she exchanging one form of worship for another?"

"Does it matter?" asked Philomene. "Is it her mind that's the issue?"

Perhaps it did not matter as it concerned the emperor, but his mother was a more volatile part of the mix. She had the ruthlessness of the moderately insane.

"I think it does matter. In the past, the emperor's acted in spates of coherence. One thing leads to another in sequence. We should be on alert. Be sure to contact the Mede regularly."

"What do you think the emperor will do?"

"It's more a question of what his mother will do. I want you to go to Gemellus in the slave market. Tell him to gather a dozen young healthy slaves. Intelligence, talent, or skills are unnecessary."

"You want tasters," she said.

"And I hope a dozen will be enough."

* * *

Philomene filled my order by the end of the week. I put half the new meat in my quarters and gave the rest to the Mother Augusta to distribute as she saw fit.

I had made inroads into the community of poisoners by removing Claudia Tuomina from the scene, but others quickly came to market. I took the added step of putting the rest on warning, and taking one man named Blackbane into my service as a consultant. He was a Greek from Epirus, where many of the deadliest poisons sprung from that rain-and-wind-swept soil. No one was more knowledgeable in the trade.

But the first moves that arose from Caelian Hill came directly. One day, while the class of palace children was enacting the Battle of Zama with wooden soldiers, the emperor appeared at the gymnasium arrayed in the silken garments of his god. The amulet that hung from his neck still held the eyes of Castinus, but the diadem that ringed his head was new and set with so many jewels it glittered in the sun and seemed to move in segments, like the fish in the great pool of the Augustana.

All the children knew him. They were awed by his sparkling presence and the Guards who accompanied him. They were twenty-four. All but the last three entered the grounds of the gymnasium in a group.

Five men were on duty from my squad that day, Thrax among them. He thrust himself to Alexianus' side, looming over him, a giant twice his size. Crysogones, their teacher, stepped forward, going nearly to the ground in a bow before the emperor.

"Welcome, my lord. We are honored by your visit to the groves of Academe."

The emperor sighted Crysogones from the fastness of his god. His whitened face and reddened lips spoke of extremes—the frozen north, the scorching south. His eyes consumed the bearded teacher limb by limb, blemish by blemish. And there were some.

"I see no trees. Nor any learning. Instead, you give me armies drawn up for battle."

Alarmed by the emperor's hostility, I stepped between them. "Will my lord join us at Zama? Will he command the legions of Scipio Africanus, or choose Carthaginians for the day?"

The emperor's gaze softened as if he wished to be pleasant. "Marcellus, you invite me into the role of Hannibal. The loser of the battle."

"No, my lord. You could still be Roman."

The emperor did not mistake my words. He seemed to want to continue his advance toward Alexianus. Slowly, he glanced around at his Guards, who occupied the flanks of the battlefield we had graveled in. Last, and briefly, he stared at Thrax.

"Warfare," he said scornfully. "I abhor the fact that my son is made to receive instruction in the art of killing men in the mass."

"It may be an art, but as my lord knows well, it often demands inspiration to be brought to a successful end."

The emperor seized the chance to provide the past with his coloring. "When I took the field against the usurper Macrinus, I did so at the bidding of the god. It was not my choice, and it should never be the choice of my son. He must reign with the God of Peace ascendant."

The emperor turned to the wooden men on the mock battlefield we had erected. They were dressed in copies of the uniforms of that ancient day, or as near as the seamstresses of the palace workshops could make them. The legions were drawn up in perfect ranks, augmented by Numidian infantry and cavalry. The Carthaginians, led by Mago's infantry, with flanking cavalry of horse and elephants, stood on the wings nearest the emperor.

"The elephant is at heart a gentle beast," he said. "He must be taught to follow the dictates of men. To perform in battle, he must be goaded and beaten to slay the enemy. We should be so wise as this beast of the wild. He could teach us a great deal."

The emperor put his foot forward and brought the silken tip of his slipper against the broad flank of the elephant, which had been constructed of twigs and covered in real hide. The beast toppled. It struck the next beast, and the next, until the entire row of war elephants cascaded to the gravel. The emperor smiled, admiring the symmetry of the fall.

"That's why they lost," he said. "The poor things became tired and lay down to rest. Who could blame them?"

"My lord, the Carthaginians lost because their war elephants bolted. When the legions attacked, they screamed and shouted, making as much noise as they could. The beasts panicked. What they could have crushed like grapes they ran from. They charged their own ranks and trampled the men they should have led into battle."

The emperor came closer, his eyes bright. "Is there a message in that, Marcellus? Do you mean to inform the Lord of All the World—by roundabout means—of his shortcomings?"

"My lord, I do not presume. I merely relate what happened at the battle that destroyed one empire and catapulted the other to glory."

"For the better?"

"Forever."

Crysogones, a good man, but unversed in the ways of the emperor, stepped up again. "We study history, my lord. Military. Civil. Whatever can be learned of greatness."

"The things learned of greatness will never be known by the likes of you," said the emperor angrily. "They must be *lived* in the god."

To demonstrate his point, the emperor drew himself up, rearing back in a strange way, like an asp rigged for harm. The hood fanned out, the fangs flickered. He held his arms wide and shuffled his feet in the pattern of his dance, moving forward yet sideways, keeping his head still, his eyes thrown high as if drawn to the invisible above his head. When his eyes whitened, he began to whirl, turning round and round, faster and faster, his garments billowing, his feet stroking the ground at a steady speed, his form blurring in the brilliance of the sun. At the moment when he seemed to become liquid, he stopped, holding a pose with limbs akimbo.

"This is what must be learned," he said, emerging from the rhythms like a guest. "This will bring knowledge."

The emperor did not require a response, nor did he wait for one. He clapped his hands, jumped in the air, and turned around before returning to earth perfectly. In the same mantic fashion, he moved into the battlefield, leaping over the heads of Hannibal's Veterans and the steeds of Masinissa's cavalry, vaulting horses and elephants, until he landed in a crouch among the massed ranks of the legions. He stopped. He looked around. He smiled at the children, who were no longer awed. Seeing one of their own, they were amused.

The emperor focused on Alexianus, his eyes gleaming like his diadem. "One day in Syria, when the sun was high in the heavens, I saw the air fill with heads. They came down over the ramparts of Raphanae. Bound in cords, we knew not what they were until we looked upon the gore. What we saw was the Family Marcianus. The family of Mammea. And Alexianus."

He pointed his finger at the boy who shared his crown. "The legions did that foul crime. Rebellious legions. Mark my words, Alexianus. These men cannot be trusted. You must keep them in hand. There is only one way to deal with them that they understand."

The emperor swept his hand across the battlefield. "I want their heads!" he shrieked. "All of them!"

No one seemed to know what he meant. The children giggled. The Praetorian Guard knew they should move on command but knew not where.

The emperor bolted toward his Guard. When he reached the first man, he jerked his sword from its sheath and turned back to our toy army. With great concentration, he brought the blade down in a long arc. The first little head in the cohort flew like a bird.

He tossed the sword back to his guard. "I want them all," he shouted. "All their heads!"

Quickly, the Guard moved to their orders. Those huge men unbound their swords and sallied through the ranks of the wooden soldiers, carving swaths in the Roman ranks. Heads fell in bunches, two and three at a time. The emperor moved with them, waving his arms like a conjurer, whipping his troops into the fury of battle.

By and bye, the slaughter was complete. Scipio's legions lay in the gravel like the ruin of the imperial playroom. The emperor surveyed his victory before turning to us. With less fervor than he had displayed toward the effigies, he pointed to the academicians who were gathered in a group behind Crysogones.

"I'll have those heads, too," he said. "Bring them along."

* * *

The next morning, we received the heads of Crysogones and his three assistants in green jars in a pickle. Carrying each head came priests of El-Gabal. They were to give instruction to the children, especially Alexianus, in the arts of leaping and dancing.

I had contacted the Mother Augusta even before we received evidence of the emperor's blood lust. Her grandson had chosen to send a message that could not be mistaken. The instruction of children, he knew, was the world in a jar.

"We know he's deranged," said Maesa. "But why does he insist on giving us proof?"

"This is a departure for him, Mother. In the past, he left the taking of heads to others, or came to it reluctantly. Now, he orders it."

"It's the purpose that matters," she said. "Any fool can see the value in eliminating his enemy or his mother-in-law. But this—"

"Is not as mad as it seems. He's decided Alexianus is more of a threat than he imagined."

"Did the god whisper in his ear?"

"If not the god, then his mother. The emperor has grasped popular opinion. Last week, when he and Alexianus appeared at the circus together, the crowd cheered the new consul, and barely remarked his colleague."

"What can we do?" asked Mammea as she walked my balcony. Alexianus' mother tried hard to concentrate, but she had been upset by Crysogones' handsome beard floating in brine.

I wondered: had there been something between them? No. Mammea was not Soaemias. A severed head always prompted thoughts of the body. Somehow, the rest never seemed quite settled or dead.

"My advice, Princess, is to accept these tutors in the mystic arts. They can do Alexianus no harm in a short time."

"And for the long term?"

"The emperor's behavior is erratic. I had the impression when he visited that he was improvising. From moment to moment, he did not know what he would do. I don't mean to alarm you, but I would have been concerned for Alexianus' safety if my men were not close by."

"I want to know one thing," said the Mother Augusta. "Can he be stopped?"

Stopping an emperor was impossible. Maesa wanted to know if her grandson could be overthrown. "It will be difficult to put a brake on the emperor as long as he has the Guard. And with Comazon as Prefect of the City, we can expect no help from that quarter."

"Then what can be done?"

"We have one course open," I said. "Subvert the Guard. They enjoyed an afternoon of mutilating toys, but that's not what they think they do best. They've never been close to this emperor as they were to Caracalla. They'll gladly serve a man, or a woman, but not a man who is woman. Discontent is growing, but to have them cross to our side while the emperor holds power— that's another matter. It can be done, but only in one way. Money. A great deal of money."

Mammea had never stopped pacing until I stopped talking. "You'll have it," she said.

"Spend it wisely," said the Mother Augusta. "We must be sure these are the last games of Marcus Aurelius Antoninus."

* * *

The recruitment of the Praetorian Guard went slowly but well. Disaffection ran deep, and deepest among those in closest contact with the emperor. I used Thrax as the bridge. He knew which men were best to approach, and how much it took to guarantee their loyalty. Those numbers were a bit less than expected. That was the most accurate gauge of their hatred.

By the end of October, I was confident if an attack were made against Alexianus, we could repel it. Our problem was that the more men who came over to us, the more likely the emperor would learn of our plan. It was impossible to keep it from him or his mother for long. When they knew without a doubt, the danger would be acute.

I had an inkling of how that would happen when on the afternoon of the Ides of November Philomene came to the office I kept next door to the Pedagogium. She seemed excited, a state that rarely pertained outside our rooms. On her forehead below her immaculate hairline were two distinct droplets of sweat that had arisen on a chill, gray day.

"I received a message from the Mede," she said. "It came by way of the Lemurian."

I moved from the table where I sat tabulating disbursements, and the duty rosters where those disbursements (Praetorian Guards) were found at every hour of the day. We took two leather chairs in the southwest corner of the room. They were far enough from the ears of the slaves who served as my scribes.

"The Mede sent a message by someone else's hand?"

"It's the second time he's done that. The first was last Tuesday."

"What does the message say?"

"He wants a meeting with my superior. He has important news, he says. It's so important he would like a bonus for dispensing it. One hundred thousand sesterces."

"He's never been bashful, has he?"

"The Mede knows what he wants. Unfortunately, it's everything he can think of."

"But he's never asked for anything like this. Money *and* personal greetings."

"I told him yes, but that's your choice," she said. "He wants to meet behind the Temple of Jupiter Libertas. In that street is a fuller's shop."

The temple was on Aventine Hill, the most southerly of the seven, convenient to nothing. If I were planning an ambush, I would have established a pattern the week before of sending a message by another hand. Nor was the Aventine a bad place for mayhem, especially at night.

"When does he want to meet?"

"In three hours."

At night.

* * *

I took Frugius, Adranos, and two of the old squad with me. Three weeks ago, I would not have removed them from their watch on Alexianus, but the Guard was thick around him now. With Thrax as their taskmaster, I felt secure leaving him in their charge.

The Aventine was not an inviting place even in daylight. Though visible across the valley from the Palatine, the expanse of the Circus Maximus shut off access to it. On its slopes and around its crown gathered small private houses and large apartment complexes. The Aventine had no important public structures except the temples of Bona Dea and Jupiter Libertas. Those, too, had been slighted by the laws of commerce and the value of real estate.

The street behind Jupiter's temple had once been the site of elaborate gardens until Septimus Severus, in need of funds to finance his campaign to Britannia, sold off the land to private contractors. What had been a lovely avenue bordered by ornamental trees and flowers was now a nest of taverns, shops, and looming tenements that far exceeded the legal height for private buildings.

Once within the broad shadows of these *insula*, shadow was all. The fuller's shop, standing in the middle of the block, was shut tight. The shutter on its front was drawn down, and the door that stood on the left side was closed and barred.

I sent two men to the back of the building and posted one across the street. Frugius I kept by my side. The Mede would not expect a man of rank to come alone in darkness.

"Your name?" said the young man in a dirty tunic who answered the door.

"Eliphias of Taursus," I said.

"You've come a long way."

"And must return quickly."

Liking the password, he swung the door open and stepped back. Frugius and I followed him through a front room that held masses of glass bottles on shelves mounting to the ceiling. All were identically fashioned. Each bottle held two pints and bore a deep indentation on the lip to accept the common Roman penis without discomfort.

Next, we passed into a much larger room where laddered wooden racks rose high, each spread with varieties of treated cloth. Along the lower walls were seven large vats that held urine or its dregs. The stench was powerful. I wondered where Rome would be if vast amounts of piss were not essential to the fuller's trade. And I wondered when I would stop feeling like Caracalla on the road to Carrhae.

When our host stopped before the largest vat, which held a full portion of its bounty, he turned to us. I barely heard his words or saw the dark bearded face that was incompletely illuminated by the candles on the wall.

"Wait here," he said.

"Where's the Mede?"

"He'll come to you."

When the young man turned and walked toward a door set in the back wall, I motioned Frugius to follow. Even before he passed from sight, a voice seemed to arise from nowhere.

"The Mede is in hiding."

Haterius, wearing his code-name like a cloak, and wearing a dagger, stepped from behind a rack of fulled cloth that had been felted and dyed. The color was the reason why in the bad light we had not seen him. The courtier was dressed as if for a Caelian banquet in silks and linens tending to pink and blue. His shoes were yellow and his face nearly the same shade, as thin and sharp as a bird's. On his head he wore a diadem that was different from the emperor's in its relative lack of jewels.

"Excuse my entrance and the very bad smell," he said, "but I bear news of great moment. Its stench, I'm afraid, is even greater."

I said nothing until I received the signal from Frugius that everything was in order. He emerged from the door and nodded, but as he was trained to do, kept his post and his distance.

I lifted from my cloak the purse of gold coins I had carried from the palace. "If what you say is true, your pay will be equal to its importance."

The Mede came closer, as if flitting through trees. His shoes made no sound. I wondered how he had made the journey over so many bad paving stones in such weak footwear.

"May I?" he asked, opening his hand.

I placed the felt purse on the edge of the vat filled to the brim with piss. "I'm listening."

His hand went out to the purse, teasing the air but not taking up the strings. "I do know you, don't I?"

"Not as well as you think."

The Mede smiled. "But you know my work."

"Intimately."

"That's the word, yes. Last night—very late last night—I was with the emperor at an intimate gathering. The charioteer was there in full gallop. As wild as a baboon but still, how shall we say, masterful. You must act, he told the emperor. Act now." The Mede flounced his long fingers toward the purse again. "Seize the day!"

"Did those words have some reference to the new consul?"

"I believe so," he said. "But I was confused. I'd just puked up a bowl of oysters in asses' milk. Said to be an aphrodisiac if it doesn't kill you. Then Hierocles began to rant as I returned. You should have seen him. Dressed in goatskins and flayed leather of doe. They'd all just come from doing a significance with the god, but that didn't stop him from looking godlike. If you'd seen him on the slopes of Mount Athos, you'd want to shoot him and mount him." The Mede laughed. "Mount him, you see."

"I do. But I'd rather know what's so important that you could not relay the information to your usual contact."

"We're getting there, aren't we?" The Mede yawned. A strange thing to do, but he was like many of the emperor's companions— so habitually giddy they could not be read.

"You have to understand there are gaps." He steepled his fingers and put them to his chin. "There were an awful lot of *words*. Hierocles shouted at the emperor. He struck him, then struck him again." The Mede bowed his head. "And the emperor cried, like a child."

I picked up the purse from the ledge of the vat and tucked it back into my belt. "That's a nice story, but not worth paying for. When you have something meaningful to pass along, send it by way of the usual channel."

I turned away, Frugius broke his vigil and began to follow, when the Mede spoke for the record at last. "When he had done weeping, the emperor offered a reward for the head of his cousin." The Mede corrected himself. "His son."

"How much?"

"A million sesterces."

* * *

I spent time verifying the Mede's story, taking him back through the "gaps," but the last fact he imparted seemed the relevant one. If true, it was important. A million sesterces would prompt action against Alexianus. Perhaps soon.

The Mede had finished his recital when the rear door burst open. The dark young man, the fuller who was the Mede's client, along with the two from my squad who had been posted at the rear, moved quickly across the room.

"Activity," said Adranos.

"How many?"

"A dozen. Maybe more."

"Get Crito in and secure the doors."

When they moved off, I turned on the Mede. "Who knew you were coming?"

He shook his head. His feral eyes were frightened. "No one. I told no one at all."

I signaled to Frugius, who removed the Mede's dagger, took him by his silken ass and dumped him into the vat of urine. The courtier thrashed mightily in the dim waters, displaying more vigor than he seemed capable of, as Frugius held his head below the surface. At thirty seconds, Frugius let him up, gasping and spouting.

"Who are those men?"

"Friends of the charioteer."

"And your information on the bounty?"

"It's good," he said. "I swear it's good."

He might have been telling the truth. The only thing that mattered was to get a warning to the palace. "Show us the way out," I said to the fuller. "The other way. And quickly."

The fuller did not hesitate. "Follow me," he said.

Crito could not be found on the street outside, so the doors were bolted and blocked against him. Quickly, we followed the fuller up the ladder to the loft. Where the rear wall appeared to go blank, he sidled into a niche corner and asked for a boost. When we lifted him up, he punched out the wooden planks above his head and pulled himself into darkness.

We made it quickly to the second floor of the building into the space beneath the hallway stairs. The fuller pried open the half-door that led into the hall, and in two steps we were out through a window onto the fire walk that circled the building outside. Almost all large buildings in Rome had the walks by law.

Everyone knew that. We were halfway to the west side of the insula, where we could escape by the fire stairs, when the call went up from the street. "They're upstairs! On the walk!"

I heard men running from two directions, converging quickly. No doubt there were a dozen or more scattered in the streets around the building. They would be the usual street thugs, no match for a soldier or a gladiator, but enough to cause bad trouble in the dark.

"A walk connects across the arch to the next building." Frugius pointed in the darkness, which was nearly impenetrable in the alley. "Go with Adranos and Gaultierus. Once across, you can make your way to the street on the other side."

"And you?"

"I'll drop down to the street from this side. Once I take a couple apart, the rest will run."

I saw his point: one man, invisible, attacking without warning, a killer whose like had seldom been seen in the arena. That could give us time.

"Good luck."

"They won't have a chance. You can leave the gay blade with me. I'll see him clear."

There was a lot I did not like about his plan, but Frugius would do what he said until he could do it no longer. I tapped him on the mail at his shoulders and moved down the walk toward the arch that spanned the closest distance between the two buildings. I felt Adranos and Gaultierus behind me, but it was only a feeling. The arch was less than that.

It was a flat surface faced with concrete sixteen inches wide. I felt both sides of the arch with my toes through the boots before I put the first foot forward. And the next, slowly. At the third step, which was more like a shuffle, I began to have bad sensations. I wished I had taken off my boots. In my stocking feet I could have felt something in my body besides the beginning of panic. That had built quickly. It was not something I could stop.

We were not high up. Sixteen feet. Twenty?

But the drop yawned. It was black and the fall would be uncontrolled. A man might survive if he were prepared to hit the ground, but not if he were struggling to stay on balance. That man would lose his footing and topple. He might strike the arch in his fall, flailing all the way to the bottom in dark space.

It was completely dark on both sides of the arch and nothing could be seen even when it was directly ahead and solid. But what was directly ahead? That seemed the easiest thing to know when I took the first step but now, by the fourth—and I should be halfway across—all sense of knowing vanished. I put my foot forward. I felt the edge, but that did not stop the feeling that death had its hand on mine. Suddenly, I felt my balance going. My legs trembled and could not be stopped. The darkness was no longer itself but a thing that had taken control of me.

I closed my eyes.

Yes, that was the way. Now the darkness moved within. I felt it pushing. And strangely, as if I could keep nothing else in my mind, I thought of Faustina. It was as if I had entered her darkness. I took a step and the arch was firm. I took another. When panic suddenly rose up again, I put my foot out and down and pushed hard against the concrete. I took one more step. My hands and then my face hit something hard. That was the side of the building.

The other side. I turned and put my hand out for Adranos. He took it. I could feel his trembling. His whole body trembled.

"Step to the right now. You're over."

Then we guided Gaultierus in. He had gone down on his belly and crawled along the arch, the only one with good sense.

When we got him onto the walk, I snapped my fingers twice to signal Frugius on the other side. He snapped once in return.

It occurred to me that he could not deal with the Mede and still drop into the street. What was he thinking?

I found out when I heard shuffling followed by a scream. It began at our level but descended quickly to the street below, where it ended in a splatter of silk and soft flesh.

I knew Frugius would drop immediately after the Mede, but I could hear nothing in the din that erupted. The street was suddenly crowded with the sound of many voices as men closed from every direction. They came in for the kill on a man who was probably dead.

And they had no idea what was coming for them.

* * *

We worked our way along the walk and the fire stairs and got down in good order. By the time we reached the street in front of the fuller's shop, hardly any sounds could be heard from the alleyway between the buildings. That was good for Frugius and bad for his opponents. Gladiators often practiced fighting blind, and often it was their own blood that blinded them.

We faced no problems until we came to the west side of the Temple of Jupiter, where a party of five large men suddenly appeared in our way. They were visible by the light of the torches at the entrance of the temple. Armed with swords and clubs but no shields, they were at a disadvantage facing gladiators.

The first of the five went down under Adranos' charge, taking the brunt with his body and losing one of his limbs to the whirlwind blade. When Gaultierus moved in on the next, even less could be seen and all that was heard was a hollow sound as the man's helmet crumpled.

I had already moved on my man, slashing with my sword in the bad light and finding no flesh. I was worried because I was no match for a gladiator, if that was what he was, especially in street conditions. I came in tight and stabbed, thinking that he had to move or die, when suddenly I realized I had no target. The man turned and ran, leaving the field to his fellows. In quick order, but not much of it, the rest followed him, scattering like shadows into the darkened side streets.

"Run!" shouted Adranos. "Run for your life, Gaurus!"

We were a block farther along, moving past the aqueduct extension, when I asked Adranos, "Did you know that man?"

"For a day or so," he said. "Gaurus was in the Guard, but Comazon brought him over to the First Urban Cohort with his pay and seniority kept by. I showed him around the barracks. He's not altogether bright, but he did well by the move."

"Were there any more from the old office?"

"I can't say, lord. There was one."

It bothered me to think Comazon had a hand in this. He was more competent than the charioteer, and his resources as Prefect of the City were substantial. It seemed clear that for Alexianus to be safe we would need all the Praetorian Guard.

I felt better when Frugius caught up to us as we approached the walls of the Circus Maximus. He bled from half a dozen wounds, but seemed his normal self.

How like the empire he was.

* * *

When I arrived at the palace three hours after midnight, I called for Thrax. In addition to being my liaison with the Guard, he was attached to Alexianus. He had first met the boy on our expedition against Verus, where he seldom left Alexianus' side. The intervening years had done nothing to improve his feelings toward the emperor, or diminish his desire to see a man on the throne. Any candidate might have appealed to Thrax, but Alexianus' nature and age seemed to bring out motherly impulses in this man who was over eight feet tall.

"There's been a serious complication, Thrax. I learned that the emperor put a price on Alexianus' head. A large price."

The giant heard with visible hatred. Everything about him was outsize, and for that reason, freakish. Of all the gigantic men I had seen—and there were many in the Guard and the arena— he was the only one who did not seem misshapen. He was simply much bigger than us. The bones in his face, which were as big as the shoulder bones of most men, clenched like fists.

"It's his own head that will roll. The False Antoninus has made the last move of his reign."

"But for the time being we have a problem. I tripled the Guard, but almost any of the palace freedmen or slaves can be bought. Our defenses can be penetrated long enough for an assassin to strike with weapons or poison. Worse, I don't see any way we can withstand an attack in force. The emperor may still be able to count on elements of the Guard. He has the Urban Cohorts and twelve cohorts from the legions he could call up from Italy."

"Then there's only one way to do it, lord. Alexianus must be brought to the Camp."

He was right. I had hoped to avoid placing Alexianus completely at the mercy of the Guard, but the Praetorian Camp was the one unassailable place in the city. It was a fortress.

"Can we ensure his safety there?"

"No better place," said Thrax. "No Guard will obey an order to harm Alexianus."

"The new prefect may give those orders. Antiochianus owes his job to the emperor."

Thrax spit on the floor. "Antiochianus," he said. "Another pussy. Let him try."

* * *

In the morning before Alexianus took any food at the palace, I sent him and his mother under protective guard to the Praetorian Camp on Esquiline Hill. The camp stood outside the Servillian walls that enclosed the city when it was a smaller place. If a line were drawn between the Palatine, Esquiline and Caelian Hills, it would form a triangle whose points were equidistant and equally inconvenient. No force of any size would be able to move from one point to the other without alerting the city.

Their safe arrival at the Camp was my signal to relax. I slept three hours and would have slept longer but for the messenger who arrived from the camp before noon. He burst into my quarters breathless from his trek across the city.

"Lord, Gaius Julius Thrax wishes you to inform you the Guard has set out to march on Caelian Hill. He begs you to understand he could not contain them. When word passed round camp that Alexianus' life was in danger, the men flew into a rage. They cannot be stopped."

"Stopped from what?"

"Lord, Gaius Julius did not say."

"But you were present at the camp."

"Yes, lord."

"What is their intention, as you saw it?"

"Lord, I believe they mean to change the government."

A politician already, the subaltern. Killing an emperor in his summer palace was not the usual means of disposal, but things like it had been done before. Thrax certainly had abetted the process. His tardy words were meant to shield his gigantic ass.

"Does my lord wish to form an answer to Gaius Julius?"

"That's unnecessary. I'd rather you fetched my horse."

The subaltern seemed insulted by the request, but he carried out the order as well as he spoke. On Bacchus I set off at once for Caelian Hill, following the course of the Claudian Aqueduct that passed between the winter and summer palaces like an enormous lattice in stone, bearing clear water from the Anio Valley thirty miles away.

I was awed by the sight no matter how many times I passed. Before the aqueducts were built, Rome was just another Italian city with hard-assed soldiers and a will to conquer. The aqueducts gave us the means to be great. A healthy population, a social ground where its citizen could meet in baths, a clean and orderly way of life. That was the Roman way, which I felt was ending. My feelings had little to do with the boy I had known as Varius, or his cousin, or the god in the stone. It was more like a light that had failed.

I arrived at the Sessorian Palace on a cool day with no wind and the sun past its zenith. This modest summer place near the crown of the hill had been built by Septimus Severus for his family, but his grandson had made it over in every inch. The stone was pink marble from Asia. The gardens, even in winter, reeled with fantastic colors, drawn from glass houses where more exotic forms were cultivated. The main motif, concealed in the columns and arches and gardens, intertwined in every ornament, was the phallus, erect.

I left my horse in the courtyard and climbed the marble stairs when I heard a distant tumult in the streets to the north. It was the van of the Guard from the Praetorian Camp. Every time I came to this suburb it seemed those huge men were bent on slaughter.

This would be a pretty place for it with no impediment in the assault. I walked through the reception hall, where young men in high dress gathered, through the antechamber, which was strangely deserted, and into the basilica before I was challenged by one of the Guard.

"You know me."

"Yes, lord."

"Where is he?"

The Guard cocked his ear to the noise from the streets that grew rapidly. He seemed to want an excuse to obey. "They're upstairs."

They would be the emperor and his husband. It might also be his mother and the Praetorian Prefect, Antiochianus. When I reached the top of the staircase, I saw the prefect in harried conversation with several of his loyal Guards. A Syrian who traced his lineage to the most effete royal house in the East, Antiochianus wore the purple cloak of the Prefect of the Guard, which was identical to the emperor's except for its shorter length. It was the only thing that distinguished him from a whore.

"Marcellus Decimus?"

"I don't have time for talk, Prefect. Your men are marching on this palace with murder on their minds. Meet them outside and try to talk them back into their cage."

He blinked his dark eyes. "What caused this mutiny?"

"Injustice."

He did not understand. Gratian Antiochianus was a small man who made up half, or two-thirds of the typical soldier in his Guard.

"But what can I offer them?"

"Try the lash."

I walked to the first room on the right, where a double brace of Guards had been posted. The one on the right moved to block my path, but the two on the left took him aside.

Had I bought those men? I could not remember their names. The last of the four simply watched as I passed into the large front room that faced the front of the palace.

It was another invention of the immature linked to the beyond. The archway was draped in plaited lilies. Within the great room was every flower in the empire in every color. They hung from the walls and stood in vases, chained by their stems in ropes. The gardens must have been culled every day, and ten ships kept in motion to fund this decadent beauty. The mingled scents were overpowering, like a single drug. Roses, having thorns, were banished, but their petals had been strewn so thick upon the floor that I could hardly walk without slipping.

The triumvirate—the emperor, Hierocles and Comazon—stood before the doors that led to the balcony. The former was dressed as the god ordered, but the charioteer had shed his animal skins for a winter tunic trimmed in moon silver. Comazon wore the uniform of the Prefect of the City in which he looked ill at ease as he saw me approach. The others turned. If their plans had gone as expected, I would not have appeared to them except, perhaps, in dreams.

"Marcellus," said Comazon. "Just the man we wanted."

"I doubt that, Prefect. You should send better men if you mean to kill a soldier."

"It's not too late for that."

"But it is."

I moved to the double doors and threw them open wide. The noise struck first, like the notes of a massive orchestra. Fresh air struck the perfumed room as powerfully. In the street below, the Guard had entered the courtyard, two or three hundred strong. They poured into the gardens on the east side of the palace, trampling the precious vegetation.

"Your Guard is no longer a Guard. Come see."

The three did not move. They must have received reports of events at the camp, but did not want to believe them. I had not seen the emperor look so confused since the night we left Antioch on fast horses. He listened as the Guard roared the same phrase over and over.

"Down with the False Antoninus! Down with the False Antoninus!"

Nothing else could be heard within the din. I put my left hand on the chest of Comazon, my right on the chest of Hierocles, and pushed them back into the room. To the emperor, I extended my hand. He looked as if he had never known its existence, or the things it had done in his service.

"I must?"

"Yes, my lord."

When we appeared together at the balcony, where he could be seen by all the men, a roar went up from the Guard. At the same time, their push onto the palace grounds halted, although nothing could have stopped them from entering and working their will.

"What do they want?"

"Your head, my lord."

If he could have disbelieved those angry voices, he would have. "And failing that?"

"If you wish to save yourself, you will have to offer the Guard what they want."

"Money," he said in a furtive voice from a place never forgotten. "I'll find it."

"That will not be enough, my lord. The Guard demands more. First, you will agree to remove the price you placed on Alexianus' head. Next, you will agree to accept your cousin as joint Caesar. He must have a separate element of the Guard that is *not* under your command."

The emperor's eyes said he saw into the past. The images that arrived were the ones he had known as a boy—Geta and Caracalla dividing the palace like fruit. Their mother passing between them as the emissary of peace. And the final act, the lustrum of blood.

"And who will this Guard obey?"

"The young Caesar."

"And you, Marcellus. You."

"If they will."

The emperor's eyes wandered to the angry men in his courtyard, still shouting the name he never wanted to hear. Antiochianus appeared at the head of the marble stairs, speaking to the Guard. He made no headway. If he spoke long enough, it might be at the expense of his head.

"Very well," he said. "I give my assent to the second Caesar. Is that enough?"

"No, my lord. You must also agree to dismiss all the cooks and muleteers you have appointed to high office."

"Yes," he said. "Yes."

"Last, you will give up your companions. All those disreputable young men."

"That can be done."

"Including the charioteer."

He looked at me as if the throne of the Roman Empire were nothing; as if the rites of his god were nothing; and as if I were his executioner. "Marcellus," he said. "I cannot."

"You must, my lord."

"If you knew what he means to me, you would not ask it."

"But I do."

He turned to the figure of his lover split in segments by the panes of the glass in the door. Was Hierocles so handsome? No doubt. Was he the finest specimen of male beauty in the city of Rome? Possibly.

"Is he worth your throne?"

"Yes."

"Is he worth dying for?"

"Yes," he said. "Oh, yes."

The Emperor of All the Romans fell to his knees. He held his chin high and bared his throat for the stroke that would end his life. I remarked he wore no paint in that vulnerable spot.

"Grant me this man, whatever you have been pleased to suspect about him. Or slay me."

To the former, I could not speak. For the latter, though I thought it much the best, I could not find the will.

THE CAMP

The emperor's promises cost him nothing. His compliance with my demands, which were the demands of his Guard, his family, and his people, would be honored as he felt the need.

For several weeks, he recollected his acquaintance with death and observed his word. He recognized Alexianus and agreed to separate the Guard. He dismissed from government the reprobates with whom he had shared the fat of the land. Even his friends were discarded, but for Hierocles. The emperor withdrew into a tight circle that included his lover, his mother, and the Vestal, whom he remarried.

He and his court did not often appear at the Domus Augustana, choosing to remain on Caelian Hill. The reports I received said the emperor had retreated deeper into his god. Days went by when neither he, his wife nor his mother were seen outside the temple. The nights, too, were often spent in worship.

I should have observed their practices more closely, but I was busy with the transition to sane rule. Alexianus was my constant companion and pupil as we moved from the classroom to the rooms of state. My only complaint was one that was usually a strength. The young Caesar listened too well to his elders, particularly his mother. Julia Mammea was a model of Roman motherhood, but one day she would have to be put in her place. And not by me.

Alexianus would do that thing, but later rather than sooner. When he came to me each day, his concern was to observe and take part in political affairs. Though his mother insisted that I correct him when he made mistakes, I rarely did. Mistakes are learning tools.

But one morning when Thrax made his daily report, I found the exception to the rule. The giant spoke to his audience of two as if to a meeting of the Senate.

"The Augustus has broken his word to Caesar, the Honorable Marcellus Decimus, and the Praetorian Guard," he said.

"The Guards on duty report that he has taken up with his old companions again. Again, he plays the woman with them."

"Will my cousin never learn?" asked Alexianus. "Can he not control himself?"

Thrax had learned how to play to Alexianus. His Thracian accent made his words sound bold and pompous. "The Augustus makes no attempt to hide his shame. He practices his vices openly. He has announced games for this week with no regard for the monies spent. Nor has he extended Caesar an invitation to share his box and the approval of the people. He has done this deliberately, as an insult to your person."

"Something must be done," said Alexianus. "Thrax, you will wait without."

"Caesar!"

The giant left the room, bowing through the doorway that would have decapitated him. Alexianus waited until the enormous shadow had gone before he took up the reed pen that lay beside his ink pot and swept down a sheet of Egyptian papyrus. I did not permit him a scribe. One day, he would tell me that writing in his own hand was a stupid thing for a ruler to do.

But this day he dipped the reed in the dark red ink. He held it over the pot but did not move it to his task. "Something is wrong?" he asked.

"Caesar can do no wrong. He may want to think about the way to do right."

"I can always tell when you disapprove," he said, letting his temper show. "Your left eye, which is motionless, casts a pall over the right. That's a stony look, Marcellus. The statues in the corridor cannot match it."

"Are you planning to write an admonishment to your cousin?"

"Yes."

"So you think he will observe your orders."

"I do not order the Augustus. I inform."

"Then you should ask two questions. Is there a chance that your information will have an effect? And do you want to produce the effect? If the answer to the first is no, then you're wasting your time and leaching your dignity. If your answer to the second is yes, you should ask why you want him to conform."

"Because he is a disgrace."

"To himself. Not to you."

"It's the same. My dignity is insulted each time he puts on a woman's face."

"And each time he does, your power grows."

"I fail to see how that can be true when my dignity suffers."

"Because there's an end to it. You should let the end come naturally. You should be blameless."

Alexianus realized what I was saying. "There's only one way the Emperor of Rome can meet his end prematurely."

"Only one."

* * *

I was rarely so sure of anything, but I did not know what event would elevate my words into history. Certainly, I did not suspect when I received a visit from Canidius Piso that all the processes of government would be accelerated.

Soon after Thrax's announcement, and on the second day of the heat wave that struck Italy, so the coldest part of the year became one of the warmest, Piso came to my office. He had been in contact with me regularly, reporting pertinent information from his job under Comazon, but this day he presented a different image. His dour face, heightened by the heavy eyebrows and a suddenly retreating hairline, seemed to have brought his mind to paralysis.

"This man Gaurus you asked me to look at," he said. "The one who showed himself by the fuller's shop. I found nothing good about him. He came with Comazon from the Guard and shortly after was on the Prefect's personal staff. That is, he does what the Prefect wants done but not known. He led the ruffians who attacked your party. He has also led his men, known as the Body Squad, on other forays in the city."

"How big is the group?"

"About a hundred and growing," said Piso. "Some have military training, but most took their education in the streets or the arena. A few were with the Guard. They performed as the emperor's special servants. Their name, I'm told, derives from when they went abroad in the city, and sometimes to other places in the empire, to locate men who had large, or freakish, private parts. These men were then brought to the palace."

"Yes."

"That sounds proper to you?"

"I saw the evidence one night."

Piso had no sense of humor. "The parts?"

"The whole," I said. "And the parts."

"In other words, they were together. Intact. What I mean is, they were not separated. Dismembered."

"Piso, the beings I observed had private parts attached to their bodies. They were intact. Whole. What I meant to say is that they were very large, or freakish, as stipulated."

He settled back in the chair. The tension in his small body did not dissipate, but seemed to arrive at a destination. "I hope you do not think I ask these questions idly."

"I know you better, Piso."

"There is a point to be made," he said. "A very grave point. It's the most disturbing I've seen in my twenty years as an investigator because it involves children. I understand that babies are put out on dunghills, some every week in various parts of the city. I know of a case where a baby was dropped from the seventh floor of an apartment building to make room for another man in the bed. Once, when a group of laborers dug up the floor beneath a bath on Quirnal Hill, we found so many tiny corpses discarded by the whores who worked there that it was like a battlefield in Amazonia. But this—" Piso grasped a patch of his hair as if the burden he carried had caused his sudden baldness. "This is of a different order."

I said nothing. It was rare that a man of Piso's experience would be so affected by a case that he felt inadequate.

"I have never seen children slain in this way," he said with muted anger. "The crimes are unnatural. At that age, their parts have no function. Not in that way."

"Their sexual parts."

"Yes," he said. "They were removed. All the bodies were missing the sexual parts. This was done while the children were alive."

"You're certain."

"The bodies were examined by Fidelis, whom you know. He guarantees that the children were alive when the excisions were made."

"Is that what they died of?"

"Their throats were also cut. Later perhaps."

"And the parts were not recovered?"

"Not to this day."

"Where did you find the bodies?"

"All over the city," he said. "There's no pattern in distribution except for one thing. The bodies were always found at crossroads. What significance this has I cannot say. We know the spirits are most powerful at these places."

"They were deliberately placed?"

"It seems so. Being scattered throughout the city, it took some days for the similarities to be noted. I was not aware of the pattern until a week ago."

"How many children were dismembered in this fashion?"

"Six," he said. "Thus far. As you know, crimes like these, which make a pattern, are often repeated. They are the product of a deracinated mind. They will stop, or be stopped, at some point, but until then—"

"You expect more."

"I'm sure of it."

"What progress have you made in your investigation?"

"There is no longer an investigation by my hand," he said. "Yesterday, I was ordered to turn over all the evidence, and any notes I had made."

"By whom?"

"The Prefect."

I did not understand what Piso was saying. I had done such things in my term in office, but only for one reason. "Piso, you're telling me these murders have a political meaning."

"I can't say with certainty. What I know is I can do nothing more with the investigation. To say they are the foulest orders I have ever received is not an exaggeration. It's the reason I've come to you. I beg you to do something about this matter. Since it began, I cannot sleep. And since it was taken from me, I cannot eat."

"You say that you turned over all your notes."

"Yes." Piso released what appeared to be a smile. "But I did not turn over my mind. Last night, I reconstructed everything I had compiled. I added everything that might be relevant to a third party who took up the investigation."

Piso was a subtle man, but only when he chose to be. He reached inside his cloak. His hands moved as he unpinned a small leather case and pushed it across my desk.

"I'll get to it when I can, Piso."

"I am in your debt, lord."

* * *

Piso was telling me more than he wanted to put into words. I knew that, so I told him I would see to it later. My resolve lasted until the evening when I took up the the leather pouch by bad light, thinking that might give me an excuse to drop it.

I tried to read without prejudice the six sheets of paper in Piso's meticulous hand. The first three pages were a more thorough recapitulation of what he related in my office. Piso had left out nothing much. The only thing I noticed was that the six sets of body parts were found on six of the seven hills of Rome. The first were discovered on Esquiline Hill, the next on Viminal, the third on Quirnal, the fourth on Capitoline, the fifth on Aventine, and the sixth on Caelian.

The locations formed a rough circle of the city, moving counterclockwise in the commission of the crimes. Piso would not have failed to note that. Certainly, he had seen one hill was missing. The Palatine.

I tried not to think of that until I absorbed the material. The next two pages concerned Piso's interviews with the parents of the missing children. Five of the six had been spoken to. They were all men and women among the lowest classes in Rome. Two parents were slaves, two freedmen, and one a pleb and his wife who ran a weaver's shop. Three lived on Aventine Hill, one on Caelian Hill, and the others in the valley between the two.

No leads of any significance had been developed from the parents except for the child of the weaver. This boy went nearly every day to the "school" of a man known as Callixtus. It was while he was on his way from the school on Aventine Hill to his home on the Caelian that he had disappeared. Piso's words on the matter were acerbic.

"It may seem strange that a child of poor people should attend a school, but this place is not as it seems. Callixtus calls himself 'The Bishop of Rome,' which means he is the leader of Christians in this city and the world. The children attend his school not to learn things to further their prosperity, but to absorb the doctrine of Christianity. Callixtus, who is a convicted embezzler, was not at a loss to supply me a suspect. His conclusion was that a man named Hippolytus, who has set himself up as a rival Bishop of Rome, must have abducted the child.

"I did not follow his suggestion immediately because it seemed the product of a doctrinal dispute among a fractious sect of fanatics. Instead, I took the opportunity to speak with two children from the school who were with the boy when he disappeared. They said they had walked with the boy, Bardas, after leaving school and until they reached the fruit market. There, they became separated.

"Investigation at the market produced the first evidence. It seems the three boys were known by the stall-keepers of the market as steady pilferers. On that day, they conducted a raid at a stall that sold Veii grapes. The stall-keeper pursued the boys, who fled in three directions, as was their custom. The survivors escaped the stall-keeper, but the boy who later disappeared was caught. He began to receive a well-deserved beating from the stall-keeper when a strange woman appeared. She is described as young, taller than average, with hair both red and gold. After intervening in the dispute, the woman offered the stall-keeper much more than his grapes were worth to release the boy. Which he did, after some haggling.

"He saw no more of the boy, who walked with the woman toward Candlemaker's Street in the company of two men who appeared. They were of a type that could serve as bodyguards for a woman of the best class, but since the stall-keeper saw them at a distance, he could not offer descriptions. The Candlemaker's Street wends east to terminate at the base of Caelian Hill. No one who lives or works there admits to seeing Bardas, the woman, or her companions. It's likely they entered a waiting conveyance. No trace of the boy was found until two days later when his mutilated body appeared on Caelian Hill.

"I have one item to add. When the woman spoke to the stall-keeper, asking him to give up his captive, she said it was her 'right' to redeem the boy. He thought nothing of her words at the time, but recalled them when questioned by this investigator.

"My question, with which I close this report, is the following: Who has the 'right' to forgive evildoers their transgressions? What kind of people, for whatever reason, would do these monstrous things to children?"

* * *

She was the one who had stayed by him. She was the one who had been chosen for her purity. The emperor had remarried her for her devotion to his cause and her dedication to the god she was called upon to serve.

The convenient thing was that Aquila Severa, Vestal—by the count the fourth and most current Empress of Rome—had been given quarters not in the palace where the nightly revels were conducted, nor in the temple where bloody sacrifices were made to the god, but in the Severan Apartments that stood between the Sessorian Palace and the Theater Castrense. Due to her position, she was accorded a watch of Praetorian Guards, but only three, who would have been overpowered if they were not already ours.

Severa was surprised when I entered her chamber unannounced so late. She was in her bedclothes, thin to gossamer, with her gorgeous hair spread like bloody gold to her shoulders; but she did not cry out. Her appreciation of reality was that keen. Even before she became empress, Severa had exercised power of a drastic sort. The Vestals had the right to excuse wrongdoing and pardon any criminal. Even a condemned man on the way to his execution could be restored to life by one of the virgins. That, if nothing else, had given her away.

"Dismiss your attendants," I said. "We will speak alone."

Having the habit of obedience, she turned to the three servants who stood by her bed and relayed my message. They left in good order, taking backward steps from the room of the woman who had held the two highest positions a woman could hold.

"We met for the first time two years ago, Severa. It was the last time we spoke alone."

"When I first saw you, I knew my life would change," she said with the authority of the superstitious. "And I believe that is true again."

"You would not be wrong, Severa. I've come to know you as the source of the corruption that surrounds your husband. It was unfortunate when you become his wife and dishonored your vows as a Vestal. It was disgraceful when you were defiled by every man in the city with love to sell. And when you collaborated with your husband in stealing the Palladium, I began to think you were a woman without a soul. This was the woman who lacked the courage to do what should have been done at the first degradation of her body."

"You wish I had destroyed myself when first I knew a man," she said with a heat that seemed to match her hair. "That would have solved your dilemma. I count it lucky that I found myself among wiser people. They think knowing a man is no sin. They think the sin lies with the religion that lies."

"The high priest told you that."

"And the high priestess."

"Which one told you to murder children?"

The truth strikes hardest with those who devise their own lies. Severa had any number put by to justify her actions, but for the last in the series she had none. It was a simple accumulation that only momentum could explain. And that she could not speak to at all.

"Aquila Severa, I came here to ask a woman why she participated in the mutilation and killing of children. If she's forthright in answering my questions, I will see she survives what is to come."

"And you know what that is."

"As you should. The emperor signed for his death in the blood of those children. His will be quick. Yours will not. You will suffer the fate of every Vestal who has been unchaste."

My threat reached her. In spite of all she had become, and every foul act she had done, she could not dismiss the image all Vestals knew if they lay with a man. A large hole was dug on Esquiline Hill as a tomb. Some food and water were placed inside. The Vestal was placed inside. And the diggers walked away.

"My husband is still the Augustus," she said, retreating stubbornly.

"He's not your husband. Nor will he be Augustus much longer. He has taken up with his old companions. The feeble countermeasures he's put in place will not help. The Guard will come for him soon."

"Feeble?" she said. "You do not understand."

"Advise me."

Severa seemed to find a route that spanned our worlds. "The way of El-Gabal is not the way of the sword. He rises above this earth. He controls the heavens." She passed her hand to the window, where the softest breezes entered the room on this night in late February. "Can you not see what he is capable of? Does the heat not brush your cheek? Can you, a mere man, turn winter into summer as he has done?"

"I acknowledge the warmth of the sun."

"Then acknowledge that your lord has brought this thing to you," she said in a strong voice. "Bow down to him!"

I did not know what she was saying, but that was always the way with the people around the emperor. Severa seemed to suggest that Marcus Aurelius Antoninus, the high priest of El-Gabal, had brought this blessing of fine weather.

"How did my lord accomplish this thing?"

"With sacrifice," she said.

I had my revelation, but slowly. I should have put the pattern together before. The ancient practices of Tanit, which were those of Syria transposed, the words of the high priest of El-Gabal on the night of the riot at the temple ("The Blood of Innocents"), the sacrifices with monkeys ("the closest to man"), led to the mutilation of children. It all had a purpose of course.

"So the emperor sacrifices children—the most blameless beings—to save fuel."

"He demonstrates his power," she said. "That power is far beyond anything you know."

"It's certainly beyond sense, Severa. You've gone past that boundary but must return. I've given the order for your burial. The pit is being dug as we speak. There is only one way to avoid your punishment. I want the name of the seventh child—the one who is to be sacrificed."

"That will not help you."

"It will help him."

"I can't," she said.

I turned to the Guard. "Take her to her grave."

She went bravely with the Guard until they put her in the carriage that awaited in the street, where she broke down.

* * *

"Sextus Coxius," said Alexianus. "Not a pretty name."

"Hardly bearable, I'd say."

"The giving of these names to my cousin, the emperor, came about as the result of a doctrinal dispute among Christians."

"Indirectly," I said. "There are two Christian factions in the city, each with a leader, or bishop. It appears the emperor approached one of them when he was collecting cult objects of all the faiths. He demanded from Hippolytus—one of the bishops—the chalice used at a last supper by their god. They call him The Great Teacher, and he was crucified. Hippolytus, however, had no chalice in his closet, so he applied to a silversmith to copy the cup for the emperor. Your cousin, knowing nothing of the object, accepted it as real."

"This holy man is devious."

"He's not alone there. The other bishop, Callixtus, is an embezzler who was condemned to the mines in Sardinia. Emperor Commodus' mistress, a Christian, had him released. Callixtus' sect understandably believes that sins should be forgiven, but Hippolytus' sect believes almost everything is a sin. This is especially true when men and women marry of the faith without his permission. He calls that fornication—a grave doctrinal error. Children born outside this curious form of wedlock are damned."

"Can they not marry properly later?" asked Alexianus. "To legitimize the child?"

"Never. The sin can never be accepted by the god—which is to say Hippolytus."

"So they go elsewhere," said Alexianus. "To the school of Callixtus."

"Exactly. They went and were accepted. All seven children."

"I see."

"Hippolytus was contacted again about three months ago. He was asked to supply the names of seven children. He found the names at Callixtus' school. They of course were beyond redemption, since the marriages of their parents had been performed by the Roman state and not his church. Their deaths do not matter to his peculiar doctrine. The deaths would also remove seven children of the opposing camp."

"So he gladly supplied the names."

"I doubt that. I understand the emperor, through Prefect Comazon, applied pressure on Hippolytus to furnish the victims. The sacrifices, let's say."

"We should release the Vestal," said Alexianus. "I mean, the empress. She's not harmless, but his flaws are laughable."

"They're laughable because she recognizes none. Only when she knew her end did she agree to talk."

Alexianus smiled like a boy of almost fifteen who found his enemy cornered. He rarely did so in my presence, which made the gesture more pleasant.

"Should we place a guard around the seventh child?"

"That has been done."

* * *

Better than posting a guard, Piso delivered the last of the children to the palace. He had always thought ahead and usually arrived at his destination before others saw it as one. Clearly, he had guessed the origin of the murders before he brought the case to me.

His genius was in allowing me to discover that myself. Though not privy to the knowledge I had drawn from the Severa, Piso had sensed the urgency of the crimes by their foulness. Large steps had been taken within the walls of the temple on Caelian Hill. They were meant to carry beyond, affecting the warp of the heavens and making the high priest of El-Gabal, and his mother, the high priestess of Astarte, masters of the wind and weather.

"I assume you placed the Guard around Caesar on alert?"

"Yes. They'll be wild when they discover Severa gave up their secrets. And they will."

Piso agreed with more than his usual gravity. "If the magic is so important to them, they will act quickly to ensure it's true. I'd expect an assault by several avenues. The Body Squad was active today. They left in a body. I believe they can be expected to fulfill their role, which is to produce bodies."

"Where has the squad gone?"

"I wasn't able to discover that," he said. "I was told by a sub-altern in dispatch they'd been ordered out secretly."

"I'd like to know, but don't want you returning to the prefect's office. We'll find a place for you in the Tiberiana. Your family, too."

"I don't think that will be necessary."

"Call it an order. I need you here."

* * *

The assault that Piso foresaw began late that evening when the Augustus came to the palace bearing a gift for his cousin and co-ruler. I was seldom twenty paces from Alexianus' side, but when I heard by runner that the emperor had entered the palace grounds, I went immediately to the antechamber where all traffic must pass before reaching the newest Caesar.

The Augustus did not announce his presence. He came quickly up the stairs, down the hallway, and passed into the antechamber with ten Praetorian Guards at his side. By now, those Guards should have been ours, but it was difficult to tell from moment to moment. The power of money, and the promises of the man who was Augustus of Rome, could turn anyone.

He stopped when he saw me before Alexianus' door. He noted the heavy guard at the entrance to the antechamber and saw the contingent of twenty more Guards that had closed up behind him in the hallway. He craned his neck to take in the sight. Although painted as usual, I saw where the makeup ended and what his cloak did not hide. He seemed composed of two distinct parts, as perhaps he always had been.

"I am happy to see my son is well guarded," he said. "That's your province, Marcellus."

"No other."

"Then I submit my request to you. I would like to attend the young Caesar on important matters of state."

"It would be better if you submitted the request in writing."

"In—" He held up his hand to his ear, but like a full stop, as if he wished never to hear what had been said. "In private, you said."

"In writing, my lord. Your request will be honored swiftly and in the proper forum."

The Augustus drew himself up, looming backward in the strange swollen position that so often preceded the dance. What stopped him from that foolishness was the only thing that could have. The door to the inner chamber swung open. Alexianus entered the room.

Dressed in a tunic without ornament, Alexianus did not seem surprised by his cousin's appearance. Advancing quickly, he drew within three paces of the Augustus.

"Father," he said.

The Augustus returned to the semblance of humankind. His face underwent a physical change, discarding the pretenses of his god.

"My son. You look well."

"It's the food," said Alexianus. "My lord's servants provide the best of everything."

"And we were worried for your health." He shrugged with his hands. "Of course, we worry most about things that few understand. The priests of El-Gabal must be concerned with more than the moment. It's eternity that beckons us."

"The Augustus speaks wisely. He knows much more of these matters than I."

"Precisely!" he said. "It's all that's on our mind. We constantly ask ourselves can Alexianus succeed us? If something happens to us, will he carry out our reforms? In particular, will he exalt El-Gabal above all other deities? Does he serve the one true god?"

He moved forward toward Alexianus. I moved with him until he stopped and focused his concentration on his cousin. "I said to myself, what can I do for Alexianus? How can I convince him of the importance of these things? How can I make my legacy his?"

The Augustus reached to his belt and withdrew a small purse. For the first time, I noticed his hands were gloved. They were skintight and approximately the same color as the paint on his face. That alerted me.

"I brought you a gift." He took from the purse a round, highly polished stone as big as the agates that children play with in the circle game. He held it up to the flickering light. "Perhaps you recognize the special glow that comes from within."

"The god?" said Alexianus.

"It is Him."

The Augustus held out the small stone. Alexianus put his hand out to accept it until I moved him aside. "Caesar thanks you. I will take your gift of the god to the palace goldsmith at once, who will have it properly mounted. It will be displayed in a place of honor."

There are advantages to knowing someone from an early age, but the chief one is being able to read his changes. Nothing altered in the face of the emperor except the movement of his eyes. They had none. Focused on me, they were like the eyes of Castinus boiled in oil.

"Very well, Marcellus Decimus."

He dropped the black stone into my hand. He saw that mine, too, was gloved.

"Guard the god well," he said, as he turned away and quickly left the palace.

* * *

"Poison?" said Alexianus.

"It's a possibility. Some work by contact. It's also said some objects are used to transmit disease. Like the leper who passes on his jewelry."

"I don't believe the emperor would do that."

"Why not? Does he love you so well?"

"He loves his god," said Alexianus. "He would not remove part of the stone of El-Gabal in order to harm me."

"What makes you think the fragment is genuine?"

Alexianus stared at the small black stone, said to be the flesh of El-Gabal, that lay in the center of the table. It glistened with an almost human quality of animation. When I held it in my hand, it seemed to throw heat through my glove.

"It's identical in color and formation," he said. "And pattern."

"Think of our conversation about the partial Bishop of Rome, Caesar. Consider that the fabrication of holy relics is one of the busiest trades in the empire. Highly skilled artisans devote themselves to the craft. Then ask yourself if it's impossible for the Emperor of Rome to do what the leader of a ragged band of Christians did very well."

"But how do we know if your idea is correct?"

"There's one way to find out."

"A trial."

"Yes."

"But if you're right, someone may die."

"We'll choose a man whose schedule is made out. Let's say a condemned criminal."

This was Alexianus' first direct contact with a life and death decision. His answer would tell what kind of ruler he would be. "Be sure to choose a man of my size and weight."

* * *

The young man brought up from prison had been sentenced to death for murdering his child. He had appealed his innocence to the presiding magistrate, saying the right of the father to wield authority over his family was absolute by the most ancient laws of Rome.

He lost the argument. His point would have been well taken in the days of the Republic, when the male head of the family was the most powerful entity in life. The advent of the empire changed that. There must be no competing center of authority. If that undermined the structure of the family, so be it. And so it was.

The man, Affectus, came filthy from his cell. I had him washed, clothed, and put in a room where he was told to hold the stone in his hand. At the end of an hour, he was taken to a room and for the rest of the day his reactions were observed.

There were none. Affectus said the stone had seemed to grow warm in his hand, and by the end of the hour, hot. Beyond that, he felt nothing.

* * *

I was more alarmed by what had *not* happened.

What reason could the Augustus have to deposit a fragment of his god, or a replica, with his cousin? The small black stone was not simply a gift. What of the mysterious heat? What did that portend for his only rival?

"I can't explain it," said Alexianus, "but I've been thinking about the children."

"Don't dwell on the morbid," said the Mother Augusta, who had joined us after her bath, which exhausted the hot water in the palace. "That's what he wants. He and his mother have regressed. They're barbarians. If you decline to enter their orbit, this nonsense has no effect."

"But it is an orbit," said Alexianus. "That's what I'm thinking."

"A circle," I said.

"Yes. The bodies of the six children, placed on the six hills of Rome, form the circle."

"But we have the seventh child."

"We have a child, yes," said Alexianus. "But others can be found. It seems to me the magic has been released already."

"The magic?"

"The magic of the marriage," he said, like the adept he might have been if his mother had not drawn a line across his life. "El-Gabal and Astarte. We know where that arises."

The Mother Augusta snorted. "Soaemias."

He nodded. "And whoever joins with her."

"Comazon, of course. He would never act independently. The children were taken by him, but for her."

"Sacrificed," said Alexianus. "With their blood, the circle was drawn. In their names, the incantations were made."

"But what's the object?"

"What lies within the circle?" he asked.

"Palatine Hill. The palace." I thought of that for a moment in which I was pleased with the subtlety of Alexianus' mind. "Now tell me the purpose of the stone fragment."

"I can't say exactly. But it's meant to act like a pointer to their target."

"You, Alexianus," said the Mother Augusta. "Perhaps all of us."

"From this point, we take no chances," I said. "The emperor may be content with magic, but those around him are not. You will go nowhere alone, Alexianus. You will eat nothing but corn meal, cold."

"An order, Marcellus?"

"Yes," said the Mother Augusta. "And one you will heed."

* * *

The next morning after breakfast, two of Alexianus' tasters took sick. The first died within an hour. The second, a slave with several years' service at the palace, had fortified himself by ingesting a variety of poisons over a period of weeks attempting to render himself immune. The measure prolonged his life for half a day, but he, too, died late that afternoon.

Not even Blackbane, my consultant on poisons, whom I kept in the Tiberiana, could determine the poison that had been introduced. His guess was that it must have been a combination of several lethal substances. The second taster provided himself with partial immunity, but they could not protect him from a battery of drugs.

The taster had also endangered Alexianus' life by trying to save his own. Since I could not know how many others might have followed the same procedure, I replaced all of them. After the substitution was made, I ordered the same sweep of cooks and servants, and rotated the Guard with replacements. I put Alexianus in my apartment and trebled the guard.

No sooner than Alexianus was safely installed than his mother came late to the apartment. She hardly cleared the door when she took me aside and delivered more bad tidings.

"The Augustus appeared at the Circus Maximus ten minutes ago for his games," said Mammea angrily. "It was bad enough that he did not ask Caesar to accompany him. Now, he and his henchman are circulating the rumor that Alexianus is on the point of dying."

"Perhaps he thinks his poisoner succeeded."

"And when he discovers otherwise—"

"He can only threaten Alexianus with the Praetorian Guard. In my opinion, that's not a viable option. They'll hold for us."

"But he must have something else in mind.. He wouldn't take such a chance if he did not. The retinue that accompanies him is large. The charioteer and many of his friends."

"Where's Comazon?"

"In the imperial box," she said.

"How many Guards are with him?"

"None," she said.

That left Comazon's Body Squad unaccounted for. They were a rogue force that did not appear in uniform or were restricted to one kind of dress. In the vast crowd that came to the circus for the games, they would be invisible—if that's what they were ordered to be.

"I may know what they have in mind," I said. "Comazon raised a band of assassins within the Urban Cohorts. He may try to use them today. You must stay here. Allow no one to see Alexianus but me."

I was sure she would follow my instructions. In the meantime, I sent for Piso, who had taken quarters on the second floor, and called for Frugius. He was healed from his wounds at the Battle of Aventine Hill, which made him eager for mayhem.

"Gather your men. Make sure they're fit for action and have them here in five minutes."

Frugius had them ready in six, which was all he could manage on a day when the games were underway and the cheers from the crowd boomed like surf in the valley below.

Piso was present by the time Frugius came again to the door. They did not smile at each other, since neither was capable of that; but they had learned to respect the other's skill on their mission to Bithynia. I knew they would work well together again.

"Frugius, go with Piso. He'll point out the men of the Urban Cohorts known as the Body Squad and isolate as many as he can for you."

"What is to be done with them, lord?"

"Place them in confinement. If they resist, destroy them."

"Where they stand?"

"Use discretion, but not to the point of forfeiting your life."

"It will be done, lord."

I decided it would not be done without me. Piso, with Frugius and his men, had already passed from the Tiberiana through the alleyway abutting the Temple of Apollo when I caught up with the rear of the formation. Surprisingly, it was a formation. Not a legion century, but seventy-five fighting men advancing at a quick pace in good order.

As they moved across the wide courtyard toward the slave quarters and the long stairway that led down to the Circus Maximus, I managed to head them. I seemed to have the knack of putting myself where death was more than a shadow on the wall. When I drew even with Piso, he pointed to the walkway above where a line of men marched toward the palace. They were close to a hundred, perhaps more, dressed in the uniforms of Praetorian Guards.

"It's them," he said. "Look, there's Gaurus."

"Back up," I said. "Protect the entrance to the alley."

My order was not heard or heeded. Frugius and Adranos had already charged the stairs to the walkway with fifty men at their backs. I unsheathed my sword and ran, alone but for six men who followed, toward the head of the alley.

When the Body Squad knew they were seen, the rear turned and presented their shields to Frugius' men. The rest, who were thirty-five or more, kept their movement toward the alley. I was sure Frugius would wheel down the broad stairs toward the alley, but that did not happen. He engaged the squad on the walk, pushing them back with his charge, and worse, pushing them toward the alleyway and the courtyard that led to the Tiberiana.

There was nothing to do but meet the front rank head on. The half-dozen men who had followed me kept close at my heels, running, lighter in their mail than the men on the walkway in full armor. I saw the scorpion on their shields. That sting could bring down any man, and it was the only poison that could overthrow Caesar. Nor did it matter if it was Augustus against Caesar.

They came into the courtyard first, where we clashed. The first rank had gone beyond us, moving fast, but the second took the brunt of our charge. And they stopped.

My first man went down with a blade in his neck. I turned, fanning with my sword, but someone in the next rank struck me on the shoulder. When I felt the steel bite through my mail and I knew my left arm was paralyzed, I threw all my weight against him and jammed his shield. He backed up before he parried. A true soldier of the legion would have taken my vitals on the end of his sword, patiently carving my bowels, but this one went for my neck. I met the thrust on the flat of my dagger, accepted it to the hilt, and pushed him off.

I struck out again, and again, before I went down. I saw a man's lips fly off his face and make a bloody hole. I saw sparks fly from the collisions of metal. When I hit the marble of the courtyard, another sword struck the chain mail on my arm. Another hit my helmet. One man stepped on my legs. The next drew on me with a slow terrible aim. I tried to parry, but barely deflected his sword. Something else did that. The bright blade flew away as my vision doubled.

It doubled again.

* * *

I awoke looking at the face of Philocrates as it hovered in the same position as the death blow. I flinched, but how irrational was my fear? This Greek had probably killed more men in his career than the legions in Parthia.

"How are you feeling?"

"I have some pain," I said, my voice loud but too soft. "But I can bear it."

The physician made a movement to someone else in the room—my room—before he gave his verdict. "I've bound your wounds," he said. "With rest, you will recover. Unfortunately, the left arm will be useless until it gains back its strength in the sinews of the shoulder."

He turned and took a small goblet from a hand that loomed in my field of vision. "A tincture of poppies," he said. "Drink it."

I drank the syrup without thinking. I was aware that I had an aversion to thought. It seemed to focus the pain, which was in several places.

"Where are my men?"

"Your subordinate is in the corridor without," he said.

"Bring him."

The physician gave a practiced nod. "I recommend complete rest. I will not be responsible if my advice is disregarded."

"Bring him *now*."

Philocrates disappeared to be replaced by Philomene. She smiled and took my hand, speaking gentle words I could not quite sort. When I looked across the bed, Frugius appeared like her genie. He wore a patch over his right eye but otherwise seemed whole.

"What happened?"

"Thrax came with a good-sized contingent of the Guard," he said. "Comazon's men threw down their arms like the cowards they are. You're the only casualty to speak of, lord."

"Alexianus?"

Frugius looked to Philomene, an uncharacteristic gesture. "The young Caesar was taken to the Praetorian Camp," she said. "When the Guard received the news that an attempt had been made on his life by poison, they rioted, shut the gates, and refused to set a guard over the Augustus. Then they sent Thrax with orders to return Alexianus to them."

"The Guard also demanded that the Augustus come to camp," said Frugius. "At once."

"Did he agree?"

"Lord, he couldn't refuse. If he walked around like a private citizen without someone to clear a path, this might be his last day."

"When did he leave?"

"Twenty minutes ago. In a litter."

"Get two horses."

"Lord, I think a carriage."

"Then a carriage."

* * *

The Praetorian Camp was like any legion garrison, enclosing the same area, but on an outsize scale, like the men who lived there. Ten thousand Guards occupied the camp, and at times their numbers were higher. They lived in barracks of two and sometimes three stories. The walls were also high and set with towers to withstand an assault by large armies. This was not only the citadel of the Guard but the place where the emperor and his court would retreat if ever Rome was put to the ultimate test.

Around the camp stood the shops, markets, taverns, and whorehouses that served the Guard. All had done a lifetime business this day, and the taverns were overflowing. As my carriage drew close to the gate, I noticed a shuttle of big men tramping to and from the camp. Giving way were crowds of onlookers, men and women from the neighborhood who had heard of the arrival of two emperors, and others who had come from far off. They were the ones whose litters had been set down in every space, blocking the streets for several hundred feet.

We could not make our way close to the entrance, so the carriage halted in the street and Frugius took me on his arm for the last fifty yards. It was a long journey. I did not feel much pain due to the poppies, but as soon as we began to move on foot, every wound burst on my body and blood flowed through the dressings. I felt it run down my back. It gathered at my belt. The sensations were slimy and distant. They seemed to bring on everything at an angle. That, I realized, was also the effect of the poppies.

"Give him to us! I'll sell *his* balls for fish bait!"

I heard the voice of the keeper at the market, but took in the words slowly. They knew the emperor was within the walls. They knew his crimes. How could he dare come here? What could he hope to accomplish? This army of armed guards hated him, and, it seemed the local people did, too, now.

"That's Comazon's horse," said Frugius. "And some other familiar ones, too. The charioteer is here to fend for his master. Look, he came in his war chariot."

Although it was already dark, I saw the car without horses. It was golden with wheels of the gods embossed on it. Only a profligate or a worried man could have left it in the street.

Grooms stood by some of the horses, while others were tied to the rail before the parade ground. They were many, but not a fraction of what it would take to challenge the Guard.

Nothing could do that today. We were called down as we came to the front gate. Frugius gave our names—and my rank—but the Guard left us stand for minutes that dragged. Finally, a centurion in battle gear put himself through the tower door. He peered at us closely.

"What party?"

"I'm the guardian of young Caesar. Marcellus Decimus. Let me pass, Centurion."

"Come to make a bid?" he said. "Where's your money bag?"

"You'll discover that when this man, whose name is Frugius the Gladiator, stuffs it up your ass. Now open the door and stand aside."

The centurion smiled. "Now there's a man with a sense of humor." He threw the door wide on its hinges.

I found out what he meant when we were inside the tower two steps from the garrison. The sounds that had been dampened by the walls rose to a steady roar. The stench of wine spoke as loud, calling to all the wild things in the world.

The camp we entered was aflame with torch light, as bright as the streets of Antioch. The giant men who made its greater shadows moved as wild and hell-bent as the *castrati* on the night of the Festival of the Great Mother. They were guardians of the emperors of Rome; they were the finest physical specimens of their kind; they were everything that was thought to be desirable in the male species; and they were under no sort of control.

On the Via Principia that bisected the camp, Guards reeled like cattle yoked shoulder to shoulder, arms locked, trampling anything in their path. If they were not singing, it was because they could not recall the words of any song. If they dropped their hold on their mates, those men fell to the ground. Some were in uniform, but most were not. This pile of brick and concrete was their home to enjoy and defile. It seemed proper that two large men reeled by, wearing the lion-skin headdress of a signifer and a trumpeter, both naked beneath their manes of fur.

Animals in the guise of animals. How far had we come from Syria? Was this the place where El-Gabal led us? Had the Orontes overwhelmed the Tiber at last?

We followed the flow of men. All movement tended to the center of the camp, where the shrine to the emperors stood. The Guard was taught to worship the images within, which were the men who ruled the empire. They were taught to die for them, but that command was as often honored in reverse. The Guard worshiped themselves. At any time they could change the names on the statues and the stones. On a night like this, they could change history.

As we drew closer to the shrine, I saw that time was near. The Guards of every cohort crowded the entrance. Already, they packed the courtyard before the temple that had been remade by Marcus Aurelius Antoninus. For his glory of his god, he had the pediment clad in gold, the steps in green marble, and the pillars with black onyx.

We worked our way to the temple, moving aside men who were as big as our shadows. Frugius did the work with his blade, always with a smile on his face and a few kind words.

"Coming through. Easy now. You could lose your nuts like that. What woman would lie with a eunuch? Your mother, you say? I don't believe it. She likes cock as well as the next bloody whore. Back up now. The gods favor the man with five fingers. It's what you use when your mother gives out. That's good. Yes, that's a good giant. Coming through."

At the top of the temple stairs stood a solid wall of Guards three ranks deep. Call them The Sober, but not The Just. Antiochianus, their prefect, stood at their head. He had discarded his purple cloak in fear he might be mistaken for royalty, but he seemed determined to hold the line against incursions.

When Frugius and I reached the long front, two sets of Guards swung their shields away and allowed us to enter the temple. I nodded my thanks to Antiochianus.

He did not return the gesture. He was too frightened.

Immediately behind I heard a clash of metal. The line of Guards closed behind us. They had held. But for how long?

"Until the men in the courtyard decide to charge," said Frugius. "I tell you, I don't like it. These bastards are crazy."

Frugius was always right about danger, even more the nearness of death. Nothing in this night meant well for anyone, not even the Guard. They had acquired, through the weakness of the emperor, an appreciation of their power. With the example of Macrinus in their minds, nothing would stop them from working their will in their camp. Nothing could stop the creation of a new emperor. The only question was who that would be. They could easily choose a man from their ranks, a barbarian or a fool, and give him any name they liked.

The inner temple of the shrine, like a mirror of the realm, was divided by loyalties. On the left side stood partisans of Marcus Aurelius Antoninus, grouped at the entrance to the quarters of the rooms of the temple priests. I saw Comazon, Hierocles, Eubulus, and a dozen others who had made it their business to milk the treasure of the empire. Payment would soon be demanded unless this gamble by their master canceled their debts and crimes.

The Augustus must be closeted in the room where they stood awaiting their fate. On the opposite side of the corridor a guard of thirty men had gathered, all of whom I knew, all in our pay. Bracing their ranks was Ulpian, the judicial prefect of the Guard. He was our man and had been for the last three months, though he had waited until the last minute to declare his choice. Greeting me with a tight smile, he opened the door to the chamber.

The well-lit room held the bowls and instruments made to plumb the livers of sacrificial animals. This was the sum of Roman religion—the practice—and yes, it wanted change. I saw Alexianus pacing before a darkened window that overlooked the courtyard to the rear. No one was with him to share this crucial time. None save Thrax.

"You're responsible for this?"

"His mother wanted him here," said Thrax. "The Guard must see their new emperor. They must acclaim him to the throne."

"Very well. Post yourself outside this room. No one enters except by my word. If anything happens to Caesar, take it in your mind to die. Or I will have you in pieces, each to a cross, until I can find no more lumber."

"Lord."

I turned to Alexianus. He was as uneasy as I had ever seen him, but had put his feelings off well. Perhaps he housed them in the chest of Lebanon cedar where I had told him to place his fear in times of stress.

Bring the lid down.

Close it slowly.

Fetter the ebony lock.

"Where is your mother?"

"She went into the courtyard at the rear minutes ago. She said that when she returned, I would be emperor."

"And you will."

"By a woman's hand," he said.

"Alexianus, there's no special way the Emperors of Rome come to the throne. No manual exists. Great Augustus fought for many years before the crown came to him. Domitian was the brother of Titus—not his son as the books say. Hadrian was adopted from a collateral family to become Trajan's heir. His adoption was done two days *after* Trajan died."

"Death is on your mind, Marcellus?"

"It's in the air, Caesar."

"What will happen to my cousin?"

"That's in the hands of the gods, whose house we share."

Alexianus looked into the courtyard again. The vast space had filled rapidly. Those Guards who could no longer press against the front made their way by the narrow walks around the rear. Caesar seemed to regret their presence; he seemed to want to flee into the night, until with an effort he turned back to me.

"Soaemias will not relent," he said. "She will prevail or die. I've heard she promised Antiochianus a share in the throne. Already she has distributed money among the centurions. It was her purse that brought on this debauchery in the camp."

"Does that surprise you? We're speaking of a woman who murdered children to devise a spell."

"Perhaps."

"You doubt that?"

"I would like to speak to my cousin," he said, drawing his cloak around his shoulders. "It's important that I do before—"

"As you wish."

* * *

I did not like Alexianus seeing his cousin, nor did I think the request would be honored, but when I sent across the corridor, the answer came quickly. Marcus Aurelius Antoninus, accompanied by Hierocles and Eubulus, walked across the corridor like conquerors with no booty. If they had arrived at an idea of this situation, they left it in the bloody temple where their plans were laid.

The Augustus entered Alexianus' room swirling his cloak, but not to begin his dance. He flung it back upon his shoulders, baring his breast to his cousin, as he held out his arms. He was calm. He seemed to have found the center of the man who for so long had disappeared, which was himself.

"My son."

Alexianus moved forward until he was nearly touching his cousin, but nothing in his demeanor said that he wished the closeness of an embrace. He spoke with forbearance.

"Varius, I want you to know I did not make this night what it is."

"I understand."

"Then also know I would not turn it back."

"We are agreed."

"It seems we have left the future of the empire to those least able to determine it," said Alexianus. "The strong arms. The Guard is not the people, nor the Senate."

"They are power," he said. "If you wish to be emperor, you must learn to deal with them. There is no alternative to their will but the eternal power of the god. My advice is to look to Him as your hope."

Alexianus lowered his dark eyes. "I do not love the god as you do, Varius. I could never love him enough to sacrifice children."

The Augustus closed his purple cloak like the halves of a gate. His face, which was unpainted, seemed not to reflect his years, but the weight of those years in the lives of his people. It was as if the grossness of his conduct had come to some meaning in his features.

"Sacrifice is everything," he said. "You may come to know that."

"But why children?" asked Alexianus. "And why the children of the lowly?"

"You should know," said the emperor, "you who shared the mountain and learned the ways of El-Gabal. What good is the blood of soldiers to the god of peace? Would he accept as an offering those sorry souls who squabble for power in the halls of the palace? Or the human refuse who tear men limb from limb in our arenas? You know the answer, Alexianus. Our god can take only the blameless to his bosom. Who are more blameless than poor children? They are the innocent of this empire. The lost. Indeed, the forsaken. Believe me when I say that if I do not prevail—if El-Gabal does not reign—they will stand in his place."

Alexianus touched the emperor's arm. "I will remember your words, Varius."

"Do more," he said. "Honor my god."

Alexianus did not answer. He waited until the emperor had taken two steps back, as if he were the servant, and passed through the door, tunneling through the massive shadow of Thrax into the corridor beyond.

"He means to die."

"Better him."

"I will not be a part of this," said Alexianus, drawing his cloak close around him. "It's important that I not be a part of what is to come."

"Caesar."

* * *

When I left Alexianus in the room alone, the mutiny changed character. A loud noise arose from the front grounds of the shrine that was echoed from the rear. The door across the corridor through which Marcus Aurelius Antoninus had passed burst open.

Soaemias emerged in a long scarlet cloak. Immediately, she put herself among her son's attendants who stood at the door and took her place like their commander. She began to issue orders that could not be carried out. No doubt she made demands that could not be met. With her hand and long fingers, she caressed the face of Comazon as if he were her hope. When she spoke to him, I stole the words from her lips: "If you ever loved me."

Comazon looked through her to me, knowing what he saw. When he was certain, he turned away from her and walked toward me.

I could not have wished for a better moment to do him harm, but I knew that time would come. I waited as he crossed the space between the statues of the gods to me.

"She wishes to speak with you."

"I could think of better times. And places."

Comazon was still a young man in spite of his cunning. He tried to pass off his panic as the measured voice of experience. "Perhaps you think you'll escape from this unscathed."

"None of us will."

He wanted to say more, but did not. He walked back across the shrine to his mistress, with whom he talked in an animated way. It lasted for longer than it should have.

"She's wearing her cunt on her face," said Frugius. "Beware."

"Can I withstand her?"

Frugius laughed, which meant he was at his most sinister. "Be careful, lord. The night before we fought in the arena, they often sent the most beautiful women in the city to pleasure us. Some were from the Palatine, too. Those were the worst. They wanted more than a fuck. They wanted to talk. About what, I asked? About how you feel, they said. So I made them feel like I felt."

"And they all loved you."

"For a fact, lord."

I should have sent Frugius as my substitute. The poppies had begun to while away and blood still crept down my back slowly. That meant the flow was thicker. The pull at my shoulder began to harden. It was possible I might scream. Anything was possible now.

The princess came in gentle pieces, treading demurely, like a lady. When she arrived at a proper distance, which was slightly beyond midpoint, she stopped and smiled. The beauty that touched her mouth had been there from the first day we met. It would never expire in life.

"You will not come halfway?"

"No."

She walked quickly closer. When she stopped at two paces, I saw all the things her smile had hidden—the fear and anger—yet her words came precisely. "Marcellus, may we negotiate?"

"You'll have to speak to the men outside. I have no power in this camp."

"You dissemble. These men are yours. So many, it seems, are committed to you."

"To the young Caesar."

"If you cannot speak for anyone but yourself, you should find another place to be. This night belongs to whomever can ride the moment."

"It will not be you, Soaemias."

"No?" Within her smile were the fatal highlights Frugius knew so well. "What of the prophecy given long ago in Britannia? Do you deny it now?"

If I had never spoken of that crucified priest, what would our lives have become? What window to the future had he raised? The gods gave these things to men, but how?

"There's something you should know about the prophecy, Soaemias."

"Be brief."

"He was not brief," I said. "The priest of the forest spoke his mind. He said your son would come to be the greatest man in the world. But he also said this: that women would rule the empire and that the name of Varius would be scorned to the ends of the earth. The Druid spoke those words with his last breath."

"*Liar!*" she said.

"Ask your son. He knows. He has always known."

* * *

The noise from the temple grounds rose suddenly. We ran to the rear of the temple, where the inner courtyard connected the temple to the shrine of the emperors. Midway in the courtyard, like an arbiter in stone, stood the statue of Mars. At the base of the statue stood Julia Mammea. I hardly recognized that familiar face so inflamed. Her eyes were hollowed by torch light into black nodes. Her bright hair whipped in the wind and her words were as brilliant.

"Men of the Guard—and I know you are men—should it be Caesar you follow?" She threw her arms open. "Or do you hold ranks for the Augustus? His service promises great things. He will provide lead paint for your face and silver nets for your hair! You will march into battle against the enemies of Rome with rings in your ears! Do not fret that these fragile things will overawe the ranks of the barbarians. They will come forward, naked, while you sink to your knees! Believe me as I speak the truth of Mars!"

The Guards who were closest in ranks sent up a cry of protest. That it was a warning did not deter Mammea. "My son Alexianus is a boy, not a man, hardly with a beard. Yet I found him one day with a slave girl from the Temple of Isis as beautiful as the dawn. I had him beaten for taking his pleasure with one so young and so mean. Condemn me if you will, but I did not know I should have taken him to his cousin for instruction in the art of giving pleasure to a man! Should I have sent him to you instead, men of the Praetorian Guard! Can you teach him to please a charioteer! Can you show him the proper way to sodomize a sheep or a cow?"

It was the poppies, I thought. Could this be the doting mother, the good woman, who stood in the courtyard of the shrine of the emperors goading the Praetorian Guard?

"You should not listen to me, brave men of the Praetorian Guard! Instead, cast your lot once more with the man who has led you to the brink of womanhood! Carry the Augustus back to his palace on your shoulders, but be sure to gird your loins. He will seek out your manhood, my friends, he will find it and cherish it, no matter how well it is hidden."

"I'll give you his manhood on the end of my sword," cried a angry voice from the mob. "Now what do you have for me, lady?"

Mammea ruled the moment with the vengeance of a goddess. She held up her right hand. Slowly, she lifted one finger. Another. Another.

"Three thousand sesterces for each man! Three thousand per man! I will not ask if men are what you are! I will assume that every Guard who stands at this shrine may find a use for the money! If he chooses to spend it on a woman, I will not condemn him! And if by his efforts he fathers a child, I will have two thousand sesterces more for his household!"

They cheered, yes, they cheered. She had put the money on the table. The rest left unsaid was their pride. They had been chewing it for three years and did not like the taste. Like one man, they spit it out. Like the gears of a machine, the Guard moved in a body toward the temple. They began to mount the stairs.

I turned to Ulpian, who was a good soldier, but better in court. "Take every man you can find and ring Alexianus' room."

Quickly, Ulpian hurried toward the corridor as an immense surge from the temple pushed him back onto the apron of the portico. The rush came from the Augustus' men.

A dozen Guards led the party, trailed by several of his companions. Hierocles was there, but not Eubulus. Soaemias was there, but not Antiochianus. Behind the vanguard, borne aloft on a shield on the shoulders of several of his friends, moving through the air without moving, came Marcus Aurelius Antoninus.

But he might have been Varius. He looked like an emperor, the purple cloak of office framing his face in the torch light. He had come to meet his fate. It was as if he had found his power again. I saw no fear in his face. When the shield stopped moving near the head of the steps, the Guard stopped. For a moment, they were awed.

"Men of the Guard!" he shouted in a voice that clashed with other voices but was still heard. "Praetorians, hear me! Remember that when you fought in Syria, I spared your lives! Did I do right by the gods? Did I spare the Guard only to menace my family?"

The sounds from the crowd did not gather coherence. Nor did they grant approval. They seemed to understand that they participated in a spectacle that would end soon.

"I've brought them here for you to see!" he shouted. "I brought my son as you requested, but others have come." He flung his hand toward Mammea, who still held at the pedestal of Mars. "My aunt who speaks so well!" He flung his hand to his side, where Soaemias stood. "My mother, the mistress of constant devotion! And the members of my government who have served you! We have come to hear your grievances! And right them!"

"You simpering cunt!" came a loud voice that held a sword. "This will right everything!"

The emperor did not heed the words that he had certainly heard. He looked beyond the source to the shrine of his forebears. "Is it a matter of your pay, Praetorians? Tell me, does that form your protest? For if it is, there is much that can be done to put things aright!"

"We want the red ruby in your navel!"

"We want the pearls that ring your ass!"

"Can I do nothing to please you?" asked the emperor, imploring. "I have no quarrel with the armies on the frontier! The people love me! But from the Guard, whom I offer my purse, I hear insults!"

"As long as you hear them, count yourself lucky!"

"Five thousand sesterces per man!" said the emperor, thrusting his hand in the air. "Five thousand sesterces!"

"And a blowjob!"

"Start with the First Cohort, if you please!"

"No rest until you're done!"

"Six thousand sesterces per man!" cried the emperor. "*Six* thousand!"

"First, the charioteer!" screamed a voice that began as one and then seemed to come from everywhere. "We want the charioteer!"

"Ten thousand! Ten thousand sesterces for each man of the Guard!"

Whoever did it was a champion, and there were some among the Guard. If in any part of the empire games were given, and one man distinguished himself above the rest, he could be taken into the service of the emperor for his eye and arm and aim.

For the path of the missile was true. The javelin came out of the mass of men like their will, almost silent in the midst of din, a trail of feathery sound. The point of the javelin struck Hierocles below the breastbone, piercing him through. He collapsed around it. The shield that he held in both hands, bearing the emperor aloft, collapsed with him.

The emperor toppled onto his lover, and as they fell to the ground, he screamed.

When the mob of gigantic men heard the sound, they charged the temple, surging up the steps. The emperor's small contingent of Guards closed around him in a half-circle, shields up. They began to retreat, but the momentum of those many men engulfed them.

I was already moving into the temple. I saw the emperor, steeped in the blood of Hierocles, as he ran down the corridor, his purple cloak trailing from his shoulders until it was stepped on by one of his retinue and torn from his shoulders. He stopped to retrieve it.

That was the last I saw him. It was said that Marcus Aurelius Antoninus escaped to a vacant room, where he hid in a trunk, and by which means he tried to escape from the camp. It was further said that when the Guard found his hiding place, they made the trunk into a living coffin as a hundred spears pierced it. When that was done, they drew him out and beheaded him.

I cannot disprove a rumor, nor dispute the fact that on March 6, 222, the Emperor of Rome, and his mother Julia Soaemias, died by being beheaded; but I believe they met their ends in a braver way. Nothing could have stopped the assault of hundreds of angry men. If the Guard had turned their wrath on Alexianus, we could not have kept them from him.

What saved us was the anger that was driven by the desire to destroy every vestige of the reign of Marcus Aurelius Antoninus. As those huge men raged, the heads of the emperor and his mother were carried through the camp on spears, displayed to everyone who had suffered during the reign of the most wanton ruler the empire has ever known.

The bodies of Varius and his mother were mutilated by every means. Tied to chariots and dragged through the streets, their headless corpses were thrown into the River Tiber.

All those who came with them to the camp perished, including Antiochianus, Prefect of the Guard and Comazon, the Prefect of the City. When those heads were taken and mounted on spears, it signaled a falling away of the last restraints. The Guard broke from the camp with their trophies. They rampaged through the city, seeking out those who had served the emperor and murdering them without exception. They did not desist until after sunrise, and even then left a trail of their passage. The people of Rome greeted the morning in a pall of smoke caused by the smoldering remains of the temple that had until that day dominated Caelian Hill.

Few things survived the holocaust, but strangely, the god came forth from the ashes of the temple. Forged in the heavens, hurtled through trackless space, the dark adamant brow of El-Gabal emerged unscathed. When his survival was reported to me, I had the stone of the sun god of Emesa transported to its home in Syria, where it remains to this day.

* * *

Marcellus Decimus, June 234
Rendered to the Imperial Archives on August 12, 242, by Eugenius Columbanus, Master of the Scrolls.

PERORATION

Marcellus Decimus Julius apparently lived to be an old man. After serving as Regent of the Roman Empire for the successor to Marcus Aurelius Antoninus, Marcellus retired to his home in Verona with his wife Annia Faustina. His last years were spent cultivating his land and composing the narrative that forms this memoir. There is no record of his death.

Alexianus, the boy he brought to manhood, ascended to the throne of the Roman Empire as Severus Alexander. Although his rule of thirteen years was marked by competent government and a judicious hand, Alexander was forced to spend much of his time dealing with rebellions on the frontier. He died in 235 on an expedition to Germany, assassinated by his Praetorian Guard.

Alexander was succeeded to the throne by Thrax, who took the name Maximus. This man, the first of the "barbarian emperors," spent most of his short reign suppressing rebellions in every part of the empire, a trend that continued for much too long. Seventy-five years of varying turmoil visited the Roman Empire. Stable dynastic rule was rarely known until the Emperor Constantine abandoned Rome and reestablished the seat of government at Constantinople in the east.

His city of seven hills reigned for more than a thousand years. Christianity, the religion that Constantine proclaimed throughout the empire, was dominant for as long. It was only challenged by the rise of another monotheistic faith from the east, Islam, which took as its cult object a black stone thrown down from the heavens.

Did you enjoy this book?
Visit ForemostPress.com to share
your comments or a review.

LaVergne, TN USA
13 January 2010
169850LV00003B/16/A